Books by R. J. Pineiro

Siege of Lightning (1993)

Ultimatum (1994)

Retribution (1995)

Exposure (1996)

Breakthrough (1997)

01-01-00 (1999)

Y2K (1999)

Shutdown (2000)

conspiracy.com (2001)

Firewall (2002)

The Eagle and the Cross (2003)

For more information on R. J. Pineiro's

novels, visit his Web page at:

www.rjpineiro.com

conspiracy.com

R. J. Pineiro

a tom doherty associates book
new york

This is a work of fiction. All the characters and events portrayed in this novel are either fictitious or are used fictitiously.

CONSPIRACY.COM

Design by Heidi Eriksen

A Forge Book
Published by Tom Doherty Associates, LLC
175 Fifth Avenue
New York, NY 10010

www.tor.com

Forge® is a registered trademark of Tom Doherty Associates, LLC.

Library of Congress Cataloging-in-Publication Data

Pineiro, R. J.
   Conspiracy.com / R. J. Pineiro.
      p. cm.
   "A Tom Doherty Associates book."
   ISBN 0-312-86908-8
   1. High technology industries—Fiction. 2. Political corruption—Fiction. 3. Conspiracies—Fiction. I. Title.
   PS3566.I5215 C66 2001
   813'.54—dc21

00-048447

First Edition: April 2001

Printed in the United States of America

0 9 8 7 6 5 4 3 2 1

For those who held my hand
during the long march,

Lory Anne, for encouraging me
Matt Bialer, for finding and supporting me
Bob Gleason, Andy Zack, and Gary Muschla,
for teaching me
Tom Doherty, for believing in me

and,

St. Jude, for making it possible

author's note and acknowledgments

Tom Doherty came up with the idea for this book. He felt that the most feared agency in the United States government was the Internal Revenue Service. I have to agree. Nothing matches the fear that coils into your stomach when you receive a letter from the IRS, other than a tax refund, of course. The IRS has more power over the citizens of this nation than any other government institution, and it is the fictional abuse of this power—and the terror that it would spread if allowed to exist unchecked—that became the basis for this story.

Many thanks go to the following individuals, who so willingly donated their time and energy to help make *conspiracy.com* a better story. All errors that remain, of course, are my own.

The awesome staff at Tor/Forge, particularly Tom Doherty, Bob Gleason, Linda Quinton, Karen Lovell, Jennifer Marcus, and Brian Callaghan. Thank you again for all of your support and for the personal attention during my trips to New York.

Matthew Bialer, my skilled agent and loyal friend at William Morris. You simply can't find a better ally in this business.

My friend, Dave, for your technical review of the manuscript.

My wife, Lory, for continuing to be the rock upon which I build my dreams.

My son, Cameron, may you find the perseverance and the vision to make your own dreams come true.

The rest of my family, for always being a source of support and inspiration.

And finally, once again, I'd like to thank all of my readers. Your letters and E-mails encouraging me to go on is in part what keeps me writing these

author's note and acknowledgments

stories. Please notice my new E-mail address and Web site, and keep those messages coming!

God bless,
R. J. Pineiro
Austin, Texas
July, 2000

Visit the official R. J. Pineiro Web site at www.rjpineiro.com, or send him an E-mail at author@rjpineiro.com.

These, having not the law, are a law unto
themselves.

                              —Romans 2:14

prologue

Lightning streaked across the central Texas sky, its stroboscopic flash illuminating the deserted alley in downtown Austin. FBI Special Agent Dave Nolan heard the rumbling thunder a few seconds later, before darkness resumed.

Wearing a black T-shirt and jeans, Nolan remained in a deep crouch, hidden from view in the narrow space between two overstuffed garbage dumpsters, listening to rats rustling over refuse. Following professional habits, he rose slowly, enough to rest his night-vision binoculars on the rusted metal edge of one of the trash receptacles.

Nolan silently cursed the stench, the shrilling rats, and the lightning storm. The binoculars, designed to amplify the available light and turn darkness into a palette of greens, flared up with the sporadic flashes, stinging his pupils before the unit's shutoff mechanism kicked in a second later.

Blinking to clear his vision from the last flash, Nolan fingered the binoculars's adjusting wheel, bringing the rear of the building across the alley into focus. He directed his attention back to one of a dozen third-story windows facing him, verifying that the curtain was still drawn—his signal to remain put.

He checked his watch, frowning.

Where is she?

His contact was late, real late. The meeting had been set up for nine o'clock this evening. Nolan had arrived an hour earlier, surveying the entire area before selecting this location to wait for the signal. But as nine-fifteen approached, an uneasy feeling began to creep up his spine. His experience told him to leave and wait for another opportunity. But his informant had indicated that her employer suspected her of trying to contact the FBI, and she now feared for her life, prompting Nolan to make an exception and hang around just a little longer.

He sighed and continued to scan the area, spending another five minutes inspecting both ends of the alley, all windows, rooftops, and fire ladders—places where a sniper could take a position against him. Twenty-five years with the Bureau had taught Dave Nolan the value of paranoia, a weapon as effective as the stainless-steel Beretta pistol tucked in his jeans by his spine.

His search yielded nothing, and the curtain in his target window remained drawn.

Twenty past nine. You have to get out of here.

Nolan hesitated, cursing his predicament. For the past few weeks the Bureau had been aware of a potential money-laundering ring in Austin, Texas, involving a high-tech corporation doing business with a local bank. The tip had arrived from a local IRS employee who had insisted on remaining anonymous. Apparently this government worker had come across inconsistencies in the tax records of those two corporations. When the IRS employee had brought the problem to the attention of her management, she had been told not to worry about it, which had implicated the IRS in this possible tax-evasion scheme, prompting her to contact the FBI to set up a meeting.

(14)

Dave Nolan, the special agent from the Washington, D.C., office assigned to the case, had flown to Austin to meet this anonymous employee, who had insisted on talking to someone from the Washington office. Apparently the informant trusted no one locally. Nolan had agreed to her terms and set up a meeting for tonight at an empty apartment leased just last week by Nolan himself under a fake name. He wasn't about to leave until he'd met this mysterious woman and made an assessment for his boss, Special Agent Karen Frost, of the likelihood that the IRS might be involved in this scheme.

To minimize the risk of telegraphing the FBI surveillance to someone tailing his informant this evening, Nolan had not brought any backup. This move, which had caused some controversy at the Washington office, had finally been approved thanks to the insistence of Karen Frost. Nolan now worried about—

He jerked back as a cloud of sparks exploded in front of the binoculars. Metal screeched. The sound of a near miss buzzed past him like an angered hornet.

Dropping the binoculars, listening to the hasty retreat of a dozen rats, one of which rushed past his feet, Nolan reached for the Beretta 92FS pistol, his thumb flipping the safety before pulling back the hammer.

What's going on? Is this a setup?

Get out of here first! Then analyze!

Options rushed to him as he sank to the ground, pulling his legs up to his chest, covering himself from all angles except directly above and in front of him. He pointed the pistol first at the narrow view of the alley facing him, seeing nothing but darkness. Then he switched it to the space above him, aiming it at the overhanging roof, barely visible in the dark.

"Where are you?" he whispered, switching his aim back and forth between his compromised areas.

Someone had fired either from a rooftop or a window, and most likely from the apartment complex across the alley in order to pin him down this easily. He felt certain that the sniper, who had to be using a silenced weapon since he had heard no report, would also be using a night-vision scope.

Nolan inhaled, clutching the Beretta, remembering the location of the other dumpsters in the alley, banking on his quarry using night-vision equipment.

Lightning flashed.

The Bureau man rolled away from the dumpster, rushing to his left, in the opposite direction from where the bullet had originated, his sneakers splashing loudly as he sprinted through a puddle, eyes frantically searching for another shield, finding one just as darkness resumed, just as a silent round ricocheted off the ground, chipping chunks of concrete.

He landed on his side behind another dumpster, surveying his new position, considering his next move, spotting an emergency door exactly across the alley from where he now stood. The door would be locked on the outside, as any emergency door would be. But if he could get it open, he would get away from the line of fire while giving himself a sporting chance inside the building. And if the door had an alarm, the siren might scare them off while alerting the police.

Aiming the Beretta at the door lock, roughly a dozen feet away, Nolan waited, wondering how long it would take the sniper to catch on to Nolan's plan.

A fork of lightning parted the skies, gleaming down the alley just as Nolan leaned forward, firing three times in rapid succession at the door lock, the reports deafening, amplified by the surrounding walls.

Another streak of lightning flickered across the sky. Nolan surged to his feet and rushed toward the door. He caught a figure in the corner of his left eye, very large, too close for him to bring his weapon around.

The blow was swift, powerful, delivered with crippling force to the side of his face, striking the web of nerves below the skin just forward of his ear.

The federal agent collapsed on the ground, dazed, his vision tunneling, the bulky shadow looming over him, a pistol aimed at Nolan's chest.

"Who are you?" the stranger asked.

Nolan blinked rapidly, clearing his vision just as lightning flashed, revealing a square face, closely cropped ash blond hair, and a pair of ice blue eyes.

15

"I'm only going to ask you one more time. Who are you? Who do you work for?"

"Where?" Nolan whispered, trying to regain his focus. "Where . . . is she?"

"You should be more concerned about what's going to happen to you if you don't start talking."

"What . . . have you done . . . to her?"

The stranger grinned. "Nothing *nearly* as bad as what we're going to do to you."

**book
one**

Career Choices

Far and away the best prize that life
offers is the chance to work hard at work
worth doing.

—Theodore Roosevelt

1

Ryan stepped inside one of the elevators in the lobby of the Fairmont Hotel in San Jose, California, and pressed the button for the tenth floor. The slight upward acceleration unsettled his stomach.

Relax, he told himself as a computerized voice announced his floor and the doors slid into the wall, exposing a navy blue–carpeted hallway adorned with vases filled with fresh flowers atop pedestals. Ornate mirrors hung on the walls behind the vases.

Swallowing with concern, he proceeded toward his noon appointment while Mozart flowed out of unseen speakers. He reached room 1020, a corner suite, at exactly 11:59 A.M.

Adjusting the knot of a tie he had not worn since his last interview two weeks ago, Ryan knocked twice, still wondering why he felt nervous about an interview that certainly didn't matter in the scheme of things. As he stood here today, Michael Patrick Ryan already had lucrative offers from Microsoft, Oracle, Cisco Systems, and even Intel—all on the West Coast, or very close to it. He certainly didn't *need* to talk to SoftCorp, an unknown company from Austin, Texas—a region of the country that was never one of Ryan's geographical preferences. Having lived in northern California all of his life, Ryan didn't relish the thought of moving too far away from family and friends. In addition, his wife, Victoria, wasn't thrilled about the prospects of uprooting her California life and moving halfway across the country. Stanford's employment office, however, had strict rules about interviews and had insisted that Ryan attend every one that it had set up for him, regardless of how many offers he already had on the table.

Relax and play the game. You're holding all the cards today.

A man in his midforties opened the door a moment later. Tanned, well built, and dressed in a double-breasted suit, the stranger smiled, making Ryan think of a toothpaste commercial. Ryan recognized Ron Wittica's face from the Internet digging he had done last night. SoftCorp's Web page included a section with photos and brief backgrounds of the management team. Ryan, a hacker at heart, had thought about breaking into their system, but had chosen to spend his time studying for finals.

"Michael Ryan?" Wittica asked, still smiling, making Ryan feel strangely at ease.

"Yes, sir," he replied, extending a hand.

"Ron Wittica. Pleasure to meet you in person." He pumped Ryan's hand firmly.

"Pleasure's mine, Mr. Wittica" Ryan replied cordially, noticing the Rolex watch hugging Wittica's wrist, probably more expensive than Ryan's six-year-old Honda. Wittica had contacted Ryan over a month ago for a brief phone screen. Then after weeks of silence, which Ryan had perceived as a lack of interest on SoftCorp's part, Stanford's employment office had sent him an E-mail to be here today for a face-to-face interview.

"Call me Ron, please. By the way, you look better in person than in your picture."

The comment caught Ryan by surprise. He didn't remember providing a picture to the employment office. *Did they get it from the yearbook?* He suddenly wished he had attempted to break into SoftCorp's system to get more insight into their operation. Before Ryan could ask about the source of the photo, Wittica put a hand on his shoulder, squeezing gently while guiding him inside the lavishly furnished suite. "We've been looking forward to talking to you, Michael."

"I go by Mike."

Wittica patted his shoulder. "Of course, Mike. I'm glad you've found the time to see us today. We know how busy you are."

You do?

Ryan followed this seemingly well-informed character inside the front room of the corner suite. A second man sat on a black leather couch, his back to Ryan as he faced the panoramic windows showing a stunning view of Silicon Valley, backdropped by the mountains leading to the ocean.

"Mike, meet Aaron Shapiro, our founder and CEO."

Although Ryan also recognized Shapiro, he certainly didn't expect to see him here. How often did the CEO of a corporation recruit candidates directly, especially new grads?

"It's a genuine pleasure, Mike," said Shapiro, standing up, extending a hand over the table separating them. Although probably in his sixties, Shapiro seemed to be in good shape, slim, with a strong handshake. His face, wrinkled with age, was framed by a full head of silver hair. Blue eyes, glinting with bold intelligence, inspected Ryan as he stood there pumping his hand.

"The pleasure's mine, Mr. Shapiro."

"Call me Aaron, please. Are you hungry?" The CEO of SoftCorp waved a hand toward a tray of cold cuts on a cart next to the sofa.

"No, thanks. I grabbed something before I came."

"Coffee? Water?" asked Wittica, standing next to Ryan.

"Water would be nice, thanks."

While Wittica walked over to the minibar on the right side of the room, Shapiro motioned Ryan to sit down on one of the chairs opposite his sofa, across from the cocktail table. A piece of modern artwork that he couldn't make out stood next to a silver coffee tray holding a pot of coffee, cream, sugar, and three cups.

"Do you like modern art, Mike?" asked Shapiro, obviously noticing his eyes.

Ryan sat back, crossed his legs, and calmly placed both hands on his lap. "I prefer the classics."

Shapiro briefly closed his eyes while giving him a knowing nod. "I know exactly what you mean. I can't ever figure out what this kind of art is trying to tell me. What do you think?"

"Art is like a program," Ryan replied. "It either works or it doesn't. Modern art just doesn't work for me. It doesn't grab me, unlike the paintings of Botticelli, Rembrandt, and Michelangelo. That doesn't mean it's bad. It just doesn't convey to me what it appears to convey to others."

Wittica and Shapiro exchanged a glance and nodded, apparently deciding that it was a good answer.

Wittica handed Ryan a glass of water before taking his place on the second chair. "You have a very impressive record, Mike," Wittica started. "Valedictorian of your high school, plus star quarterback, which got you a double scholarship to Stanford for athletics and also academics. You completed your bachelor's in electrical engineering in three and a half years instead of the regular four."

"While fulfilling your end of the deal on that football scholarship," said Shapiro.

"Even after your knee gave during your sophomore year. You never missed practice and even played in a few games. That's remarkable." said Wittica.

"After your bachelor's," added Shapiro without skipping a beat, almost as if they had rehearsed this, "you turned down Cisco System's full-time offer, as well as several others, to pursue a master's degree in computer engineering, even though such a decision would force you to take out a student loan because both scholarships expired at the end of your senior year. You completed your master's in just over a year and a half, instead of the regular two, mostly due to the success of your virtual-reality database-access software, which earned you three patents and even more lucrative offers from Microsoft, Oracle, Cisco, and others."

Impressive, Ryan thought, especially since neither of them held a single piece of paper in their hands.

Before Ryan could reply, Wittica picked up the ball, reciting Ryan's other accomplishments at Stanford, including two-time president of his IEEE chapter, member of Stanford's elite president's list for maintaining a 4.0 GPA during his entire college career, and other awards and recognitions.

"Seems like you've done your homework," he said, somewhat relieved that they had not mentioned his hacking activities back in high school and during his freshmen year in college. Either they didn't know about it, or they had chosen to ignore it for now. Either way it didn't matter. The episodes had been mild at best, a mere slap on the hand in high school and no action at Stanford because they were never able to trace the break-ins back to him. After that Ryan had somewhat reformed himself, though he occasionally visited classified networks, especially from the corporations that interviewed him. He made a mental note to research SoftCorp a little more thoroughly. Ryan also wanted to do *his* homework.

"We can't afford not to be thorough, Mike," said Shapiro. "You see, we're not a large company like Microsoft or Cisco. We're fairly small in size but quite large in sales and profits."

"Last year's reported revenue surpassed two hundred seventy-five million dollars," said Ryan, recalling his limited Internet research. "At only seventy employees, that puts the revenue-per-employee ratio at the very top of the industry. You only recruit a couple of candidates per year out of the top five percent engineering schools in the nation."

Shapiro smiled. "Here's a question whose answer is not posted on our Web site: We have kept pretty much the same head count since our sixth year in business, even though we have continued to hire at the rate of two engineers per semester. How is that possible?"

Ryan shrugged. "In this industry people change jobs a lot. They move around."

Wittica nodded. "That's a good answer for other companies, Mike, but not for SoftCorp. We never lose an employee to the competition."

"If they don't leave to go elsewhere then how . . ."

Both executives stared at him. Ryan realized that he was being tested. The answer came to him a second later.

"Early retirement?"

"Exactly," said Shapiro, smiling first at Ryan and then at Wittica, like saying, *See, I knew he was smart enough to figure it out.*

"Financially independent?" Ryan asked.

"With enough money to never have to work a single day in their lives," said Shapiro, reaching for the coffee tray, turning over one of the cups, and filling it halfway.

Ryan shifted his gaze between the two SoftCorp executives. "At what age?"

"Early forties for the most part," said Wittica as Shapiro leaned back and sipped coffee. "Sometimes a little younger."

"One engineer left us at thirty-seven, after only fourteen years," said Shapiro in tag-team fashion. "She now lives in the Florida Keys."

Ryan considered that for a moment. These guys were good—*damned* good—at their recruiting job, to the point that they'd already piqued his interest in a job he would not have considered just five minutes ago. As he decided that he would definitely need to research their operation further, it dawned on him that aside from checking Ryan's ability to think beyond textbooks, these two characters weren't here to *interview* him but to *sell* him. They had already done all of the homework they needed to do on the technical competence of Michael Patrick Ryan, even to the extent of obtaining information that wasn't publicly available.

He decided to continue playing their game. "What are your products? Your Web page was vague about that."

Holding the cup to his lips, Shapiro glanced at Wittica, who nodded solemnly, leaned forward on his chair, and rested his elbows on his thighs, narrowing his gaze, as if about to disclose national secrets. "We specialize in custom software for the government. That in itself helps keep our overhead low. We don't need to advertise or sustain expensive sales and marketing departments, like Microsoft and Oracle. SoftCorp is made one hundred percent of engineers, minus a few clerical assistants and the unavoidable security staff of any high-tech firm. We don't have the large manufacturing headaches of semiconductor houses like Intel, Motorola, and AMD, or the huge advertising expenditures of Microsoft and other software companies. Our primary asset is our intellectual property, our engineering staff. That's where all of the money goes, keeping them happy and focused on their work. No other company can compete with our salaries, bonuses, and other benefits, Mike. *No one.*"

"Don't you run the same risks of so many other government contractors? Can a shift in Washington politics cancel your contracts?

"Not a chance," said Shapiro before Wittica got a chance to reply.

"How can you be so certain?"

"Because, Mike," said Wittica, smiling while glancing over at Shapiro before focusing on Ryan. "We have managed to make ourselves quite . . . indispensable. This particular government agency, which has been around for a very long time, could never survive without our services."

"How do you keep from losing your contract to another company? If this is as big an opportunity as you claim, there would certainly be other parties interested in wrestling the fat government contracts away. Doesn't your client have to go through a bidding process each time contracts are up for renewal?"

Shapiro nodded.

"Then how do you keep the competition out? Whenever there's money to be made, start-ups begin to pop up everywhere to grab a piece of the action. Some years back, when the need for networking computer chips rocketed in order to support the exponential expansion of the Internet, the initial companies that got in were able to make huge profits overnight, but soon after other start-ups got in the game, driving the prices of networking chips down as the supply grew, until the profit margins were minimal at best. Why is your situation any different?"

Wittica took a deep breath. "Damn good question, Mike. The answer is that at SoftCorp we have created a leading edge in technology and we continue to keep it by constantly thinking outside the box, by hiring nothing but the very cream that the industry has to offer—and hanging on to them for their entire careers. We have managed to develop the finest environment in the industry for the birth and growth of ideas. We don't have to worry about losing an employee after investing years of training. By hanging on to our people we hang on to our most precious investment. Our mode of operation resembles that of a think tank more than that of a large corporation. That keeps us always ahead of the pack whenever contracts need to be renewed. No one can touch us, and believe me, there have been many who have tried."

"What agency?" asked Ryan.

"Excuse me?"

"What government agency does your company support?"

"That's confidential," said Shapiro. "Only full-time employees of SoftCorp can know."

Ryan nodded, well aware of company confidentiality in the high-tech sector, and of the extremes to which many corporations went in order to protect their intellectual property. In fact, a significant portion of the virtual-reality database-access software that he'd developed for his thesis comprehended extensive fire walls designed to keep hackers out.

Ryan decided to take a different tack to get a little more information. "You mentioned custom software as your end product. Can you elaborate without revealing anything confidential?"

The SoftCorp executives exchanged a glance and concurred that it was a fair question.

"Sure, Mike," started Ron Wittica. "It's all C++ code. We are Unix based and develop all of our programs on workstations."

"Is the C code for development or production?"

"Our client has a wide variety of requirements, from development of new applications to bookkeeping of its huge database. Along with that comes all of the required software and hardware to protect the system from outside interference."

Ryan looked away, considering how he could best contribute to such environment. "What type of systems does your client use?"

"A wide variety, actually," answered Wittica while Shapiro poured himself more coffee and watched Ryan carefully, even as Wittica spoke, obviously trying to read Ryan's reaction to the explanations. "They have an army of mainframes, some of them dating back to the seventies, interfaced with latest-generation supercomputers. All of that is networked with new workstations and personal computers."

"Sounds like a very eclectic system. A big monster, actually."

"It is," said Shapiro.

"But that's our job," said Wittica, nodding at his CEO. "Keeping it all working together in harmony. Old and new hardware running a mix of old and new software."

Ryan considered that for a moment before asking, "Do you have any plans to upgrade the entire monster to a single platform? Nothing like trying to maximize simplicity and uniformity in the already challenging world of computers."

Again, the SoftCorp executives exchanged a glance, nodding in unison. Shapiro put down his cup of coffee and also leaned forward, staring at Ryan in the eye. "Do you have any recommendations?"

Another test question. Ryan cleared his throat and began describing a hypothetical scenario where an intelligent computer platform is introduced, coupled with the latest virtual-reality database-access software. The nature of this platform allowed it to be adapted to satisfy the needs of many different divisions within a corporation, including engineering, legal, marketing, sales, quality assurance, and even administrative and security. He explained how his thesis was based on this scenario. His patents, which he had been awarded just a month ago, covered the application of his artificial intelligence code to allow his hardware-software platform to learn not just from the inputs of a particular division but also from its own mistakes as it received feedback from its users, just as a person would. He spent ten minutes touching on the basics of the implementation phase and the required training, again based on the model that he had developed in school.

"So," said Shapiro, his eyes now regarding Ryan with respect and admiration. "You've introduced the concept of artificial intelligence to the field of database management."

"Not really," Ryan admitted. "AI has been around for a long time in many fields, from the medical industry to oil refineries, financial services, the military, and NASA. Database management has been an integral part of most of those applications."

"So how is your research different from previous developments?" asked Wittica.

Ryan nodded and smiled. "Good question but a lengthy answer, so please bear with me. The classic concept of artificial intelligence is computer software that performs tasks we would consider intelligent if done by a human. These tasks comprehend providing expert advice based on a set of inputs or observations made in natural languages, like English. Because of their goal of providing expert advice, these artificial intelligence systems were—and still are at some levels—commonly referred to as 'expert systems.' An example of this traditional approach is Project Myacin, an expert system developed at Stanford during the 1970s to diagnose treatment for certain blood infections. In order for doctors to perform a proper diagnosis of blood infections they have to grow cultures of the infecting organism, a process that usually takes around forty-eight hours. But if doctors waited that long before providing a treatment, their patients might be dead. So doctors make educated guesses about likely problems based on the available data—like symptoms and medical history of their patients—to provide a general treatment to deal with likely problems until a final diagnosis can be generated from the cultures. Myacin was developed to explore how doctors, in this case the experts, made these very educated guesses on partial information. The expert system translated the doctor's knowledge into a complex series of if-then rules with certainty factors. For example, *if* the infection was primary bacteremia, and *if* the site of the culture is one of the stelire sites, and *if* the suspected portal of entry is the gastrointestinal tract, *then* there is an eighty-five percent certainty that the infection is bacteroid. Are you with me so far?"

Both executives nodded with interest.

"So," Ryan continued, reciting a portion of his Ph.D. dissertation, "Myacin used a backward-chaining reasoning strategy, which was pretty much the same concept applied to most traditional expert systems. My concept transcends that classic view to a higher level: the multiagent protocol system, or MPS. Unlike traditional AI views, which promote a computer system thinking on its own to the point of replacing a human, MPS maintains the human at the center of the universe but provides him or her with numerous smart agents, or SAs, classically known as expert systems, to accomplish hugely complex tasks. MPS in essence links many expert systems in hierarchical fashion to accomplish much larger tasks than individual expert systems, like the Myacin Project. I'm sure you still remember HAL, the smart computer in *2001: A Space Odyssey*, which performed many intelligent tasks but at some level under the master control of a human. MPS is very similar to that concept, but it's all executed through a virtual-reality interface that takes its inputs in plain English and replies to its ultimate master—the human—also in English. In this VR world, similar to a three-D video game, the human user moves through a citylike environment where buildings can represent the multiple sites of a corporation and streets are the high-speed connections linking the company. MPS agents may be represented by anything the customer prefers, from a man in a business suit guiding a corporate executive through a complex planning task to a cartoon character explaining to a nine-year-old how to access the school library system. These agents, at the request of the user, will go into buildings and retrieve the required information, or work with other agents to coordinate transfers of information, or develop plans that are presented to the user, or anything else that the user might require."

"Interesting," said Wittica.

"What's really interesting," said Ryan, whose master's work had also earned him three patents in the field of artificial intelligence, "is its ease of use once the MPS concept has been customized to a particular task. Take your eclectic system, for example. You have many versions of software operating on different versions of hardware all linked through the Internet, right?"

He received simultaneous nods.

"First we create expert systems, or agents, for each unique software-hardware platform. We do this by reviewing the system and interviewing the experts, like the doctors in Project Myacin, generating agents which in essence are modules that will act as interface, or liaison, with that particular software-hardware environment. Once we do this for every unique instance, in the process creating a hierarchy of junior agents, we step back up to the master, the human user, who provides overall guidance to the agents. We would also create special expert systems for security, quality control, and maintenance, to randomly roam the entire system looking for problems like illegal entries, corrupted software, and expired software licenses. Independent agents are the checks and balances of the system and a great asset to the human user to get another perspective on the activities of the entire system." Ryan spent an additional twenty minutes diving into the detail of how his concept could be applied to SoftCorp, at least to the level of detail that he could based on the limited information the executives had released on the operations of their company.

"Impressive," said Wittica.

"Thanks. I felt that I had created a very practical concept to help solve some of today's high-tech problems, like dealing with too much data."

Shapiro leaned forward, resting his elbows on his thighs, interlacing his fingers. "Listen, Mike. It's obvious that we're very interested in hiring you, and we would love to fly you and your spouse down to Austin so that you can take a look at the area. It's quite different from all other cities in Texas.

27

In many ways it looks and feels like California, only without the crowds. Austin is very young and still growing. I know you and your wife will love it there."

Ryan nodded thoughtfully. "Could you describe the typical responsibilities of a new hire?"

"They vary," said Ron Wittica, sitting sideways on the chair facing him. "We believe in nurturing the natural interests of our new hires, letting them grow at their own rate. We can afford to do that because we hire nothing but the best—the geniuses—and one can't really force a genius into a cookie-cutter position and expect him or her to shine. Our approach is quite refreshing and a bit different from the rest of the industry. We empower you from the beginning to pursue your ideas if they make sense to our business—and more specifically—to our primary client. We also provide you with the resources to carry out your vision. In many ways, Mike, your vision is quite aligned with ours. I think your background in artificial intelligence coupled with advanced virtual reality fits right into our current development efforts."

Ryan didn't know what to say. Wittica had just described the ideal position for an engineer. Do what you like and get paid for it. *Are these guys for real?*

"Does that answer your question?"

"Just a moment," Ryan said, standing up, walking behind the chairs, arms crossed. "You mean to tell me that if I accept your position I would be allowed to incorporate my VR-MPS concept into your current software-hardware development?" The mere thought of being able to do this made Ryan salivate. No other company had taken a real interest in his thesis beyond using it as a gauge to measure his technical competence and ability to work in their own software development efforts.

"If the integration makes technical sense, yes," said Wittica.

"And so far it makes a lot of sense," said Shapiro. "Personally, I can't wait for a demo of what such a system can do, especially your methodology for integrating artificial intelligence with VR. This could very well be the final link in our current effort to find an alternative to our client's eclectic system. The challenge of revamping what is one of the most complex, diversified, and in many ways archaic computer systems in the world—without disturbing our client's daily operations—has kept our engineers quite busy for years, developing what I believe is one of the most advanced and complex AI systems in the world. Problem is, we have not been able to work out a good interface for its users. In the meantime, we continue to Band-Aid—or patch, if you will—the existing systems to keep the entire machine running at its current level of efficiency."

"Actually, Aaron," said Wittica, "at it's current level of *inefficiency*."

Shapiro grinned. "The brightest minds from MIT, Caltech, Berkeley, and Princeton, among other schools, have been unable to work out a good user interface. The question is, do you think your MPS solution is versatile enough to handle a large number of expert systems working in parallel under the control of multiple users across several geographical locations?"

Ryan gave him a single nod.

Shapiro stood and went into one of the suite's bedrooms.

"How's your knee, Mike?" asked Wittica, switching subjects.

"Fine, though not good enough to play in the pros."

"What position did you play?"

"Defensive back."

Wittica inspected him for a moment before saying, "You look small for a defensive back."

Ryan smiled. "I made up for that with speed. Before my knee gave I broke the record at Stanford for the most tackles in a single game."

Shapiro returned holding an envelope, which he handed to Ryan. "Well, Mike, we are dead serious about convincing you to come and work for us. From here on out money should never again be a problem for you and your wife."

Ryan took the envelope in his hands, opened it, and for a moment wished he had been sitting down.

2

Under the grayish glow of fluorescent lights, FBI Special Agent Karen Frost followed a plump, black woman wearing a lab coat to the basement of Brackenridge Hospital, in Austin, Texas.

Karen's collection of turquoise-and-silver necklaces and bracelets, a constant reminder of her Texas heritage, rattled as she went down a flight of stairs. The sound mixed with the clicking of her snakeskin boots, echoing lightly inside the claustrophobic concrete stairway. The powerful Desert Eagle .44 Magnum pistol, secured in a chest holster beneath her dark cotton jacket whose sleeves Karen had rolled up to the middle of her forearms, reminded Karen of her profession. At six feet tall and just under a hundred thirty pounds, Karen Frost was an effective field agent, capable of controlling thugs of any size. Her regimen of exercise kept her arms and legs solid and her stomach flat—something Karen maintained not out of vanity but out of necessity to survive in the streets. But it was her voice that added command to her persona. It was low toned, and a bit raspy from the damage she had caused to her vocal cords during her cheerleading days in high school.

Her shoulder-length hair bounced slightly as she continued down the steps, a dark olive hand on the metal railing. Her stomach rumbled, telling Karen that she had not had a bite to eat in the past twelve hours. But food had not been a priority for the field agent while on a special assignment to search for a missing FBI agent: Dave Nolan.

"The service elevator's reserved for equipment and also bodies," Noemi Johnson, the graveyard shift supervisor, before looking over her left shoulder. "We get a lot of them from east Austin. Bad neighborhood."

Karen knew all about bad neighborhoods, having worked out of the nation's capital for the past ten years. A temporary-access pass clipped to the front pocket of her stone-washed jeans, Karen gave Noemi an easy knowing nod and a flicker of a smile. Every city had at least one hospital that catered to victims of violent crimes, especially those from the worst neighborhoods. The ERs of those hospitals typically had the best trauma teams in the city, capable of handling anything from stabs to gunshot wounds. Because of their efficiency in handling trauma, those ERs also treated victims from the worst auto accidents, fires, and even attempted suicides. It seemed logical then, that such a hospital would also receive city funding to support a large morgue, housing the bodies of those who'd died shortly after arriving at the hospital, or those who were pronounced DOA, until family members could claim them. Some bodies, however, were never identified and therefore never claimed. The city usually held them for a couple of weeks before cremating them.

Such hospitals were the best places to look for missing persons, especially for Karen Frost, who didn't want anyone aside from the director of the FBI to know she was in Austin. That included the local FBI office.

Cracking criminal networks operating inside the United States was what Karen Frost did best. Her recipe for success included maintaining utmost secrecy during a mission to avoid inadvertently tipping the enemy of her intentions—a mistake that FBI agents usually paid for with their lives. Criminal networks were not merciful when it came to a federal agent trying to expose their operations, and Karen Frost feared that Agent Dave Nolan had fallen victim to the network he was trying to crack—a fear she shared with Roman Palenski, the director of the FBI. Palenski, an old hand at the Bureau, kept a handful of very senior agents reporting directly to Karen Frost and trained for deep undercover assignments. Dave Nolan had been one of those agents, and when he had failed to report for three days in a row, Palenski had ordered Karen down South to find him. Although she usually received direction from Palenski, on paper Karen reported to Russell Meek, the FBI's deputy director, Palenski's right-hand man. Meek, a former desk agent responsible for modernizing the Bureau's computer networks, had little street experience and usually just stayed out of the way in these matters—though he had objected to deviating from the book and sending Nolan here alone.

And he'll raise even more hell when he finds out that I came down here by myself.

Palenski had opted not to tell Meek about Karen's last-minute trip until she had discovered Nolan's fate.

Noemi Johnson pushed a white metallic door at the bottom of the stairs. An old sign painted at eye level read:

Morgue
Brackenridge Hospital
Restricted Area
Passes Must Be Displayed at All Times

The fed smiled when noticing the word *Passes* missing most of the letter *P*, which had been peeled off the door.

"It happened last week and no one seems to be in a hurry to repaint it," Noemi said as she inserted her ID card in the reader next to the door.

"You gotta keep a sense of humor," Karen commented.

The red light on the card reader turned green.

"You sure you want to do this, honey?" the supervisor asked. She stood six inches shorter and almost a foot wider than Karen, her hair trapped inside a black net, her face relaxed, even showing a hint of dark amusement that probably came from working in a place like this. "It ain't too late to change your mind."

Karen, who had flashed her credentials to the graveyard shift supervisor to get her cooperation, simply said, "I can handle it."

"All right," Noemi said with a shrug. "But I'm warning you, I've seen some of the toughest cops lose it in here, especially in the section where *we're* headed."

"I'll be all right," Karen said reassuringly, hiding her annoyance at the overweight woman leading the way down a short corridor. There were two doors on each side and one at the end. With some luck Karen might be able to convince her not to make a report of her visit.

The supervisor went straight for the door in the rear. "This is where we keep the ones who haven't been identified."

Karen felt the skin of her exposed forearms goosebumping the moment she entered the room, but not from fear. The place was freezing, in sharp contrast with the hot and humid city where she had landed just past midnight, four hours ago. She immediately rolled the sleeves of her cotton jacket down to her wrists and braced herself.

"Some of the bodies have decayed beyond recognition by the time we get them," Noemi said while leading the way.

Karen frowned. Decomposed bodies always reminded the federal agent, ironically enough, of her years growing up in south Texas, near the border town of Eagle Pass, where her father had been the sheriff. A week during the hot season never went by without somebody stumbling upon the mortal remains of another illegal alien who had fallen victim to the scorching sun. Karen herself had found at least a half dozen of the poor bastards over the years while keeping her father company during his rounds. Many of the bodies had decomposed beyond recognition, oftentimes thanks to the hungry coyotes and vultures, which struck the moment the Mexicans succumbed to the extreme heat while traveling north on foot.

Karen Frost inspected the morgue. Three walls of refrigerated steel cubicles bounded the large white-tiled room. The gray door to each cubicle measured two feet square and each wall held close to twenty of them. A stainless-steel table next to a cart covered with surgical tools stood by a small bassinet in the center of the room, under a grid of fluorescent lights, of which one flickered, inducing a slight stroboscopic effect in the room.

"Too bad's four in the morning," Noemi said while working her fingers into a pair of green latex gloves. "The last forensic shift ended at midnight, and the next one isn't until six. Otherwise you'd have been treated to quite a show."

"Lucky me," said Karen while taking a shallow whiff of the antiseptic smell saturating the room.

"How far back you want to start?" Noemi asked while inspecting a brown clipboard hanging from the side of the stainless-steel table.

Her brown eyes on the cubicles, the fed asked, "How old is the oldest one you have?"

Keeping her gaze on the scribbled forms clipped together, the supervisor said, "Eight days."

Nolan had last called in just over three days ago. Shaking her head, her silver earrings swinging, she said, "That's too far back. How about any adult male brought here starting three days ago?" Karen didn't expect to find the female informant here, but she would have been disappointed if Nolan's body was missing. All criminal networks followed certain unwritten rules. One such rule was the guaranteed disappearance of informants. They simply were never found, unless one was willing to dredge every lake and river in the region for months. Captured FBI agents, however, were usually tortured in medieval ways before their bodies were dropped off at some street corner to send a message back to the Bureau.

Running a sausage-fat finger down the list and suddenly looking to her right, the supervisor left the clipboard swinging from the end of a chain, proceeded to open a shiny hatch at waist level, and pulled a sliding table holding a corpse under a white sheet.

"This one drowned in Lake Travis sometime Thursday night," Noemi said, lowering the sheet.

A shrunken face the color of gunmetal stared at the ceiling with dead eyes. Most of his forehead was missing, allowing Karen to see right into his brain cavity.

She felt a cramp.

"We think he must have fallen off a boat and got struck by something on the forehead, perhaps a propeller," Noemi said.

"Or maybe he got hit in the head first and *then* dumped in the lake." Karen's stomach churned when noticing the puss oozing from his ears. *Lovely.*

"No way to tell. Is this your man?"

"No," Karen said, looking away with the same disgust as when her father had to douse rotting carcasses with gasoline before setting them on fire to prevent the spread of disease.

"Not easy to get used to it, is it?" Noemi asked without really expecting an answer while she covered him, shoved him back in the cubicle, closed the latch, and opened the one below. "After a while you learn to simply treat them like objects. You even laugh at some of the jokes."

"I bet."

Noemi lowered the sheet and Karen felt her stomach knotting. Annoyed at herself for feeling this way, she focused her attention on a face that resembled burnt meat, missing all facial features. The corpse's seared neck displayed the hole of an emergency tracheotomy.

Fighting back the sudden nausea, Karen said, "What a way to go."

"We got three just like this one in the past month, all suspected homeless. Looks like someone's started a trend of pouring gas on them and setting them ablaze. Believe it or not, this one managed to run to a nearby fountain and put out the flames. He was still breathing when we got him upstairs. Didn't last long though. Can't survive with burns like these."

Fortunately.

Karen swallowed hard and took a deep breath. Shaking her head and closing her eyes, feeling as if she'd swallowed hot coals, she wondered what kind of scum would pour gas on a human being and set him on fire?

Unfortunately she knew the answer: the same kind of scum she had been hunting down for the past twenty years. The same kind of trash who had murdered her husband years before.

But at least I got even, Mark, Karen thought, her left thumb toying with the silver band on the ring finger of the same hand. A number of years ago Karen Frost had exposed a mafia ring in New York that profited from gray-market sales. Unfortunately, the people at the very top, who she discovered had been responsible for her husband's brutal death, had managed to escape to South America. Karen had caught up with them in Colombia, where she'd opted to take the law in her owns hands instead of having to deal with complex extradition procedure—

"Well?" asked Noemi Johnson.

Karen blinked once and gave the corpse another reluctant glance. "No." In spite of the extensive damage, Karen could see that the body was too tall to belong to Dave Nolan. "Any others in the past three days, male or female?" Karen asked, wondering not only how many more she would be able to endure but also whether she would find him here.

"Two more. Both males," Noemi Johnson said in an indifferent tone of voice after checking the clipboard once again. She walked to an adjacent wall, slid out the next corpse, and lifted a white blanket. "What do you think?"

Karen came face to face with a grossly burnt and disfigured man. The skin over the cheeks, mouth, and chin had vaporized, leaving soot-filmed jawbones and teeth exposed in a permanent leer. The same had happened to the throat and neck, letting Karen stare straight through to the man's spinal column. Still, what was left of the face didn't match Nolan's. The chin was too thin, the face too long.

Karen shook her head and took a step back, momentarily closing her eyes.

"You all right, honey?" the black supervisor asked. "You want to take a break? Maybe use the restroom?"

Karen winced, fighting a spasm. "I'm . . . I'm fine," she finally whispered.

"Of course you are," said Noemi while pointing to the sink next to the sterile surgical instruments. "But just in case chalk white isn't your normal color, feel free to use that sink. *Many* have, including yours truly. Around here vomiting is as common as urinating. You should see this place during Labor Day weekend. We call it puking day weekend because of all of the bodies."

Karen whispered, "Thanks for sharing that with me. Who's next?"

"All right," she said with a long sigh. "This last one even grossed *me* out. If you don't lose it here, you will set a new endurance record in this room for a visitor."

"I don't plan to stick around to receive any awards," remarked Karen, trying to use humor to shave off the edge.

Noemi pulled out the next corpse, her gloved hand reaching for the sheet. "A garbage truck found him inside a dumpster infested with rats. Not a pretty sight."

Noemi Johnson unveiled it, and Karen's stomach contracted hard. She clenched her teeth while gazing into what was left of the face of . . . *Dave Nolan!*

"The sick thing about this one," the morgue's supervisor added, "is the cause of death. There are some signs of torture. He is missing all fingernails, and his tongue was sliced off by a razor. But what killed him were the hundreds of bites from rats. They ate him while he was alive. Just like the two Roman candles back there, this poor bastard was killed by some sick son of a bitch."

Anger displacing her queasiness, Karen Frost inspected what was left of her subordinate. The eyes had been chewed away, as well as the ears, and most of the nose and lips.

But it's him all right.

"Let me see the rest of the body, please."

Noemi slid the tray all the way out and completely removed the sheet. The rats had eaten their way through the chest cavity and abdomen,

35

devouring internal organs, nibbling ribs clean of flesh, consuming his genitals as well as most of the muscle tissue from the thighs and calves. But the lower forearms, wrists, and hands were intact.

She focused on the left forearm, spotting the jagged scar Nolan had gotten while training at Quantico, the FBI training academy.

"Is this it?"

Karen shook her head. "No." Identification meant lots of paperwork, proof that she had been here, and the possibility of telegraphing her moves to the enemy, which also meant the risk of her ending in the same spot.

Karen told Noemi that she needed to go outside and get some fresh air—which wasn't too far from the truth—and that she would return in a moment to fill out the appropriate access forms. Then she left the hospital.

Karen had to call Palenski. The director of the FBI was not going to be pleased.

3

"Eighty thousand dollars per year?" said Victoria Ryan, rapidly waking up, her sleepy eyes blinking while staring at the offer letter in her hands before regarding her husband with a mix of surprise and admiration. Ryan had not had the heart to wake her up until now, the morning after the interview. Victoria, also a graduate student at Stanford, had been literally sleeping for the past two days after successfully completing all of her final exams. She would receive her MBA in finance next week, in the same graduating ceremony where Ryan would pick up his master's degree in computer engineering.

"That's . . . almost fifteen thousand higher than any other offer you have," she said, sitting up, white cotton sheets receding to her thighs.

"And that's just the base salary, honey," Ryan replied, curling up in bed next to his wife in the tiny bedroom of their married-student apartment just outside the main campus. "Keep reading."

Victoria battered her eyelashes in disbelief and lowered her gaze to the document in her hands, which were already beginning to tremble. She said, "Plus a quarterly bonus based on net company profits adjusted according to seniority and current base salary."

"What that means," said Ryan, remembering Wittica's explanation of the employee bonus program, "is around fifteen to twenty grand every three months if SoftCorp continues at its current level of earnings. And that's the going rate for new grads. Bonuses get progressively fatter as you move up the ladder."

Ryan smiled as she looked into the distance, obviously doing the math in her head. She looked lovely, wearing only a pair of black panties and one of his old football jerseys, currently raised up to her midriff.

"That's another sixty to eighty thousand more per year. Is this for real?" She licked her lips, which were dry from sleeping.

"It gets better," he added, reaching for the benefits package in the large manila envelope that Wittica had given him, and fishing out an Austin real estate brochure. Unfolding it, Ryan pointed at the picture of one of several homes displayed in full color, above drawings of their respective floor plans. "The Austin home market is a world away from this area. See here, a nice three-thousand-square-foot home in a good neighborhood goes for around two hundred and fifty thousand. That's roughly a *quarter* of the price of something even remotely similar in this area."

The Ryans had been pricing homes in Silicon Valley for the past three months. What they had found utterly depressed them. The housing market in this area was incredibly overpriced, with small three-bedroom homes in an average neighborhood starting at half a million dollars. And the homes themselves left a lot to be desired. Most were thirty or more years old and in need of serious upgrading, which the prospective buyer had to take into consideration before committing to the purchase. Not only was SoftCorp's offer far more generous than any other offer Ryan had gotten, but eighty thousand dollars per year—plus bonuses—bought a hell of a lot more house in Austin than in the valley.

Victoria was silent, her eyes fixed on the brochure. She had been in tears just last week, after it had become evident that the Ryans would be renting an apartment rather than purchasing a house for the foreseeable future. First they needed to save enough to come up with a sizable down payment, and that's after their combined salaries got to the point where they could qualify for such a mortgage.

"And," Ryan added. "Texas doesn't have a state income tax, which amounts to an additional eight percent salary increase over my other offers."

She put the brochure down, leaning her head back. "When something's *too good* to be true, it probably *isn't*. Mike, there *has* to be a catch."

He shrugged. "If there is one, I haven't been able to find it yet. I went on-line the moment I got back from the interview and was able to break into their network and—"

"Mike! You promised me never to—"

"It was quick. No one would be able to trace it. Besides, I had to get more info on them to check what they were telling me."

Crossing her arms, she asked, "And? What did you find?"

"So far it all matches. But we'll get a better chance to verify everything they've told me."

She regarded him with a puzzled stare.

Ryan tapped the business card stapled to the front of the brochure. "SoftCorp is springing for two round-trip tickets to Austin plus a two-night stay at the Four Seasons, classy joint. We've been invited to a company picnic Saturday morning to get the chance to meet the team and their families. Then this realtor is going to take us around the area and show us homes within our price range. Sunday we get the rental car of our choice to explore on our own."

She put a hand to his face. "Honey. I love you, but we can't buy a house, not even with this high salary and in Austin. Not only do we need to save for a down payment first, but you're forgetting about our student loans." Like Ryan, Victoria had also received an academic scholarship, but the financial assistance had not covered her master's degree. As they sat in bed this morning, they owed over forty thousand dollars in loans, which although they were low-interest loans still had to be paid back in full.

Ryan grinned. "Part of the benefits package includes payoff of any student loans, plus I guess I forgot to mention my sign-on bonus." He pulled out another envelope. It contained a check made out in the name of Michael Patrick Ryan for the amount of twenty thousand dollars.

Victoria Ryan wasn't an easily impressible woman. But at that moment she gave him the most incredulous look that Ryan had ever seen. "They just *handed* you this check and let you walk away without making you sign a contract? And they're willing to pay off your student loans?"

He turned the check over and pointed at the fine print above the endorsement line. It stated in legal jargon that cashing of this check implied his acceptance of the job offer. "They pick up loan payments the moment I sign up, and they pay it off in full after my first year at SoftCorp, assuming of course, a positive review from my manager. I am bound, though, to work a minimum of three years, or I'll have to give it all back." The practice of binding engineers was pretty common in the industry when a company had to shell out money up front to hire someone.

"How—how can these people afford to do this? I mean," she said, now holding his face in her hands, "don't get me wrong. I *adore you*, and I think that you're brilliant . . . but, honey, you're just a *new grad*. Why are these people treating you as if you're a Nobel Prize winner?"

"And I forgot," Ryan said, reaching once more into his magic envelope. "I get a car allowance."

"A what?"

"An car allowance. Five hundred bucks a month. I get to buy or lease anything I want."

"Mike, why are you getting such royal treatment?"

"Everyone does at SoftCorp," he said, taking her hands in his, kissing her on the cheek, and going on talking about how SoftCorp employees retired in their late thirties or early forties with money to burn.

"I've never heard of . . . Mike, I'm getting a bad feeling about this."

"Have I told you how sexy you look when you behave with such paranoia?"

She pushed him away and crossed her arms. "Someone has to balance that insane *optimism* of yours. I'll continue to keep my feet on the ground while you're up there trying to snag stars. I just hope you don't get burned by one."

They locked eyes, reading each other's minds. Victoria and Ryan had met at the beginning of their freshmen year but didn't date until late in their sophomore year. Instead, they had been simply good friends, confiding in each other for that year and a half, developing a mutual trust that was completely alien to couples who dated from the day they met. That friendship, combined with the love that followed, formed a powerful bond between them, a bond that allowed them, with a simple stare, to convey any imaginable feeling. And right now Ryan saw true concern in his wife's stare.

"Who are these people, Mike? Why are they being so generous?"

"Look," he said. "I've checked them out on the Web. The company is legit. They have a huge government contract and hire only the very top talent from the top schools. They are really interested in my MPS software along with the VR interface. It just might be the solution to their customer's database problems."

"You don't have to sign away any of your patents to them, do you?"

Ryan shook his head. "Patents are mine. My task would be to customize a solution for their customer starting at one site and then expanding it into a network linked through the Internet." He went on to explain how his approach could apply quite elegantly to SoftCorp's eclectic software-hardware dilemma. Victoria followed the conversation and asked intelligent questions about the details of the implementation. She had taken several computer science courses along with her finance degree. In this day and age it was almost crazy not to get some formal training in computers along with any discipline.

She exhaled heavily the moment Ryan finished his explanation, pushing out her lower lip as she did so, ruffling the bangs of auburn hair over her forehead.

"I won't consider it if you don't want me to," he said matter-of-factly as they sat cross-legged facing each other. And he really meant it. Victoria was more than his wife and best friend. She was his soul mate. They would do this together or not at all.

"You're willing to leave California?"

Ryan tilted his head. "Sounds radical, doesn't it? On the one hand, we do have a great life here, with our families nearby and so many outdoor activities, great weather. But on the other hand, how are we ever going to get ahead with the high cost of living? How about if we look at this as an opportunity—call it a shortcut if you wish—to improve our financial situation and then return to California with a solid enough cash base to start our life as we had once envisioned it?"

"How is the banking industry in Austin?" she asked, raising a brow.

Victoria had put off any serious interviewing until Ryan's job situation had settled. They'd figured that a magna cum laude from Stanford's graduate school of business and finance could land a job in any financial district. She just hadn't thought that his job would take them that far away from their home. Both had been born and raised in northern California. Victoria's parents lived in Oakland, across the Bay from San Francisco. Ryan's mother lived in Sacramento, about two hours away by car. Ryan's father had passed away a few years ago. This area was all they knew and all that they had wanted to know until SoftCorp had come along.

Ryan smiled shyly. "I almost forgot." He browsed inside the manila envelope once again and showed her a business card. "This is from a fellow named Angelo Rossini, the president of Capitol Bank, the institution in Austin handling SoftCorp's financial needs, which, by the way, includes low-interest home loans for SoftCorp employees." He winked. "He's expecting your call, Vic."

"He is?"

"Yep."

"They just *happened* to have this business card handy?"

Ryan thought about it. "No, actually, they produced it, along with information on home loans, when they gave me the real estate brochure because the low-interest loans are part of the incentive package."

She stared at the card for a moment. It had a very clear color photo of its owner.

"Well, he is a handsome devil," Victoria said, flashing Ryan a mischievous smile.

Ryan rolled his eyes, frowning, caressing her hands. Her fingers were slim, with a couple of calluses and unkempt finger nails. Victoria, a tomboy at heart, never concerned herself with certain aspects of femininity. She wore little to no makeup, preferred blue jeans and starched long-sleeve shirts to dresses, kept her hair very short though cut stylishly, and would rather spend the weekend roughing it at Yosemite National Park than in a resort at Lake Tahoe. Ryan always felt that this aspect of his wife's personality was best reflected in her shoes. Victoria Ryan's dress shoes were penny loafers. The rest were weathered sneakers and hiking shoes or boots. But she was naturally beautiful, with light olive skin, lips that models would die for, perfect teeth, and hazel eyes that Ryan had grown to love so much.

Those eyes now flashed him an ironic look. "And I suppose this good-looking Italian guy is going to offer me . . . a *job I can't refuse?*" She said, lowering her tone of voice and hissing the last few words.

He ignored her comments about Rossini's looks, which she had thrown in just to annoy him. "They're not the mafia, Vic."

"They sure *seem* like it. And this guy Rossini reminds me of Al Pacino. Looks to me like they're doing you *a lot* of favors."

"It's a business deal, Vic. Nothing more and nothing less. I do my job and they pay me for it. And between you and me, I think I'm worth it."

They laughed for a moment, before turning serious again.

"Are you sure you want to do this, Michael Patrick?"

Ryan thought about it before responding. Victoria—and Ryan's own mother for that matter—never called him Michael Patrick unless they were either dead serious or really mad at him. Right now Ryan suspected it was the former.

"Let's just visit Austin and go through the motions. I can't see the harm in doing that. *Then* we'll make our decision, okay?"

"Okay."

Ryan kissed her. "Thanks, Vic. You're not going to regret it."

4

Karen Frost filled her lungs with warm air as she left the hospital and walked for several blocks to reach a vehicle she had parked just one block away. She did this out of habit, to check for surveillance—though she didn't expect to find any. But if she made an exception today, she would make others later. When trouble struck she could be caught unprepared—a mistake younger agents paid for with their lives.

She approached the rented Taurus from the rear, carefully inspecting the backseat before unlocking the front and getting inside, and locking it again as she closed it. She put the car in gear and pulled off the curb before using her cellular phone to dial a Washington extension she had long committed to memory. It belonged to the director of the FBI.

After two rings, Palenski's booming voice came on the line. "Yeah?"

"Morning, Chief," Karen said, her eyes gravitating to the rearview mirror, making certain that she was not being followed.

"Karen? Found anything?"

"Is it safe to talk?"

"Hold on." A light static sound invaded the connection. "Okay."

"The operation was compromised," she said with deceptive calmness, left hand on the wheel, right hand pressing the small unit against the side of her face.

Silence, followed by, "Nolan?"

"Dead."

"Are you certain?"

"I just saw what was left of him at the morgue." She steered the Taurus toward I-35.

"What was left—?"

"This wasn't your typical interrogation and torture, Chief. *Rats* ate him alive."

"Ate him . . ." His words trailed off for a moment before he added, "What about the informant?"

"Our lady friend is probably no longer with us."

Another sigh, followed by, "All right. What's your next move?"

Accelerating as she reached the ramp for the highway, Karen spotted a large billboard on the side of the road. It showed a cowboy in an aluminum boat holding a fishing rod while trolling in waters filled with smiling catfish and turtles. Texas State Parks, the Perfect Weekend Getaway.

"I'm going fishing," she said, her calculating mind thinking through a scenario with the same icy, uncompromising attitude that had allowed her to crack many criminal networks in the past. Cold, frosty, like her name, Karen knew of only one way to fight fire: with a blizzard, without emotions, chilling her enemies' operation to the bone, to the breaking point, until she exposed them, until she took them down.

She remained in the right-hand lane. Her exit, Oltorf Street, was less than a mile away, according to the tourist map spread open on the passenger seat.

"Did you say *fishing?*"

Karen spent the next minute explaining her plan.

"Very risky," Palenski commented.

"It's the only way."

"What about backup?"

As she exited the interstate and turned left on Oltorf, she said, "No, Chief. No backup. The moment I start digging, I'm very likely to become a target, just like Nolan. That'll make *everyone* around me also a hot liability. Besides, there's a chance that Nolan talked. He knew that if something were to happen to him that I was next in line to pick up this investigation. If he did confess—and I have to assume that he did—then there's a pretty good chance that I'm already in grave danger."

"Careful, Karen. I don't relish the thought of having to send *another* agent down there to find out what happened to you."

"I'll handle my end, sir. Please handle Meek. He's not going to be pleased when he finds out."

"I'm not worried about Meek. I'm worried about those barracudas in Congress. I'm going to have a hell of a time getting my budget approved, especially after Nolan's death hits the press."

"Is Senator Horton at it again?" she asked, well aware of the difficulties in getting budgets through Horton's scrutinizing eye.

"With a vengeance, but that's my problem. You're sure you don't want some backup? I can send you a couple of old hands from the New York office. People you've worked with before."

"I'm afraid they might end up in that same morgue, Chief, right next to Nolan."

"Or next to *you*, if you don't watch your ass."

Karen frowned. "Look . . . I've been in tight spots before. I can handle it, but I have to do it alone."

"All right," Palenski said reluctantly. "How are you doing on hardware?"

"Brought my old faithful and my backup. Anything else I may need I'll put it on the card," she said, referring to a Bureau-issued Visa for one of her undercover names. Karen also had a Washington, D.C., driver's license under that fake name. Following basic undercover rules, she had left her personal identification—anything that could link her to the FBI—at a locker at the airport.

"Don't take any chances. Call once a day, as arranged."

"Will do."

"And I'll contact Nolan's family and take care of all of the necessary arrangements."

Her stomach cramped.

"Good luck, Karen."

"Thank you, Chief."

The ravaged body of Dave Nolan flashing in front of her eyes, throwing a translucent veil over the long street, Karen ended the call and set the mobile phone on the passenger seat, over the map. The heart-wrenching pain of having lost a fellow agent attacked her insides with the same intensity that those rats had when devouring her subordinate . . . *while he was still alive!*

Karen Frost swore at that moment to avenge Dave Nolan's death, just as she had avenged her husband's.

Coldly. Without mercy.

The thought brought her back to Colombia, to a rainy night at a mountaintop villa outside Bogota. Karen remembered the sentries guarding the perimeter fence, she could still hear their guttural sounds as she sliced their throats, their dark figures falling on the muddy ground already corpses. She could feel the soaked cotton fabric of her drab olive fatigues sticking to her back, her breasts, her legs. She tasted the sweetness of the tropical rainwater dripping down her cheekbones and into her mouth. She studied the backlit silhouetted figures inside the mansion. They were relaxed, vulnerable, never expecting the long arm of the FBI to strike so soon after they had escaped via Mexico and Central America. But Karen Frost had tracked them down. She had bribed Mexican officials, threatened a customs agent in Nicaragua with castration, listened to the conversation of two high-ranking officers in the Panamanian government, and had finally reached Bogota, where an underpaid bank official told her a tale about the eccentric foreigners who had recently transferred dozens of millions of dollars into his bank and had purchased an estate formerly owned by a drug lord.

R . J . Pineiro

The rest had been simple mechanics, coldly executed, just as she planned to carry out this operation.

A frost is coming to town, you bastards.

She reached Oltorf and drove into the parking lot of a Days Inn hotel—her home for the foreseeable future.

5

"Dammit, Roman! I told you we shouldn't have sent Nolan alone! Damn!"

Palenski sat back on the leather chair behind his desk on the top floor of the J. Edgar Hoover Building and regarded his freckle-faced subordinate with dark amusement. FBI Deputy Director Russell Meek had the day off today, but Palenski had pulled him away from an early-morning golf game to let him know that Nolan was dead. Meek had always been quite predictable, and today the desk agent continued to live up to his reputation.

"Relax, Russ. You know that sometimes these things don't go as planned."

Meek, a hefty man with orange hair, removed his baseball hat and sat down across from Palenski. "If we followed the book a little more, sir, *these things* would *not* have to happen as often as they do."

Palenski's stare hardened, but he didn't reply. He actually indulged his subordinate, whose lack of field experience was more than made up for by his administrative and computer skills. Although the Yale graduate in computer science had not fired a weapon in years, his work to modernize the Bureau had given him access to every department inside the FBI. Meek knew all of the ins and outs of the federal agency. He could cut through red tape when ordered to, and throw enough of it on an issue to stall it for as long as Palenski demanded. In addition to improving efficiency, Meek provided overall discipline in the FBI, a refreshing balancing force in an agency that had a natural tendency to lean in the opposite direction. Meek was also one hell of an asset when it came time to obtaining federal funding, especially in light of fiascos like Waco and Ruby Ridge. Meek's attention to detail when documenting the accomplishments and plans of the FBI in perfectly crafted color foils provided Palenski with a great tool to fight off the standard wave of skepticism and criticism in Congress.

But Russell Meek could also be one royal pain in the ass during times

R . J . P i n e i r o

like this, when his textbook view of the operations world tended to clash with reality.

But that's why they pay me the big bucks, Palenski mused. *To handle people like you.*

"Great," said Meek, crossing his sunburned arms alive with the same orange freckles that moved across his face as he frowned. "This incident's going to look *just* great in our files, Roman. Horton's going to have your head in Congress next month."

Palenski hated budget reviews, and he used the well-crafted presentations generated by Meek's technical division to handle those Capitol Hill piranhas, who had no idea how difficult it was to run and coordinate the complex activities of the FBI. They loved to focus on the few things that had gone wrong while ignoring the Bureau's many accomplishments.

"We're the world's largest *and* finest law enforcement organization, Russ. I can promise you two things. One is that this kind of problem will happen again, and two, that we will always find a way to deal with them. And don't worry about Senator Horton and the rest of his kind on the Hill. Let them complain. At the end of the day they go home to their families and sleep safely and peacefully thanks to people like you and me, who work around the clock keeping the world's loonies from blowing up this country."

"Roman," Meek said, shaking his head. "I hear you. But every time we screw up it goes on the record. We can't keep—"

"Halt," Palenski said, deciding to try to get through to his subordinate one more time. Meek was worth the effort. He was a straight shooter trying to do the right thing. Problem was he didn't have the experience to know what the right thing was all the time and needed coaching on situations like this one. "Listen up. If we don't lose a battle sometimes, it means we're playing it too safe. It means we're being too conservative with an enemy who is willing to take *many* chances, to get caught *many* times as long as it gains ground, slowly, like a cancer. Our enemies don't care if they lose fifty men a month as long as their empires grow. In order to fight back effectively, we also must be willing to take chances, risks, go out on a limb, *deviate* from the book. Otherwise I can guarantee you that in the end we will lose the war. The problem is that most people don't realize this, especially here in Washington. They see one problem and think that the world is coming to an end at the FBI, while in reality we are winning. The streets are safer. Crime is down. We're catching more bad guys than ever—and *before* they get a chance to strike. We do that by risking the lives of our agents, by sending them to the field to do a job no one else wants to do because it's too damned difficult and there could be terrible repercussions, reprisals against oneself and also one's family, like what happened to Karen."

Meek exhaled heavily, looking about him. "I get the message. Speaking of her . . . does she know?"

Palenski, who had strategically chosen not to mention this minor detail until now, said "She's in Austin, Russ."

"In—why?"

"She's the one who identified Nolan."

"Who went with her?"

Palenski just stared at him.

Meek leaned forward, his tone of voice deepening. "Any local support?"

The director of the FBI just kept staring.

Meek jumped to his feet and slapped Palenski's desk. "Dammit, Roman! We just lost one top agent this way! What are you trying to do? Lose them all one at a time? Is that your idea of running an agency like the FBI?"

Palenski let that one go. He liked Meek, and he knew the deputy director had just finished going through a painful divorce. Apparently not only had his wife left him for a younger man but she had pinned him with one a hell of an alimony payment in addition to sticking Meek with the college tuition and living expenses of their two kids. And to top it all off, just last week, the computer wizard had also received an invoice for the legal fees of his ex-wife's lawyers. Apparently, she had managed to convince the judge that he should pay for her litigation expenses.

Palenski motioned his subordinate to sit back down, disappointed that he just didn't seem to get through to Meek on the bigger picture of what the FBI was trying to accomplish. He decided to move on. "Nolan's death actually presents us with a unique opportunity."

Meek settled back down in his chair and gave him a puzzled look. "You've lost me."

Palenski explained Karen's plan.

After a moment Meek stood again and calmly walked to the windows on the right side of Palenski's corner office. A postcard-perfect view of the Capitol under a clear sky filled the tinted panes.

"Very risky, Roman," Meek said. "Very, *very* risky."

"But think of the potential upside. We could force a breakthrough in the investigation. This was what I meant by taking chances in order to win the war. We could play it safe by shipping an army of federal agents to Austin and just blanket the place with security. But all that's going to do is force the crooks to go underground for a while before resurfacing someplace else. We would accomplish nothing, except spending taxpayers' money."

"But for all we know they are already going underground because of Nolan. We have to assume he talked."

Palenski nodded. "Criminal networks of the size that I suspect we're

49

dealing with here won't vanish on account of one agent. They've told us that by allowing Nolan's body to surface."

Meek narrowed his stare.

"Russ, the bastards sent us a message with Nolan's body. They maimed him in horrible ways and then fed his living remains to the rats. Those bastards are telling us to leave them alone."

"Then what's the harm of sending more agents if they already know we're investigating them?"

"To bank on their arrogance. If they see just one lone agent going after them they will be far more willing to show themselves again than if they see a dozen."

Meek took a deep breath, apparently understanding Karen Frost's suicidal strategy. "So she's staying down there to draw them out?"

Once again Palenski just stared at his subordinate.

"And when they do come out?"

"That's when it gets hairy," agreed Palenski. "But Karen feels confident that she can turn the tables on them."

"And you think she can handle it alone?"

Palenski nodded. "She's a big girl."

"She's setting herself up as bait," Meek said in amazement.

Palenski didn't reply.

"All right, Roman. For the record, I don't agree with this approach. It's just plain crazy."

"Your opinion has been noted, Russ."

Meek stood up to leave. "Is there anything else?"

"Yes. When will I see the draft for this year's report to Congress?"

Meek tilted his head. "In about a week."

"All right. Go back to your golf game."

Meek left the office.

Palenski turned to the windows. On one hand he was concerned about Meek's ability to see the big picture. On the other hand, the experienced agent in Palenski forced him to consider his subordinate's point of view for a moment. What if Meek was right about this one? What if something were to happen to Karen? How many more agents would Palenski be willing to sacrifice before sending in the cavalry?

The director glanced at the pictures of his son and daughter at their college graduations almost a decade ago. He rarely heard from them now that one had become a hotshot Wall Street lawyer and the other a college professor at Indiana State. As for his wife, Palenski had not seen her since their divorce over fifteen years ago, soon after their kids went to college. She had left him just as abruptly as Meek's wife had, tired of his working hours and the unavoidable stress that he would bring home at the end of the day. Marriages and FBI careers simply didn't mix. Too bad they didn't teach that at Quantico.

He leaned back in his swivel chair while gazing at the blue skies over Washington. His mind drifted to Special Agent Dave Nolan, eaten alive by rats. On his desk was the letter Palenski had already drafted for Nolan's widow and children.

He groaned while reaching for a pack of gum on his desk. He unwrapped a stick and began to chew it while wondering just how much suffering was too much for an FBI agent. In his days with the Bureau, his men had been stabbed, shot, strangled, drowned, set ablaze, and even buried alive. Being eaten alive by rats was certainly a first.

Palenski wondered if he was getting too old for this job. He also wondered just how he would go, when his turn came. Would he die of cancer like his parents, or did destiny hold something else in store for him, like one of the brutal methods that criminals liked to reserve for federal agents—and their bosses?

Will I die alone?

Palenski glanced at the picture of his kids once more before getting up and heading for a meeting.

(51)

6

Ryan and Victoria leaned against the railing on the upper deck of the party barge as it cruised down the middle of Lake Travis, just west of Austin, Texas. The midmorning sun shown high above the forested hills surrounding the man-made lake. The wind caressed Ryan's face as he looked to the east, where ridges rose to meet a blue-gray heaven. The terrain slanted down to the base of the hills, where the water had eroded the land, exposing layers of whitewashed limestone, twenty or more feet high in some places, marking the varying levels of the lake.

Ryan peered at this angled wall of hunter green, speckled with the pastel hues of luxurious homes nestled amidst cedars and oaks. Long stairways, and in some cases automatic lifts, connected the residences to boat slips by the water's edge, where yachts and sailboats rocked gently in the shallow swells blown by the wind.

Light music flowed out of multiple speakers spread across both decks, mixing with the soft whistle of the lake breeze, the sound of water lapping against the boat's hull, and the near-hypnotic drone of the stern screws. The smell of barbecue catered from a place called the Iron Works made his stomach rumble. The food line was scheduled to open at 11:00 A.M., according to the activity agenda posted around the large vessel.

They had flown into Austin the night before. A limousine driver had greeted them at the gate. Following a night tour of downtown Austin, they had reached the Four Seasons at around ten. The same driver had picked them up at nine this morning and brought them to the lake, where Ron Wittica and his girlfriend had met them by the dock. Ryan and Victoria had wondered what to wear for such an occasion, finally settling on dress shorts, a polo shirt, and Topsiders for him and a summer dress and white sandals for her. He had been relieved to see Wittica and the model-thin blonde accompanying him wearing similar clothing.

Introductions had followed, as Wittica had taken the young couple around the boat. Several engineers eventually migrated to one section of the boat, dragging Ryan along to talk shop while the wives' club pulled Victoria aside for their own conversation.

"They grilled me technically," Ryan commented to Victoria later, out of earshot from anyone milling about the upper deck. This was the first time that they had been alone since boarding the large boat. He sipped diet Coke while enjoying the view.

Victoria laughed before whispering, "At least you could talk on even terms with them. All those women wanted to chat about was home decorating and babies."

"Babies, huh? I'm sure the Farrah Fawcett look-alike with Ron wanted to chat about anything *but* babies."

"Her name's Cherry."

"Figures," Ryan said, spotting her in the distance hanging on to Wittica's right arm, her hair flowing in the breeze. She looked at Ryan and waved while flashing a smile. He waved back while commenting, "Do you think Ron's paying her by the hour?"

Victoria leaned over, adding, "She might be great at hooking or stripping, but she can't hold a normal conversation." She touched her left temple. "I didn't detect much up here."

He shrugged. "That's all right, Vic. There's plenty below her hood to make up for that."

She stabbed his ribs with a finger.

He grinned. "But nowhere near as much hardware as what you're packing beneath that cute little outfit."

This time he got a smile in return. She looked stunning this morning. Her moussed hair, brushed straight back, accentuated her eyes and her high cheekbones, giving her a natural aura that she further enhanced with a touch of lipstick and eye shadow, all in the pastels that blended beautifully with her bronze skin tone. For a moment he wished he were alone with her.

Ryan was going to give her another compliment but held it back. Sensitive about being confused with dumb beauties like Cherry, Victoria didn't care for too many such compliments, preferring instead to be treated according to her level of intelligence and academic accomplishments.

Instead, he asked, "What do you think so far?"

"That's the one I like," she said, pointing to a Mediterranean-style mansion snuggled in a relatively flat spread of land two-thirds down a hill. Opulent oaks shadowed it and the large deck overlooking a dock housing a beautiful yacht, a ski boat, and two personal watercraft.

"I think we'll have to do something illegal to get that one."

"As opposed to what we're doing now?" she said, leaning back against the railing, crossing her arms. Victoria had contacted Capitol Bank yester-

53

day and had gotten through to Angelo Rossini. They'd spent an hour on the phone talking about everything from her schoolwork and career aspirations to the differences between life in Austin and Sunnyvale. Rossini had insisted on meeting her in person before she headed back to California. He had given her the impression that Capitol Bank could be making her a competitive offer based on the outcome of this face-to-face interview.

"Stop being so paranoid and enjoy the ride."

She gave him an admonishing look. "I grew up poor, Mike, and so did you. You *should* be 'paranoid' of anyone being so generous."

"You're missing the whole point, Vic. They're not being generous. That's how much our education is worth."

She was about to reply when Wittica and Cherry approached them.

"And how are our guests of honor doing?" he asked, smiling, his face sporting the handsome damage of many weekends sailing and horseback riding.

"We're having a great time, Ron. Thanks."

Wittica winked, flashing another perfect smile before leaning closer to Ryan. "I heard you really impressed the boys back there."

Ryan gave him a half-embarrassed shrug. "I just answered their questions. They're a very smart lot."

Wittica turned to Victoria. "Is he always this modest?"

"Only when he's after something," she replied, frowning with humor while glancing sideways at Ryan.

Wittica smiled. The blonde giggled and said, "My! They look so cute together!"

Cute?

"Don't you think so, Ronny?"

Ronny?

Wittica glared at Cherry in the same manner that a father uses to admonish a misbehaving child.

Blondie either ignored him or didn't get the subtle hint to zip it, because she added while pointing at Victoria, "See, Ronny, I told you she looked like a movie star."

Victoria glanced at Ryan, who smiled, and said, "Great, now the two of you can audition to be extras in *Bay Watch.*"

Wittica burst out laughing. Blondie looked confused. Victoria shot him a look that could cut steel.

A horn blared.

Wittica glanced at his Rolex watch. "Lunchtime, folks. Shall we?"

As the foursome headed for the stairs leading to the main deck, Michael Patrick Ryan glanced at the distant hills once again, the breeze in his face, deciding at that moment to make Austin home at least for the next three years. The only question left in his mind was how soon they could move down there.

7

Karen Frost leaned back and rubbed her eyes before reaching for a two-day-old issue of the *Austin American Statesman* in one of the reading rooms at the central branch of the Austin Public Library, where she had spent the last hour searching for articles on missing women in the past week.

According to the FBI database, which Karen had convinced Russell Meek to check earlier this morning, three women had been reported missing since Nolan's last call. Two were teenagers. The third was a woman in her sixties. None of them fitted the description of a female employee at the IRS.

Well aware of the limitations of that database—which was only as good as the underpaid government clerks updating it from the data flowing out of fifty states—Karen had opted to cross-check her information through the Internet, where many missing-person services kept fairly accurate records—services that didn't require Karen to reveal her true identity and thus tip the enemy to her activities. That search, however, had yielded nothing beyond what she had found in the FBI database, probably because Nolan's informant had been missing for no more than a few days. That had led her to the local paper, where she had hoped to find related stories. So far she had found a back-page article about a sixteen-year-old high school girl who'd vanished four days ago. She was one of the missing teens in the FBI database.

Karen flipped through the newspaper, finding no additional information. She also saw nothing of interest in yesterday's edition of the *Statesman.* Replacing that newspaper with today's edition, she resumed her hunt. Five minutes later her eyes zeroed in on the Metro and State section. Janet Patterson, a twenty-seven-year-old woman, had driven off a cliff in west Austin and was found dead moments later by a truck driver, who called the police. An autopsy revealed an alcohol level of 0.2 percent, four times higher than the state limit of 0.05 percent.

Karen reviewed the obituaries, scanning the short write-ups, finding the one for Janet Patterson.

Janet Michelle Patterson, 27, died on Friday from injuries sustained during an auto accident. She is remembered by her parents, Greg and Louise Patterson of Westlake, a community west of Austin, and by her coworkers at the Internal Revenue Service, where Ms. Patterson worked for five years following her graduation from the University of Texas. A memorial service will be held Sunday at 3: 00 P.M. at St. John Newman Catholic Church in Westlake. Arrangements by Cook-Walden Funeral Home. All services donated by the Internal Revenue Service.

She froze, reading the entry two more times before flipping back to the metro section and reviewing the article.

"Son of a bitch," she hissed.

Two people from a table next to hers looked up, frowned, and resumed their reading.

She ignored them, her mind racing through the facts she had just learned, her logic exploring possibilities, options. If Janet Patterson was Nolan's informant, and if she had indeed been killed because of what she knew, then that knowledge put her parents also at risk. She felt certain that their lives were being monitored to see if they made any attempt to reach the authorities. Contacting them without putting them in danger would be quite challenging. She knew how these networks operated. Their primary objective in a situation like this was to sever the link in the investigative chain. First they had removed the FBI's primary link, the informant, followed by the agent leading the investigation. Now they were focusing on her parents to make sure that Janet didn't leave something behind, like a videotape or some other record of her knowledge in case she met with misfortune. This, Karen knew, was a very tricky balancing act for the criminal network, who wanted to avoid any unnecessary attention to keep its operation from stalling, and therefore wouldn't just barge in and eliminate her parents because that in itself would attract a lot of attention so soon after their daughter's accident.

So they are just monitoring them.

And that, Karen admitted, would be the case only if Janet Patterson had indeed been Nolan's informant. The timing of her death and association with the IRS could still be coincidental, particularly since in many cases informants usually vanished. They didn't show up in the obituary section of the newspapers. But then again, the staged accident might have been set up to keep her parents from getting suspicious.

Possibilities. Theories.

But only one truth.

And the calculating agent in her knew of only one way to find it.

**book
two**

Plug and Play

I think there is a world market for maybe
five computers.
        —Thomas Watson, chairman of IBM, 1943

A metallic blue-gray sky, broken up by charcoal clouds with imperfect edges, covered the 256-color cyberscape. Ryan stood in the middle of a neon blue street, which contrasted sharply with green buildings, white sidewalks, and the red-and-violet figure of the agent representing the expert system designed to assist him during this demonstration. A plane of motion-sensitive diodes built into his head-mounted display read the motion of his eyes as he shifted them about this digital world, verifying that his last edits to the program had indeed highlighted the access door to the data bank that he intended to use on this run.

The virtual-reality system had painted the entryway to this archive down the street to his left as a large garage door, which would open at the actual blink of his eyes after he got past the security protocol. The diode plane not only registered Ryan's eye motion but it also activated whatever object he had been looking at the moment he blinked. This last aspect of his VR scheme—a departure from traditional VR controllers like tactile gloves—had been the most difficult to master, many times resulting in the wrong items selected or the wrong agent dispatched when Ryan blinked at the wrong time. For that purpose, Ryan had added a neutral zone for normal blinking or simply to rest his eyes: the imperfect clouds, which governed the digitized skies of his multiagent protocol system. The evolution from tactile glove to eye control, however, had allowed Ryan far better system reaction time to his commands as he cruised through this carefully tailored land. Despite all of the technological improvements made in recent years to tactile gloves, particularly in the spatial detection of the position of his fingers as he moved them about to issue commands, Ryan's patented diode plane and associated software could far better detect the position of his eyes and blinks than the best tactile gloves in the market, especially after Ryan had spent a year making the eye scan user friendly.

Accompanying Ryan on this MPS exercise was Ron Wittica, the magenta-and-silver figure to his immediate right, standing by the agent waiting for his direction. Like Ryan, Wittica wore an HMD that housed the dual LCD displays, the diode matrix, headphones, and a connection for the throat mike. But unlike Ryan, Wittica's interface lacked a key feature in the diode matrix—the ability to detect blinks. He could gaze about in this digital environment, but he could not select or activate anything. He was just an observer. Ryan was the driver. In addition, Ryan had attached an electronic rope to Wittica so that his boss remained glued to his side and could not get lost in the VR city as they made their run.

Ryan moved his head to the right and left to check out his flanks and also test the VR system response. The software detected this head motion and responded with minimal latency, presenting his brain with a very fluid stereoscopic image to match his head movement at the respectable rate of twenty frames per second. Both negligible latency and reasonable frames per second were required in order to achieve good VR immersion—the degree of realism achieved by the virtual-reality environment. The more the user couldn't tell the difference between the VR experience and reality, the better the immersion. Latency was the delay between the user's head motion and the system's response to shift the digital scenery according to that motion. The frames per second drove the fluidity of the image presented. A minimum of fifteen frames per second was required to permit comfortable use of a VR system. Anything below that tended to slow down the action, creating a delayed effect between the head motion and the image presented to the brain. This in turn would result in discomfort to the user as the image displayed to the user lagged behind the position information communicated to the brain by the semicircular canals of the inner ear, inducing dizziness, motion sickness, even vomiting.

Ryan remembered the many times when he had to take medication in order to minimize such effects while spending many hours strapped to an HMD developing his system. Due to a mix of prototype hardware and immature software, the early versions of his VR-MPS system would not always deliver small latency and fluid images, which prompted him to always have airsick bags nearby. Ryan had actually lost ten pounds over the year-long development period.

"All right, Ron," Ryan said, his throat mike picking up the message, amplifying it, and broadcasting it in cyberspace as a powerful baritone voice in Dolby digital surround sound. "If you begin to feel queasy just close your eyes and the feeling will pass. We're going to access the database of a fake corporation, which I used for my thesis. Here we go."

Ryan moved his eyes down the street in front of him and blinked. Forward motion started as the VR city came to life. Footsteps clicked hollowly over the neon blue pavement, mixed with the digitized sound of a light breeze as Ryan walked up the deserted street, heading toward the first database entryway in this very simple exercise, which he had set up to give Wittica a taste of the capabilities of his system. In a real run, there would have been not only many entryways, marked in an array of easily distinguishable colors according to their security levels, plus a small army of agents, also color coded according to their security clearance, but also traffic on the streets as users retrieved information from various databases.

The virtual-reality model moved around Ryan as he strolled up the street, displayed by the one-and-a-half-inch LCD screens in front of his eyes. The images painted onto his field of view broke down into pixels sprayed by the software onto an array of 1024×780 pixels, the same resolution of a high-end computer display, but curving along the vertical and horizontal planes to cover Ryan's entire field of view, including his peripheral vision. This image was further enhanced into a high-quality picture by the HMD's holographic filters, which removed the staircase appearance of diagonal lines by filling the empty space that existed between the individual pixels and the LCD screen.

Ryan stepped off the street and onto the white sidewalk as he neared the garage door, pale green in color, depicting the lowest level of security but still requiring an access password. A three-dimensional barrier made of bright green lines that resembled lasers—crisscrossed into an impenetrable web that extended halfway into the sidewalk—covered the door.

61

"What's that, Mike?" asked Wittica in his digitized voice.

"The firewall. Let's try to enter without proper authorization," Ryan said, and stepped right into it.

The hatched lines forming the barrier turned bright red. At the same time Ryan jerked back slightly as tiny electrodes built into the HMD zapped him with a very mild electric charge.

"Ouch!" complained Wittica, who, electronically linked with Ryan, was equally punished for the attempt to break in without a password. "What in the hell was that?"

"That's the system using visual and sensory stimuli to let you know that access was not granted. The same sensors used to detect your head motion and thus allow you to navigate are also used to zap illegal users."

"Is that your idea of fun, Mike?"

"Actually," replied Ryan, "it was part of my thesis work in the area of database security. My proposal postulated that if hackers got electronically punished every time they attempted to penetrate a secured system illegally, they would think twice before doing it again in the future. As it stands today, hackers don't have to pay any penalties unless they get caught. When they try to enter a system without a password, the system just denies them access, but does not attempt to retaliate. Hackers just keep trying to break in with different passwords until they succeed. My system would zap them every time, with the magnitude of the discharge increasing on each failed attempt. And if they happen to be using a regular terminal instead of an HMD, my system would fire an electronic torpedo at their system, crashing it."

"Interesting, but what keeps HMD hackers from just putting a piece of tape over the electrodes to isolate them from your skin?"

"That would only make matters worse. See, the electrodes must close the circuit with your skin in order to detect your head motion and therefore navigate. No electrode connection, no navigation, meaning you can't go anywhere in the system. But there are two levels of security on top of a plain password. First, the diode plane of the HMD runs an eye scan every time you request access to the system. The digital signature of the user's eyeballs must match the user's password before access is allowed. Second, the password itself needs to be spoken. The voice-recognition system will digitize the words and compare the digital sound with the one on file, which is also linked to the eye scan. If everything matches, the eye scan, the voice, and the password itself, the system will allow access. Otherwise, the user gets a zap through the electrodes. If a hacker decides to get cute and navigate right up to the protected door and then tape over the electrodes so that he or she won't feel the pain while trying to break in, my software will detect that and deploy security agents armed with laser guns, which they will use to dilate the illegal user's pupils with multiple bursts of light. I'm also working on an enhancement that will fire an acoustic bullet to the hacker with the same intensity as a gunshot, making his ears ring for several minutes. Trust me, no hacker will ever want to set foot anywhere near a system protected with MPS, because it not only protects, it bites back."

"Amazing," Wittica said.

Ryan glanced over at MPS-Ali, his agent.

MPS-Ali, a figure digitized from a 3-D image of former heavyweight boxing champion Muhammad Ali, flexed his muscles with natural fluidity under a crimson-and-indigo bodysuit, and turned toward Ryan.

"Nice touch there, Mike," said Wittica.

"The best fighter that ever was," replied Ryan, a boxing fan.

"Direction?" MPS-Ali asked in a deep voice.

"Database access."

The cyber pugilist nodded as he asked, "Password?" Every expert system was linked to its own database and was the only one that could interface between the database and the user, including granting or denying entry.

"Dance like a butterfly and sting like a bee," Ryan said.

"Stand by for eye scan. Please refrain from blinking," said MPS-Ali.

Ryan looked straight ahead while the system scanned his eye signature, which would then be compared with the spoken password for a match.

"Access granted," said MPS-Ali a moment later.

The light cage surrounding the entryway dimmed until it vanished. Ryan stared at it and blinked once. The door hissed as it slid into the wall at great speed.

Ryan stared at the open portal and blinked, moving inside the cavernous interior. They walked to the middle of a large open lobby, overlooked from all sides by the open balconies of five stories of cubicles. Potted plants adorned the slick lobby, floored with red-and-white tile. Dozens of figures, all faceless, roamed the lobby, the stairs at the far side, or the open hallways above. Some moved fairly slowly or stood still. The large majority dashed by at great speed, leaving behind a trail of gray that slowly faded away, like contrails marking their path.

"What are those?" Wittica asked.

"That's the normal traffic that you would see on any database," explained Ryan. "Each figure standing around the lobby represents a user, like you and me. The figures running about are the expert systems, doing the legwork for the users as they browse through the database, viewing files, copying them, moving them, cataloging them, just as we are about to do. For this specific exercise, everyone around us, except for the agent we brought with us, represents the output of a program that I have running in the background to simulate multiple users working files at random so you can get a feeling for the system. In a real application, each of the users will have a face and an identifier so you can tell who is who. You can walk right up to any of them and start talking. If the user is using an HMD, he will be able to talk back, just like you and I are doing now. If the user is on a workstation, then a window will open on the screen, alerting him that you are trying to start a chat session. Also, in a large network, like Soft-Corp's, the VR scenery would be much more complex than just a few city blocks. It would probably be best represented as a large planetlike sphere, with multiple cities and other objects on its surface to represent the various directories and paths between them. But today we'll keep it nice and simple."

Ryan turned to his agent. "Graphic representation of production output in the memory division for the past year by quarter."

MPS-Ali raced toward the stairs at the end of the hallway, leaving behind digitized smoke, returning a moment later, before his original contrails had vanished, coming to a screeching halt in front of Ryan and Wittica. A second later a graph materialized next to him.

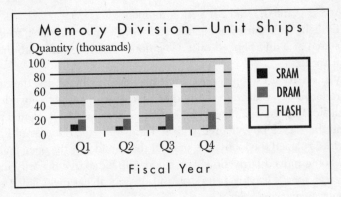

"Is the graph acceptable?"

"One moment," said Ryan, turning to Wittica. "This database doesn't contain any graphs. It is strictly thousands of files of numbers—figures—but organized such that expert systems, like MPS-Ali, can run an extract of the desired information and graph it at the blink of an eye."

"Can MPS-Ali assist you in interpreting this information?"

"Yes." Ryan looked at the graph and blinked.

MPS-Ali began his dissertation. "This is the unit volume ships by quarter by product for the memory division. SRAM memory shipments continue to decline quarter to quarter while DRAM memory and FLASH continue to grow as a result of strong demand from the computer market."

"How about ASPs?" asked Ryan, using an industry acronym for the average selling price of a product.

A moment later a second graph materialized out of thin cyber air right above the first one.

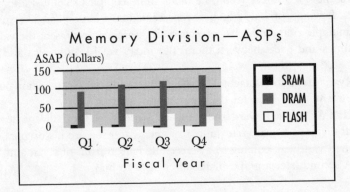

"As you can see," continued MPS-Ali in his monotone voice, "average selling prices eroded for both the SRAM and FLASH markets while DRAM prices grew through the year due to stronger demand.

"How about sales figures?"

A moment later a third graph appeared in front of them.

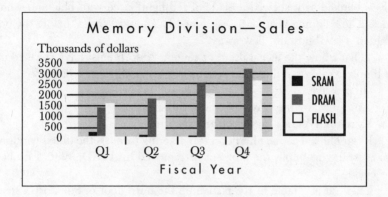

"As you can see," said MPS-Ali, "the higher ASPs generated comparable levels of sales for DRAM and FLASH. However, given that both products have the same manufacturing expense, the net profit from DRAMs overwhelms FLASH by an order of magnitude, as shown in the following graph for the fourth quarter."

Ryan and Wittica spent another ten minutes reviewing several graphs, all materializing in front of their eyes upon request, followed by MPS-Ali's dissertations. In the middle of this, an alarm went off, its blaring halting the business presentation. All activity stopped in the lobby.

"What's happening, Mike?"

"Another simulation," Ryan answered. "Watch."

A moment later a dark figure appeared on one of the balconies on the top floor. It paused before turning toward the stairs at great speed. Three bright figures darted past Ryan and Wittica, their contrails marking their path up the stairs toward the runaway dark figure, which had already made it down to the third floor, but doubled back up to the fourth as its pursuers closed in. A moment later they had it surrounded, drowning it in intense light, which also encircled the arresting agents. This sphere of light descended to the lobby and left the building. Activity resumed a moment later.

"MPS security froze the illegal user and is now taking him to a holding cell while an agent was dispatched to the home page of the originator of the illegal search. In this simulation the illegal user was able to roam the system for just three seconds before security caught up with him. Of course, this was only a simulation. In reality, the illegal user would have had to get past the firewall checks before getting inside, and even if he did get through my eye- and voice-scan checks, his bodysuit would lack the surface signature that every legal user is issued by the system administrator. Mobile security tracking units, affectionately referred to as orbs, roam the halls of every database, checking users for proper bodysuit signature. There comes one."

A silver sphere the size of a softball floated by them. Red and green LEDs blinked as it spewed a blade of red light, laced with blue and white lines. The scanning beam cross-sectioned Ryan and Wittica, before the orb emitted a few blips and flew away.

"That's how the illegal user got caught. An orb must have sneaked up to him, registered an illegal bodysuit signature, and alerted security."

"Impressive."

"And that, by the way, concludes this exercise."

Ryan and Wittica logged off the system.

Ryan blinked as the afternoon sun, filtering through the tinted windowpanes, stung his pupils the moment he removed his HMD. Wittica rubbed his eyes.

They sat at a table in Ryan's lab on the third floor of SoftCorp's steel-and-glass building atop a hill overlooking Lake Austin, the name given to the Colorado River downstream from Lake Travis, as it approached the city, where it was dammed once again to form this lake. Ryan spotted several boats cruising the narrow lake, folks getting an early start on their weekend. After this last dam, the river continued into the city, through downtown Austin, where it was renamed Town Lake.

The lab, set up by Ryan just four days ago, after officially starting work at the firm, had been his entire world while at SoftCorp.

"So," Wittica said. "Nice demo. I'll need you to hook up with Agi on Monday and explain to him the details of the VR interface. He will go over the big picture of our artificial-intelligence effort and then take you through the technical details of one of the many sections to use it as a test vehicle for your VR software. Depending on how the VR software works on one section we may consider extending it to the entire project."

"No problem," said Ryan. Agi Maghami, one of SoftCorp's senior scientists, was Ryan's technical advisor on this project. Unlike other companies, SoftCorp didn't have a classic reporting structure. Instead, the engineering organization was arranged like a think tank, with a number of engineers doing research in parallel with one or more technical advisors "mentoring" them through their tasks. Although the arrangement promoted independent thinking and focused efforts, it kept most employees isolated from each other in their daily tasks. Ryan still had no clue what anyone else was doing in the company, beyond the general description of creating one of the world's most sophisticated artificial intelligence systems. He'd met most of the engineers, but knew little of their actual work. Everyone seemed to be working on some classified project, just like Ryan, in their own personal lab. And also unlike other high-tech companies, SoftCorp didn't have the typical ocean of cubicles but rather just hallways and doors to the many labs, conference rooms, and the executive area on the fourth floor, where Wittica and Shapiro sat. The first step of cross-functional visibility came at the technical advisor level. Agi Maghami, an engineer from India who had received his Ph.D. from Berkeley a few years ago, mentored a dozen engineers and reported to Wittica, who, as chief technical officer, coordinated the efforts of several technical advisors while also making time to personally review the progress of each engineer.

Although the relative isolation of having his office and lab area in one place, out of sight from everyone else, had bothered him the first couple of days, by day three Ryan had gotten into the swing of things and had grown to enjoy spending all of his day working on his newly purchased hardware. The 2-GHz PC he used as an engine was an order of magnitude more powerful than the 266-MHz PC he had used at Stanford to develop VR-MPS. In fact, Ryan was quickly realizing that the lack of interruptions made him so productive that he was able to integrate his software with the new hardware in just two days, a task that would have taken him at least a week at Stanford with so many hourly interruptions by other students and professors.

"Also," said Wittica, "I've set up an appointment for you Monday afternoon to have a working meeting with a representative from our client. His name is Gam Olson. He will be here at two o'clock. Use the time to interview him and get a better feel for how he currently goes about his job with his existing system. His team will be the initial users of the first-pass adaptation of your VR software with our AI development."

"Ron, you never did tell me who this client was." Ryan had wanted to know that since arriving here this past Monday, but the boxes of computer gear, plus an assortment of top-notch virtual-reality hardware—helmet-mounted displays, mikes, and interfacing hardware and cables—had diverted his curiosity. He had not expected Wittica to acquire the stuff so soon after Ryan had accepted the job offer and moved to Austin. Besides, along with the sophisticated hardware—whose worth Ryan had estimated at around one hundred thousand dollars—was a memo from Wittica requesting that he have the VR-MPS software running on the new hardware by the end of the week.

Wittica touched his forehead and smiled. "Sorry, Mike. I forgot. Our client is the Internal Revenue Service."

Ryan set the HMD on the lab table and regarded Wittica for a moment. SoftCorp's chief technical officer was dressed very casually in a pair of khaki slacks, a polo shirt, and loafers. He looked ready to hit the lake with his blond friend. Mike was dressed in jeans, a Stanford T-shirt, and sneakers. "I guess that makes sense," he finally said, thinking of Wittica's description of his client's eclectic system during his interview.

"Agent Gam Olson is from the Internal Audit Division. The Service would like us to create a VR environment for IAD agents to go into their databases and seek out tax violators. The Service's current system for tracking down tax evasion and fraud is quite manual, antiquated, requiring considerable effort across all ten tax processing centers in the United States. The first phase of the adaptation of your VR system with our artificial intelligence system will be targeted at assisting IAD agents as they cruise not just through IRS databases but also the databases of other federal agencies and private corporations."

"Private corporations?" Ryan asked.

Wittica smiled, sunlight gleaming on his bronzed face. "Our solution will allow the Service to get instantly linked into every industry, public or private—as well as all government agencies, federal or state—through the employment division of each company or agency. The link actually exists now, but it's highly manual and quite decentralized, with different processing centers owning part of the required information while operating with incompatible software and hardware."

Ryan considered that for a moment. Wittica's comment didn't make sense. "Software and hardware incompatibility was solved with the birth of the World Wide Web," he said. "What better solution can we provide in terms of accessing databases than the Web?"

In the beginning there was the Internet, a hardware link that extended across the United States. However, it required above-average technical skill to use those links. There wasn't a universal software interface to create the cyberspace known today as the World Wide Web. Users had to know the physical location of the site they wanted to access, then dial it with a modem, go through the required electronic protocols and required passwords, and finally access the information, which consisted mostly of text. The process would have to be repeated over again to access other locations. The World Wide Web created a virtual interface between users and the physical hardware, eliminating the need for extensive user intervention to access a database halfway across the country. The Web was linked virtually through hubs known as Internet service providers, where users would log in only once before they simply pointed and clicked to navigate through the vast amount of information available. After the Web came the search engines, facilitating the process of accessing information by searching the billions of data files available by the use of key search words or phrases. Graphics quickly replaced text, making the entire system even more user friendly, extending its usage to the computer illiterate. This metamorphosis solved the old problem of interfacing with incompatible software-hardware platforms. The universal programs driving the World Wide Web system transcended all known software and hardware incompatibilities, making it transparent to users. A user could check the latest football scores posted on the ESPN home page, and then turn around and make a flight reservation to Europe, and then order a book from an online bookstore to read on the plane, and then shop for luggage on another on-line service, and so on, cruising from system to system with the click of a mouse, without having to know where, physically, those on-line services resided.

Wittica smiled. "I apologize for not being specific enough. You're absolutely correct about the Web, to the extent of solving the software-hardware incompatibility of systems that were *intended* to be accessed. What I was referring to was systems that are *not* readily accessible by the average Web surfer. These are the highly classified files in many corporations or government agencies that aren't there for public access, though criminal hackers break into them from time to time. And there are even more secret files, those to which illegal access would be devastating to the average citizen. I'm referring to private records, Ryan, medical records, employment files, the kind of stuff that simply can't get out into the public domain because it would cause a commotion of unprecedented proportions in this nation. You see, everyone, and I mean *everyone*, is concerned about the loss of privacy that has come with the Web. People are concerned about their most precious secrets being online for the wrong eyes to see. And so, many of those files, those records, are kept in systems that are not accessible by the Web as you know it today, requiring another level of interfacing in order to ensure their protection in the event that some hacker manages to break in. Those are the databases I'm referring to, the very jewels of our society, our private information."

"I see," Ryan replied, taking that in.

"IAD agents now have to go through each database manually due to security reasons. We don't have a powerful enough software fire wall to feel comfortable about integrating all of those databases, spread across the nation, into a centralized platform like the Web for fear of what a hacker could do if he or she broke in. The way it is set up right now, a hacker will have to break into each individual system, minimizing the exposure of private files. The price of that, of course, is that IAD agents have to go through the same level of pain to get to them, and after they do, there is no intelligent engine to guide them through their data-retrieval process."

"So hackers will have an equally difficult time."

Wittica nodded. "I know it sounds like a backwards way of protecting something, but believe me, the files we're talking about are too valuable to take any chances. That's why we're so excited about your VR solution, Mike. It departs from the classic software world, making it all the more difficult for a hacker to break in."

"And if they try, they will be punished," Ryan said.

Wittica smiled. "Aaron will love that special touch. For years he's been after me to find a real way to make hackers pay for their mistakes, to hit them where it hurts."

"That's how I feel too," said Ryan, for a moment thinking of his own hacking background. It now felt strange to be on the other side, working to prevent people like him from breaking in.

"So," Wittica said. "The intent here is to provide centralization through your virtual-reality system in combination with our artificial-intelligence solution. Our expert systems act as intelligent software interfaces to these special databases, and your virtual-reality system brings them all together, operating in a safe and secure environment. That initial objective will empower our client to have instant access to the personnel records of any individual, as well as their credit records, bank accounts, criminal records, and anything else that you might think of. For example, say we want to investigate the status of John Doe, currently single and unemployed, but who during the past twenty years married and divorced three times, changed jobs a dozen times, and lived in four different states. An IAD agent would have to search through many different databases from corporations and states to generate a history file, which the agent can then compare to Mr. Doe's tax records from the past twenty years. This last task is further complicated by the incompatibility of the systems within the IRS. All of this adds up to make the Internal Audit Division's job quite challenging. In the meantime, our client suspects that many Americans slip through the system paying less than their fair share of taxes. At last week's estimate, the IRS, under a nondisclosure agreement with our firm, indicated that this hole in the system is causing around five billion dollars per quarter in lost tax revenue to the U.S. government."

Ryan tried to grasp the magnitude of the task. Suddenly he didn't feel all that certain that his MPS solution could swallow something that big and complex.

Wittica must have read the expression on his face, because he added quickly, "But don't worry much about trying to solve the big picture, Mike." He patted him on the back reassuringly. "I was just giving you a taste for the entire project. It's always good to know the ten-thousand-foot view before one dives in to address a small portion of it. Your initial job will be to get a limited VR solution working in the local IRS branch, while using our own security interface for the time being. We'll test yours later. Agent Olson will be your primary point of contact. He has a lot of incentive to assist you. Right now his men spend too much time performing manual tasks that could be automated. Your system has the potential to make his job a hell of a lot easier. Olson's also qualified to give you a basic rundown on the IRS, its procedures, and even some history on the agency."

"All right," Ryan said, his mind trying to digest the waterfall of information that Wittica had just dumped on him.

Wittica checked his watch. "Gotta meet my girlfriend at the lake. Do you have any big plans this weekend, Mike?"

Ryan stretched. He had worked his butt off for the past few days and was looking forward to the weekend. He was going to pick up his company-leased car, a red Porsche Boxster. Vic had already gotten her new car, a Honda Accord, which she had purchased through a low-interest car loan from Capitol Bank. In addition to the cars, the Ryans were scheduled to do more house hunting this weekend. "I'm getting my new car tomorrow."

"Great! Did you settle on the Boxster?"

Ryan nodded.

"What color?"

"Red, with gray leather."

"Nice. What about the house?"

"Vic wants to do a little more house hunting before making a decision."

Wittica looked confused. "Oh, I thought you'd settled on a home over in Lost Creek," he said, mentioning an upper-middle-class neighborhood in west Austin.

Ryan sighed. "That's what I thought, but apparently the realtor has found a few houses in Lakeway that Vic now wants to check out tomorrow afternoon." Lakeway was a community bordering Lake Travis.

Wittica smiled. "If you do buy there, I'll have to throw you a welcome-to-the-neighborhood party. You kids are moving up faster than I did at your age."

"Just because we may live in the same neighborhood doesn't put us in the same league, Ron. I've seen your house. We're looking at a new development in Lakeway that's more affordable than the rest of the area but still keeps us close to the lake." Wittica's Mediterranean-style mansion, six thousand square feet in size, backed onto the lake, where a boat slip housed a beautiful forty-two-foot yacht, which Wittica had pointed out to the young California couple during their lake cruise a month ago.

"Great things are just around the corner for you and your wife, Mike. Anyway, I hope you get in."

Ryan nodded and stretched. "So that's the plan for the weekend. Have fun on the lake with Cherry."

Wittica raised a brow. "Ah . . . it's *Joanna* now. Not as cute as Cherry but she can actually hold a decent conversation."

Ryan shook his head. Wittica patted him on the shoulder one more time and left.

The Stanford graduate stood alone in the lab, facing the panoramic windows. Emerald green hills, starred with luxurious homes, overlooked Lake Austin. He gazed at the scenery in silence for several minutes before powering down his system and heading out of the lab. He closed the door behind him, making sure to listen to the customary blip that indicated that the magnetic lock had engaged. Access to his lab could only be granted by entering the correct six-digit code into the keypad next to the door.

71

Ryan proceeded down the hallway toward the elevators, walking past a dozen doors all sporting similar access keypads. Suddenly one door swung open and a large man dressed in a security guard's uniform stepped out.

"Hi!" said Ryan.

The tall guard, his bulging muscles pressing against the dark uniform, momentarily regarded Ryan, a mix of surprise and hostility in his blue-eyed stare. His ash blond crew cut and chiseled features reminded Ryan of a Nordic warrior. He eyed the badge hanging from a chain around Ryan's neck, gave him a slight nod, and rushed off toward the stairs adjacent to the elevators.

Strange.

Ryan shrugged it off and continued toward the end of the hallway, past the open door, peeking inside. An array of TV monitors, dozens of them, covered the wall opposite the entryway.

Security cameras.

Ryan stopped, natural curiosity creeping in. Each black-and-white monitor displayed a different interior or exterior view. For a moment he wondered if there was a camera inside his office that he wasn't aware of.

Ryan took a step closer to the doorway. The glaring screens didn't display the interior of laboratories or of any other part of the building that Ryan knew, such as the lobby. Instead, they showed views of what appeared to be different homes, of people moving about inside or outside. Audio jacks beneath each screen provided a hookup for headphones.

What is this? Who are they monitoring? Is this another project?

His eyes drifted to the only monitor that had an audio jack connected to a pair of headphones. It displayed an attractive woman in a sports jacket standing by an elderly couple. Her stance, combined with her large, round eyes, high cheekbones, and small pointy nose reminded Ryan of actress Susan Sarandon. Tall, elegant, yet hard, portraying strength. The camera had zoomed in on her as she talked to the old couple, though Ryan couldn't hear about what. But he could see the distress lining the faces of the elderly couple. In fact, the old lady looked in tears as she covered her face with her hands.

What in the hell is going on? What are these guards doing monitoring—

"Hey!"

Ryan jerked back, looking toward the stairs. Two guards were walking in his direction. One guard spoke on a radio. He had a neatly trimmed beard.

"What are you doing?" asked the second guard, his booming voice echoing in the corridor.

"I . . . I was heading home and saw this door open. I thought—"

"Please step away from it," the guard demanded.

"Sure. No problem. I just thought that—"

"That room is off-limits to all personnel."

"Didn't they explain that to you during orientation?" asked the bearded guard after replacing his radio on a hook on his thick belt, from which also hung a side arm.

Ryan remembered now. The human-resources lady had told him that every room was off-limits at SoftCorp, except for his own lab, the office of his technical advisor, a handful of conference rooms, the restrooms, and the cafeteria.

"Sorry, I forgot. I—"

The bearded guard cocked an index finger at Ryan. "That's not an excuse for—"

"That will be enough," said a familiar voice from behind. Ryan turned around. Aaron Shapiro was emerging from the stairs alongside the guard with the blond crew cut. The CEO of SoftCorp was dressed casually but his face was drawn tight with alarm, with concern. It was obvious to Ryan that something terrible had happened and he had just been lucky enough to have walked right into the middle of it. What it was, Ryan had no clue.

"But, sir," the bearded guard insisted. "I caught him looking in—"

"He's new and doesn't know the drill yet. He's a good kid, so cut him some slack."

"Yes, sir."

All three guards went inside the large room. One of them snagged the headphones connected to the monitor Ryan had been looking at before the guards found him. Shapiro stayed with Ryan for a moment.

"Aaron, I was just heading home when—"

Shapiro raised a palm. "I know. We just got a little emergency here and the guards are on edge. Don't worry about it." Lowering his voice, he extended a thumb toward the door while lowering his voice a few decibels, as if wanting to confide something in Ryan. "They're good guys, Mike, but tend to overreact at the smallest thing. I'd better go in there and solve it for them. Have a nice weekend."

"You too, sir."

Shapiro closed the door after him, and Ryan found himself in the middle of the hallway trying to make sense of what he had just witnessed. Why were SoftCorp security guards monitoring what appeared to be private residences? And what had gone so wrong that it not only put all the guards in an altered state of mind but also required the immediate presence of Shapiro?

Ryan headed for the elevators, wondering exactly what he had just seen, and who was that woman in the TV monitor talking to the elderly couple.

73

2

Smoke roused her. Thick, suffocating, it veiled the room. The throbbing in her temples made her dizzy and nauseated, or was it the smoke?

Karen rolled over on her belly, showered by sizzling plasterboard raining from the burning ceiling.

Move out of the way.

She kicked her legs against . . . something, couldn't tell what. The heat smoldered as she clambered on all fours away from the sizzling debris, keeping low, her face against the carpet, where the smoke thinned.

Whooshing flames pulsated across the ceiling, licking it in near-hypnotic waves of orange and red-gold.

Pressing a sleeve against her mouth and nose, she breathed slowly, shallowly, cautiously, lest she risk burning her lungs. Tears clouded her eyes, mere slits of glinting agony, savaged by the inky haze, struggling to find a door, a window, anything beyond the collapsing . . . *There!*

She crawled toward a window at the opposite end of the room, adjacent to the kitchen, where just moments ago . . . *Where are they?* Doug Patterson had stood by the kitchen while his wife fetched them some coffee. Karen had gone to the living room, leisurely inspecting the artwork on the walls.

Determination fought dizziness, triggering more recollection, comprehension. She remembered the hissing noise from the kitchen, the smell of methane assaulting her nostrils, the ensuing explosion. Wood had creaked, nails popping from the frame with the sound of rattling machine guns. Incandescence had swallowed the house. Screams mixed with the booming blast propelling her toward the back of the living room with animal force.

And then nothing.

Until now.

Full awareness awakened. A fist of flames roared through a gaping hole in the ceiling, above the gas stove, amidst charred wires, twisted plumbing, and darkened wooden planks. Karen crawled away from the blaze, reaching the side of the living room, beyond which extended a yard sloping down to a forested creek, barely visible in the half-light of the room and the darkening glass of large windowpanes. Through thickening heat, she crept on hands and knees toward the translucent image of her escape route, framed by burning draperies, its smoked panes obscuring beams of sunlight shafting through the hovering soot.

Her hands searched for an object, anything to crack the windows, the darkened images of dancing flames reflecting on the glass. The heat grew intolerable. She had to break free, *had to breathe.*

Fingers groped for an object, curled around the base of a small table next to a sofa. Mustering strength, Karen hoisted it over her head while rising to a deep crouch. Eyes closed, her breath caught tight in her throat, she threw it at the pulsating images.

Glass shattered, projected outward by the differential pressure created by the accumulated smoke and rising heat. Karen staggered forward, scrambled toward the opening, ignoring the cuts on her arms and legs as she dove through, as air gushed inside to feed the growing inferno.

Recently trimmed grass cushioned her fall as she landed on her side, grunting from the impact, going into a roll to get away from the breathing path of the fire. A second later a horizontal column of flames growled out of the opening, the force cracking the window from the frame, shooting it toward the rear of the property like a flaming catapult shot.

She staggered away from the scorching structure, fresh air relieving her lungs, clearing them. Coughing, tears clouding her eyes, Karen breathed deeply over and over. Instinct forced a hand inside her jacket, fingertips verifying that her chest holster still held the Desert Eagle.

Serenity replaced shock. She continued to move away, toward the ravine bordering the south end of the property, toward the dry creek materializing as her sight cleared. A backward glance, disbelief filling her that she had survived relatively unscathed, Karen Frost steadied her retreat. Smoked billowed skyward, swirling glowing ashes across the pale-bright leaves of neighboring cottonwoods. Sirens blared in the distance. Fire trucks, ambulances, and police cruisers approached the scene.

Help. But not for her. She had to get away, remain invisible, just as she thought she had done for the past few weeks, operating solo, following her senses, monitoring the activities of Janet Patterson's parents, searching for signs of surveillance, formulating the best way to contact them.

Fallen leaves crunched under her weight as Karen moved gravely, brushing past a line of cedars bordering the ravine, out of sight from the emergency crews shouting commands over the roaring fire. One final backward glance revealed bright streams of water arcing down over the blaze, shimmering in the sunlight before disappearing in the swelling flames.

The tree-studded terrain sloped steeply, strewn with boulders and exposed roots. She descended twenty or so feet to the bottom, layered with fallen wood, leaves, and river stones. Fallen branches creaked, snapped as she pressed on, following the winding rift. The chaos above yielded to the autumn breeze rustling the leaf-littered ground, swirling her short hair.

Karen sighed, puzzled. *What in the hell went wrong?*

She had obeyed professional habits, abided by her experience, her intuition, honed to near perfection after so many years of field operations. She had followed the Patterson's daily routine, their trips to the flower shop before driving to the cemetery. She had watched them replace the flowers alongside a new headstone amidst freshly laid dirt, had seen them comfort each other in tight embraces, had felt guilty for prying into such private moments. She had followed them on foot during their evening strolls to a nearby church, where they attended nightly services, and the endless chats with the priest afterward, in the courtyard behind the church.

Not once had Karen spotted a tail.

Her initial contact had been clean, a visit to a flower shop at the other end of town, a sealed message, orders to deliver flowers to the mourning parents. The message in the sealed envelope had directions on how to contact Karen without using their own phone due to the likelihood of an illegal tap. The Pattersons had called Karen the following day, discussed arranging a meeting at a place other than their home, settling on the house of another retired couple, close friends on extended vacation abroad. The Pattersons were looking after their house, watering their plants, sleeping there a couple of nights a week to give the impression that someone lived there.

Karen could not see the hole in her plan. The Pattersons had not discussed the contact with anyone, just as Karen had requested both in the note and during their phone conversation. And yet . . . *damn.*

Now they were dead, just like their daughter, assassinated by this elusive network. The unexpected attack also told Karen that she was no longer invisible—not that she had ever been, based on this unfortunate turn of events in her covert investigation. The enemy knew for certain that someone was investigating the death of Janet Patterson. The question was just how much they knew about the investigation. Did they know Karen's name? And how much did they suspect she knew?

The meeting, however, had not been a total failure. Although the late Janet Patterson apparently had not had any conversations on the matter with her parents, probably to protect them, her parents did know the name of her supervisor at the IRS: Pete Rubaker. Karen now faced a new challenge: if the enemy suspected that she had learned this much from Janet's parents before they could be silenced, then Pete Rubaker was in great danger since he represented the next link in the FBI's investigative chain. The recent explosion, still ringing in her ears as she tramped through the woods, reminded Karen of the swift, brutal way that organized crime dealt with liabilities.

That possibility, however, also provided Karen with an opportunity. If she could get to Rubaker before the enemy did, she might be able to strike a deal with him: his life for information. The danger, of course, was that Rubaker would be watched much closer than the Pattersons, and probably terminated at the slightest hint of trouble—that's if he wasn't already dead. And if the enemy knew her name, then her life was also at risk since she presented an even larger danger to their operation.

But Karen Frost was used to being a target. And besides, she didn't really have much to lose anyhow. After Mark's death everything else, her own life included, had taken second place to cracking criminal networks. She had gone to chilling extremes to accomplish just that, and she felt quite willing to do it again. In her professional mind this recent attack only confirmed her suspicions: she was on the right track. Organized crime avoided taking such drastic steps unless it was absolutely necessary, like a federal agent closing in on their operation.

But such operations resembled an onion, with layer after layer of buffers, of expendables, of front companies, all strategically placed to slow down, or even stall, an investigation while links in the investigative chain were severed, guaranteeing the survivability of the establishment.

Cracking them required patience and perseverance, strong character traits in Karen Frost's personality. Her training, combined with her personal motivation, put her in a unique position to strike back.

Midafternoon sunlight pierced the woods, reflecting off mirror-smooth pools of rainwater. Insects clicked, mosquitoes buzzed around her but didn't settle. Moths danced in shafts of light forking through the tree canopy, fluttering out of sight as Karen walked past. She climbed up the ravine, reaching the edge, pausing, resting her hands on her thighs as she bent over, catching her breath, sweat filming her. Though in good physical shape for a forty-five-year-old, she was definitely not the same energetic agent of ten years ago. But the age-induced loss of stamina Karen balanced with experience—and with the cold, unyielding determination to keep going, to disregard her personal safety as long as she made progress, as long as she could instill fear in her opponent's life. And that determination forced her now to keep going, to increase the gap, to ignore her throbbing leg muscles. She needed to get away, live to fight another day.

She exited the woods several blocks away from the inky funnel of smoke streaming skyward at the other side of the neighborhood. She had parked her car just three blocks away, but it might just as well have been three hundred blocks away. The rented Taurus was compromised, as well as her FBI-issued identity and everything else that associated her with her investigation of the Patterson couple, including her hotel room. Being a target,

77

however, could also be turned around and used to bootstrap her investigation. All she had to do was capture her would-be assassin, break him, and run up that chain before someone caught up with her and broke it. Needless to say, it meant placing herself in great danger in order to draw the assassin to her, which she could do by returning to her rental car or hotel. But Karen was not that desperate yet. For now she had a name, a lead. She just needed a new identity before pursuing it.

And a new plan.

As she reached a convenience store at the end of the neighborhood and used a pay phone to call a taxi, that plan began to take shape in her head.

3

Sitting behind his desk at the FBI headquarters, Director Roman Palenski hung up the phone and rubbed his eyes. He was exhausted, having spent most of his Friday at Capitol Hill being grilled by senators and congressmen alike while he defended his budget proposal for the coming year. So far he wasn't having much luck, even with Meek's awesome color foils. The problem was Senator Jack Horton from New York, the Senate majority leader and major contender for the Democratic ticket in next year's presidential elections. The senator had a lot of pull around Washington—too much pull in Palenski's opinion, and one of his campaign promises was to create a new FBI.

Palenski closed his eyes. *The man knows dick about security, and he wants to transform the FBI.*

He shivered at the thought of the Bureau being handed to someone with little experience and a big ego, handpicked by the newly elected president, and ratified by a Congress he also controlled.

Still, the day had not been a total waste. He did get the basic budget approved, meaning no one would be losing their jobs and all existing operations would remain in place, as well as all planned equipment upgrades and salary increases. But Horton had moved to cut the Bureau's large expansion budget—almost 30 percent of the entire package—under the claim that the FBI was run too inefficiently. Palenski had asked for an additional week to show further evidence of how well he ran his agency and why those funds were critical to support planned FBI operations in the coming year. A reluctant Congress had granted him the extension.

He put aside the presentation that Russell Meek had begun to craft this afternoon and made several phone calls to ship overnight to Karen the gear she'd requested to carry out the new twist in her plan. Palenski did this without having to reveal to anyone inside the Bureau, Meek included, that she would be the user of that equipment. He accomplished this by using a system of buffers that mimicked those in organized crime. In fact, Palenski had chosen to keep Meek in the dark for the time being not only because he knew how his textbook subordinate felt about this maverick-style approach but also to keep him focused on cranking out the new congressional reports.

He tried to resume his work but couldn't get his mind off the situation down in Austin. Karen continued down the right path, but the body count was rapidly getting out of control. Still, he couldn't bring himself to pull the plug on this one, not while she had so obviously pushed the right button. Nothing like having people wanting to kill you to know that you had definitely stuck your nose in the wrong place—or the right place, depending on your perspective. As a street agent during the '60s and '70s, before his superiors recognized his talent and promoted him several times in the course of a decade, Roman Palenski had pushed many such buttons, and had lived to tell his story. He could empathize with Karen Frost.

Palenski stood and walked toward the windows facing the Washington skyline. A full moon hung high in the night, its glow dimming surrounding stars. He watched it in silence.

4

An autumn dusk beneath a partly cloudy sky. Wooded hills extended beyond the edge of the property, angling down toward the water. Lake Travis murmured. Somewhere birds chirped. The sun hung just above the western rim, splashing burnt orange hues across the sky, staining the surface of the lake, rippled by sailboats.

Michael Patrick Ryan stood beneath an oak, staring into the distance, a mild breeze swirling his hair. A hawk wheeled aloft, riding the thermals in wide, lazy circles.

Everything felt good. The location, the floor plan, the amenities, the nearby clubhouse with a pool and tennis courts.

And even the price.

Things actually looked *too good*, to the point that Ryan was beginning to get suspicious that something was terribly wrong with this whole picture. But he wasn't certain what had triggered that emotion. Up till now, Victoria had been the paranoid one.

Was it the incident yesterday afternoon on his way out of work? But what if that was nothing out of the ordinary, as Shapiro had indicated. The guards' reaction, however, certainly tended to contradict that. And what were they monitoring? Were they testing some kind of security software? Perhaps someone else's project? After all, SoftCorp was sort of a think tank more than a production-oriented software company, like Microsoft and Oracle.

"I don't see anything wrong with it," said Victoria, her auburn hair glowing in the dying sunlight. She walked up to Ryan and held his hand.

Ryan nodded, glancing back at the house. Large windows glowed while reflecting the setting sun, backlighting the silhouette of Gail, the real estate agent who had been showing them properties in Lakeway all afternoon. The last one had been just across the street—though the view wasn't anywhere near as spectacular as this one. And just a few blocks down the street was the neighborhood's clubhouse, where, in addition to the pool and tennis courts, Gail had shown them the large party room, two conference rooms, and even an office outfitted with a fax machine and a computer with an ISDN line. The place, which overlooked Lake Travis from a long ridge atop a forested hill, was designed to handle everything from small receptions to business meetings.

"I don't see anything wrong with it either," he said, looking away.

Victoria batted her long eye lashes. She looked stunning in a business suit, her long hair pulled back, accentuating her bronze coloring. She had to work Saturday morning and had come straight to Lakeway from the bank, meeting Ryan for lunch before heading over to the real estate agency, which happened to be owned by Capitol Bank.

"The terms are perfect," she said, holding a manila folder. "We qualify with plenty of margin, and we have even more buffer because of the low-interest loan from Capitol Bank. And the best news of all is that we can move in right away."

"We can?"

"We've been preapproved through my work."

"I'm sure we have." He shoved his hands in his khaki trousers, shaking his head, yesterday's incident still bothering him, though he had chosen not to share it with his wife for now. "I don't get it, Vic. Why is this house so underpriced? It's clearly worth much more than the asking price. And why do I get the feeling that someone's out there working quite hard to make our lives so easy?"

"Gail says the owners are going through a divorce and need to sell it quickly. The bargain of the year, she calls it. As for the easy loan . . . you knew about that before we even came down here."

"Surely, Miss Real Estate over there can find another buyer willing to pay more for *this* view, especially wearing that low-cut dress to show off her boobs."

She slapped his shoulder. "Be nice."

"I'm being nice. She's the one doing everything she possibly can short of getting me in bed to make this sale."

"Mike!"

"I'm serious, Vic. A guy can tell. She's been leaning down in front of me way too many times today while you're in another room, showing me what has to be breast implants, and also her black-lace lingerie, plus she has this habit of getting just a little too close when talking. And not that a guy minds that. God knows she's very attractive, but the question is why? Why is she trying so hard to sell us this house? It's obvious that she could get far more for it. I'm telling you, Vic. Something isn't right."

Dark humor washed her fine features as she said, "Now, darling, you're beginning to sound like me. Have I rubbed off on you?"

He took a deep breath, exhaling heavily. "I guess I just never thought we would own a house like this one so soon, especially right after college."

"Dreams do come true sometimes," she said, snuggling against him. "Let's enjoy it while the going is good."

They stared at the western sky until the blood red disk had sunk beneath the hills, until the first stars sprang forth in the indigo sky.

5

Karen Frost moved swiftly, quietly, with purpose, blending herself with the night. Perspiration covered her face, her neck, soaking the black T-shirt she wore along with black jeans and sneakers. She had left her turquoise and silver jewelry at her newly leased apartment, lest she risk glittering metal betraying her otherwise stealthy approach up the forested hill surrounding Rob Roy, one of Austin's premier neighborhoods.

An owl hooted overhead, its high-pitched shrill echoing in the country-side, breaking the cool green silence enveloping her. The predator winged skyward, past clusters of tree limbs, rustling the canopy, searching for prey.

Bird of prey.

Karen's features tightened at the thought. Her instincts continued to steer her in the right direction, toward her *own* prey. The average price in this neighborhood surpassed half a million dollars—certainly outside the range of IRS lower management. This was one of the clues that Karen sought when trying to identify someone associated with organized crime. Pete Rubaker was an individual whose spending ratio greatly exceeded his documented income. The IRS, classically chartered with flagging such in-dividuals and bringing them to the attention of the FBI, had failed to do so in this case for obvious reasons: a conflict of interest. This situation resem-bled a case she had worked six months ago in New York. A U.S. Customs chief, who also ran a gray-market smuggling ring, used his position to pro-tect his shadowy but highly profitable enterprise. Karen had tracked him down after the FBI received a notification from the IRS on mismatches between his reported income and his level of expenditures.

Karen continued up the slippery hill, ankle-deep in wildflowers and pine needles, mosquitoes buzzing around her. She clambered over moss-slick boulders, tugging on branches, slowly making her way up the steep incline, reaching the edge of the woods. A manicured lawn extended beyond the tree line, toward the rear of a large house—Rubaker's, according to county records. A silver moon reflected off the rippling surface of a large pool monopolizing the right side of the backyard. A hot tub built a foot over the level of the water, amidst a clump of huge boulders bordering that side of the property, cascaded its overflow into the pool, its gurgling sound mixing with the incessant humming of mosquitoes, and Karen's heavy breathing as she paused to recover from the strenuous climb.

A limestone path, whitewashed by the moon glow and further outlined by accent lights, connected the pool and hot tub to the rear of the house, where a covered patio led to three sets of French doors. Landscaping seemed generous. Manicured hedges surrounded the far side of the pool, creating a natural barrier to the neighbor's property, where the boulders continued all the way to the front. Three levels of flower beds tiered down from the boulders, hugging the hot tub and pool. An array of vegetation, highlighted with artistically arranged accent lights of varying colors, conveyed a sense peace that pleased the senses as much as the soothing sound of running water. Between the pool and the main house stood a smaller structure resembling a pool house, its sliding glass doors facing the limestone decking surrounding the pool. A few trees blocked the moonlight on the left side of the yard. These too were manicured, each trunk not only enclosed by a bed of flowers but also with an array of spotlights flooding the branches to continue that sense of balance.

And all purchased with the salary of an IRS supervisor.

On the take.

Feeling anything but peaceful, Karen frowned, more determined than ever to force a break in the case. As beautiful as this place was, it had been bought with blood money—blood from Dave Nolan, the Pattersons, and the many more who had been killed before them to protect the monster.

Panoramic windowpanes reflected moonlight as Karen settled herself in the moist underbrush, a pine resin fragrance mixing with the musk of her own sweat.

Her hands reached for a pair of small field binoculars strapped to her belt, pressing its rubber ends against her eyes, fingering the adjusting wheel while scanning the width of the mansion.

She spotted activity in one of the rear rooms, two men . . . no, make that three men, all in suits, standing about. But she couldn't make out much more than that. She had to get closer, listen in, even at the risk of detection.

Karen had not spotted any sentries, but she wondered about dogs. After all, beautiful places needed protection to keep them beautiful. An untrained stalker would have quickly written off dogs as a possibility because of the lack of a fence to contain them, to keep them from wandering off in the woods. But she knew about invisible fences, where a perimeter was defined by strategically placed directional radio transmitters, all broadcasting in a frequency that matched the receiver strapped to the dog's collar. The moment the animal neared the high-frequency wall, a light buzzing sound would alert it to the upcoming electric shock, so that it retreated quickly back inside the yard.

Concerned about being surprised by such a system, Karen spent ten minutes scouting the perimeter of the property, checking for any signs of guard dogs, satisfied that there were none—but just in case screwing a silencer to her small Walther PPK/S pistol. Tonight Karen would use the backup gun rather than the larger Desert Eagle .44 Magnum, which couldn't be silenced. While scouting, she preferred stealth rather than brute force. But she still hauled the Magnum in a shoulder holster in case she was forced to escalate her firepower.

In her business it paid to be paranoid.

She advanced silently over recently watered lawn, the pistol in her right hand, muzzle pointed at the star-filled sky. She reached the limestone path, crossed it, hiding behind a row of bushes, scanning for sentries, finding none.

Past the wrought-iron furniture beneath the slowly rotating ceiling fans of the back porch, beyond the tall French doors, Karen Frost focused on three men standing in the living room. She saw the brusque arm movement, their twisted expressions.

She crept closer, leaving the cool grass, her elbows and knees now pressing against concrete, wedging herself between a patio table surrounded by chairs and the side wall.

Stop. Listen. Move again. Stop again. Listen some more.

A few words now came, broken, sporadic, with the rapid change in intonation typical of an argument.

"... are we going to ... one of us ... Dear God."

"We can't ... damn ... told you ... would happen!"

"... blame yourself!"

The men beyond the glass were definitely arguing. One was tall, well built, even handsome in a Hispanic or Italian kind of way. The second was short and fat, and kept patting his forehead with a handkerchief. He was obviously sweating. The third man, young and muscular, remained several feet away from the other two, not saying anything. Karen couldn't follow the heated discussion, even as she listened intently for nearly a minute. The glass panes on the doors were double glazed, which reduced heating and cooling costs but also improved their soundproof quality. She caught a first name ... someone named Aaron. He needed to be informed of ... she missed the rest.

Get closer.

She did, hoping that the bright overheads inside the house would prevent them from seeing out, from spotting her as she crawled right up to the right-most door, hiding behind a pile of neatly stacked firewood.

Who are these people? Who is this Aaron? IRS?

Her ears perked up at the sudden mention of Rubaker, of his impending fate now that his name was—

The doorbell rang. The young guy went to answer it, reappearing moments later with two other men, also wearing suits. One was old but in seemingly good shape, based on how brusquely he moved, how he began to stab the air in front of the Italian guy and his fat friend. A full head of silver hair framed an intense look as he started shouting at the others. The second man, huge, built like a wrestler, with hard-edged features and closely cropped ash blond hair, remained behind the old man as he lectured the pair. Karen slowly pressed an ear against the lowest pane of the French door.

"... but, Aaron, we—"

"Damn you two! Can you fucking think for yourselves? I told you to take care of the problem when you first spotted it! Heads will roll when Washington realizes that we've let it go this long!"

The fat one started to say, "But Aaron, we don't have the resources to—"

"Just shut up, Jason! Let me think!" The old man crossed his arms, asking after a long pause, "Where is he?"

"In the pool house," answered the Italian-looking man. "Tied to a chair."

"Has anyone contacted him?"

"He claims he hasn't been. But we can't be certain."

"Then what are you waiting for?" The man called Aaron turned to his large assistant. "Todd, call the others."

Setting her gun down and grabbing a felt-tipped pen from her pocket, Karen scribbled the three names she had heard thus far on her forearm. Pocketing the pen, retrieving her gun, she crawled away from the door as Todd, the blond giant, produced a cellular phone and began to dial it. She backed herself off the patio and onto grass. Cool dew soaked her T-shirt, chilling her bosom. She stood, weapon in hand, rushing in near darkness toward the far end of the pool, near the small structure. The indirect lighting registered her shadow dashing across the night, taking a position behind the waist-high hedges.

Karen parted two branches just enough to peek through, to see beyond the sliding glass doors of the pool house, spotting the silhouette of a man sitting on a chair, hands tied behind his back, a gag on his mouth. The image vanished as the porch lights switched on, followed by floodlights on the roof, bathing the yard in yellow light, reflecting off the sliding door.

Karen inched back just a bit, the brightness stinging her eyes. The group emerged from the patio moments later, marching down the limestone path, Aaron leading the way, obviously in command.

Todd slid the glass door out of the way, switching on the overhead lights in the pool house. The image of the bound man reappeared, but much clearer now. His head turned toward his captors, eyes widening in fear. The party went in and Todd shut the door behind them.

Karen frowned as a heated argument broke among them. The group encircled Rubaker, who appeared more awake now, shifting his head from face to face. She could see but was too far away to listen. She needed information, needed answers, and she felt certain that she would find such information in the dialogue inside that room, answering the questions swirling in her mind.

Who were these men? Who did they work for? Were they higher ups in the IRS ladder? Karen had to assume so for the time being. Janet Patterson had gone to Pete Rubaker, who in turn had probably gone to one of those characters, who in turn . . . and so on, going up the chain. She wondered how many levels were represented inside that room? From the looks of it she guessed at least two, the original trio and then the silver-haired Aaron.

Curiosity superseded her sense of caution, luring her beyond the protection of the evergreens, toward the humming pump and filter wedged between the stucco wall of the small house and the hedges, cleverly planted to shield the pool equipment from anyone standing on the decking surrounding the pool. The bright overheads inside the pool house would reflect off the sliding door, turning it into a one-way mirror, preventing them from seeing out, just like in the main house—or so Karen hoped, justifying taking this risk as she started toward the rear of the small structure, bordering the hedges in case she needed to make a hasty retreat. The evergreens brushed against her right shoulder as she reached the whirling pump.

She paused, disappointment tightening her features. The pump, albeit fairly quiet from a distance, grew quite noisy when standing just a few feet away. It would certainly impair her ability to eavesdrop on her quarry. She considered her options, reaching for a control panel on the wall, opening it, eyeing the twenty-four-hour timer, noticing that the pump was programmed to go on three times a day for about two hours.

So it would be normal for it to go off, she decided, turning the programming wheel until the timer clicked off, all the while keeping her eyes glued to the door a few feet to her immediate left.

At once, the purring stopped, and a moment later the water stopped cascading, its gurgling replaced by the chirping of crickets and other insects.

She waited, hiding around the corner, out of sight should anyone peer outside to see why the pump had stopped.

No one did.

Confidence gaining over apprehension, she came around, creeping closer, slowly now, back on all fours, inches at a time, until her head just barely reached the glass, near the bottom, the lawn's cool moisture once again chilling her.

Her right hand clutching the Walther, Karen pressed her ear against the glass, making out some words, slowly, sporadically.

". . . no choice . . . onto you . . . confessed under torture . . . please . . . keep quiet . . . wife and kids . . . disappear . . ."

Karen concentrated, struggling to catch everything, desperately seeking to hear the information that would once again draw her closer to her objective. It came a moment later. *SoftCorp.* There was a problem at SoftCorp and at the IRS regarding some kind of transaction with Capitol Bank. And just as she heard this, a loud voice echoed in the night.

"Hey! What are you doing?"

She turned, momentarily stunned. A large man stood by the main house, in plain view, the porch lights washing his hardening features, his narrowed eyes. His posture was balanced, professional, hands off to the sides, free, ready, one of them suddenly reaching inside his coat. She watched the silhouettes of three others running out of the living room and onto the porch, all dressed casually, but assuming the stances and readiness of specialists.

Instincts overrode surprise.

Move!

Karen rolled away from the house, rushing through the bushes. She could identify herself as a federal agent, order them to surrender. The operative in her, however, chose against it. Four armed men by the house plus the party in the pool house. She didn't stand a chance in such an unbalanced playing field.

She fled the mismatch, considering what kind of target she would present to potential shooters. A moving object at night at roughly a hundred feet away. Only an excellent marksman could make such a shot. And a silencer would further degrade accuracy. Lacking noise suppression, they might chose not to fire for fear that the reports would draw unwanted attention.

Her brief postmortem analysis supporting her trained reflexes, Karen dashed across the deck, past the hot tub, its light projecting her shadow against the wall of boulders as she approached the woods, and she reached the tree line.

Shouts behind her, followed by hastening footsteps clicking over limestone. She had to get away, reach safety, decipher what she had heard, had learned.

Angry voices echoed in the night. Karen risked a backward glance. Flashlights torched the darkness, their piercing beams converging on the underbrush she'd crushed moments—

89

A low branch scraped her torso, nearly impaling her. She exhaled, then tensed, the sudden pain arresting, biting into her. Wincing, she pressed on, ignoring the welted skin throbbing against her damp T-shirt.

More shouts, foliage rustling, yellow light shafting down the hillside, mixing with the silver moon glowing through breaks in the canopy overhead. Karen shoved the Walther in her jeans' waistband as she began her descent, needing both hands as she dropped fast to the gorge between hills a few hundred feet below, following a different path than—

A silenced round buzzed past her, splintering bark from a cottonwood to her right, the sound unsettling, telegraphing their intentions, further confirming her decision to flee.

Another bullet shot by, also silenced, like an angered hornet, ringing in her left ear long after it had struck another tree.

Birds shrilled, took wing. Her chest on fire, breathing heavily, Karen Frost lurched toward the bottom of the hill, struggling for balance, her legs unsteady, her arms flailing, hands grabbing onto branches, vines, trunks, anything to control her hasty retreat.

Increase the gap. The thought flashed in her mind over and over, as she swung down on a thick branch, landing a few feet below, ignoring her protesting knees. She scrambled farther down the slope, turning to see how close they were, her spine tingling in anticipation of a hollow-point round.

Karen slipped on something, losing her footing. Arms stretched, she tried to reach for anything, fingers brushing a thick limb, failing to grasp it. Then she was falling, her head jerking back, eyes momentarily glancing at the moon through a break in the branches.

Then everything turned into a blur as the branches, the moon, and the ground swapped places. Tumbling down, Karen protected her chest, her stomach, her face, assuming a fetal position, head tucked in, hands over her face. She struck something, momentarily breaking her fall. She felt blood oozing down her side, felt its warmth, its stickiness. And then she was falling again, out of control, sinking below the trees around her, landing against something very hard, raw pain shooting up from her left kidney, feeling as if something had ruptured her skin.

Tangled in vines, laboring to control her breathing, to manage the pain, to focus, Karen fought to break free, ripping through the surrounding vegetation. She staggered to her feet, half blinded by the impact, by the pain, feeling weak, taking another moment to realize she had reached the bottom.

Her pursuers' lights momentarily lost uphill, Karen cut left, hurrying through the darkness on what appeared to be a game trail winding between ridges. She had to increase the distance from the incoming threat, from the search beams that once again pierced the night above and slightly behind her.

She counted three lights. Three pursuers. More if they shared flashlights.

A pain invaded her stomach, telling her that she was pushing too hard, taxing her endurance. She grew nauseous, her body demanding rest. The climb uphill had been difficult, draining. This sprint through the woods, plus the fall, had further eroded her strength.

Reality demanded a change of tactics. She had to escape but could not outrun them. She had to alter the rules.

Karen stumbled upon a fallen log, its vine-laced trunk blocking the trail, one end resting on a large boulder. She ducked, rolling under it, instinctively switching tactics, obeying her instincts, reaching for the silenced Walther, her hand slapping her own flesh behind her, by her spine. The pistol was gone, probably fallen as she'd stumbled downhill.

A sinking feeling spread through her at the thought of having lost her only silent weapon. The Magnum, strapped to a shoulder holster, lacked a silencer. The report, plus the muzzle flash, would betray her position if she fired it, yielding her only edge. The crisscrossing lights near the gorge told her that she had momentarily lost them. She couldn't allow them to catch up. She was too tired to outrun them.

She had to act quickly. Soon they would find broken branches, footprints. Perhaps—

No more time to analyze! Just do!

But movement meant noise—meant risking giving away her position. Doomed if you move and doomed if you don't.

Karen made her choice, remaining put, searching for a silent weapon, finding a thick branch resembling a curved club, its center hard, solid. She held it in her left hand, feeling the weight, satisfied with the blow it could deliver. Her right clutched the massive Desert Eagle, in case her initial strike failed to incapacitate her quarry.

She receded behind the boulder supporting the fallen log, pressing her back against the wall of the ravine, fallen leaves cascading over her, further concealing her presence from everyone coming up the game trail.

"Which way did she go?" a voice said.

Karen stopped breathing, listening apprehensively.

"Not sure," said another.

A third added, "Split up. You go up the opposite hill. You go down the ravine, and I'll sweep the other side."

Karen dropped her eyelids at the order, at her chance to even out the field, at turning the tables.

Divide and conquer.

She waited as the search party split up, as one men headed in her direction, probably armed with a silenced weapon, with orders to shoot on sight.

Gray moonlight reached down into the gorge, its gleam casting a long shadow on the incoming figure, who stomped confidently—and noisily—toward her position, crushing leaves and other debris as he neared the fallen log.

False confidence in numbers.

That gave Karen another edge, on which she intended to capitalize.

The stranger paused.

Tensing, Karen inched forward, slowly, quietly, like a coiled viper, ready to strike.

Slowly bending over, the stranger scrambled under the log, his face away from Karen, checking the opposite side of the gully from where she stood. He clutched a shiny pistol with a silencer screwed onto its muzzle.

Karen lunged, striking the man on the side of the head, just as she'd been taught at Quantico.

As expected, the stranger dropped unceremoniously, like a sack of coal.

She shoved the Magnum back in its holster and grabbed her victim's pistol, a compact Colt .45. The man carried it already cocked, ready to fire. That the gun did not go off by accident didn't surprise Karen. The Colt had a handle-grip safety, which locked the trigger the moment he'd let go of the weapon.

She checked for a pulse on the fallen man, finding one. Then she checked for identification, finding none.

Professionals. She would learn nothing from him, and she also assumed that the other two were also clean—not that she had the strength or the desire to go after them.

Having bought herself precious minutes, Karen considered her best escape route. One man down and two still looking for her, but in the wrong direction.

Flipping the Colt's safety, she shoved it where her Walther had been before she'd fallen, pressed against the small of her back.

She doubled back, charging up the same hill she had descended, her sneakers slapping against the soft soil layering the angled walls of the ravine. A hand on the fallen log, a foot on the boulder, and she got on top—all the while glancing behind her, toward the darkness that still cloaked two of her pursuers.

With considerable effort, she climbed roughly one-fourth of the way before cutting left, away from everyone, toward the entrance to the exclusive neighborhood, which connected to Loop 360, the highway circling Austin's west side. No one would think of looking for her this way for a while, at least until they realized what she had done, how she had outfoxed them. And by the time they did, Karen Frost planned to be back at her new apartment, soaking her cuts and bruises in warm water while she thought this through. She needed to rest, to consider what she had learned, to report it to Palenski, to map out a new course of action, one that would take her one step closer to this criminal network.

Her body ached. Her lungs burned every time she breathed. The cuts and bruises on her torso continued to broadcast waves of pain, intensifying as the adrenaline boost faded. She took the pain in resigned silence, focusing her efforts on the terrain ahead.

But in spite of her physical condition, Karen was elated. She had learned considerable information, the kind that this shadowy network would not be able to dismiss or eliminate so quickly, the way they did with the Patterson's, as they were now doing with Rubaker. Individuals could be eliminated a lot more easily than corporations. The latter presented many difficulties, especially if corruption ruled their businesses, as Karen suspected. They simply could not vanish without answering endless questions, without investigations, without probes, making the whole process far less appealing than leaving things as they were and fighting it another way.

Which is what they'll do.

Karen felt certain that today marked the beginning of a new fight, one that she would have to carry on at a different level. SoftCorp and Capitol Bank, somehow in association with the IRS, would bring up their defenses, while at the same time come down on her.

Hard.

But first they have to find me, she thought. *And when they do . . . I'll bury them.*

93

6

Aaron Shapiro paced the lawn by the pool, tense, finding it difficult to focus, the palms of his hands sweaty as he rubbed them together. The intruder had escaped, had slipped right through Hausser's men. Now he had to deal with the damage that might bring to the operation.

Walking by his side was Jason Myrtle, the overweight deputy chief of the IRS's Austin Processing Center—a man *owned* by Shapiro. Myrtle's face, bloated and puffy from a life of excess, had turned chalk white when Hausser, upon returning from his failed attempt to eliminate the intruder, slit Rubaker's throat. The IRS executive knew he was next in line.

"What—what are we going to do now?" Myrtle asked, his words choked with emotion, perspiration beading over his upper lip and also running down his cheeks.

Shapiro forced control into his external appearance. He had to remain calm, show why he was in charge of the Austin operation.

Angelo Rossini stood behind Myrtle. Rossini was the president of Capitol Bank. Although a hopeless womanizer who had probably slept with every female at the financial firm, Rossini was a damned good banker, and an even better money launderer, responsible for funneling hundreds of millions from SoftCorp's corporate accounts into numbered accounts in the Cayman Islands, the Bahamas, Brazil, Colombia, and a half dozen other places. For his discreet services, Rossini, along with a handful of carefully selected Capitol Bank employees, received handsome quarterly bonuses—tax free.

Rossini hadn't said a word since Hausser eliminated Rubaker, and Shapiro knew what was running through both of their minds.

"Gentlemen," Aaron Shapiro said, turning on the soft grass to face his audience of two. "This situation has turned *critical*, but it is not by any means *out of control*. However, we must bring it to closure as soon as possible in order to keep everything running per the expectations of our superiors in Washington."

"What will happen to us if our names make it to the FBI?" asked Rossini, adjusting the knot of his tie. "Is your man over there going to . . ." The banker ran a thumb across his neck before pointing to Hausser, who was busy shoving Rubaker's body into a plastic bag while two of his men cleaned up the pool house.

Aaron Shapiro wasn't so certain about their immunity to termination if they ever stumbled into the path of an FBI probe. Washington, however, paid him handsomely to handle the operation down here, and whatever problems might crop up. He slowly shook his head, gave them a fatherly look, and said, "You have *nothing* to worry about. We are *not* foot soldiers. We are *not* expendable."

That alone had a visible effect on both of them. They momentarily relaxed, breathing with obvious relief.

Shapiro continued, trying to believe his own words. "We are needed to run each of our respective organizations. I am needed to handle SoftCorp. You, Angelo, must continue to run the banking side of the operation. And you, Jason, are needed to keep on signing the contract checks to SoftCorp while keeping the agents in the Internal Audit Division and Criminal Investigation Division out of our hair."

Myrtle shoved his hands in his pockets and stared at his shoes before lifting his gaze and leveling it with Shapiro's. "I think I know how to handle that, even without Rubaker."

Shapiro gave him a brief smile. "Good. Right now I need you to focus on that, while keeping your eyes peeled for any—and I mean the *slightest*—sign of wrongdoing by your own people. My guess is that the FBI probe has come to a halt with Rubaker. They probably don't know how to proceed from here or what is even going on inside the IRS—much less our business arrangement. However, if we panic and do something stupid, then we *will* give them something to continue their investigation. Right now they're just fishing. They're rustling the branches to see what shakes out, see what they can catch. They have nothing concrete to move on, just indirect pointers, like the sketchy information that the Pattersons might have provided, which apparently was good enough to lead the FBI probe to Rubaker. Now we have eliminated the link in their investigation by preventing Rubaker from talking to them."

"So we just go back to our lives and pretend nothing has gone wrong?" asked Rossini.

Shapiro nodded. "With the caveat that you must keep a close watch on your people in case the FBI sticks its nose into your business again, especially at the IRS, Jason," Shapiro said, staring at the plump government bureaucrat. "That's where it all started anyway, so it's very likely that this female federal agent might try to contact other people within your organization."

Jason Myrtle took a deep breath, produced a handkerchief from a pocket, and wiped off the sweat on his forehead and neck.

Shapiro kept up the pep talk for another five minutes before sending them on their way.

After they left, the CEO of SoftCorp remained by the pool, hoping his subordinates had bought his story. Inside, however, he was in turmoil. The female agent had been savvy enough to get Rubaker's name from the Pattersons. If she had managed to hear anything tonight, the entire operation would be in jeopardy. He had to close this, and soon, before it got so far out of control that it required Washington's involvement.

Taking a deep breath, his eyes on Hausser and his team inside the pool house, Aaron Shapiro considered his options. He had enough money stashed away in personal accounts in three overseas banks to vanish, to take his wife and daughters and disappear, just like in the movies.

Right.

He knew it wasn't that simple. His girls, now grown up, had their own lives. If Shapiro disappeared, the shadowy men from Washington would retaliate.

He had to play this out and hope to shut down the investigation before it reached him, before he ended up in a body bag similar to the one Hausser and his men now hauled out across the lawn.

"Let's start at the beginning," said Ryan, laptop ready to take notes as he sat at a round table in one of several conference rooms off to the side of SoftCorp's sumptuous lobby, which conveyed the sense of wealth and power that had grasped Ryan during his first visit over a month ago. Employees walked the lobby, some meeting with equipment suppliers, others stopping by the small branch of the U.S. Postal Service, set up a year ago by Shapiro for the convenience of his team. Two ATM machines stood next to the post office. SoftCorp employees could perform any transaction without fees.

The early morning sun streamed through the cracks in the drawn blinds, softening the gray glow of the room's overheads. Ryan would have preferred natural light, but the bright afternoon glare would have made the screen of his IBM ThinkPad impossible to read.

"What happens after a taxpayer turns in his income tax return to the IRS?" Ryan asked, trying to gain insight into his customer's needs.

Across the table sat Internal Audit Division Agent Gam Olson, a well-built man in his midforties dressed in a gray suit, with a full head of salt-and-pepper hair, slit eyes, and a chin that portrayed strength. He regarded Ryan with a poker stare before saying, "Well, Mr. Ryan. The first thing—"

"Mike, please."

"Excuse me?"

"I go by Mike."

Olson raised a brow. "I'm more comfortable with last names, sir."

"Ah . . . okay . . ." Ryan frowned internally. He should have realized that Gam Olson was a last-name kind of guy after he had introduced himself simply as Agent Olson, giving no hint that he wanted to be addressed in any other way. Perhaps the IRS was like the armed forces, where everybody addresses each other by their rank and last name. "Please continue, Agent Olson."

Olson nodded. "The moment you mail in your 1040–hopefully prior to April fifteen–it goes directly to one of ten IRS service centers."

"What are those?" Ryan asked while typing away.

"They are colossal processing facilities, Mr. Ryan, where your return begins its long IRS processing queue. First thing that happens is the removal of any attached checks. Those are sent off down their own channel to be deposited immediately. Meanwhile, your 1040 form makes its way to data entry, where operators transcribe the information from your tax return into the computers."

"Manually?"

"Yes, sir. Unless you filed electronically. But electronic filing amounted to less than ten percent of the volume of returns received by the IRS last year."

"I see. So these operators have to essentially retype my entire return? That sounds like room for human error."

"There is some, yes. But do keep in mind that IRS data entry operators only transcribe about forty percent of the information on your 1040, and they do cross-check what they entered to ensure maximum accuracy."

"Only forty percent?"

"Yes, sir. They capture all of the essentials, leaving out intermediate computations."

"What happens to the original 1040?"

"The paper copy goes to the National Archives warehouse in Washington, D.C."

"Okay," said Ryan, "Let's go back to these . . . service centers?"

"Yes, sir?"

Ryan was quickly getting tired of the "sir" thing but decided to indulge the federal agent. "I take it that the service centers are spread out by geographical regions of the country?"

"Correct, Mr. Ryan."

"And they're responsible for processing all returns from that region?"

"That's right. They get returns from all local offices in their region."

"Is this the way the IRS has always processed returns?"

Olson shifted his weight on the chair while looking into the distance. "Back in the early fifties, income tax returns–due on March fifteen instead of April fifteen–were turned in to local tax offices. These offices handled everything locally, answering tax payer's questions, reviewing the 1040s, performing audits, processing returns, et cetera."

"That sure seemed convenient," said Ryan, thinking of his own tax return from last year. The newlyweds had had a few questions regarding the tax changes with their new marital status but had been unable to get all of the answers from their local tax office.

"It was from a taxpayer's perspective. The overall system, however, was too inefficient, too manual, too decentralized. The first major move toward centralized handling came in 1955, when the 1040A returns from several districts in the Midwest were sent to Kansas City for centralized handling. The so-called Midwest Service Center was born that year from the old Kansas City IRS office. This location was outfitted with modern computers, which at the time were just becoming widely available, to streamline the process. By 1959 there were seven such service centers operating across the United States plus a central computer hub in West Virginia that serviced all accounts."

Ryan took detailed notes of this historical perspective, the IRS's initial steps toward automation. He listened intently as Gam Olson described in great detail how the IRS came of age in the computer revolution that swept through the nation during the '60s and '70s, plodding ahead in its quest for full automation. Olson described the concerns from the general public, fueled by the media, about the IRS growing into a monster with centralized computing capable of sorting and analyzing every bit of personal information from every American citizen. Would the IRS learn about taxpayer's religious affiliations based on charitable deductions? Would the IRS extract medical data based on medical expense deductions? The Service tried to quash such concerns with assurances that all taxpayer information was secured and protected by the IRS's state-of-the-art systems. Over the years such concerns slowed the Service's ability to make progress in automation, and more so recently, with the advent of hackers and computer viruses.

And that's where I come in, thought Ryan, while listening to Olson's historical dissertation. His virtual-reality system would initially empower agents like Gam Olson to extract the information they sought quickly and efficiently, using SoftCorp's existing security system. Later on, Ryan would add his own layer of security, further safeguarding the personal and confidential information embedded in those tax return forms.

"Ron Wittica mentioned that your division needs to go through considerable manual effort to track down the information you need to catch tax violators."

Olson frowned while adjusting the knot of his tie. "The problem that we face is that too many of the systems we need to access are not compatible with one another. Some of that was solved by default with the advent of the World Wide Web, but we still can't access many confidential databases easily, and on top of that we have difficulty digesting the massive amount of information required to process our cases efficiently."

Ryan nodded, remembering the conversation he'd had with Ron Wittica on Friday.

"But that's what your company is solving for us, Mr. Ryan," the federal agent added. "And I understand from Mr. Wittica that you will be integrating the multiple expert system interfaces with an all-encompassing virtual-reality environment."

The Stanford graduate nodded again. Other engineers in the firm had been working to design smart interfaces between a common software platform and the IRS's eclectic computer system. Lacking the ability to just replace the incompatible systems across many divisions, SoftCorp had opted to create a common denominator for all of them so that Internal Audit Division agents could easily access their information by just dealing with a single operating system, very similar to the way the World Wide Web works, but on a much smaller scale. Ryan's initial job was to facilitate navigation through virtual reality. "I've been tasked to tailor a VR interface to your requirements."

"All right, then," Agent Gam Olson said, for the first time this afternoon displaying interest. "Why don't I tell you exactly how we operate. That will give you a good idea where to start."

"Sounds good."

Crossing his legs, Gam Olson began. "I'll start with the simple case: the taxes of an individual. We'll cover corporate taxes later since they are far more complicated, though it is here that we lose the larger portion of our tax dollars."

Ryan remembered reading an article some time back about the rapid spread of tax shelters among corporations to dodge taxes. "Okay," he said. "Let's start with the simple cases."

"It all starts at data entry," Olson began, "where operators are transcribing part of the information in the 1040s into the mainframes. IAD—that's us, the Internal Audit Division—has agents monitoring flags, which can be set whenever a return deviates from the norm."

"For example?" asked Ryan.

"Charitable contributions exceeding a certain percentage of the reported income. Or medical expenses that seem out of line with previous years. Anything that sticks out more than a few percentage points from the historical data of a taxpayer."

"I see. Please continue."

"The flagging process is actually fairly straightforward. After the information has been scrubbed by a data entry supervisor to make sure it is error free, we get the request for further investigation. This is where the problem starts. We get literally thousands of these cases every day—too many to go after in any efficient manner given the highly manual state of our investigative procedures. So the first thing that my division does is rank the flags according to their level of severity. The taxpayers who deviated the most from either history or from what we have established as prudent given their unadjusted income go into one category. Those with slightly lesser deviations go next, and so on. In total we have six different categories. We currently only go after the top two with a reasonable degree of effectiveness, which means that we bag the bigger fish, but a lot of smaller fish get through our imperfect net. We're hoping that your system will allow us to tighten things up, to increase the granularity of our search."

"Wittica estimated the lost revenue at the IRS because of this inefficiency in the system at around five billion dollars per quarter."

Olson shrugged. "No one knows for sure. I think that it is probably larger than that. What we know for certain is that the loss in tax revenue from the corporate world is bigger than that from private individuals. Just to give you an example, in 1999, the tax court found that United Parcel Service had engaged in a long-running scam to evade more than one billion in taxes. One billion, Mr. Ryan, from just one company."

"So why not go after the corporations first?" asked Ryan.

"Although there are far fewer corporate cases than individual cases, they are much harder to break, oftentimes requiring hundreds of more resources than what's required to go after a single taxpayer. And those resources could be tied up for years, as they fight their way through the tangled web of legal loopholes that some of these companies can weave, keeping us chasing our tails for some time. On the other hand, private individuals, although much easier to catch, yield modest amounts in the bigger picture. So we opt for a balance, allocating some resources to go after key corporate cases and others after top-ranked private individuals. But in both cases many slip through our imperfect nets because we're stretched way too thin to be very effective. In fact, we know for a fact that many corporations are now playing the tax shelter game, banking on the fact that we won't have the people to go after them. Kind of playing audit roulette."

"Amazing," said Ryan, taking it all. "So, back to ranking. What happens after you have ranked the cases and have identified those you can go after?"

"We go after them, Mr. Ryan. In the case of an individual taxpayer, for example, who happened to have claimed excessive medical bills, we follow up with the hospital, doctors, insurance company, even his or her employer, to make certain that the story holds together. In some instances we find that it does, and we opt to drop the case. Other times we find enough evidence to pursue it further."

Tapping keys, Ryan asked, "At what point in time does the taxpayer realize he or she is being investigated?"

Olson looked away, apparently considering how to answer that. "It varies," he replied a moment later. "Sometimes we find evidence almost immediately to conduct a full-blown audit. Other times it may take us six months or longer to gather enough evidence to proceed."

"Is it true that in some cases taxpayers are never notified until after the IRS has seized their properties and frozen assets?" Ryan decided to risk the question. He remembered reading such articles in the newspaper from time to time.

"In some cases, yes."

Ryan decided to push his luck. "Is it really necessary to go to such extremes?"

Olson sighed, uncrossed his legs, and leaned forward, resting his elbows on the table. "Mr. Ryan, my agency must do what's necessary to ensure that those trying to live for free in this country are brought to justice and forced to pay what they owe the government of the United States. Our nation offers a straightforward deal: you get to live here and enjoy one of the safest and finest standards of living in the world, and in return you pay taxes. Plain and simple. Now, there are those who think they can get away with the best of both worlds. When we identify those individuals, we go after them with a vengeance—and please do understand that we're not talking about your average mistake on a 1040. Our intention is not to frighten the American public. Unfortunately, the few instances when we do make a mistake, the media has a field day with it."

Ryan considered what seemed like a perfectly reasonable explanation from the IRS's perspective, unless of course, you happened to be the poor bastard under their magnifying glass.

"What kind of flags do you get from a corporation that might be trying to dodge taxes?"

Olson leaned back again and crossed his legs, apparently more comfortable with this last question. "We usually find them through random audits. Some time back, for example, AlliedSignal, sold its investment in a petroleum company at a profit of over four hundred million dollars. The company would have owed close to one hundred forty million dollars in taxes, but it shifted the profit to a partnership created with a Dutch bank. AlliedSignal later took back the profit from the partnership—untaxed. This one's currently in the court of appeals. We figured that something was seriously wrong during the audit, when the four hundred million dollars in profit had vanished overseas."

Ryan shook his head in disbelief. "But . . . didn't AlliedSignal know that it could get in trouble?"

"Audit roulette, Mr. Ryan. Corporations simply play the odds, which usually are in their favor. And so what if they get caught once in a while, as long as they succeed the other twenty—or a hundred—times they try to dodge taxes?"

The conversation continued for another thirty minutes, time which Ryan used to get more details on the IRS thought process, procedures, policies, and background information that would help him best customize a VR system for the IAD, linking all of the expert systems already created by SoftCorp.

At the end of their three-hour-long chat, Ryan had typed almost ten pages' worth of notes, which he planned to spend the next day sorting out and prioritizing before diving into the code, which, based on his experience at Stanford, he estimated would take him roughly five weeks to complete. Ryan's technical advisor, Agi Maghami, was supposed to send him an E-mail with all of the links and required passwords to retrieve the expert systems created by other engineers in the firm. One of the expert systems, for example, represented the product of many more interviews with the IAD over the past year to emulate the thought process that agents went through during the prioritization of violation flags from the data entry department. Another expert system handled the highly manual tasks of accessing the huge database of the American Medical Association, plus its thousands of classified links into the databases of hospitals across the country, to retrieve information to corroborate a taxpayer's medical deduction claims. There were also several expert systems designed to access financial data, credit reports, state records for child support, alimony payments, prison records, and so on. These expert systems were part translators, allowing the auditor to easily view and download the desired information, while also providing analysis capability based on more interviews with seasoned IAD agents. Ryan would take all of those expert systems, which Maghami had estimated at over two hundred, and give them all identifiers in a virtual-reality world.

After thanking the IAD agent, Ryan headed upstairs to his lab. Wittica caught up with him in the elevators. The chief technical officer looked as if he had just returned from a photo shoot for *Gentlemen's Quarterly*.

"Hey, Mike. How did that meeting go?"

Ryan shrugged. "Okay, I guess. Got what I needed. Now I have to get busy with the code."

"Good. We're running the first test in three weeks."

Ryan stopped. "*Three* weeks? No way, Ron. I need five minimum."

Wittica slowly shook his head, extending the ring, middle, and index fingers of his right hand, as if giving Ryan a Boy Scout salute. "Today is Monday. I'll schedule a demo two weeks from this coming Friday."

"But—"

"I know you can do it, Mike. That's why we hired you. Now, tell me about your weekend. How was it?"

Ryan frowned. So much for negotiating schedules in this place. He could feel the screws rapidly being tightened. Momentarily accepting his superior's terms, Ryan nodded and started to walk again. "My weekend? Probably not as exciting as yours, Ron. And based on *your* development schedule, I guess the next couple of weekends won't be much fun."

Wittica laughed while patting Ryan on the shoulder.

Ryan didn't see the humor in his last statement.

"Did you get the Boxster?"

"Saturday morning. It's awesome."

"Good. By the way, congrats on the house on Rowley Drive."

Ryan froze. He had not seen Wittica since Friday, and he clearly remembered not telling him which houses he would be seeing on Lakeway. Ryan himself didn't even know that until Gail had brought them there on Saturday.

"How did you know that?"

He winked. "I've got my sources."

Ryan grimaced, not certain how to take that. It seemed that every move he made in or outside of work was being monitored. For a moment he thought of the monitors in that room down the hall from his lab, and couldn't help but wonder if—

"Relax, Mike. I'm not stalking you," Wittica added, obviously noticing Ryan's face as they stepped inside the elevator. He smiled sheepishly. "I know Gail . . . *very well.*"

Figures, Ryan thought.

Wittica leaned closer to him. "I paid for her . . ." He cupped his chest. "Nice job, huh?"

Ryan exhaled in exasperation.

"Anyway, she called me on Sunday. Told me all about it. Sounded like a great deal."

"And it was, Ron," Ryan said. "I guess I'm just used to my privacy, that's all."

"And you should be entitled to it," he replied, seriously. "I just take a personal interest in all of my guys. I want to see you and Vic do well in life. You kids are very smart, hardworking, and deserve nothing but the best."

Ryan breathed deeply, deciding to ask the question that had been bothering him since closing the deal on Saturday. "About the house, Ron."

"Yes?"

"Well, it was almost like . . . the deal of a lifetime. I strongly suspect that Gail could have sold it for far more than we paid. SoftCorp didn't have . . . anything to do with that, right?"

Wittica regarded his subordinate for a moment before asking, "Are you happy with the transaction, Mike?"

"Yes."

"Is Victoria happy with the house and the price."

"I think *thrilled* is a better word. We're moving in on Saturday."

"Then enjoy it, my friend. You've worked very hard. Now it's time to reap the benefits."

The elevator door slid open. Wittica motioned for Ryan to go in.

He did. Wittica remained in the hallway. "We're here to help you, Mike. We want you to be successful and make yourself rich while making SoftCorp rich. Is that such a bad deal?"

Ryan shook his head. "The best deal in town."

Wittica gave him one of his ear-to-ear smiles, dazzlingly white, contrasting with his bronzed features and his million-dollar posture, all wrapped inside an expensive Italian suit. "That's my man. And don't forget about the three weeks. I'm looking forward to taking our IRS clients through a run in the VR system."

The doors closed before Ryan could reply. His own feelings betraying him, he made his way to his lab, slowing down as he walked past the double doors halfway down the antiseptically clean corridor.

Let it go, Mike. Do your job. Make a bundle of money. Return to California in a few years. Buy the house you and Vic had always wanted overlooking the ocean. After all, that was their plan, right? Ryan and Victoria had not discussed it much since their arrival here. Was that still their goal? Or were they slowly being wrapped in this golden web, craftily woven by SoftCorp for the whole purpose of locking them in, of making it very painful for them to leave?

Ryan remembered his initial interview, Shapiro's comment about no one ever leaving SoftCorp unless they retired. How did Ryan's plan fit in with this unique company trend? What would happen in three years, after his new-hire bond expired and he turned in his resignation to return to the West Coast and work for another company? He didn't recall any clauses on the papers that he had signed during his first day at orientation. Was there some clause or stipulation that he was not aware of? Or was it possible that people simply didn't want to leave SoftCorp? Was the lure of so much money such a powerful motivator?

As he reached his office and keyed in the access password, Ryan recalled the look filming Victoria's eyes after they had signed the agreement papers on Saturday evening. He remembered the way in which she had clasped his hand, had kissed him when Gail left them alone to remove the For Sale sign off the front lawn. He had never seen her act that way, so . . . thrilled? Ryan wondered if they would be able to turn their backs on all of this in a few years and return to overpriced California, where the quarter of a million dollars they had spent on a beautiful home in Lakeway would only buy them a small two-bedroom, thirty-year-old home in a run-of-the-mill neighborhood in San Jose?

As he settled behind his desk, he decided to call Victoria at work.

"Capitol Bank, this is Victoria. May I help you?"

"In more ways than you think," he replied.

"Hi, honey!"

Ryan smiled, feeling better just listening to her voice. "How's my favorite girl?"

"Being worked to death by my boss," she replied with a heavy sigh.

Ryan dropped his lids at the reply. "Oh? Want to tell me about it?"

"I guess that's what happens when you work directly for the president of the bank. He's dumping all of his dirty work on me. He's just dropped a big stack of loan applications on my desk to get my risk assessment on them." Victoria's current position was that of risk management officer. She was one of a handful of risk officers on the hook for reviewing the history of any corporation seeking funding, including its profit-and-loss statements, financial outlook, current assets, and a hundred other indices, before assigning the loan application a risk factor and associated recommendation to Rossini, who would review the recommendation personally before approving or rejecting the loan application.

"Is he giving you more than you can handle?"

"No. He's treating me pretty much the same as the other officers. But I'm still going to be working pretty hard for the next few weeks. Probably even weekends."

"That's funny," he replied.

"Perhaps to you," she said. "I'm the one buried in paperwork."

"No, no. That's not what I meant," Ryan said, before telling her about the executive pull-in on his own schedule.

"Well," she said. "Look at it on the positive side. At least neither of us will be lonely at home waiting for the other one."

Ryan was surprised at her response. Victoria seemed to be taking this whole overworking business a lot better than he was.

"But you are off this Saturday, right?" he asked, dreading the thought of having to deal by himself with the move from their SoftCorp-leased apartment to their new house—not that they owned that much stuff anyway. The Ryans had shed most of their college belongings before heading to Texas.

"Relax, honey. I'm not going to stick you with that shit job—though I'm sure we should be able to wrap it up in a half day."

After agreeing to be home by nine to have a shot at an evening together, he hung up and began to review the notes he had taken during his interview with Olson, momentarily wondering if all of this was worth it, and if he would be able to walk away from it all once he got used to this life.

As he dove into the writing of the code for his VR solution, Ryan's inner voice told him that the longer he stayed at SoftCorp the harder it would be to leave.

8

Karen Frost had worked undercover for as long as she could remember. Shortly after graduating from the FBI academy in Quantico, Virginia, she got assigned to the San Antonio, Texas, office, where she underwent her first identity change to catch cartel lord Jose Pineda. Posing as the owner of a small bank in San Antonio secretly founded by the FBI, Karen had lured Pineda and his goons by offering money laundering services. Over the following nine months, she monitored hundreds of financial transactions and videotaped dozens of Pineda's meetings, resulting in the arrest and conviction of Pineda and many of his local contacts.

Her career continued to grow as she went on to assume dangerous assignments in other regions of the country, always going after organized crime, always managing to prevail, to survive, to bring criminals to justice. It was during one of those missions that Karen had met Mark Frost, a senior FBI agent in New York. They'd spent many weeks engaged in an FBI task force to crack a local mafia ring, in the end not only succeeding but also falling in love, and marrying soon after. But her romance was short-lived. The mafia didn't forget the blow inflicted by the FBI task force, costing them tens of millions in lost revenue from gray-market sales. A car bomb claimed the life of Mark Frost, propelling Karen into a rampage to achieve retribution, an obsession that had led her to the jungles of South America, to the darkest chapter in her life.

Karen looked at the silver band on her ring finger and frowned. *But I caught those bastards, my love.*

"Just as I intend to bag *these* bastards," she whispered, fingering the red pointer floating in the middle of the keyboard of her notebook computer, bringing the cursor to the About Our People menu selection of SoftCorp's public Web page.

The modem connection began to download the information from the

Internet, painting it onto her screen. Karen reached for the mug of steaming coffee next to the laptop and took a sip, breathing deeply, her bruised ribs stabbing her torso as she did so. The package from Washington, which included the laptop, had arrived at her apartment that morning, less than twenty-four hours after contacting Palenski following her hillside adventure. She had spent the balance of that evening, plus all of the following day recovering, resting, planning her next move.

The screen displayed the photos of SoftCorp's management team on the left side of the screen, adjacent to a brief bio on each.

Karen tensed the moment the photo of the silver-haired man back at Rubaker's house materialized on the plasma color screen. Aaron Jerome Shapiro, founder and CEO of SoftCorp.

"Son of a bitch," she hissed under her breath. "Hello, Aaron."

Her heartbeat rocketing with the knowledge that she was making mounds of progress, Karen continued browsing down the list, arranged according to pecking order. A handsome man was next, Ronald S. Wittica, chief technical officer. She spent the next five minutes reading about each engineer in the company, all graduated with honors from top universities: MIT, Harvard, Yale, Stanford, Caltech, Georgia Tech, Rice, and others. She clicked on the printer button and a moment later her Hewlett-Packard laser jet began to hum, sucking a sheet from the tray.

She printed the list of SoftCorp employees and moved on to Capitol Bank, where Karen connected the Italian-looking fellow at Rubaker's with the photo of Angelo Rossini, president of Capitol Bank.

The beauty of the Internet, she thought. *Information at your fingertips.*

But not enough. She had been unable to get any info from the local IRS processing center beyond instruction on filing taxes.

She frowned, getting up, walking to the bathroom while undressing, leaving a trail of clothes. She turned on the shower and spent the next fifteen minutes letting the hot water caress her back, her neck, filling her lungs with the rising steam. Forcing her mind to relax, Karen shampooed her hair and rinsed it thoroughly before reaching for a sponge and a bar of soap. She cleaned her arms, her chest, her legs, scrubbing hard, until her fair skin tingled. Then she just stood there, beneath a stream of water set as hot as she could take it. She had read once a long time ago that the Japanese scrub themselves clean with soap and sponge before immersing themselves in pools of nearly scalding water to achieve *yudedako,* a sublime state of mental and physical relaxation, which allowed them to think clearly. Karen had adapted that custom to the shower, using it every time she had to clear her mind.

Turning off the water, she dried off with a towel and stepped out of the shower, pausing in front of the mirror over the sink.

The lines of age, quite fine and barely noticeable, were beginning to mark her once smooth skin, particularly around her eyes. But she still considered herself an attractive woman—not that it really mattered. Mark's assassination had killed off the love interest in her life. She didn't care about her looks any more than what was required to remain physically fit to do her job. On occasion she would wear makeup if the job required it. Otherwise, her eye shadow, eye liner, lipstick, and a few other items remained at the bottom of her suitcase.

For reasons she could not explain, however, it did bother her that her breasts had begun to sag five years ago, coinciding with her fortieth birthday. She had always been proud of her bosom, full, uptilted, with small brown nipples—and all natural, God-given, not purchased at the local cosmetic surgery center. She cupped them and raised them about an inch, to the level they had once been.

"You're not getting any younger, darling," she told her reflection in the mirror.

At least she had managed to maintain the same weight of her younger days, refusing to get fat like so many other "old hands" at the Bureau, including the once robust Roman Palenski.

Time for a metamorphosis. Her enemy had taken a good look at her the other night. She needed a change in looks. Grabbing the bottle of hair dye on the sink, Karen read the instructions on the box next to it and spent the next thirty minutes turning herself into a blonde. She rinsed her hair in the sink, toweled it dry, and regarded her reflection again, raising a brow in approval. But the effect was not natural. The color in her eyes did not match her new hair. Reaching for a case of contact lenses, she unscrewed the right container and used the tip of her right middle finger to remove the lens. She had done this many times before, when an operation called for a quick change in looks. She put it on, blinking a few times until the lens adhered itself to her right eyeball, turning her brown eye blue. She did the same to her left eye and smiled approvingly. The extended-wear colored lenses had no magnification. She could wear them for up to a week without having to take them off, at which point she could insert a fresh pair from the package she had received from Palenski.

"Hello, beautiful," she whispered, thinking of a couple of blonde jokes.

Putting on a robe—part of her shopping spree at a nearby mall once it became evident that she would be spending some time in Austin—Karen Frost refilled her mug and brought it to the living room windows, overlooking her complex's parking lot and the highway. The apartment was nondescript, out of the way, and best of all, the landlady had not even registered Karen's name after the federal agent had paid in cash for three months in advance.

Staring at the traffic on I-35, she wondered how high up the corruption reached inside the IRS. Was the head of the Austin office involved? Perhaps one or more of his subordinates? Was it confined to Austin, or were other centers involved as well? How about Washington? Who could be trusted?

There was only one way to find out. Karen needed to make contact with someone on the inside, someone who would be willing to assist the FBI.

But who?

She finished off her coffee and got dressed, starting with the money belt she had purchased at a travel shop at the local mall, made of waterproof nylon, perfect to carry her emergency cash, and a second set of FBI-issued identification, which included a Texas driver's license and a Visa card. She slipped into a new pair of jeans and a black T-shirt—she never wore any undergarments. She put on a fresh pair of socks and sneakers before strapping the compact Colt .45 pistol, minus the silencer, in the same ankle holster of the Walther PPK/S she had lost on the hill outside Rubaker's house. She then donned the lightweight shoulder harness supporting the large holster of her Desert Eagle .44 Magnum, also securing the Colt's silencer in a Velcro strap on the same shoulder harness. She would wear the new light cotton jacket hanging in the closet to cover the large weapon in public. A lifetime of undercover work had taught her the value of living and sleeping with emergency funds and two weapons on her immediate person.

She returned to the table, where she began to inspect the sheets she had printed out. Somewhere, buried in the list of employees of both companies, was her key to taking the next step.

Karen spent the following three weeks zeroing in on her quarry, following a number of potential candidates while also performing multiple Internet excursions, not just to the Web pages of SoftCorp and Capitol Bank but also to other sites, including Stanford University, as she narrowed down her search and selected her final candidates. She changed the color of her hair and eyes religiously every week, going from a blonde with blue eyes to a redhead with green eyes, back to her natural brunette look, and again to a blonde.

A chameleon, Karen Frost thought, finalizing her strategy and her time line to execute it. The chameleon who came in from the cold, bringing with it a frost that would chill her opponents and make them wish they had never been born.

Shades of magenta, cyan, and violet merged into a thick whirl the moment Mike Ryan jacked into his virtual-reality system, enveloped by this psychedelic cloud while trying to familiarize himself with the network. It was Thursday, the day before Wittica had scheduled the demo. It amazed him that three weeks had already gone by.

Ryan sighed. He had not even gotten a chance to enjoy his new home, and neither had Victoria for that matter. Their jobs saw to it that the young couple spent just enough time at home to sleep before having to head back out.

He had spent most of his time stuck in this lab alone with his VR equipment. Although he had not yet completed the finishing touches on his interface, he had hammered out enough code to take a test drive. If this run through the VR system went as expected, Ryan felt certain that he could wrap it up in the next twenty-four hours.

Ryan used a set of standard library cells to interpret the thousands of directories in SoftCorp's computer network, arranged according to Agi Maghami's level of security. The veiling haze was his VR system's imaginative interpretation of a low-level security access shield, which he had to clear before being allowed permission to enter this net. His library, which Ryan had developed over the course of two years while working on his master's thesis, had visual interpretations of every known hardware or software element in a network. While a directory or program might appear like an icon on a screen, which the user would click to gain access, Ryan's VR system mapped that view into something far more visual, more meaningful.

He spoke his password and the throat mike digitized it. At once the cloud vanished, and Ryan found himself floating in front of a huge spherical cloud—the network's home directory, where files generally available to employees resided, like company goals, mission statements, phone lists, and

R. J. Pineiro

organizational charts. Many silver figures zoomed about in this space. They
were SoftCorp users, whom his initial version of the library cataloged ge-
nerically, making them all appear the same in his eyes. Ryan's next version
of the VR system, the one he would show Wittica, would personalize the
users with the photos from their personnel files.

Ryan's system enabled him to fly in any direction by merely looking
that way and then blinking. He did so, dropping through this hazy layer
like a descending jetliner sinking in the clouds during a final approach.

Slowly, the images beneath this cyber atmosphere materialized, revealing an Earth-like sphere, dark brown and covered by multicolored three-
dimensional structures—portals—each representing a file or subdirectory on
the system. Users went in and out of those portals, whose colors conveyed
their accessibility.

Ryan felt like an astronaut circling Earth as he cruised over this cyberscape, recognizing the many 3-D symbols he had crafted during countless
nights at the lab back in Stanford. He knew most of them by heart. Those he
didn't identified themselves with the blink of an eye.

Ryan dove toward one, a white portal shaped like a pre-Columbian
temple, columns surrounding a glyph-etched limestone slab blocking the
entryway. His thesis mentor at Stanford had particularly liked the detail in
the columns and the glyphs adorning this portal, which Ryan had reprogrammed to represent the file containing the company's history. The white
color code indicated that he did not need an additional password to get in.

The limestone slab creaked open, the grinding sound of stone against
stone echoing in his headgear. Ryan landed softly in the exposed passage-
way, the flickering glow of torches bracketed against the stone walls revealing a shaman dressed in a colorful ceremonial gown and a feathery
headdress. His face needed some work, though, and Ryan made a note to
fine-tune that before showing it to Wittica. The shaman, standing in front
of a glowing fire, described the beginnings of SoftCorp, founded over ten
years ago by Shapiro and Wittica. The information came to Ryan fast. Data
in the form of both video, emerging from the flames, and Dolby digital
surround sound, filled his senses. The start-up, financed with venture capital
from Capitol Bank, had only four employees, chartered with capitalizing on
the computerizing frenzy of the late '80s, when systems had become more
and more affordable, allowing most businesses, big and small, to introduce
computers into their daily operation, from doctor's offices to retailers and
restaurants. The young company acquired a lot of market share during its
first few years, mostly thanks to the technical brilliance of its founders, who
developed hardware-software solutions that were not only quite elegant and
innovative but also highly efficient, enabling SoftCorp to offer five-star services at a three-star price. But the company as a whole wasn't growing sig-
nificantly. During its first five years in business only four more engineers

joined the firm, bringing the grand total to eight. But that all changed in 1992, when the IRS selected SoftCorp as one of several firms contracted to modernize the ancient IRS computer systems.

Ryan listened intently as the shaman continued to relate the company's story, aided by timely images and video clips, which materialized out of the flickering flames. In the beginning there were eight contractors providing computing services to the IRS's Austin Processing Center. Over the following two years the list was pruned to only SoftCorp. Ryan found nothing in the company's historical archives that explained the circumstances that had led to competitors abandoning what appeared to be quite profitable government contracts. But they did, one at a time, leaving SoftCorp as the sole provider of computing solutions and services to the local branch of the IRS. By then SoftCorp had grown to thirty full-time employees and moved to this building, where they continued to increase in size until reaching its current staffing level. The letters *EOF*—end of file—flashed beyond the images of SoftCorp's opulent headquarters and of a group picture on the front lawn.

Ryan pulled back up, once again circling this virtual planet along with dozens of other users, their silvery shapes glinting under the white cloud coverage. He descended in front of a mausoleum, dark gray, a pair of stone gargoyles looking down at him. The entryway, however, glowed bright yellow, requiring an additional password. Ryan recited it and the yellow faded to white and then vanished altogether, granting him access to a copy of Cemetery, an expert system designed by another SoftCorp engineer to access the records of the deceased. The expert system, which Ryan's VR environment showed as a tall, pale, and bony mortician dressed in a black tuxedo, could access the database of any hospital or police department across the country and extract the information an agent from the IRS's Internal Audit Division might want as part of an investigation.

Ryan spent a few minutes inside this complex directory and its large number of files, all linked together in a massive decision tree designed to emulate the thought process of an IAD agent gathering information on deceased tax payers. The mortician could handle the special protocols and handshakes to interface with hospital records, police records, the nationwide FBI database, and even extract information from all cemeteries across the nation with records on-line. He performed a brief test, ordering the mortician to access the morgue at Brackenridge Hospital. The software interface had up-to-date access passwords courtesy of the Internal Revenue Service in cooperation with all hospitals, police departments, the FBI, cemeteries, newspaper archives, and any other location where records of deceased were entered.

In an instant the landscape changed. A gleaming white room swallowed the mausoleum and Ryan found himself staring at walls of steel cubicles.

Floor-to-ceiling hatches with bright handles held the records he sought. A single blink commanded the mortician to open a hatch. An image of the deceased materialized in front of Ryan, as well as all registered records, which the mortician read out loud for Ryan. There was, of course, a far easier way to find information than randomly checking cubicles. Ryan spoke the name of a woman he knew had died based on today's newspaper. A moment later the mortician levitated to a hatch close to the ceiling on the wall to his right, and slid a tray out of the wall. The image of a middle-aged woman materialized in the mortician's open palm while he related all known information, including personal data never released to the media. Ryan then asked for a summary sheet of all entries in the past twenty-four hours, and the mortician complied, providing a list of photos and statistics on each entry in the morgue's log. He could search through this list in any order he wished, alphabetically, by time of death, by type of death, by age, by race, by gender, and any other of dozens of sorting mechanisms designed into the expert system from interviews with IAD agents.

Satisfied, Ryan returned to the mausoleum, where he commanded the mortician to give him a list of all hospitals where he could access information. The list was enormous, presented with a default sorting by state and then alphabetically. Ryan then went into statistical analysis, requesting a number of specific graphs, like the top ten hospitals with the highest reported breast cancer deaths, or the largest number of trauma victims, or the smallest number of stillbirths in the nation. He then came up with a fictitious name, K. Smith, and released it to the mortician with instructions to locate all K. Smiths deceased in the past forty-eight hours. He received a reply just over ten seconds later. There were three, a Kate Smith from Indiana, a Keith Smith from California, and a Kevin Smith from Louisiana. The mortician then asked Ryan if he wished to find additional information on any of them. Ryan asked for more data on Kevin Smith from Louisiana. The mortician produced several photos, along with all known data on Mr. Kevin James Smith from Monroe, Louisiana, age seventy-eight.

Convinced that the expert system, at least on the surface, appeared to be doing its job, Ryan departed the mausoleum and circled the Earth-like sphere once again, landing on other expert systems, including those designed to access medical history, employment history, school transcripts, driving records, and similar information routinely used by IAD agents to track down tax violators.

Ryan spotted a blue portal, its color making it beyond limits for his existing security clearance. His VR system, however, presented it as a video camera, which attracted Ryan enough for him to descend in front of it, adjacent to SoftCorp's technical library, appropriately displayed as a large tome.

He walked up to the bluish light shrouding the lens, careful to remain just outside the perimeter of the sensors—the turquoise lines lacing the cloud. If any of the beams were broken, an alarm would go off marking an intrusion.

Ryan sensed a presence behind him and he turned around. A light, powerful and penetrating, blinded him, pushing him back into the bluish cloud. Alarms blared. A powerful jolt made him tremble, colors exploding in his mind before all went black.

"Mike? Mike? Are you all right?"

Someone was shaking his shoulders. Ryan tried to open his eyes but the bright overhead lights stung them, so he kept them closed. He recognized Wittica's voice, strained with anxiety.

"Damn, Agi!" Wittica shouted. "You never told me that the active security system was on-line!"

"You—you asked me to put it in place as soon as possible, so I did. I–I didn't know he was going to be poking around in the–"

"You're his technical advisor, dammit! You need to keep an eye on— wait, he's coming around."

Ryan opened his eyes, blinking, using a hand to shield his narrowed stare.

"Are you okay, Mike?"

Ryan took a deep breath. A headache pounded the back of his eyeballs. He peered around the room, his lab, where he lay on the floor while Maghami, Wittica, and two security guards looked down at him. One of the guards clutched a first-aid kit in his right hand.

"You got any aspirin in there?" Ryan asked the guard, who opened the case and began rummaging through it, finally producing a pack of aspirin.

"That'll do," said Ryan, slowly getting up with the help of Maghami and Wittica, settling on his chair. The guard ripped open the packet and handed the pills to Ryan, who pointed to a half-drunk bottle of springwater on the table, next to the VR system. Wittica handed it to him.

"You gave us quite a scare there, pal," said Wittica, smiling while Ryan downed the aspirin. He could see strain in Wittica's eyes.

"Just when you thought it was safe to jack in," Ryan mumbled to himself. "Why was I attacked?"

"A sentinel detected you near a restricted portal," said Maghami in his heavily accented English. Sweat formed beneath the Indian's armpits.

Ryan set the bottle on the table next to him, closed his eyes, and massaged his temples. "I landed short of the . . . technical library. I guess I misjudged. . . . In any event, I never came close to disrupting the security lasers, until the flash threw me into the portal. Something in the security system overreacted."

Wittica turned to Maghami. "I thought we discussed trimming back the sensitivity level until we performed more tests."

Maghami frowned. "That was the plan on the spec sheet. I'll have to check with Vijay. He owns Sentinel."

Although his head felt as if it were being squeezed in a vise, Ryan remembered clearly his conversation with Wittica over three weeks ago, when SoftCorp's CTO had told him that no one was working on an active security system that punished hackers. This little on-line episode certainly contradicted that. Either Wittica stole Ryan's hacker-punishing idea and had someone else develop it—very unlikely given that only three weeks had gone by since that discussion—or they already had such project under way, and Wittica had chosen not to disclose it to him. He decided to ignore that for the time being.

"Sorry about that, Mike," said Wittica. "We'll have Vijay adjust that so you can cruise through the network to get the information you need for your project."

Ryan remembered Vijay Parma, one of Maghami's engineers working on classified projects, like Ryan. Although Ryan felt angry at having been tricked, the hacker in him chose to suppress the feeling for the time being, opting instead for getting even at the right time.

"What I need is the password or something that identifies me as one of the good guys to any on-line security system. I don't feel like getting zapped again while trying to do my job."

Maghami and Wittica exchanged glances. Then Wittica spoke. "We'll work it out, Mike. Agi will get Vijay to adjust Sentinel."

Ryan shook his head. "That's not good enough, Ron. What other surprises are out there that I haven't been told about yet? Three weeks ago you told me that SoftCorp didn't have an active security system in place, so I took no precautions while I went poking around the network, getting myself familiar with the environment, kicking the tires. Then, *wham*, I get zapped—and I wasn't even violating anything! I don't work like that. I'm either a part of the team or I'm out."

Wittica looked away for a moment before returning his gaze to Ryan. "You are a *key* part of this team, Mike. I'll see to it that you get all of the information that you need to do your job, including any required passwords. However, I do ask that you be sensitive about SoftCorp's security

R . J . Pineiro

requirements, especially given the privacy required by our client. There will still be directories that are off-limits, but they will be clearly marked, and as a SoftCorp employee your user ID will carry a qualifier that will prevent you from getting zapped by Sentinel, or any other active security system roaming our network. You'll just get denied access, but no physical harm."

Ryan stared at him.

Wittica frowned. "We've been working on active security systems for a few years now, Mike. Vijay is in charge of that project. Sorry about the withhold of information. At the time I thought you didn't have a need to know. My mistake."

Ryan just nodded, not feeling like carrying on the conversation. He had made his point. Besides, the headache was flaring up.

Wittica motioned Maghami and the guards to leave them alone.

"I'm really sorry about this, Mike. Really. Part of my job's making sure that you have everything you need to do your job, not only efficiently but also safely. I failed at the latter. You have my apologies and my assurances that I'll do my best to make certain it doesn't happen again. And just to show you that I mean what I say, you will have your required access passwords in the morning. Also, I'll postpone the demo scheduled for tomorrow until Monday. Maybe that will give you a little personal time. I know I've been working you hard in the past few weeks. Say, why don't you take the rest of the afternoon off. Go and enjoy your new house. It's on me."

Ryan wasn't sure if he felt concern or admiration at Wittica's willingness to admit his own mistake and also to make a serious attempt to amend the damage. It wasn't every day that a senior executive at a high-tech corporation admitted fault. He decided to give him the benefit of the doubt for now and agreed to his terms. However, he also promised to himself to never again jack into the network without some protection of his own. The hacker in him also vowed cyber revenge against Maghami for having tricked him.

"All right, Ron," Ryan finally said. "All right."

Most women took pleasure in visiting a jewelry store, or browsing through a furniture store, or perhaps trying on a few outfits at a designer clothing retailer. But Victoria Elizabeth Ryan got her kicks at REI. The large outdoor sports retailer had an outlet in a shopping strip overlooking the hills of northeast Austin. She drove there during her lunch hour, browsing through the store with interest, excited about the prospects of purchasing new gear to replace the old and worn-out equipment they'd left behind in California.

Victoria missed hiking, missed the woods, the trees, the sweet resin fragrance of the forest in the morning, the dew collecting on maple leaves, the chirping of birds at dawn as she stirred inside an oversized sleeping bag with her husband.

And she was determined to get that life back. The house was nice. The cars were nice. The recently delivered furniture was also nice. But being alone in the woods . . .

She remembered those weekends backpacking in Yosemite National Park, or any other of the many state parks in northern California, where the young couple would lose themselves for days, leaving their old world behind, entering a mystical one. The experience was one of mental and physical rejuvenation, of transformation, of learning to notice, to appreciate, the simple things all over again, of transcending the lack of creature comforts and experiencing the essence of nature.

She missed that inward purification, which she could not achieve by any other means. She needed to get away, be alone with Ryan in the woods, clear her mind, sever her ties with Capitol Bank, with SoftCorp, with home mortgages and car loans, with deadlines and seventy-hour weeks—if only for a short while. But their old and worn backpacking equipment had been among the items they had sold prior to their move, figuring that they would get better gear after settling into their new life.

And the time had come.

She unzipped her purse hanging loosely from a shoulder strap and pulled out a shopping list, which she unfolded, running a finger over the items that Ryan and Victoria had jotted down during the few moments they had alone this morning before rushing to get to work.

First Victoria inspected the features of a new portable gas stove, remembering her old rusted one, which she had sold to a pair of freshmen for a few dollars the week before the move. She selected a single-burner stove, ultralight for backpacking. She also picked a pair of lightweight lanterns before walking about the tents set up among the camping gear. She settled on a very light but rugged tent, capable of withstanding a strong wind and heavy rain. The sleeping bags were also quite light, but with a nylon taffeta outer shell and a flannel liner. And all of that equipment went perfectly with Victoria's selection of external frame packs. Made of an ultralight but very strong aluminum alloy, the backpacks offered plenty of attachments and zippered pouches, along with padded adjustable shoulder straps for comfortable wear on long hikes.

She continued shopping for another ten minutes, picking all of the items to which she would entrust her life in the wild for years to come. She piled it all in an oversized shopping cart before proceeding toward the checkout counter.

With some luck, Capitol Bank and SoftCorp would cut them some slack this upcoming weekend so they could test drive their new gear on a short trip. She had already checked out the Web sites of a couple of state parks nearby that would do for now. Later this year they might try driving up to Arkansas or west to New Mexico for serious backpacking in real mountains.

She paid with her Visa and pushed her cart through the automatic doors. As she maneuvered her load toward the parking lot, a blonde came out of nowhere and accidentally bumped into her.

"Sorry," the stranger said before rushing off, disappearing inside the store, not waiting for a reply from Victoria, who shrugged and continued toward her Honda.

120

12

Karen Frost risked a backward glance the moment she entered the store, watching the tall, slim brunette reaching a silver Honda sedan. She hated doing what she had just done, but the federal agent was out of choices. She had to force a break in the investigation, and Victoria Ryan, employed by Capitol Bank and married to Michael Ryan, employed by SoftCorp—both recent hires—ranked at the top of her list for potential informants. They were young, smart, probably still unstained by the shadowy network operating beneath the surface—something Karen felt was an asset rather than a burden. She had selected the Ryans because she doubted they'd been involved in anything illegal so soon. This way she could first appeal to their sense of decency and hopefully turn them, then train them, teach them to gather the proof that she so desperately sought.

Karen crossed her arms, watching Victoria Ryan drive away, praying that the young couple was as clever as their records at Stanford seemed to indicate. They would certainly need their combined intelligence—plus a little luck—to avoid ending the same way as the Pattersons, Dave Nolan, Pete Rubaker, and anyone else silenced to protect this corrupt organization.

Victoria Ryan returned to her small office in the executive area of Capitol Bank, where all of the risk officers reporting to Angelo Rossini were situated. Banks lived and died by the return on their investments—their loans. Bad loans meant losses, and Angelo Rossini seldom approved a loan that turned bad. He accomplished this by keeping his advisory committee of risk officers under close supervision.

As she began to work, the phone rang.

"Capitol Bank. This is Victoria. May I help you."

"Vic, I need you in my office in five minutes," said Rossini. "Bring your assessment of Baulkner Eight Seven Six."

"Yes, sir," she said, hanging up and pressing a button on the small black stand of her Palm V, a handheld computer that Victoria used to take notes, keep a to-do list, her personal calendar, E-mails, and notes on specific loans she had worked in the past week. The Palm V was connected to her desktop PC via the serial port. Software allowed her to synchronize the files in her PC with those in her Palm V by pressing the Hot Sync button. She could then just take the Palm V with her to meetings and read E-mails off-line, reply to them, or simply delete them. Upon returning to her desktop PC, she could perform another Hot Sync and the software would update her E-mails and any other files or notes that she may have added, edited, or deleted since the last Hot Sync. In addition, the Palm V had an infrared port that allowed it to communicate with other Palm Vs in the same room. Risk officers used the little gadget to silently transmit messages back and forth during long meetings.

She removed the Palm V from its cradle after the Hot Sync finished and used the Palm's picker—a pencillike instrument, but much smaller—to select items on the two-inch-square screen of the Palm V. The small system recognized taps and strokes across the screen as inputs just as a personal computer received its inputs from the keyboard and mouse.

Victoria browsed through her small system, checking the headers of her loans, finding one titled Baulkner Construction–Loan App# 0700876.

As backup, she also grabbed one of many manila folders resting on their sides on a long wall organizer behind her desk. She read her own handwriting across the top. Baulkner 876.

The executive area of Capitol Bank occupied the seventh floor of one of many high-rises in downtown Austin. Victoria's office was just to the right of the elevators. Rossini had the largest corner office on this floor, overlooking west Austin.

She walked up to Rossini's assistant, an attractive woman in her late thirties clicking away behind a desktop PC.

Victoria pointed at the closed door. "Is someone in there with him? He just called me to review a file."

"No. He's expecting you. Just knock," the assistant said, flashing Victoria a brief smile before resuming her work.

"Thanks," replied Victoria, knocking twice.

"Come in!" came Rossini's deep voice.

Victoria went inside, leaving the door open.

"Please," he said walking around his desk, motioning Victoria to close the door. "I don't want to us to be disturbed."

Angelo Rossini, impeccably dressed in a dark suit that fell smoothly from his wide shoulders, smiled at Victoria. He reminded Victoria of Ron Wittica in the way he dressed and handled himself, and also in the fact that he too was a bachelor—which probably explained why a large percentage of Rossini's risk officers were attractive women. Ruggedly handsome and well built, Angelo Rossini also had a large cruiser on Lake Travis and lived just a few doors down from Wittica. He was very handsome, well packaged, and very refined—someone she would have certainly considered dating if she were single.

She closed the door and took her seat at the small round table on the right side of his large office, where Rossini usually handled his business with risk officers.

As she sat down, Rossini walked to the minibar adjacent to the round table. "Can I get you something to drink, Vic?"

"No, thanks," she replied.

Rossini grabbed a soda and sat next to her. On her first day Victoria had felt a bit uncomfortable at the close proximity that Rossini liked to maintain while working with his subordinates, but after realizing that he did this with everyone, including male risk and loan officers, she'd decided to let it go.

The president of Capitol Bank pulled out his Palm V, identical to Victoria's, got his picker, and began to select items on the monochrome screen. Due to his proximity, Victoria could see the Palm's screen as he picked his way through a few directories. At two megabytes of memory, the tiny units could hold a lot of files and messages. Victoria caught a glimpse of the names of several files, like Passwords, Miscellaneous, Accounts, and Confidential.

"Where is it?" he said to the little unit in his hand, reaching his E-mail directory and browsing down several E-mail headers. "Oh . . . here you go." He pointed the front of the Palm V, where the infrared port was located, toward Victoria's Palm V, which she still held in her hands."

Victoria looked down at the Palm V in her hands and saw the Beam Detected message flashing, indicating that her Palm V was about to receive data from another Palm. She clicked okay and the message changed to Receiving.

The moment the screen changed to Transmission Complete, Victoria tapped the screen and read the short E-mail. Baulkner Construction had defaulted on loan number 0700876 yesterday, officially notifying Capitol Bank of their bankruptcy filing. The primary reason was a huge error misjudging recent construction bids.

She shook her head, selecting the file on the Palm V containing her recommendations for this loan and beaming them to Rossini while saying, "This loan carried a high degree of risk, Angelo." Rossini had insisted on first names from day one. "That Baulkner defaulted is not at all surprising."

Rossini regarded her with admiration after reading the beamed message. "You're something else, Vic."

She crossed her arms, not certain what he'd meant by that. "Something else? Is that good or bad?"

He smiled. "*Very* good, Vic. Very good indeed." He patted her shoulder, keeping his forearm resting on the back of her chair. "Out of a dozen risk assessment officers you're the only one who called this one."

She ignored the arm. "You mean others made a recommendation on Baulkner? I thought that was *my* account."

Another pat on the shoulder. "It is, but being that important and also given your level of experience, I decided to seek out additional opinions. In the end I should have just listened to you . . . which is what brings me here."

She narrowed her stare, not really knowing why her heart began to race.

"I'm considering promoting someone next year from the existing risk assessment pool to oversee the entire division. I'm running out of bandwidth with our recent growth, but I can't afford to let just anyone run it. I need someone with a good nose."

"I've just started, Angelo. There are other officers in the team who have spent far more time than—"

"I'm not looking for seniority here, Vic. I'm looking for someone who can smell bad loans, just like you did on Baulkner. Most officers out there are great at following guidelines and procedures, but they lack instinct. You don't. That, however, will mean spending a lot of time with me, briefing me on issues."

"I'm still not sure if I'm the right person for this—"

"Why don't you come over to my place tonight to discuss it further," Rossini said, moving his arm from the back of the chair to her shoulders, squeezing gently. "I know I can convince you over some vintage wine that this would be the best career move you'd ever make."

Alarms blared in Victoria's head. She felt a little dizzy and hated herself for feeling this way.

What's wrong with you, Vic? You're married! You love Ryan!

She was momentarily confused. This was not the first time someone had made a pass at her since she had started dating Ryan, and she had always managed to push those proposals aside without a second thought. So why wasn't it the same with Angelo Rossini? Was it his looks? Or his clothes? Or his refinement? Rossini was certainly *very* smooth. Feeling color coming to her cheeks, all Victoria could say was, "I'm happily married, Angelo. I don't think that going to your home this evening to sip wine would be very appropriate."

There. She had said it, and she felt a wave of relief sweeping through her.

Rossini shrugged and gave her a mischievous smile. "So you have a husband. . . . What if I told you that he'll *never* find out? I can arrange it so that it appears that you've been working late at the office."

Victoria couldn't believe this, especially in this day and age. Wasn't Rossini aware of the hundreds of sexual harassment suits floating in the corporate world?

"Once again, Angelo," she said, slowly gaining strength in her position, "I'm *happily married*, and even if my husband never finds out, I still couldn't do this."

"Marriage is a contract, Vic," he insisted. "And contracts can be bent without breaking them."

She slowly shook her head and gently moved his arm off her shoulders while standing up, looking down at him.

"Wrong, Angelo," she heard herself say. "Marriages are not contracts, they are *covenants*. They are for life, and I intend to keep mine exactly as it has been. Once again, I don't feel that I should be promoted so soon, but would be willing to discuss this matter further, at work and during regular office hours. Is there anything else?"

"You're an amazing woman, Vic. Now you have made me want you more than ever."

The comment made her angry.

"Perhaps with time you'll see that all I want is to help you grow, help you find yourself."

"Angelo, I have a lot of work piled up. If there is nothing else—"

"That's all for now, Vic. Again, good call on the Baulkner account."

"Thank you."

As she stepped outside, Rossini's assistant raised her gaze from her work, flashed Victoria another smile, and asked, "Everything all right, dear?"

Victoria forced control into her voice and returned the smile while saying, "Everything is just as it should be."

Ryan intercepted Victoria in the foyer the moment she closed the front door.

"Michael Patrick!"

Ryan grinned while tackling her from behind, nibbling at her neck.

Victoria let go of her purse, which landed on its side, spilling its contents over the wooden floor. Although momentarily annoyed, she responded quickly, turning around, embracing him, kissing him.

Ryan took her right there, on the Oriental rug in the foyer. He found her unusually responsive as they rolled amidst hastily shed clothes, her pantyhose caught on her left ankle, her dark brassiere still strapped on, but lowered to her waistline, rubbing against him as they writhed in a pleasure that had been denied to them for longer than could be withstood. Despite their best attempts to get home at a decent hour every day for the past weeks, one of them had wound up stuck having to take care of some last-minute detail at work, and on top of that they had each put in over ten hours on Saturday and another eight on Sunday. This was their first chance in days, and they took it, rolling off the rug and onto the wooden floors, eyes closed, moving in unison, until they climaxed, then stopped, panting, Ryan on top, still inside of her, feeling Victoria's cool wetness against him.

"How was your day, honey? Anything interesting happened?" he whispered, his face buried in her hair, his elbows supporting most of his weight.

Her hands caressed his back while her left ankle moved up and down the back of his right thigh. "Somebody made a pass at me today," she said, matter-of-factly. "Otherwise, it was uneventful. I had fun buying our backpacking gear. It's in the trunk of the car."

He lifted his head to look into her hazel eyes. "What was that first thing again?"

"It happened after I returned from REI, after lunch," she continued, pressing her pelvis against him to keep Ryan from slipping out as he shrank. While she did this, she also contracted the muscles in her vagina, squeezing him.

He absolutely loved this, and he knew that she knew this. Still, her comment lessened its otherwise highly pleasurable effect. "*Who* made a pass at you?"

"My boss."

Ryan rolled beside her, and he could see her displeasure as he did so. Victoria enjoyed keeping him inside of her for as long as possible.

"Tell me everything."

She shrugged, reaching behind her waist to unfasten the brassiere. "There isn't much," she said, toying with the black straps. "He asked me for a drink at his place tonight to chat about career opportunities."

Ryan transitioned from surprise, to disbelief, to anger in a few seconds. "That's . . . *sexual harassment.* You need to report him."

Victoria put a hand to his face. "Now, calm down, darling. No need to overreact. I politely turned him down and explained in a very nice way that I'm happily married. He understood and withdrew the offer."

"Was he the guy on that business card?"

She winked. "Angelo Rossini. Very good-looking."

He frowned. "And I assume that *Don* Rossini is married with kids, right?"

"Single, like Ron Wittica. Has a nice boat too—and a nice ass." She giggled.

"That wasn't funny."

"Like I said, honey. I handled the situation."

Ryan had not felt jealous since their early college years, when a day never went by without someone from the male population at Stanford making a pass at Victoria. But unlike some of his previous girlfriends, who had used such opportunities to their advantage, flirting with other males to manipulate Ryan, Victoria had been loyal to the bone from the day they had gone steady—though she did joke on occasion that she reserved the right to change her mind if Mel Gibson or Tom Selleck propositioned her.

"I hope there are no repercussions because of this," he finally said, trying to forget the image of his wife with this man. "How do you know that the Don isn't going to hold this rejection against you in the future?"

She continued to regard him with a tranquil stare. "His name is Angelo, honey. My choices, though, are pretty clear if that were to happen. Don't worry about me, though. It isn't the first time someone's made a pass at me. I'm a grown-up. I know how to handle it."

He nodded, in a strange way feeling jealous that very few females had ever flirted with him. Guilt replaced jealousy when he realized that he should be on his knees with gratitude that he had found Victoria, someone who was as faithful as she was beautiful and smart—a very hard combination to find these days.

"So, what else happened today?" he asked, deciding to forget about Don Rossini for now. He ran a hand over her smooth torso as they lay on their sides facing each other.

She tilted her head from side to side. "Aside for my brief shopping spree at REI, just work, work, and more work. I'm in loan risk assessment hell."

He laughed. "I'm in C++ programming hell, but Ron gave me until Monday to get the code ready."

"Really? How did you manage that?"

When he told her about the incident during his VR run, Victoria crossed her arms over her breasts, her eyes becoming slits. "That was very dangerous, Mike! You can't be doing that! That's your brain you're messing with. I thought you told me this VR stuff was safe."

Now it was his turn to calm her down. "It's all right, honey. I know what went wrong. Agi screwed up and I got careless, thinking that it was safe to jack in alone while browsing through the network of my own company. Won't happen again."

She shook her head. "So this light just blinded you and then you passed out?"

"Not exactly. The head-mounted display also zapped me. That's what knocked me out. What really bothered me the most about the entire incident, though, was that Ron had told me that there was no active security system development going on at SoftCorp. In fact, he was excited about my active system to zap hackers. As it turned out, Agi and another guy had been working on such a system all along and had put it on-line without any warning, catching me off guard. I got zapped. I also found out later that two other users, who happened to be in the vicinity of the network when I was attacked, got the hard drives in their PCs corrupted from the fallout of the electronic attack—which is a serious flaw in Agi's security system. It hurts not just the violator but those in the vicinity as well. Like I said, it won't happen again."

"And you feel fine?"

"You tell me," he replied, leaning down and kissing her breasts. They were perky and a shade lighter than the rest of her, with small pink nipples.

She slapped the back of his head gently. "Stop that. Here I am, all worried about you, and all you can think of is—"

He kissed her hard, rubbing himself against her, entering her moments later. She embraced him, locking her ankles behind his thighs as they moved in unison again, momentarily forgetting about SoftCorp, about Capitol Bank, about unethical bosses and virtual-reality programs. Victoria cli-

129

maxed first, trembling, clinging to her husband. Ryan followed seconds later, tensing, releasing, then relaxing, and tensing again as Victoria contracted her groin muscles, massaging him in ways that purged his mind of all thoughts.

This time he remained inside for some time, kissing her, caressing her, nuzzling her neck, her ears.

"I've missed you," she said, finally releasing him.

"We're never going this long again," he rolled off her and sat up.

"You've got that right, mister."

"How about a shower?" Ryan asked. "I'll wash your back if you wash mine." He winked.

"Deal," she said, winking back. She sat up and reached for the personal articles that had fallen out of her purse. "Just let me put–" She stopped.

Ryan sat up as well. "What?"

"This," she said, holding a small envelope.

"What is it?"

"Never seen it before." She shook her head while ripping it open and sliding out a white sheet of paper, which she unfolded and held in between them.

Your house is under surveillance. Do not discuss this out loud inside your house or car or on the phone. People are watching you and listening to your conversations. Harm may come to you if you do. Things are not what they seem at Capitol Bank and Softcorp. If you want to stop the killings and help us reach the truth, meet me at 9:00 A.M. this Saturday on Town Lake, by the gazebo across from the power plant. Careful.

–a friend

He read it twice, then stared at Victoria while remembering the monitors he had seen in that room at SoftCorp.

Is this for real?

His mouth suddenly going dry, Ryan stared at Victoria, whose face reflected what he felt.

Victoria was about to say something but Ryan reacted quickly, pressing an index finger to her lips before leaning over and kissing her. He pushed the paper aside and pretended to nibble her right ear.

"Don't say a word," he whispered, so softly that he wasn't sure if she had heard him. "I think we're being watched."

She tensed and tried to move away, but Ryan gently held her next to him. A hand behind her back, pressing her against him. "I know," he added. "They might have seen us making love. They could be looking at us now. But you must pretend that all is normal. Okay?"

She nodded while muttering. "I'm afraid,"

"Just do as I tell you," Ryan whispered, praying that he knew what he was doing.

He stood and offered a hand to his wife, who was still sitting on the rug. "Come, darling," he said out loud. "I think it's time for a shower."

They left their garments behind and went straight into the oversized shower, built with two shower heads. Ryan turned on the water and let it warm up. When he looked back at Victoria, her eyes were filled.

He guided her inside the spacious shower stall and closed the frosted-glass door, placing his head under one of the shower heads, letting the steam rise and fog the mirrors—and any camera lenses that could be prying on their privacy inside the bathroom.

"What are we going to do?" she whispered, holding him, resting her head on his shoulder, her lips an inch from his ear. Water dripped from her face and onto his shoulder.

Ryan spent a minute telling her about the video monitors he had seen the other day at SoftCorp.

"So you think that this note might be for real? That we've been watched all this time? . . . *Oh, God.* They have us on *tape?*" She put a hand to her mouth.

Ryan's fear turned to anger. If this was indeed the truth and SoftCorp was responsible for such intrusion into their private life, then—

"Why?" she asked, her gaze narrowing, glinting contempt. Her wet hair stuck to the sides of her face, framing it. Dark makeup ran down her eyes. "Why are they doing this?"

He shook his head. "I'm not sure, but I intend to find out on Saturday."

"So we're going to meet this . . . friend?"

Ryan nodded.

"But it's only Thursday. What are we going to do tomorrow? Just pretend nothing's happened?"

He gave her another nod. "That's the only thing we *can* do until we get a grasp on what we're dealing with."

The steam continued to rise, matching Ryan's anger. If this was true, then they had all lied to him, to Victoria. The elegant Shapiro. The trend-setter Wittica. Ryan had been drawn into something that he didn't understand, but that, based on what he had observed, could be potentially dangerous.

There's always a catch, Mike.

Ryan dropped his eyelids while washing Victoria's back, a task that under other circumstances would have been quite arousing. Instead, it was just mechanics, something to do while they talked, keeping their voice at whisper level. They discussed the signs they had seen all along, the subtleties, the indicators that SoftCorp—and later on Capitol Bank—seemed too

(131)

good to be true, far too generous, all too willing to make their life as pleasant as possible. The large amount of information SoftCorp had on him during his interview, followed by an equally incredible job offer, a sign-on bonus, the payoff of his student loans, the car plan, and the opportunity to continue working in his field of virtual reality, should have tipped him that something was seriously wrong. But they had chosen to ignore the warning signs, their logic veiled by the intoxicating haze of money. Then it had been Victoria's job, so tailored for her, almost as if someone at Capitol Bank had read up on the interests outlined on her résumé and then created a position to match her career objectives. And again, they had ignored the signs of potential trouble. Then it was the house, priced strategically below market, but only enough to get it just within their affordable range—made even more afford-able by the surprisingly low-interest mortgage from Capitol Bank. There was also his company car, the shiny new Porsche Boxster, plus the low-interest loan to buy Victoria's Honda—also from Capitol Bank. And most recently, Ryan had been pleased by the zero-percent financing from an assortment of department stores to furnish their new home.

He exhaled, placing his palms against the simulated marble wall, letting Victoria wash his own back as they were absorbed in their own thoughts.

They got in their usual sleeping garments. Victoria preferred silk pa-jamas while Ryan slept in one of a dozen Stanford football jerseys and gym shorts. Figuring that they should do nothing unsual—nothing that would raise suspicions in those used to their evening routines—the Ryans did what they had done during the past weeks: collapsed on their bed after another killer day at work. In a way Ryan was glad they did that, not only to minimize the risk of someone figuring out that Ryan and Victoria knew they were being watched but also because the sooner they went to sleep, the sooner they would wake up and leave their house and have a regular conversation, perhaps at a nearby coffee shop before driving in to work.

Victoria took a couple of Tylenol PM caplets and fell asleep twenty minutes later. Ryan opted for the natural way, but he found himself re-gretting the decision two hours later, as he lay there facing the ceiling fan, Victoria peacefully snoozing sideways to him, her head on his shoulder, a leg over his.

Feeling her warm breath on his neck, Ryan struggled to fall asleep but couldn't. Thoughts, questions, continued to creep into his mind.

Who was this so-called friend? And why contact Victoria and him, out of all the people in both companies? Was it because they were brand-new? Was it because they were involved with both companies? And what was SoftCorp and Capitol Bank doing that was illegal? Ryan was aware of the public aspect of the business relationship between the companies. SoftCorp employees used Capitol as their banking institution for direct deposits, loans, and other services owing to their highly competitive rates and convenience, including the fee-free ATMs in the lobby. Wittica had also mentioned that SoftCorp maintained all of its major accounts, including payroll and reserves, at Capitol Bank.

But it now seems as if there's more beneath the surface.

What, though?

What could be so vital that it required SoftCorp and Capitol Bank to go to such extremes as to monitor the activities of their employees? Banks dealt primarily with the movement of money, of assets. Whether granting loans, collecting payments, or transferring funds, financial institutions handled money transactions, making their profits through fees and interest payments. He'd learned that much from Victoria. Some banks, however, had made more than their fair share of income by performing covert transactions for special clients, clandestinely moving money from one account to another, in some cases to overseas accounts, to avoid paying taxes on unreported income—an activity also known as money laundering. But assuming for the moment that such was the case here, for whom was Capitol Bank laundering money?

SoftCorp?

But SoftCorp was tied up in government contracts with none other than the Internal Revenue Service, the agency most feared by money launderers. Surely, with the IRS so close by, the risk of attempting such a scheme would be astronomical. Unless . . .

He suddenly wanted to wake up Victoria and have another discussion, particularly since he had deduced a possible explanation that involved not just the high-tech industry and the financial world but also the IRS. His wife, however, was out of commission for the next several hours.

Sighing, trying to fall asleep and failing to do so again after another few minutes, Ryan got up and went into the kitchen, where he poured himself a glass of milk and snatched a pack of cookies from the pantry, finally settling by the kitchen table.

He stared out the window and quietly ate his midnight snack, for the first time accepting the fact that if the message was accurate, if SoftCorp was indeed involved in something illegal enough to justify running full surveillance on its employees, then he was stuck. He couldn't just pack up and leave. His contract with SoftCorp required him to work a minimum of three years before he could resign, unless he was willing to repay the sign-on bonus, the student loans, and the first monthly lease on the Boxster. And Victoria would also have to repay her sign-on bonus since they would be leaving together. Trouble was, they had spent most of it on the down payments for the house and Victoria's car, not to mention the cash they had put down to purchase the furniture. In addition, their Visa was close to its limit after the three thousand dollars' worth of home furnishings like blinds, rugs, and curtains, and backpacking gear. The Ryans were certainly living the American Dream, but they were also seriously in debt, relying on those paychecks to stay ahead of their bills.

He frowned. *No place to go.*

Like the mafia, SoftCorp and Capitol Bank had the Ryans in their clutches for now. They could, of course, declare personal bankruptcy, let the house, the cars, and the furniture get repossessed, and just return to California, but Ryan feared that they would never again be able to work in their fields. He felt certain that SoftCorp and Capitol Bank would put the word out in the high-tech industry and the financial world about them. No reputable company would ever touch them after pulling a stunt like that on their former employers, who would make themselves look like the victims of two immature professionals. All the years in school would have been wasted.

Of course, if those two companies were up to something real bad, trying to quit now could have worse repercussions than just future employment opportunities.

We're trapped.

Ryan gazed around his beautiful house, at the designer kitchen, at its granite countertop, at its stainless-steel appliances. His eyes gravitated to the living room, lavishly decorated under the soft glow of recessed lighting. And it was at that moment that he realized that the entire place was nothing but a first-class prison, a luxurious jail—all with guards and security cameras monitoring the activities of its unsuspecting inmates.

There has to be a way out.

But how?

Think, Mike.

Sitting at the breakfast table, Ryan struggled to figure a way out of his predicament. The anonymous message, however, told him that things were likely to get even more complicated. Just how much, Ryan had no earthly idea.

Ron Wittica enjoyed the distraction of watching the monitors inside SoftCorp's MSCC, Monitoring Systems Control Center, at least once a day, especially late at night. At times he found it far more exciting than watching porn flicks, particularly the little show that Mike and Victoria had just performed for him and the shift security guards manning the control room. That had been the real thing, uncensored, unedited, unrehearsed, and to top it all off he knew every actor in every real-life drama developing in front of his eyes. Wittica, however, had not been too pleased at Rossini making a pass at Victoria Ryan. There were enough beautiful women around to not have to pick on the ones at work.

Don't shit where you eat.

Wittica had had this conversation with Rossini in the past, but Rossini had basically told him to mind his own business. Shapiro, the fatherly figure in the Austin operation, had convinced Wittica to let it go. After all, Rossini had managed Capitol Bank for over ten years without any problems. Somehow he had managed to keep it under control. Messing with Ryan's wife, however, was like messing with Ryan himself, and that affected Wittica far more directly than some other woman at Capitol Bank whom Wittica didn't know. He decided to take this up with Shapiro again.

"Definitely a nice piece of ass," said Todd Hausser, the husky leader of SoftCorp's security team, whose job extended well beyond that of a typical high-tech firm. Two of his men assisted him this late evening monitoring the private lives of every SoftCorp employee, except for Wittica, Shapiro, and the guards. The MSCC also monitored the lives of certain Capitol Bank employees, as well as any critical IRS worker—a precaution that had paid off when Janet Patterson had come across incriminating information linking the IRS and the two corporations and had brought it to the attention of her superior. Ms. Patterson had been placed under immediate surveillance by the MSCC, who discovered her secret dealings with the FBI. The MSCC had then opted to monitor her parents' activities twenty-four hours a day, in the event of a further FBI probe, and once again the precaution had paid off, though not as much as Wittica would have hoped for. The Pattersons had been eliminated, but the FBI agent had escaped, and she was still an agent on the loose, threatening to destroy this very lucrative arrangement.

Wittica regarded the ice-cold blue eyes on Hausser's square face, beneath his military-style crew cut. He said, "You can say that again, Todd. That Mike Ryan is one lucky bastard."

Hausser nodded. His team of guards, mostly former members of some elite military force or intelligence network, were charged not only with the protection of SoftCorp's property and grounds, along with the intellectual property being developed within these walls, but also with ensuring the safety of an underground pipeline transferring money from IRS accounts into private accounts somewhere beyond his reach, or the reach of anyone he knew. Neither Hausser, nor his team—not even Wittica, for that matter— knew all of the aspects of this very complex operation, masterminded by someone from Washington. He wondered how much Shapiro knew.

Ron Wittica switched his headphone connection from the display monitoring activities at the Ryan's to Agi Maghami's house. The brilliant Ph.D. from Berkeley had visited his hometown in India last year. His family had arranged a marriage for him, but due to visa problems his wife had joined him in Austin only last month. The bottled-up hormones of the newlyweds had resulted in many hours of entertainment for the monitoring crew at SoftCorp, whose operating practice was to install three cameras in each household, covering the foyer-living area, the kitchen, and the master bedroom. Some statistical report a while back had claimed that those three areas represented the locations in the home where most conversations took place, particularly in the bedroom, along with occasional hot action—a rewarding benefit for what was otherwise a mundane and highly boring job.

"Agi sure married Miss India," commented Wittica, staring at Devi, a tall and lithe woman with a million-dollar face and a provocative mouth that awakened the most primitive of desires in him. "Too bad she doesn't like to walk around naked."

"She's actually quite naughty when Agi's not around," said Hausser. "I saw her masturbating in the bedroom last Tuesday. The bitch had my morning shift up in arms. I guess all those years repressed in India finally caught up with her." The large guard ran a finger over her figure on the monitor as she sat in bed reading a book. They could hear a toilet flushing in the bathroom, and Maghami appeared a moment later. Short, fat, and downright ugly, Agi Maghami had obviously relied on his rich and influential family back home to negotiate a great arrangement for him. Maghami crawled into bed, turned off his night-light, rolled over away from his wife, and closed his eyes. Miss India glanced over at him, slowly shook her head, and continued reading.

"No wonder she's playing with herself," added Hausser.

"Guess the honeymoon's over," said Wittica.

"Looks to me like your typical case of marital neglect," commented Todd. "Maybe he can't get it up because you're working him too hard, Ron," said Hausser.

"I'd find the energy," said Wittica.

"If I were Agi, I'd fuck her every day," said Hausser.

"And twice on Sundays," added Wittica.

The MSCC guards laughed.

Ron Wittica switched to another monitor, glad to see the guards relaxing for a moment. Ever since the Patterson and Rubaker incidents, Aaron Shapiro, who had left for Washington that morning to show support for the IRS high-tech bill that Congress would be voting on in the coming days, had been riding Hausser and his security team quite hard to stop the bleeding. The guards needed a break from the demanding Shapiro.

Wittica sighed, not certain what to make of Shapiro's sudden trip north. In the years that SoftCorp had been the Austin Processing Center's sole high-tech contractor, Congress had never rejected a single one of SoftCorp's proposals. Wittica suspected that Shapiro had been *summoned* by the powers that be. Before leaving he had given his team an ultimatum about taking care of this FBI probe by the time he returned tomorrow night. So far, though, Hausser and his team had found nothing. The FBI agent had vanished from view after disabling one of Hausser's men near Rubaker's home. Shapiro, however, certain that the feds would try to make contact with someone else, either at SoftCorp, Capitol Bank, or the IRS, had ordered Hausser to increase the surveillance, including pinning tails on their employees according to a priority list based on their best guess at who could be next in the investigative chain.

Although the mood was somewhat cheery inside the control room, Wittica knew better. They used humor to mask fear—the fear of ending up just like Rubaker, who had been unlucky enough to have his name revealed by Doug Patterson to the FBI, turning him into an instant liability. Wittica, however, felt he was far enough away from the real action not to be in serious danger. After all, as an engineer, Wittica's role in this highly profitable arrangement consisted of developing technical solutions for the IRS. SoftCorp was a real company, providing technical services to the Internal Revenue Service. Anyone curious enough to try to scrutinize their operation would find nothing more than a private enterprise under contract with a federal agency, and using Capitol Bank as the banking institution handling all of its financial needs, from payroll to company-subsidized IRA accounts.

So why are you worried then?

Because the same group of men sitting behind the glaring monitors laughing with him would just as easily slit his throat and dump him in Lake Travis if it ever became necessary to assure the survival of the operation.

Like the Mafia.

Or worse.

But the decision to accept both the risks and the huge rewards was one which Ron Wittica had made a long time ago. There was no turning back now. He could only hope that Todd Hausser and his men found a way to sever the investigative probe before it reached him. In the meantime, he would do what he did best, put up the cool, relaxed front that always made people feel at ease with him.

And perhaps pray.

**book
three**

The Puppet Master

There is no peace, saith the Lord, unto the wicked.

—Isaiah, 48:22

1

A solitary man sat on a rocker.

A cold wind rustled the forest surrounding the complex in Virginia, swirling his thinning hair as he teetered back and forth, creaking the stained pine planks of the rear porch of his mansion. A blanket warmed his legs. He sipped steaming Cuban coffee from a tiny cup.

The man stared into the distance at the streaks of light breaking the vast expanse of darkness enshrouding the mountains to the east.

Dawn.

He had been up for two hours now, waiting for the report from his subordinate. The waiting angered him. He had little patience, particularly on an issue as dangerous to his organization as an FBI probe.

The coffee felt good inside his mouth. This particular blend from Camaguey, Cuba, had made its way to him through his contacts in Cuba and Mexico.

The phone on his lap rang. He answered, *"Dígame?"*

"Ya llegó el Senador Horton. Lo llevamos a su officina, como usted ordenó."

"Muy bien. Voy en un momento."

Orion Yanez hung up the phone and continued to sip his coffee. The report from Esteban, his nephew and also chief of his personal security, calmed him down some. At least everything appeared to be in order regarding this emergency visit from Senator Jack Horton, and also from a subordinate from Austin, Texas. Otherwise Esteban would have alerted him already.

The streaks of golden light cut deeper into the night sky, breaking it up in pockets of darkness among jagged rivers of light. Stars faded slowly as the crimson horizon outlined the eastern rimrock.

2

Aaron Shapiro sat on a sofa in a strange room, blinking to clear his sight after having been blindfolded for the past two hours, ever since getting inside the limousine that had been waiting for him at Dulles International Airport, in Washington, D.C. He had been scheduled to land at midnight, but his connecting flight out of Chicago had been delayed for three hours due to mechanical problems.

Tired, nauseated from lack of sleep, the CEO of SoftCorp struggled to maintain his composure. He had never been summoned to Washington before—ever. But he had heard rumors of others who had, rumors that he quickly shoved aside. Not only did they terrify him but he needed his mind clear, needed to think. The conversation he was about to have with the head of this organization could easily be his last if he didn't convey progress and the right sense of urgency.

He adjusted the knot of his tie, the uneasy feeling that he was being watched descending on him. The possibility made him look alert, energetic, ready to tackle any—

"Aaron," a voice boomed through unseen speakers.

Shapiro jumped, but quickly settled back down. "Yes?"

"You have much to answer for." The voice had a heavy Hispanic accent.

His heartbeat felt like a piston inside his chest. Before he could speak, the door swung open and two men entered the room, both in their late twenties, very muscular, casually dressed. Their expressions conveyed nothing. They stood in front of him, impassive stares gazing down at him as he struggled to remain calm. He tried to start his well-rehearsed speech but fear would not let him move his lips. His body was frozen in terror by the realization that he might die today.

"You have served me well, my friend," the voice continued. "Over ten years of loyal service, always managing to handle your end of the issues without my intervention, always meeting your profit goals, always doing your part of this arrangement. Your security team is the finest that I've ever seen, always on top of every issue, of every potential problem."

Shapiro clenched his teeth. He had used this tactic many times before, getting a subordinate comfortable through praise before reaming him.

"But now it seems that we have one problem that you have not been able to take care of. Frankly, I do not care to hear the reasons why you have failed. In my mind they are just excuses, justification for not having accomplished your job. I, however, have always been a firm believer in using incentives to get people to do what's necessary to ensure the survival of the operation. Do you agree?"

"Yes, sir."

"Good, then. Since your salary and bonuses are apparently *not* enough to get you to fix this problem, then perhaps additional incentives are in order."

One of the guards produced a manila envelope and handed it to him. Shapiro opened it and then gasped while staring at a surveillance picture of his wife, taken while sunbathing at the Austin Country Club. His wife, albeit in her late forties, still maintained the slim figure of her youth thanks to a healthy diet and a fitness trainer at the club. Behind that snapshot was a photo of Melissa, his youngest daughter, walking around the campus at Harvard, where she was majoring in finance. And right behind that picture was one of Mary Beth—Shapiro's oldest daughter—and her husband and twin babies going to church. And last was his daughter Katherine, a Harvard attorney, strolling the streets of New York City in a business suit while chatting on a cellular phone, presumably going to her work at a Wall Street law firm.

"Those beautiful daughters and your very attractive wife, Aaron, make you pretty vulnerable.

Shapiro was barely listening now, shoulders drooped, his wet stare fixed on the photos in his trembling hands. He had been concerned about his *own* safety, about making a widow of his wife, about orphaning his daughters. But he had never worried about the safety of his family. That had never been a part of the deal. This threat went beyond standard operating practices at the firm. The family of an employee was *always* taken care of if something happened to that employee. Families were never targeted. Rubaker's wife and kids had been taken care of through an immensely generous life insurance policy. He'd expected the same if something happened to him.

Shapiro took a deep breath, forcing discipline into his thoughts, into his behavior. He had to appear calm, in control, capable of handling any job, able to take care of any problem, whatever it might be. And although the threat was indeed highly unusual, he knew better than to complain.

"So, Aaron, I'll make sure there are no problems in Washington. You make sure our issues are resolved in Austin. I'll be sending my finest guard down there to make sure you get all the help you need to take care of business. Are we clear?"

Shapiro straightened himself, forced confidence lifting his chin as he stared at the guards. "Yes, sir," he replied. "Crystal clear."

3

"Do you trust him?" asked Senator Jack Horton, sitting across Orion Yanez's desk while watching the rectangular flat plasma screen monopolizing a large portion of the left side of the high-tech office. It currently displayed two guards escorting a blindfolded Aaron Shapiro into a waiting sedan.

Orion pressed a button on his desk. The display went blank and receded into the wall as an original Picasso slid in its place and a pair of curtains dropped from the ceiling to flank the painting, blending the wall with the rest of the traditional decor of the plush office. "I trust he will do as I have requested, but not because I *trust* him."

"Then how do you know he will comply?"

Orion looked away. He planned to order Esteban down to Austin to work with Shapiro's security team. "Never underestimate the persuasive power of fear, my friend. It will serve you well after I get you into the White House."

The elegant senator, tall, slender, with a full head of silver hair, grimaced, shifting his weight while crossing his legs. "I'll be elected because of my reputation, because the nation needs the strong leadership that I can provide."

"Save those words for your campaign, Senator. I'm not one of your . . . *constituents*," Orion said, waving a hand in the air, reaching for a box of Cuban cigars, opening the lid, tilting it toward Horton.

"No, thanks."

"*Smoke* with me," Orion insisted.

Reluctantly, Horton reached in the box and took one.

"Trust," Orion said, slicing one end of his cigar with an eighteen-carat clipper before lighting it with a matching gold lighter, which he then offered to Horton. "I've never trusted a man who would refuse to smoke one of my fine habaneros with me."

Horton regarded the cigar with indifference.

"You hold the fruit of many Cubans' work in your hand, Senator. My father was among them, working all of his life like an animal in the tobacco fields while my mother rolled the habaneros," said Orion.

"Sounds like a hard life," Horton conceded

Orion nodded absently. "Do you know what melanosis is, Senator?"

Horton shook his head.

"It's a type of skin disease. One way of contracting it is by prolonged handling of tobacco leaves without gloves. The chemical in the leaves stains your hands green, and over time degrades the epidermis, triggering this unique form of the dreaded disease. Some call it an occupational hazard, just like coal mining. I call it murder. The government makes those peasants work the tobacco factories without any protection. At least Batista gave the peasants gloves. Castro gives them speeches. The disease killed my parents, just as it kills hundreds of my compatriots in Castro's Cuba every year, so that you and I can enjoy this moment, smoking the fruits of their hard labor. And you can't complain, otherwise the bastard sticks you in *gavetas*."

Horton shook his head. *"Gavetas?"*

"Translated literally it means 'drawers,' because that's just what the cells look like, like fucking drawers, just barely large enough to fit a person. They resemble those cubicles in the morgue, only the bastards are still alive."

"Jesus," said Horton. "I had no idea."

"Yeah, well, most people don't. One of my uncles spent three years locked up in one of those *gavetas*. His joints froze beyond repair. He is a quadriplegic for all practical purposes. Another relative of mine served ten years for the crime of verbally insulting one of Castro's militia after standing in a bread line for eight hours and being told to go home because they had run out of bread. He served them at the infamous Isle of Pines prison, where, from 1961 to 1967, he watched fifteen thousand men pass through that hell on earth. He saw men get shot, point-blank, or stabbed with bayonets, or arbitrarily pulled out and punished—which often meant having lit cigarettes extinguished in the anus, or having electricity applied to their ears, anus, and testicles. Everything in that prison was designed to break your spirit, to force you to publicly declare your wrongdoing in front of your peers and join the revolution."

Orion continued his well-rehearsed anti-Castro speech for another minute. His operation hinged on being able to convince this man that he hated Castro with all his might, even though reality was just the opposite. Orion's father had died like a hero of the revolution, fighting against the CIA-backed invasion force at the Bay of Pigs. Raul Yanez had singled-handedly killed eight of the invading *gusanos* before a grenade blew him apart. He had been buried with honors alongside other fallen heroes of the revolution.

Horton gave Orion a grave nod while taking a puff before saying, "I came here today because you said it was important."

Orion briefly remembered his father's funeral in Havana while inspecting the burning end of his cigar. Then he put the past away and shifted his gaze to the next president of the United States. Orion had made one phone call—*just one*—and the eminent senator Jack Horton from New York, congressional leader on Capitol Hill, ahead in the polls for the Republican ticket next fall by over twenty percentage points, had dropped everything he had been doing, canceled all of his appointments, and had rushed to see Orion Yanez, a little-known Cuban-American businessman residing in a hundred-acre estate buried in the hills of Virginia.

That was power.

Orion Yanez, a Cuban expatriate, was now, just fifteen years after stepping out of the Cuban vessel *Mariel*, one of the richest men alive. But unlike Michael Dell, Steve Forbes, and Bill Gates, Orion didn't appear in a *Fortune* 500 list. He didn't have to endure the burden of being so wealthy. He didn't need an army of lawyers to fight Washington bureaucrats in order to hang on to his empire. Orion Yanez *owned* those bureaucrats. He didn't have to advertise or slash prices in order to stay in business. He just eliminated his enemies, his competition, using methods mastered while working his way up the echelons of the Cuban government—a government that had taught him everything he knew, but a government that had to evolve in order to survive. The Soviet Union was no longer around to subsidize Cuba—had not been around for a very long time. And so Castro had opted to diversify, to capitalize on everything he possibly could while maintaining the facade of the ideological Cuba of his revolutionary years. The Cuban leader had tried everything, from luring European and Asian investors to build world-class resorts by the crystalline beaches of Havana, to drug trafficking—anything to sustain his army, his dream.

But we have to evolve, Fidel, Orion remembered telling Castro. Cuba had to change or risk following the same fate as Romania and Yugoslavia, of Czechoslovakia, of the Soviet Union itself.

Change or die.

So a plan was masterminded to funnel huge amounts of American capital into Cuba, to inject the dying nation with new blood.

Orion Yanez, on the surface a self-made billionaire, *forced* the powers that be in Washington to bend in his direction, unlike Bill Gates and the rest of them. This naturalized American capitalized on the inherent weaknesses of the chosen form of government in America to achieve a larger goal, to preserve Cuba, to keep it from becoming just another puppet of the United States, like during the Batista regime.

"Tell me about the closed session yesterday," Orion said, once again admiring his cigar, in his mind remembering his beloved homeland.

Horton smoothed his tie with two fingers. "It went pretty much as we had hoped. The vote will take place this afternoon. I expect it will go through with a majority of the vote."

Orion nodded. That would be another four-hundred-million dollars contract for the expanding Austin Processing Center, the IRS's development vehicle to take the next step in modernization. The report he had read from Shapiro indicated that by the end of the year the Service would have its first fully operational virtual-reality database management system.

At the budget price of seventy million dollars.

The balance of the contract would be piped through SoftCorp and Capitol Bank into accounts in the Cayman Islands, Mexico, Spain, Venezuela, and Brazil—out of reach from anyone in this country.

And under my direct control to finance Cuba's future.

"How's your campaign fund?" Orion asked.

Horton grinned, flashing the million-dollar smile that had captivated the nation in recent months. "Over a hundred million so far."

"More will come," said Orion, who couldn't contribute directly to Horton's campaign in any significant way without arousing suspicion from the multiple investigative probes scrutinizing the campaign contribution, as well as the personal life, of every candidate. But there were many other ways to inject funds into Horton's campaign. Orion's power reached many places, could influence hundreds of corporations across many states, all of whom gave generously to elect America's favorite politician to the highest office of the land next November. From high-tech industries and banks to insurance companies, communications networks, securities companies, casinos, import-export companies, retailers, real estate agencies, resorts, restaurants, a host of Internet companies, and dozens of legal firms sprinkled across the nation, Orion Yanez managed a vast empire in America, which he used not just to empower and control dozens of politicians like Horton but also to perform a large number of money-laundering schemes, funneling billions into overseas accounts. Cuba, a nation with an annual gross national product of just under $13 billion, benefited significantly from the additional billions provided by Orion's organization, funds being used wisely by Castro to build the economic infrastructure required to carry his revolution far into the twenty-first century.

As president, Horton would have the power to sway the nation toward policies that could benefit Cuba, that would allow limited trading, that would further bolster its economy, that would disregard CIA warnings about the possibility of Cuban officials acquiring nuclear weapons from Russia and Ukraine. As president, Horton would make Orion Yanez the most powerful man in America.

They smoked their habaneros and chatted about the future, about the upcoming election, about the prospects for additional funding in the next budget cycle, about the new yacht that Orion had purchased in Miami but kept in the Bahamas. Then he surprised Horton, who, as a former navy officer, loved the sea but couldn't afford a yacht of his own with a senator's salary.

"And yours is docked next to mine, my friend."

The senator leaned forward. "*My* yacht?"

"Not as large as mine, of course. I got you a forty-eight-foot Sea Ray. Three private cabins. Two large heads. A gourmet galley."

Horton's expression changed from surprise to concern. "But . . . the investigative probes. They'll nail me to the wall if they find out I accepted such a significant gift."

Orion shook his head. "Relax, Senator. It's all legal. The boat is registered under one of my leasing companies. You get to rent it just like anyone else, only everyone else gets charged an exorbitant price per hour. You don't. That essentially gives you full rights to use it any time you wish for a modest price. Plus it's in the Cayman Islands, out of reach from anyone investigating your assets in this country.

Horton thought about it for a moment, and then a smile broke over his concerned face. "I . . . I'm very grateful, Orion. That was very nice of you, especially considering how much I love the sea."

"That's nothing, my friend. Here's something you can *really* thank me for." Orion produced a small manila envelope, which he slid across the smooth surface of his desk over to Horton.

"What is it?"

"A gift. Open it."

He did. Unfolding the sheet of paper inside. Horton looked up from it. "There's a long string of letters and numbers. What does it mean?"

"That number will grant you access to a numbered account in the Cayman Islands. Its current holdings exceed five million dollars."

Horton's face went ashen, quite aware of what that meant. Nobody could trace the numbered account to him. It was the ultimate tax-free gift in the world, his safety net if the world ever came crumbling down on him. Just a flight to the Caribbean island, and he could buy himself the right to to live incognito on his yacht in full luxury for the rest of his life.

"I . . . I'm speechless, Orion. This . . . goes beyond our agreement. I–I don't know how to begin to thank you for your genero–"

"Just get into the White House. You have already won the election. All you have to do is avoid doing something stupid, like getting caught screwing some college girl."

Horton smiled. "Don't worry. Is there anything I can do to repay this most unexpected but highly generous gift?"

"There is . . . one small thing you might be able to—never mind."

"What?"

"Nothing. I hate to bother you with my problems."

Horton set his arms on the desk, pointing the cigar at Orion. "*Your* problems," he said, before pointing at himself, "are *my* problems, my friend."

Orion regarded the politician through the swirling smoke. "Are you sure you don't mind?"

"*Anything* for you, Orion. What is it?"

"All right," Orion said, leaning back, the cigar in the corner of his mouth, his eyes drifting to the large windowpanes on the right side of the room. He knew the gift would work. It went beyond the arrangement that he had struck with the then-senatorial candidate Jack Horton six years ago. Their deal had been a simple one: political advancement in return for his assistance getting IRS funding. Orion had bankrolled Horton's election through his many contacts and business associates, making it totally untraceable when investigators looked into Horton's campaign contributions, though Orion did own more than his share of investigators. Orion had gotten him elected in New York twice, partly by funding him, but also by discrediting Horton's opponents with media scandals. All Horton knew about Orion's operation in Austin was limited to generous contracts between the IRS and one of his corporations. Nothing else. And Horton had *never* received anything as direct as what Orion had given him today. "I'm afraid one of my businesses might be under investigation by the FBI."

"Those *bastards*," said Horton. "They totally screw up in Waco and Ruby Ridge, and drop the ball on preventing the bombings of the World Trade Center and the federal building in Oklahoma City. Instead of doing their job they're out harassing taxpayers like yourself." Horton took every opportunity he could to stab the Bureau whenever the FBI went to Capitol Hill seeking funding. "Where is the probe?"

"In Austin."

Horton breathed deeply. He knew that Austin was a critical region in Orion's business pursuits. "What happened?"

"It might be nothing, but you know how paranoid I get about anyone interfering with my business deals."

"I don't blame you," said Horton, pocketing the sheet of paper. "The business world today is cutthroat. Only the paranoid survive. What can I do?"

"Congress is going through it's budget cycle, right?"

Horton nodded. "Every agency is coming forth with their plans and budget requirements."

"And that also includes the FBI?"

"We already went through theirs. I've recommended a serious cut."

"Is it final?"

Horton narrowed his gaze. "Not until the end of next week. . . . Where are you going with this?"

Orion Yanez exhaled. "I wouldn't want you to do anything that could make you uncomfortable, my friend."

Horton stared at Orion for a moment. "You want me to change my position on the budget as a bargaining chip to get information from the FBI?"

"There are ways of doing so without making it an illegal practice. Any good politician or businessman knows that."

Horton frowned.

Orion continued. "Anything you can get on the ongoing investigation will be of great assistance to our cause. And time, of course, is of the essence."

Horton appeared skeptical. Up to now it had been easy for him to simply appear in Congress as an IRS sympathizer. There was little risk in that. Now Orion was tightening the vise a bit. He added, "It would be . . . *unfortunate* if my operation in Austin was exposed . . . and the trail led to your campaign contributions."

Now he had Horton's undivided attention. The senator's cheeks reddened as he uncrossed his legs and cleared his throat. Up to this point Orion had demanded little of the senator while being quite generous to promote his career. Orion had saved those favors for a rainy day. And that rainy day had come. It was time to start capitalizing on the investment, letting Horton know subtly that he was quite tied to the operations of Orion Yanez, who had financed his political career.

"That *would* be most unfortunate," Horton finally said.

"Such an embarrassment to your good name, to your career, to your family. And if the district attorney gets his way, there might fines, even some jail time—though I would do my best to prevent that from happening."

The senator didn't respond.

"So we understand each other, my friend?"

Jack Horton gave him a single nod before leaving the office.

Orion Yanez returned to his back porch, sat on his rocker, and regarded the sunrise, the new beginning of his beloved Cuba, the prospects of his return home once Horton had been elected, once he had secured the weapons his government needed to ensure its survival.

4

The Ryans arrived at a Starbucks in west Austin at 6:45 A.M. and ordered two cappuccinos before settling at a corner table. Their morning routine, which had been quite stressful today as they went through the motions of getting ready to go to work while being watched, made them realize that they couldn't possibly go on living like this. Their privacy was not a negotiable item in their business agreement with SoftCorp and Capitol Bank. Something had to change. Just how they would change it the Ryans were not certain yet. Perhaps tomorrow's meeting might provide them with some alternatives. For the time being, they had to continue to pretend that nothing was wrong, at least until they knew exactly what they were dealing with.

"What do you think this is all about?" asked Victoria, looking quite formal in a business suit. She even had a touch of makeup on, accentuating her lips.

"Don't know, Vic. But I do know that whatever it is, it's not worth having if it means giving up our privacy."

"I'll drink to that." She appeared much calmer now.

"How about the meeting tomorrow?" he asked.

Victoria hitched a shoulder and frowned. "What do you think?"

Ryan had pondered this last night. "I think we should meet this so-called friend. It could provide us with some options. Right now we're pretty much narrowed to two."

She set her cup down, planted her elbows on the table and interlaced her fingers, as if she were praying. "And *neither* is very appealing. I don't relish the thought of having every moment of my life on video, and I also don't feel like switching careers if the bastards ruin our professional reputation in our respective fields."

"And that's if they let us get away."

She didn't say anything.

"Okay," he added, also setting his cup on the table and reaching for her hands, holding them in his. "Let's think about this for a moment. If indeed there's something illegal going on, it has to involve SoftCorp, a high-tech company doing business with the IRS, and also Capitol Bank, which has a very close relationship with SoftCorp—in fact *too close*, if you remember how quickly they got you the job of your dreams in order to convince me to head down here."

"Where are you going with this?"

"I'm considering probing the network at SoftCorp. I get the feeling that I might be surprised at what I find."

"But . . . that's dangerous. What if—"

"I *won't* get caught again. I'm going to force them to grant me more control of their network than they really know they're giving me."

She narrowed her hazel eyes at him. "How?"

He grinned. "I'll tell you later. Right now I need to know what to look for after I break in. I won't have much time to browse around hoping to stumble onto something significant. I need a crash course on banks, Vic. They transact money. They open accounts, move liquid assets from one to another. What if Capitol Bank does more than just support SoftCorp's financial needs. What if they're involved in moving large amounts of money under the table? Could you tell me how's that done?"

"Are you referring to money laundering?"

"Precisely. There's circumstantial evidence of this already. SoftCorp appears to make just too much darn money for the services they provide to the IRS. What if Shapiro and Wittica got something illegal going with Capitol Bank executives, who, by the way, were the ones who financed the high-tech company in the first place? Maybe SoftCorp makes too much profit from its IRS contracts and the execs want to keep more than their fair share to themselves, so they use their close friends and allies at the bank to launder the money."

She shook her head. "You're reaching, Mike. Besides, no company would be crazy enough to be laundering money when the IRS is so close to them. After all, Mike, the IRS knows how much money it's paying SoftCorp for its services. If SoftCorp tries to report less than their true income, surely the IRS would be all over them."

"That's right," he said, smiling. "Unless . . . they're in on it as well."

"The IRS? No way."

"Why not?"

"Because . . . because they're the *IRS*."

"And the IRS is run by people," said Ryan in a casual tone. "The IRS has the power to check on everyone else, but no one can check on them. They're in an ideal position to pull this off."

153

"Again, Mike, you're reaching."

He shrugged. "Maybe. Maybe not. Let's shelf that for a moment and chat about money laundering. What do you remember from Stanford?"

Victoria pushed out her lower lip and narrowed her hazel eyes while staring back at her husband. She had moussed her hair and brushed it back, exposing her forehead, giving her a serious but elegant look, which went well with her business suit. "We covered the topic in a few of my courses. There are many known money-laundering techniques," she said, "and they are usually monitored to some degree by members of FATF."

"Of what?"

"FATF, the Financial Action Task Force, a Paris-based organization created to monitor and expose international money laundering. There are twenty-six member nations in FATF, including the United States, the United Kingdom, Canada, most of Europe, Japan, and a handful of other countries in Asia. FATF has affiliations with most law enforcement agencies, like our own FBI and the Interpol. Unfortunately, there are many countries that do not participate in this international program, including many South American nations."

"Which is the place where the laundered money usually heads to, right?"

She nodded while sipping her coffee. "Part of the job of FAFT, and its affiliated agencies, is to intercept illegal funds while they make it through international channels, before they reach accounts in nonparticipant nations."

"What about catching the source?"

"Once the funds are intercepted, or at least the illegal channel used is identified, then an agency like the FBI can try to work its way back through the channel to the source—assuming that the channel is intact. Many times channels are used only once and then a part of it is discarded, so anyone investigating it will reach a dead end."

"Who are the typical money launderers?"

"Organized crime, like the Italian mafia, the Japanese yakuza, the Colombian cartels, and lately Russian and Eastern European criminal enterprises. These organizations deal in a large range of criminal activities, from embezzlement, fraud, extortion, and loan sharking, to prostitution, arms trafficking, and even slavery."

"They taught you that at Stanford?"

She nodded. "Financial crime. I took it during my senior year, remember?"

Now he did, and the memory made him wish for those simpler times. "Yeah. How do they launder the funds?"

"There are many known laundering techniques, and I'm sure there are many more that are still to be discovered. The most traditional ones are in the banking sector. Accounts are set up under false names or the names of individuals or corporations operating on behalf of other beneficiaries. Now, these so-called *beneficiaries* might be attorneys or accountants representing shell companies used to transfer funds from one false account to another. After repeating this process three or four times, the trail gets sketchy, difficult for the authorities to follow. By then the various levels of beneficiaries have vanished, as well as the front companies, often leaving just empty warehouses and office suites for the authorities to rummage through in their search toward a likely dead end."

Ryan remembered some of this from their conversations about their respective course work or upcoming exams. He also recalled something about the size of the transfers triggering an alarm, as well as the use of foreign banks to dispose of the illegal funds. He mentioned that to her.

Victoria nodded. "The problem is that the alarm goes off *after* the transfer has occurred, after the money has passed through the pipe."

"There are no policies to hold the transaction in question until an investigator can verify the legality of the transfer?"

She smiled while shaking her head. "Think about it. Transactions go on every day between individuals, between corporations, between individuals *and* corporations. The international money market is huge, with millions of transactions occurring every hour varying in size from ten dollars to ten billion dollars. That monster can't be halted to wait for some government probe to sanitize each one. First of all, no government could ever be equipped to do so in a timely manner. The sheer volume of transactions makes it impossible. We can only flag certain transactions and investigate them postmortem."

"If transactions can indeed vary so much, how do you tell the good ones from the bad ones? After all, money is money."

"You do it by using qualifiers during the flagging process. For example, we would flag activity in accounts if the amount of money moved is greater than that which we would ordinarily expect given the legal nature of the account holder's business. Probing those transactions sometimes leads to poor documentation of the reason for the activity, which could be anything from loan payments and purchases to sales and contracts. Also, the businesses in question often have only been recorded with the local chamber of commerce for a short while, and in some cases the transacting parties are related."

"What about using foreign accounts?"

She sipped her cappuccino and agreed. "That's another flag. Illegal funds would sometimes end up in the hands of representative offices of foreign banks, which accept the deposits and then wire the funds to their own accounts with a local bank in their own country without disclosing the identities of the original depositors and beneficiaries.

"And there are other money-laundering techniques outside the banking sector, like using a *bureau de change* because they tend to not be as heavily regulated as banks and other financial institutions. Of course, the oldest technique is still in use: common smuggling. Criminals will go to the extent of purchasing businesses engaged in the shipment of goods and hiding tainted money inside the product. There are also other industries that facilitate the process, like casinos and insurance companies."

Ryan made a face. "I can see how casinos could easily dispose of large amounts of cash, but how would an insurance company go about it?"

"Simple. A launderer would purchase insurance policies at a premium and then redeem them at a discount. The balance becomes available to the launderer in the form of a sanitized check from an insurance company. Single-premium insurance bonds can also be used as guarantees for loans from financial institutions. So a launderer takes out a one-million-dollar insurance bond using illegal funds and then turns around and uses that bond to get a loan from a legal banking institution. Also, don't forget about the securities industry. Here you could have front companies or beneficiaries buying or selling securities for other fake entities, who eventually may lead to a legal business owned by yet another shell company."

Ryan rubbed his chin. "Amazing. What about the Internet?"

"That's one of the emerging threats. Cyber payments are on the rise, opening new avenues for smugglers by providing them with the ability to conduct transactions anonymously and entirely outside the banking system."

They finished their coffee, walked together to their cars, which they had parked adjacent to each other's, kissed, and went their separate ways. A half hour later Ryan found himself staring out of the large windows of his office lab, going over his plan to get himself more latitude in this computer network. His hacking skills slowly resurfaced as he prepared to do something he had not done in some time: a deep probe into a system.

What if you get caught?

You have no choice in the matter. You need to give yourself some options. Besides you have the skills.

But do you still have the nerve?

Ryan made his decision and dove into his code, reverting back to his hacking days, fine-tuning the virtual-reality database access system to cater to his clandestine needs, integrating the expert systems created by the other engineers in the firm. He did this not only to facilitate his planned breach but also because he had a project deadline and didn't want to give anyone the impression that something was wrong by missing his schedule.

At noon he drove out to a nearby deli and got a club sandwich, which he brought back to his lab. On the way, he walked by two security guards, whose impassive stares betrayed nothing. Ryan gave them a single nod. One of them replied, "Good afternoon, sir."

Did those two watch Vic and me last night in the foyer? If so, they sure didn't seem to show it.

Ryan returned to the lab and ate his lunch in between thirty-second keystroke sessions. When he finished, he got into it again for two solid hours, completing the user-figure identification match, as well as adding the finishes touches to a new, more powerful version of MPS-Ali, who Ryan would use as his primary bodyguard during all future excursions into cyberspace. Ryan had also built a few extra features into MPS-Ali to comprehend the money-laundering discussion he'd had with Victoria this morning.

Reaching for the helmet-mounted display, Ryan jacked in, waiting a few seconds for MPS-Ali to materialize through the psychedelic cloud shielding the network. The muscular figure of his agent, dressed in a brand-new silver-and-black uniform, and wearing a thick utility belt—packed with Ryan's own brand of hacking gadgets—floated next to him. Ryan used his basic SoftCorp password to blow past the swirling haze, emerging on the other side, finding himself hovering over the Earth-like spherical representation of SoftCorp's cyber domain.

First he commanded MPS-Ali to deploy a dozen SSPs, security sensor probes, which resembled geosynchronous satellites orbiting Earth, except that SSPs were stealthy, shrouded by a mirroring program that hid them from any sentinel programs created by Agi Maghami and his programmers. The satellites, which positioned themselves in a pattern that mimicked the global positioning satellites over Earth, covered every square inch of virtual land on the surface of the planet SoftCorp. The SSPs represented Ryan's early warning system in case someone detected his planned illegal breach and tried to send sentinels in his direction, giving him time to launch countermeasures.

Feeling a bit like Superman, Michael Ryan stretched the legs of his video accelerator, test-driving his speed and maneuverability through cyberspace in case the satellite system detected incoming danger and he needed to get away quickly. MPS-Ali, also hooked up to a similar video driver, kept up the pace with his master, dashing across the vast emptiness of this virtual-reality atmosphere, past dozens of users, their silver-and-black silhouettes now attached to faces and names he could recognize. No one, however, could pick out his presence while protected by the same cloaking software hiding his satellites and MPS-Ali.

Ryan ordered MPS-Ali to release a clone version of Ryan, nicknamed MPS-Mike, into the system. A moment later a silver figure appeared, floating through space along with the other users, and descending according to a preprogrammed sequence, legally accessing normal databases of SoftCorp.

The figure retained all of Ryan's system qualifiers, including his user ID and password.

Satisfied that he had built himself a perfect cyber alibi, Ryan continued toward his primary objective this afternoon: the three-dimensional video camera enveloped by a high-security blue bubble—to which Ryan didn't have a password. Ron Wittica had graciously provided access codes for some of the engineering databases—the ones currently being visited by MPS-Mike, his clone—so that Ryan could get a better feel for the work under way. But this video portal, and several others like it, still remained locked.

Ryan stood in the same place as yesterday, in front of the blue bubble laced with turquoise-colored laser beams. He frowned. The first rule in hacking was that *no* system could be locked—provided the hacker found a way to steal the access key. The second rule—and just as important—was to avoid getting caught in the process. Ryan intended to obey both rules this afternoon.

Standing aside, he commanded MPS-Ali to send a decoy probe—a dark figure representing a file with Agi Maghami's user ID and network address—into the bubble. A shadow detached itself from his agent, assumed a human shape, and rushed into the cloud, breaking the laser and triggering a breaching alarm. The shadow then just stepped aside.

5

Agi Maghami relaxed in his leather swivel chair, resting his feet on the desk, holding a mug of steaming herbal tea in his right hand as he watched network activity flash on his screen. He felt like a god, sitting back, observing the activity of his dozens of engineers from the vantage point provided to him by his system administrator privilege. Ownership of root password allowed him, at any given moment, to monitor who was doing what, for how long, and even detect moments of user inactivity, which would automatically go on that engineer's record to be reviewed and questioned at weekly one-on-one meetings. He oversaw the activity of many senior engineers, loyally cranking out the code for the expert systems that would be integrated into Mike Ryan's virtual-reality environment.

Maghami decided to check up on Ryan, finding his user ID accessing one of the expert system databases. The young engineer from Stanford was trying out the passwords Wittica had released to him.

Maghami took a sip of tea. He didn't like Ryan, feeling that SoftCorp had shelled out way too much money to snag him and his VR program, according to the offer letter he'd had to sign as the hiring manager. Maghami felt that given enough time and resources he could also have produced such an elegant VR solution. But in his current position, having to spend most of his bandwidth baby-sitting engineers, Agi Maghami had little time left for actual development.

Plus his lonely wife wanted him home for dinner every night.

The native of Bombay shook his head. As lovely as Devi was, she was also turning out to be quite demanding. His mother had never questioned his father's hours at work. Why was Devi questioning his? For reasons he could not comprehend, Devi didn't seem to accept her place in their marriage, making demands that took him away from his work in the evening and weekends.

Maghami frowned. His father had warned him about marrying a beautiful woman. They were high maintenance.

But all of that will change, Maghami thought, remembering his father's advice about having babies to force a wife to settle down into her role as a—

Maghami spilled hot tea over his khaki trousers as his system began to flash a red icon shaped like a bell while the computer speakers began to whistle in a high-pitched siren.

Security breach!

Quickly brushing off the tea burning his thighs, Maghami frantically reached for the keyboard and began to type furiously, pulling up a status log. The breach had occurred in disk sector 27C, home of a directory of video and audio data requiring super-root privilege to access. He could tell this by the color of the bell, which prohibited its access to anyone but Aaron Shapiro and Ron Wittica, the only owners of super-root passwords at SoftCorp—in addition to the security system's software sentinels, which could access any directory in order to protect it in case of a breach.

He verified that a sentinel had been automatically deployed by the on-line expert system handling security.

As Maghami followed the path of the sentinel, programmed to zero into the breach, his screen froze.

What's going on?

He tried to reset it but the keyboard had also frozen. As he reached beneath the system to flip the power switch and force a hard reboot, two guards burst into his office.

6

Michael Ryan nodded thoughtfully when a gleaming white sentinel dropped from the sky and blasted the dark intruder, before making it vanish. Following its own programming, the sentinel issued its super-root password to access the database and attack anyone who might have gotten inside.

This was exactly what Ryan had been waiting for. MPS-Ali, invisible to the sentinel, intercepted the super-root password and injected the unsuspecting software sentinel with a virus, designed to add a ten-second loop to the beginning of its execution program. The sentinel froze under the spell of this loop, temporarily unable to reach any of its programmed options. MPS-Ali then punched him hard with an electronic left hook, containing a new C++ program, whose starting point was the end of this loop, forcing the sentinel to issue a signal acknowledging to the network administrator that it was now entering the breached directory—even though it was not.

In the same instant MPS-Ali issued the intercepted super-root password to the classified directory. The turquoise lasers in the cloud vanished for five seconds, before reengaging again, but not before Ryan and MPS-Ali had dived through the opening, dragging the spellbound sentinel along.

While MPS-Ali fed the sentinel the information that it would then convey to the system administrator, Ryan started a countdown, giving himself five minutes inside this directory. He figured that Agi Maghami and the guards would be busy sorting out what had happened in that time, including questioning why Maghami had tried to enter a restricted directory.

To a regular user, the interior of this directory would have appeared like thousands of video and audio clips, ordered according to dates, but without any names or other information describing their contents. Ryan's MPS-Ali, however, read in the nearest one, dissecting its header in nanoseconds, decoding the user-specific information, and mapping it to a table of possible descriptions, including obvious ones, like names, addresses, titles, and projects. It then rearranged the files according to their headers and presented them to Ryan in the form of a huge three-dimensional Rolodex.

Ryan floated over this virtual Rolodex and went after the digital archives first, his eyes doing most of the driving, blinking his way through the selection process, zeroing in on his personal video and audio clips, sorted by date. He found three sets of video and audio files, one set per camera installed in his house. He reviewed the files from last night in one minute, using the VR system's frame-freeze and fast-forward capabilities to verify their contents: the Ryans' private life, taken from well-hidden cameras in the foyer–living room area, the kitchen, and the bedroom. Controlling his anger as images of Victoria and him rolling on the foyer floor flashed on a screen in front of him, Ryan deleted the record. He then commanded MPS-Ali to extract all clips showing any undressed scenes. The virtual agent was smart enough to discern between dressed humans and undressed humans by the pattern of clothing on their bodies. A moment later Ryan watched in surprise a strange man and a woman copulating on a sofa. It belong to a D. Keller, someone at SoftCorp whom Ryan didn't know. Before he could reprogram MPS-Ali to give him *only* the images under the Ryan video directory, another image flashed, displaying an amazingly clear video of a beautiful woman lying in bed, the fingers of her right hand prodding her vagina. She moaned while masturbating. Ryan was a bit in shock at the sight—and especially so when reading the name at the bottom. A. Maghami. Now that he looked closer, the woman did look Indian, and the date was this past Tuesday at ten in the morning.

While Agi was at work.

He shook off the thought, reprogrammed MPS-Ali, and was about to start viewing his own private moments when he decided to take a shortcut. He ordered his agent to delete *all* of his video records, except for those from one full week two weeks ago, when he clearly remembered doing nothing but waking up in the morning, rushing to work, returning to work, eating supper, and going to sleep. That weekend they had spend working in their new house. He would rather delete these records as well, but he needed them for the next phase of his plan.

While MPS-Ali was busy erasing away, Ryan selected the files flagged Live Recording, opening the one matching his user ID. A screen materialized, displaying three views of the interior of his home, again taken by the three cameras planted there. First, he connected the seven days he had saved from MPS-Ali's erasing frenzy, linking the end of the first day to the beginning of the next day, and so on, adding one final link to the end of the seventh day to loop back to the beginning of the first day. Having completed this week-long loop, he synchronized its time and day of the week with the current recording of his home. Then he switched the source of the cameras from Live Recording to his special seven-day-long file, which

Ryan named Live Recording to keep any security guards from suspecting its origin. He also added a software shield to this video file in case someone tried to open it. In addition to preventing anyone from opening the file, and therefore discovering Ryan's handiwork, the shield would send Ryan a page to alert him of the intrusion, and also start a thirty-minute counter to give him time to get home. At the end of the thirty minutes the shield would erase the recorded file—therefore destroying all evidence of his wrongdoing—and also switch to the real Live Recording, to make everything seem normal. Ryan hoped that thirty minutes was enough to get home, just as he hoped that a week's worth of recorded activity would be long enough to keep anyone from suspecting the switch. As a final safety feature, Ryan commanded MPS-Ali to delete the video records of ten other engineers at random. That way if someone decided to look, he would find many files missing, not just Ryan's.

Ryan moved on, checking the timer. He had fifty seconds left.

Deciding not to push his luck, Ryan exited the directory, along with MPS-Ali, who had completed his previous task and awaited his command.

They reissued the access password, opened the portal, and raced outside, dragging the hypnotized sentinel along, and letting the lasers engage behind them. As they flew away, MPS-Ali fired a virtual torpedo at the frozen sentinel, erasing the appended code, releasing it from the cyber spell. The sentinel returned to its programmed directives, issuing an all-clear signal to the system and vanishing from sight.

Ryan checked the status of his alibi clone, verifying that it still continued to access its approved directories. Now that he had ensured his privacy at home, Ryan ordered MPS-Ali to find any portal that resembled Capitol Bank while using a special filter to screen out anything that might have to do with employee matters, like direct payroll deposit, home or car loans, and retirement accounts. The filter did make special provisions to include Ron Wittica and Aaron Shapiro in the search. MPS-Ali came back a moment later with nothing.

Frowning, Ryan tried another tactic, ordering his agent to scour the surface of the sphere with the cyber equivalent of a radar surface search and to compare the returning signal with a visual image of the same landscape. He then subtracted the visual image from the radar scan and lapped the remainder over the original sphere.

"Show the difference in blue," Ryan ordered, and a moment later all portals vanished on the sphere, whose surface suddenly resembled that of a desert, its vast ocean of sand sporadically broken up by blue pyramids, marking the locations where SoftCorp designers had placed hidden files in the network. Hiding files from regular users was a fairly standard practice in the industry to eliminate cluttering the network with too many system files that normal users had no need to know about, like those used to

163

support log-in protocols, or search protocols. But there were also other hidden files, which the network kept cloaked because of their highly classified nature. These latter files were the ones that Ryan sought to find, and, he hoped, penetrate. But first he needed to separate the many system files from what he suspected would be a handful of classified files.

In order to accomplish this task, Ryan relied on the fact that system files were usually compiled, meaning that they had already been translated from a human computer language, like C++, into an executable language, or computer code, the ones and zeroes that a computer can understand. Eliminating these files from his search would yield files with regular text or graphics—which Ryan hoped would house answers to his questions about SoftCorp and its clandestine relationship with Capitol Bank.

Ryan ordered his cyber pugilist agent to perform this screen, and a moment later the landscape began to rumble. The earth opened and the sand began to swallow all pyramids in sight at a staggering rate in a dazzling digital display.

As the virtual dust settled, Ryan commanded MPS-Ali to take him to the nearest remaining pyramid.

The landscape blurred as Ryan and his agent rushed around the sphere, like cruise missiles, flying just a few virtual feet above the golden desert, making brusque altitude adjustments to avoid colliding with sand dunes, stopping with astounding precision in front of a huge blue pyramid. That was one thing Ryan loved about the virtual reality world: it transcended the laws of physics. He could go from zero to sixty in a nanosecond and stop just as fast. He could shoot up vertically and perform high-speed acrobatics that would make an air force jock's head spin. Michael Patrick Ryan was Superman in this cyber world, and MPS-Ali was his sidekick.

Ryan checked the status of the system, verified that his clone was still following its preprogrammed sequence, and then ordered MPS-Ali to release a shadow probe against the turquoise lasers blocking the entrance to the virtual stone structure. The dark figure, carrying Vijay Parma's user ID, attempted an illegal breach of the portal, triggering a new alarm. The pyramid's color changed from neon blue to bright crimson.

7

"What do you mean, it wasn't you?" asked Ron Wittica, a mix of concern and anger filling him at the thought of someone having breached the video system. "Your own security system pointed at you as the user attempting to enter a super-root directory. You know the rules. Those are off-limits to everyone but Aaron and me."

"I . . . I don't understand what happened," replied Agi Maghami. "I was monitoring the system and then—"

"I've heard that already, Agi. That still doesn't answer my question."

"It must have been a glitch—something in the code. I don't know, but what I do know is that *it wasn't me*."

Wittica considered the explanation for a moment. Agi Maghami had been a loyal SoftCorp employee for five years, looking the other way when on occasion the wrong thing was said at the wrong time in some hallway conservation. He was a team player, aware that there was something else going on beyond the everyday activities of SoftCorp. On a few instances he had brought certain observations to Wittica's attention, like the time when, during a Y2K-compliance test, a number of E-mails had gone to the wrong addresses, including one from Capitol Bank, which had ended up in Maghami's account instead of Shapiro's. Maghami had instantly reported it to Wittica, who'd commended the engineer for his loyalty and discretion.

Ron Wittica exhaled, regarding his obviously nervous subordinate, fidgeting with a mechanical pencil while staring at the carpeted floor. He seemed quite small and fragile while flanked by Todd Hausser and one of his men.

The SoftCorp executive waved the guards out of the office. Hausser nodded once and complied, saying, "We'll be right outside if you need us, sir," before leaving with his subordinate in tow.

"Listen, Agi," Wittica began, trying to find the right words to break the news to him. "I believe you. I don't think that you are responsible for the attempted breach."

"I would never do anything that would break the trust that you and Aaron have placed in me."

"Like I've said, Agi. I believe you. However, I also hold you accountable for letting someone get far enough into our system to attempt to break into one of the most classified directories in the company."

Maghami stood. "It won't happen again, sir. I swear it. I'll figure out what happened and make absolutely certain that it never happens—"

Hausser stormed back into the room, his face tense with concern.

Wittica turned to him. "What is it?"

"We've just had another breach. It's Vijay Parma."

8

Repeating the same process to snag the password from the sentinel, MPS-Ali followed with a virus injection, momentarily freezing it before adding the code that surrendered its control to Ryan.

A moment later Ryan, MPS-Ali, and the hypnotized sentinel were inside the pyramid, dashing down a long corridor, ignoring the many access doors flanking the long hallway. MPS-Ali had already found the main chamber, buried deep inside the virtual structure. They reached it a second later, only to discover that its access was protected by another set of turquoise lasers.

Ryan checked the system timer and decided he was running out of time on what he could safely accomplish on this network run. The nested security chamber, however, was far too tempting for the hacker in him. Lacking this password, which he suspected might not even be within the access of the sentinel, Ryan saw only one option, whose exercise would also close down all other portals until the system went through a reset.

He gave MPS-Ali the order, and the virtual boxer summoned the sentinel, ordering it to pierce the turquoise lasers.

Under Ryan's cyber spell, the sentinel did, and a moment later sirens blared hollowly inside the enclosure. The sentinel had been forced to pierce this highly classified file, whose access password, as Ryan had suspected, was not in its possession, otherwise the sentinel would have issued it. In performing this illegal breach, the sentinel in essence had been forced, through Ryan's virulent code, to commit suicide because the network, realizing that the breach had been committed by its own security system, would shut down the security system immediately.

As expected, the sentinel froze as the system disabled the security software, leaving the network open to anyone for just a fraction of a second, before a safety feature in the network closed access to all files, regardless of their security level. That small time gap, however, was all the time that Ryan needed. The moment the security shield was momentarily lowered, he rushed inside at the speed of light, along with his cyber servant.

Now he had to hurry. He had triggered a major system event. No one could access any files until the system was rebooted. Those inside a file, however, could continue to access it until the reboot sequence kicked everyone out.

Seconds, perhaps a minute, was all he had to browse through the data in this file, which MPS-Ali had already begun to dissect, presenting a graphic form of the information.

They were financial transactions between the Internal Revenue Service and SoftCorp for software and hardware installations. Ryan saw the sizable invoices, along with dates for services rendered. Next to the invoices were the payments, which matched the invoices to the penny. The payments were wired straight into SoftCorp corporate accounts at Capitol Bank.

Nothing abnormal there, he thought, until MPS-Ali, programmed to think like Victoria, pointed out the quantities on the invoices, also explaining that SoftCorp had a revenue of $275 million last year, yet these figures indicated a much higher number than the one reported on the company's Web page. MPS-Ali showed Ryan three invoices in the past six months totaling over $280 million—all deposited in their corporate accounts at Capitol Bank. MPS-Ali spent another twenty seconds displaying additional transactions, which added up to $410 million this year alone, and there was still another two and a half months to go.

So, Ryan thought, *either SoftCorp is having a much better year than last year, or* . . .

Now he needed to find a way to get into Capitol Bank's system to continue the trail, to find out what happened to the money. He stared at the corporate account numbers and struggled to copy them. In his current situation, however, Ryan could not move—or copy—any data out of the locked directory. He decided to brute-force it, grabbing a pen from his pocket and feeling for a pad on the table in the real world, finding one, and jotting down the account numbers blindly.

He was halfway through the fifth account when a bright flash stung his eyes. Then everything went dark. Somebody had rebooted the network.

Frowning, Ryan set the pad on his lap and removed his helmet-mounted display, blinking to clear his sight. The late afternoon sun streamed through the blinds on the windows.

He stared at the hastily written sequences of numbers and nodded approvingly. Now he had something of substance to use during a run through the Capitol Bank network, which he planned to do as soon as he—

Someone knocked on his door.

"Come in," he said, calmly turning the pad over and setting it on the table, next to the computer system. He stood just as the door swung open.

"Hi, Mike," said Wittica, dressed in one of his silk suits, flashing Ryan a smile. "How's it going?"

"Not so great," Ryan replied as he saw Maghami walking right behind Wittica and closing the door behind them. "The system just went down."

"That's what we're here to talk about. Do you have a minute?" asked Wittica.

"Ah . . . sure, sure. What's up?"

Maghami looked over at Wittica, who said, "We have a little problem, Mike."

Ryan's heart began to race, though he forced an intrigued expression rather than one of alarm across his face. "Anything I can do to help?"

Maghami lowered his gaze while Wittica spoke. "The system shut down because we had multiple security breaches in the past ten minutes."

"Are you kidding?"

Maghami shook his head.

"Damn. Did we lose any files? Was anything corrupted?"

"No. We got lucky . . . *this time*," Wittica gazed at Maghami.

"Do we know who did it?"

Wittica shook his head. "Not yet, but we intend to. In the meantime, though, we can't afford to take any chances. So Agi had an idea."

Maghami raised his gaze. "I've taken a good look at your security system, Mike."

Ryan crossed his arms. "Yes?"

"And we feel that it's far better than anything Vijay or any of the other engineers can produce at the moment, especially the eye- and voice-scan software required to match a password before granting entrance. Had we had something like that in place, we probably would not have had these breaches."

Ryan simply nodded. So there were more engineers than just Vijay Parma working on security code. This whole thing was getting more interesting by the moment.

Maghami continued. "Your security software is top-notch, plus the sentinels in your environment are very precise in their strike, not harming any users nearby, and so far we have not been able to break it."

Ryan leaned forward. "*Break it?* How? I never gave you a copy."

Maghami smiled sheepishly. "We made a copy two weeks ago. We've been trying to find weaknesses since. So far it looks solid."

"Why wasn't I informed about it?" he asked, displaying true annoyance. Then he added, "I could have saved you a lot of time and effort if you would have told me what you were planning to throw at it."

Maghami nodded. "I know, I know. We just didn't want you to lose focus on your first project."

Ryan frowned. *Right.*

"Now, though," Maghami continued, "we need your best version of the MPS security system to put it on-line as soon as possible. Our system was breached three times before it shut itself down."

"Mike," said Wittica, "our client's records are sacred. If the IRS ever gets a whiff of this breach it will be all over for us."

I doubt that seriously, Ryan thought while forcing concern in his stare.

"We really need your help," insisted Wittica. "You have my word that no one will copy or browse through any of your files without discussing it with you first."

The critical edits that he had done to his MPS system in order to perform the hacking run were safe from Maghami, Vijay Parma, and Wittica in a hidden directory. And even if they found this directory, they would not know which of the thousands of files had his clandestine edits. And even if they got lucky and pulled the correct file, they would only find tens of thousands of undocumented lines of C++.

"All right," Ryan finally said. "You have my full support."

Wittica gave him one of his million-dollar smiles.

Ryan also smiled. He had accomplished *exactly* what he had set out to do: empower himself to browse through the network with negligible chance of getting caught. He had been lucky during today's session, running a few red lights while staying one step ahead of the police. Next time he might not be so lucky. Having SoftCorp *adopt* his security system, however, gave Ryan total control of the environment that he intended to hack. It was the ultimate hacker's dream, the equivalent of controlling not just the traffic light system but also the police.

Closely followed by his two bodyguards, FBI Director Roman Palenski made his way through the evening crowd waiting to be seated at Palomino's, a popular restaurant in the heart of Washington, D.C. According to the unexpected invitation he had received two hours previously, his dinner companion would be expecting him at eight o'clock sharp at a reserved table in the back of the busy establishment.

Palenski had just finished speaking to Karen Frost, getting the details of a meeting the federal agent had set up for this Saturday with a potential informer. Karen had chosen to keep the identity of the informant secret for now, at least until she could secure cooperation.

Palenski sidestepped just in time to miss an incoming waitress hauling a ridiculously large tray, jammed-packed with dishes. He resumed his search, inspecting the tables toward the rear, almost getting run over by a waiter pushing a dessert cart, finally spotting Senator Jack Horton, sitting precisely where the note had stated. Four agents from the U.S. Secret Service, assigned to Horton after it had become evident that he was the front runner for next year's presidential election, occupied the tables on either side of the senator. All four were inspecting the crowd. One of them gave Palenski a single nod as he approached Horton. The director of the FBI returned the informal salute before motioning his own bodyguards to sit with the Secret Service agents.

Palenski took off his coat and handed it to one of his bodyguards before settling on the chair across from Horton. The constant hum of dinner conversation mixed with the delicate clatter of silverware and the sudden pop from a waiter opening a bottle of wine—which caused two of the Secret Service agents to reach inside their coats, before relaxing a moment later when realizing the source of the noise. The crowd didn't even flinch at the sight of so many bodyguards. A lot of political VIPs frequented Palomino's every day.

Palenski breathed heavily, gave the place another look, and settled his curious stare on the aristocratic Horton, who unbuttoned the coat of his silk suit as he leaned back, running a finger down his chest to smooth his tie, which hung from a perfect knot.

"So," Palenski finally said, loosening his own tie before rolling the sleeves of his white shirt up to his elbows. He moved aside silverware and glasses to make room for his exposed forearms, which he planted over the tablecloth, interlocking his fingers. "Here I am, Senator. Now would you mind telling me why you invited me to dinner after putting me through two weeks of *hell* in Congress?"

Horton started to reply but their waiter arrived holding a bottle of red wine, which he proudly displayed to Horton, waiting for the senator's nod before producing a corkscrew.

Palenski grew impatient as the waiter went through the opening cere-mony. Horton tasted the wine, gave the waiter another nod, and motioned him away.

"Would you care for some excellent sauvignon, Director?" Horton asked.

"Sure," Palenski said after a short pause. *What the hell.*

"What if," Horton began as he poured Palenski a half glass, keeping their conversation out of everyone's earshot, including their bodyguards, "I can get Congress to reverse the decision on your expansion budget?"

"Don't screw around, Senator," replied Palenski, also in a low voice, leaning forward. "I'm not in the mood."

"I mean it," reply Horton, pouring himself some wine. I believe I have the power to swing the vote back in your favor."

Holding the glass by its delicate stem, Palenski swirled the wine. "Why would you do such a thing?"

"Because deep inside I believe that you're trying to do the right thing."

"But?"

"But I don't believe that you've outlined all of your undercover oper-ations."

Palenski shrugged. "There are always a certain number of operations in any law-enforcement agency that must remain secret in order to protect the agents involved, at least until after the cases have been solved."

"I agree that confidentiality is of the utmost importance, especially when it comes to the witness protection program. And it's quite appropriate to describe completed operations, as you did so eloquently over the past two weeks. But you also need to appreciate the fact that we, the people footing your budget, have a need to know a little more about ongoing operations than the general statements you threw at us. We're not asking for excruciating details, Director, just a little more insight into key operations. This is why I went against your expansion budget. *But* there's still time . . . if you're willing to help me understand your operation—just enough for me to get a sense of where you're going, so I can justify in my mind the additional expenses."

Palenski thought about that for a moment, trying to find the harm in cooperating. After all, Jack Horton was slated to become the next president of the United States. If a president couldn't be trusted, they might as well all pack it up.

"You better not be trying to trick me, Senator," said Palenski, still trying to decide. He took a sip of wine. It was excellent.

Horton's face became solemn. "You have my word. If you're up-front with me, I'll support you in Congress, just as I support other federal agencies, like the IRS and the FDA. I'd also keep in mind your cooperation today if I'm elected to the White House next year."

Palenski nodded, remembering his irritation at the relative ease with which the IRS had slipped in and out of Congress with every dollar of its budget approved.

If you can't trust a president, who can you trust? The words repeated in his mind over and over. Despite their differences, Palenski felt that Horton, albeit a self-centered politician, did care about the welfare of his constituents, even if he did so for the sole purpose of promoting his political career.

Like every other politician you've ever met.

"All right," said Palenski, taking another sip. "I will level with you, but if you divulge information and jeopardize the lives of my agents, I will have you arrested."

Horton pressed his lips together, nodded, and said, "Fair enough."

"Also, I want this arrangement to remain between us."

"That's my wish as well. I have a lot to lose if word leaks out and gets misinterpreted by the press."

Palenski considered that. As a presidential candidate, Horton indeed had far more at stake than he did. He leaned back, and said, "In that case, Senator, what would you like to know?"

Horton smiled. "Why don't you start by telling me how you're really fighting organized crime, beyond the nice foils you showed us in Congress. Then let's get into the growing threat of militias. And spare me the details. I just want to get a good feeling about the operations and their potential for success."

Palenski began to speak, relating to Jack Horton the basics of several covert operations, including the one being led by Karen Frost in Austin, Texas.

The man in the tan windbreaker held a gym bag as he stepped out of the taxi and walked across Sixth Street, in the heart of the nightlife in Austin, Texas. Medium height, clean-cut, the loose windbreaker and khaki slacks hiding his athletic built, he merged easily with the river of humanity crowding the bars, live music clubs, and restaurants flanking the popular street. College students from the University of Texas, tourists, and professionals enjoyed a cool and breezy Friday evening.

His eyes scanned everyone around him without really focusing on anyone in particular, checking for signs of FBI surveillance. After the information he had received in Washington, he couldn't be too cautious.

Following directions he had committed to memory, the man turned left on Colorado Street, and left again on Second Street, giving the block behind him one final check before going inside an apartment complex. The instructions had been simple and clear: reach unit number 347 and knock four times, slowly, followed by a coded message.

He pushed the elevator button for the fourth floor, inspected both ends of the hallway, and used the emergency stairs to climb down to the third floor. He inspected the long corridor, verifying that number 347 was adjacent to the stairs.

As instructed he knocked on the door before saying out loud, "Delivery for Mr. Brickmann."

A moment later he heard a voice through the door. "Mr. *James* Brickmann from Indiana?"

"No, Mr. *Peter* Brickmann from Connecticut," he replied, completing the code.

The door opened and he recognized the tall, broad-shouldered man with closely cropped ash blond hair and intense blue eyes blocking the entryway.

"Esteban," said Todd Hausser. "It's been—"

"A very long time, yes," interrupted Esteban Yanez, waving the over-sized security guard aside as he stepped into the small living area, his eyes quickly assessing the place, the cheap sofa facing a small television set playing some action flick. He walked up to the windows facing downtown Austin. From here he could see the crowd on Sixth Street. "How have you been?"

"Better," replied Hausser.

"That's why I'm here. Did you get my list?"

Hausser nodded and pointed at the kitchen table.

Esteban took off his windbreaker, folding it as he walked into the small dining area, and draping it over one of the chairs surrounding the table containing his wish list of weapons. After a brief inspection of the dozen or so pistols, he selected a Colt .45 semiautomatic in a blued finish. His finger moved automatically, releasing the magazine, inspecting it, and verifying that it was fully loaded before reinserting it. He pulled back the slide, chambering a round, before flipping up the weapon's safety lever so he could carry it with the hammer pulled back, "locked and loaded." That's why he loved the Colt semiauto above all other pistols. He could carry it with the hammer pulled back and the safety on. To fire it all he had to do was flick off the safety with his thumb and apply a slight pressure to the trigger. This weapon had saved his life on more than one occasion during his Sandinista days in Central America, before Orion Yanez, his uncle, had redirected his efforts to run his personal security in America in the late '80s.

He shoved the gun in the small of his back before checking the contents on the table once more, choosing a small Beretta, also in blue steel, and already secured inside an ankle holster, as his backup piece. Again, trained fingers checked the weapon before he rested his right foot on the chair, wrapping the Velcro strap around the middle of his lower leg, high enough so the gun wouldn't show if he sat down and crossed his legs, yet low enough for easy access should he ever need it.

Next he pulled up the metal snaps of a long and flat case next to the pistols, housing a disassembled Heckler & Koch PSG-1 sniper rifle in individual foam-protected sections. He assembled it in under thirty seconds, adding the scope at the end. Esteban swore by this rifle. He had killed more than his fair share of Contras during the ten-year war with one just like this one. It was not only one of the most accurate sniper rifles in the world but also included a twenty-round magazine for follow-up shot capability in case of multiple targets. Based on the instructions he had received on the way up here, there was a high probability that he would need to use this additional feature of the weapon.

"Anything else we can do?" asked Hausser.

Esteban told him only what Hausser needed to know about the plan he had worked out on his way here, after his uncle had explained the problem. Six years ago Esteban had come down to Austin to handle another problem for his uncle—the elimination of the obstinate CEO of one of SoftCorp's competing firms. The month-long job—which Esteban successfully set up as an auto accident—had gotten him quite familiar with the area. This time around, however, time was of the essence, pretty much narrowing down his choices to an assassination.

Esteban dismissed Hausser so he could get some rest. The flight from Washington had been very bumpy, followed by a long layover in Dallas before he could catch the shuttle down to Austin. Ignoring his body's demand for rest, Esteban had ordered the taxi driver to take him on a one-hour tour of the city at night—time he'd used to make certain no one was following him. The precautions, however, had drained him. He wasn't the same thirty-year-old Marxist rebel of yesteryear. Back then he could hike through the mountains of Honduras and Nicaragua for days without needing much rest, hunting down his prey, leading hit-and-run missions designed to demoralize the Contras. But over fifteen years had passed since then. After Nicaragua, Esteban had also fought alongside Marxist guerrillas in El Salvador and Shining Path guerrillas in Ecuador. That was all before dedicating his life to protecting his uncle's business in America, helping it grow by eliminating the competition, by strong-arming his way into the corporate world with the help of a small but loyal band of former Sandinistas, put out of business by the fall of communism in Central America.

Esteban Yanez approached the windows and closed the blinds while Hausser bagged the other weapons and left without another word.

Alone, lying on the sofa, he used the remote to shut off the television set, and closed his eyes, trying to relax. He thought of Cuba, of his days growing up in Havana during the '50s. He remembered the bearded rebels fighting in the Sierra Maestra, the mountain range in the western section of the island, slowly gaining on the demoralized army of Fulgencio Batista. The fall of that right-wing regime had been sudden, stomped by the legendary bearded rebels in the olive-drab fatigues and red bandannas who stormed across Havana in January of 1959, soon after Batista had fled to Miami. He recalled the Castro militia liberating Batista's political prisoners, heroes of the revolution, some of whom didn't live to see that glorious day. His own parents had been caught by Batista's troops just days before using a radio to advise the rebels in the mountains of the activities in Havana. They had been executed in the driveway of their home after the officer in charge labeled them as traitors.

Esteban rubbed his eyes. He'd never forgotten what he had seen on that dusty driveway forty-five years ago. He had swore then, just as he swore now, to fight against American imperialism, as his parents had, until his body fell victim to age and exhaustion. And he had kept that promise, fighting to liberate Nicaragua, El Salvador, Ecuador, anywhere the cause took him. But his uncle had pulled him back from that nomadic life and tasked him with organizing and training a world-class security force to protect his growing empire in America, with the goal of preserving Castro's ideologies in Cuba long after the dictator passed away.

And his uncle might also be the only man in Esteban's opinion who was strong enough to pick up the reigns after Castro. Cuba had remained communist for this long only because of Castro's vision and determination, because of the no-nonsense way in which he dealt with his enemies, with dissidents, using extreme but justifiable methods to either make them believers in the revolution or to kill them. Such were the sacrifices of true freedom, and Orion Yanez was among the few men capable of continuing Castro's crusade for an imperialist-free Cuba, a crusade that Esteban had devoted his entire life to support.

Esteban stared at the slow-turning ceiling fan, thinking of rain forests and ambushes, of agonizing screams and horrifying amputations, of field executions and kidnappings, of everything he had witnessed in his fight to defend the rights of the people against American-backed governments.

Now his uncle had masterminded a plan to keep Cuba alive by injecting it with the capital it needed to survive in the twenty-first century. He had accomplished the first step by helping attract foreign investors to build resorts and casinos on the beaches of Havana and other oceanfronts of the island. Now he needed more than that, plus the insurance that the United States would not try to pull a Panama or Grenada after Castro's death. And that assurance came not just by putting Orion's puppet in the White House but by the acquisition of nuclear weapons. Having a sympathetic president in the Oval Office was just a bridge, something that would end a few years later, when a new official got elected. But that would be long enough to get Cuba the weaponry it would need to command fear. Fear of nuclear retaliation was the key to respect, the tide that raised all ships. But in order to succeed, the funds needed to keep flowing through his uncle's network. They had not yet achieved the financial critical mass to pull this off. They were close, but not there yet. Each of Orion Yanez's dozens of money-laundering channels—the IRS–SoftCorp–Capitol Bank connection being just one of them—had to continue fattening their overseas accounts for at least a few more years.

And Esteban Yanez's current job was to make certain that those interfering with his uncle's operation were swiftly and silently eliminated.

Karen Frost kept a steady pace down the jogging trail bordering Town Lake, the branch of the Colorado River crossing through downtown Austin. Wearing a dark jogging suit and sneakers, her recently dyed red hair bouncing gently, she blended perfectly with the dozens of Austinites exercising this early Saturday morning. Sweat filmed her face, partly because of the exercise, but mostly due to the Kevlar vest she wore beneath the suit, a precaution she had taken after getting shot at outside Rubaker's house. The weapons she hauled probably added to her fatigue. They seemed heavier than when she had started. The Desert Eagle .44 Magnum semiautomatic burned a hole in her shoulders as it hung from a chest holster beneath the jogging suit, and, combined with the Colt .45 compact model strapped to her ankle, made it difficult to keep her steady pace.

Bright sunlight had burned off the light fog that hazed the jogging trail when she arrived an hour ago. Karen had spent most of that time inspecting the meeting grounds.

Cool air filled her lungs as she trotted by the gazebo across from the power plant for the fifth time, expecting to see the young couple, but finding no one.

Where are they?

Had they failed to follow her instructions and said the wrong thing in their home or cars?

Karen shoved the thought aside, concentrating on the people around her, whom she inspected from behind a pair of oversized sunglasses that almost qualified as a mask, further altering her looks. Their mirror finish prevented anyone from seeing her green eyes, courtesy of colored lenses. Some people walked. Others, like her, jogged. A few had dogs. There were even some riding bicycles.

Karen continued for another half mile before doubling back, making a stop at a water fountain on the side of the busy trail, near a family of ducks sitting by the grassy shore. A few boats broke the smooth surface of Town Lake. One had several oarsmen slaving to the shouts of their coxswain, sitting by the bow with a megahorn. Karen picked up the pace again, this time spotting the Ryans as she made her way up the trail toward the large wooden gazebo.

Like Karen, Ryan wore a jogging suit and sneakers. But he wasn't running. He was stretching his legs against the gazebo, where the trail met the grass. Victoria stood next to him, also in full running attire.

Karen approached them, wondering how they would react to her presence. The Ryans turned their heads toward her as she got near.

"Michael and Victoria Ryan?" Karen asked from a good fifteen feet away. If there was one thing she had learned at the FBI it was not to get too close to any stranger initially. Fifteen feet was about the minimum distance until she decided that the Ryans meant her no harm.

They both nodded.

"I'm glad you decided to—"

A powerful blow to the middle of her back made Karen jerk forward. Crash-landing on the gravel trail, her sunglasses flying off, Karen skinned the palms of her hands as she thrust them out instinctively.

Stunned, squinting in the sunlight, arrested by the crippling pain, she rolled toward the hedges framing the side of the trail next to the water.

Someone with a silenced weapon had shot her from behind.

Grateful that she had worn the Kevlar vest, but her back nevertheless burning from the impact, Karen heard the hastening steps of joggers approaching her, including the Ryans, curiosity and concern mixed in their stare.

Where was the shooter? Among the crowd approaching her? Or farther away, perhaps in one of the many trees in the area? Or maybe even across the river? And who had betrayed the meeting place? The Ryans? No one but they and Palenski knew about—

No time to analyze!

Move!

Strangers approached her. Karen had to find the shooter among them, and fast. Instinctively, she reached inside her suit for the Desert Eagle, ignoring the pain in her right palm as she clutched the weapon, freeing it from its holster.

People screamed the moment she pulled the massive gun out from beneath her suit, aiming it at everything and everyone around her, including the Ryans. As expected, the crowd panicked and stampeded away from her, letting Karen concentrate on anyone lingering behind.

An invisible fist punched her in the stomach, knocking the wind out of her, pushing her light frame against a large oak on the water side of the trail, its opulent limbs projecting over Town Lake and also shading the trail.

Fighting her blurring vision, gasping for air, Karen staggered to her feet, her abdomen ablaze, her breath caught in her throat.

Amazed that she still clutched the Magnum, the fed pressed her back against the trunk for balance as she blinked rapidly, struggling to clear her sight, succeeding a moment later, but unable to find the shooter among the havoc of people screaming and running away.

The ground exploded just beyond the oak in a cloud of dirt and gravel. The shooter was still hunting her.

But from where?

Wincing in pain, Karen watched the Ryans reaching the sidewalk, joining the dozens of joggers escaping from the woman holding the large black gun. She wanted to call out to them, explain her actions, but not only did she not have the time as she searched the area for the sniper, she also didn't want to identify herself in front of so many people. After all, she was running a covert operation. And even if she had wanted to shout after the young couple, the pain from the multiple gunshots made it nearly impossible to speak, much less shout.

She watched them disappear from view, her mind focusing on her own predicament.

Get away from here. Live to fight another day.

Karen had little to gain and much to lose by hanging around. She couldn't find a target, and because the weapon used on her was silenced, no one else knew that a firearm had been discharged. All anyone saw was a jogger stumbling on the trail before producing a pistol and triggering a general panic.

Albeit light-headed, Karen spotted two men running toward her from across the street. Their massive figures and military-style haircuts belied their civilian clothes. Neither held a weapon, which told her that there was a third person, the shooter, still hiding somewhere. She suspected that the incoming pair wanted to force her back into the open, into the sights of the sniper. But these two could just be civilians, or cops out of uniform trying to overpower an armed suspect.

Then Karen recognized the taller of the two, the man with ash blond hair who'd been at Rubaker's the other night.

Todd.

He reached her side of the street first while holding a two-way radio to his lips.

Mustering strength, ignoring her protesting ribs and back, she lifted the heavy gun and aimed it in his direction. Todd immediately dove for the cover of a tree. His companion did likewise as Karen stood her ground, resisting the temptation to leave her cover. However, her training also told her she was a stationary target. Todd could be redirecting the shooter—*or shooters*—toward a better vantage point.

Doomed if you move and doomed if you don't.

As she cursed her situation, Todd reappeared from behind his hideout, this time clutching a pistol, which he aimed in Karen's direction but didn't fire. Instead, he dashed across ten feet of grass toward another tree, gaining ground on her, perhaps positioning himself for a better shot.

Karen aimed the Desert Eagle just to the right of the trunk, at the spot where she expected the large blond head to appear. A moment later he did, and she fired.

The .44 Magnum cartridge cracked in the morning air like thunder. The round missed its intended target, splintering a cloud of bark, which broadsided Todd as he stepped away from the tree.

The blast pounded her ears, but through the heavy ringing she could still hear Todd screaming as he dropped to his knees while holding his left side. The shot had not been a total waste. She had managed to temporarily incapacitate one of her pursuers.

Capitalizing on the diversion, Karen lunged, ignoring her protesting abdomen, her burning back, using the distraction to get away, dashing down the edge of the trail, remaining beneath trees, cutting left toward the street while holstering the Desert Eagle.

The gamble worked. The second stranger remained hidden from view, unknowingly letting Karen escape. Breathing heavily, she rushed away from the trail and crossed First Street, cutting left on Lavaca Street, slowing down to a fast walk and taking a right on Third Street, flagging a taxi, quickly getting inside.

"Where to, lady?" a Hispanic driver asked, inspecting Karen through the rearview mirror.

"Drive," she said after a moment, struggling to catch her breath, the pain crippling. "Just drive."

"Yes, ma'am."

As the taxi sped away from the curb, Karen decided she would call Palenski the first chance she got. Someone had intercepted her information, and Karen doubted it had been the Ryans. They seemed genuinely surprised, and they had run in a different direction from the two gorillas who had tried to flush her toward the sniper.

Unless someone followed them.

She quickly discarded that thought. If someone had indeed followed the Ryans, Karen would have expected a less organized strike since the enemy really didn't know who or how many people would be meeting with the young couple. Karen also didn't think the Ryans would have been able to get away as easily as they had. Someone would have certainly terminated them on the spot to keep them from talking to her.

Just like the Pattersons.

Another possibility was that the Ryans were in on it. Maybe they had read the note and decided to approach their employers, who may have coached them on how to attend this meeting.

Once again, she faced many possibilities.

The taxi left the streets of downtown Austin behind. Karen continued checking behind her, satisfied that she had not been followed. She then gave the driver instructions to take her to her car, parked several blocks away from Town Lake, from any possible danger.

As the driver steered the taxi back to the city, Karen frowned. If the Ryans hadn't approached their employers before, they might do so after what had taken place today. In their minds all they saw was a woman approach them, fall, and then point a gun at them.

Damn!

She closed her eyes, wondering if she would indeed get another chance at connecting with them. She hoped that they would head home sometime today, perhaps after taking some time to discuss what they had seen. She also hoped that the Ryans—if they were indeed innocent—would not panic and contact their employers after this incident. If they did, she felt certain that they would end up in the same morgue where she had found the grossly maimed remains of Dave Nolan.

Of course, if the Ryans were clean, then she had even greater problems because the information on the meeting had leaked through another source, and that source was Palenski, the only other party who knew about the meeting.

Karen shook her head, refusing to believe that Palenski would double-cross her.

So it has to be someone inside the Bureau who must have intercepted the information.

And if that was the case, then everything that Palenski knew was compromised, including Karen's current residence in Austin and the rental car that the taxicab was taking her to.

Shit.

As the Austin skyline grew bigger, Karen decided to play it safe and gave the driver a new address.

She then reached for her cellular phone, her fingers aching with the desire to contact Palenski right now, even at the risk of the driver overhearing the conversation.

Wait, she told herself. *Palenski isn't going anywhere.*

Roman Palenski kissed his wife and climbed into the rear seat of his Bureau sedan. He headed out for the golf course on this sunny Saturday morning— along with his two bodyguards, one sitting next to him and one in front, next to the driver.

He checked his watch as he rode in the rear of the bullet-proof sedan. His tee time was in just forty-five minutes—barely enough time to make it to the club and hit a few practice balls at the range to warm up.

Palenski leaned back in his seat, forcing himself to relax, to momentarily forget about all of his ongoing operations, about his conversation with Horton. He simply gazed at the suburban Maryland scenery while thinking about his upcoming golf game.

The driver abruptly cut the wheel sharply to the left.

Palenski was shoved against the door, crashing the side of his head against the tinted glass, realizing a moment later why his driver had made such drastic turn. A cement truck had run a red light and was coming straight at them.

Dazed from the blow to his head, Palenski tried to scream as the truck's front bumper filled the side window.

The FBI director found himself staring at the very face of death.

The impact came a fraction of a second later, ear piercing and powerful, lifting the sedan with the force of a freight train, flipping it, ramming it a second time as it landed on its side, shoving it against a city bus, where it was crushed like a beer can.

His body pressed between the collapsed roof and the floor, Roman Palenski tried to move but couldn't. He was trapped, and so were his bodyguards. For a moment everything was quiet.

Then he smelled gas.

And began to pray.

Witnesses would never forget the agonizing screams coming from inside the sedan seconds after the vehicle, still on its side, ignited in a sheet of flames that quickly engulfed the truck and the city bus. The passengers in the bus managed to escape with minor bruises and a story to tell. The truck driver also walked away from the accident, but he didn't hang around for the police and emergency crews already on their way to the scene of the accident. He used the confusion following the crash to slip away. The truck had been stolen just an hour ago. No one would be able to trace it back to him.

He turned the corner and climbed inside a waiting van, the maddened howls from inside the burning sedan piercing through the morning traffic.

The rented Mustang Ryan had picked up the night before started on the first crank. He put it in gear and stepped on the accelerator, leaving the curb behind—and the chaos of what had become their morning meeting. Panting from the short sprint out of the Town Lake area, he gave his wife a brief sideways glance. Victoria buckled up and ran her hands through her short hair, taking a deep breath.

"Damn, Mike. What in the hell just happened?"

Ryan shook his head, confused. "That woman . . . I'm not sure what happened. One moment she was walking toward us . . . then—"

"She pulled a gun and aimed it at us! *That's* what happened!"

Ryan frowned. Something just didn't add up. "I know, Vic. I was there too. But she was aiming it at everyone, not just at us."

"What are you saying?"

"That something was very strange. Have you ever seen someone falling like that before?"

She shook her head. "That *was* strange. It looked almost as if some-one . . ."

"Pushed her?"

"Right. But there wasn't anyone else."

"*Exactly*," Ryan said, glad that they had decided to rent a car so they could speak freely, without the risk of being monitored by whoever it was that ran SoftCorp and Capitol Bank—according to this *friend* of theirs who had pulled a gun on them. "And it didn't happen once but twice."

"When was the second time?"

"Right after she grabbed the gun, just as everyone began to scream and run in all different directions."

"The same invisible push?"

"A push, a shove—*something*. But this time it hit her stomach, doubling her over and sending her crashing toward a tree at the edge of the trail."

Victoria pinched the ridge between her eyes while closing them. "It doesn't make sense."

"What *doesn't* make sense is that somehow we've been sucked into the middle of something big . . . very big."

"And pretty darn scary."

"True, and I'm not sure *what* it is or how far it goes, but I'm certain that it will be up to you and me to find a way out of it."

Victoria crossed her arms. "I doubt anyone's coming to our rescue."

"We have to fend for ourselves, honey. Just like in the past," Ryan said while checking the rearview mirror to make sure no one was following them. Although he had not seen anyone at the park who looked even remotely familiar, the paranoid hacker in him told him he couldn't be too careful.

"What should we do?" asked Victoria.

"We continue to do *exactly* what I did last Friday: use our positions—our skills—to dig up more information, to find out what in the hell is going on, and then use that information to set ourselves free."

She nodded. "I can certainly think of a thing or two at my job that I can do, including finding out a little more about the accounts you jotted down yesterday."

Ryan gave her a nervous smile, the adrenaline rush making it difficult to settle down. "That's a good start. I'll do the same from my end, but it would be very helpful if I could have a couple of passwords to get started."

"There's at least two or three that I should be able to get right away. Where are we going?"

"To get some coffee. I sure could use some."

Esteban Yanez used the scope on the PSG-1 sniper rifle to observe the commotion on the opposite shore of Town Lake, cursing his stupidity for not having given the federal agent more credit. At first Esteban had been amused at her attempt to disguise her presence by simply changing the color of her hair and wearing those oversized sunglasses. Esteban had scrutinized the videos provided to him by Hausser, the ones depicting the final minutes of the Pattersons. He had memorized her facial features. Hair dye might be enough to throw an amateur, but not a trained professional. But in a way the FBI woman had fooled him. She had been wearing a bullet-proof vest and had reacted quite professionally, seeking cover and holding her ground when confronted by Hausser and his best man, before creating a diversion and rushing away. Fortunately, both Hausser and his subordinate had also gotten away before the police arrived, amidst blaring sirens, which Esteban could hear across the Colorado's slow-flowing waters.

Time to retreat and reconvene.

Frowning, he took the rifle apart, storing it in a large gym bag. Zipping it shut, he shouldered it before climbing down the oak, ignoring the curious stare from a couple of joggers.

Calmly, he made his way down the jogging trail, reaching a parked sedan a half mile away, and storing the rifle in the trunk before driving away.

Orion Yanez sipped his coffee while enjoying the cold and invigorating morning. The call from his men in Washington had been quite encouraging. The elimination of Roman Palenski not only mitigated the FBI threat to his organization but it also presented him with the unique opportunity to influence the activities in the Bureau by manipulating the deputy director, who, according to Jack Horton, would be far more willing to cooperate if given the appropriate congressional budgetary incentives.

One of his subordinates brought a phone to him. It was connected to Orion's secured line.

Orion took it and said, *"Dígame?"*

"It's Horton. My assistant told me this was critical."

"I'm afraid there has been a terrible accident," said Orion before taking another sip of the strong coffee. "It's Palenski."

"What happened?"

"He was just killed in an auto accident."

Silence, followed by, "Oh, God."

"People die, my friend," said Orion. "It's a part of life. Let's focus on the living, shall we?"

"Yes . . . of course."

"Good. Now, if I remember what I learned from my American citizenship class years ago, the president of the United States will have to appoint a new director, and the Senate will have to ratify it, right?"

Another moment of silence, followed by, "Correct."

"Good, then. This is what I need you to do."

Orion hung up the phone a minute later as one of his subordinates approached him.

"Mr. Yanez?"

"What is it."

"It's Mr. Isonov."

Orion finished his coffee and handed the cup to his guard before replying, "Show him to my office and offer him a refreshment. I'll join him shortly."

Orion Yanez was a very calm man. He had seen enough death and destruction in his life to last him twenty lifetimes, but along with such experience came a sense of peace, of serenity when it came to dealing with problems, with issues. Today, however, excitement trickled into his bloodstream at the prospects of closing this deal. His superiors in Havana would be most pleased at this key milestone.

Standing, he walked inside the house and went directly to his office.

"Sergei," said Orion, extending a hand to the Russian diplomat—at least according to the State Department. In reality, Sergei Boris Isonov was second in command of the Russian mafia in the United States, controlling everything from gambling to prostitution in several states.

"My friend," replied Isonov, a slim man in his late fifties, with thinning white hair and large, thick glasses, which magnified his alert eyes.

"Please," Orion said, waving a hand at the chairs flanking a fireplace opposite his large desk. "Nothing like a fireside chat with a good friend to close the deal of a lifetime."

Isonov smiled and sat down, staring at the glowing fire. "All of the arrangements have been made," he said after sipping from a glass of water.

"Any complications?"

Isonov shook his head. "Nothing beyond the usual. Several officers in St. Petersburg are now enjoying their new dachas overlooking Lake Ladoga."

Orion nodded. "And the transportation is on schedule as well?"

"Spy satellites will be unable to detect the disassembled missiles this time. They are not being transported on the decks of vessels, like the last time."

Orion wondered how the Soviets could have been so stupid as to carry missiles in plain view of American U2 spy planes in the early '60s, triggering the legendary October missile crisis of 1963. "The special resort near Pinar de Río is ready to receive them," he said, referring to a large compound that he had built near the Cuban coastal city, a hundred miles from Havana, to house the missiles. The entire place had been designed to look like just another beach resort, three more of which Orion was also building in the same region to avoid arousing the suspicions of the ever-vigilant CIA.

"Including the covered receiving dock?"

Orion nodded again. The "resort" included a large covered marina, built to resemble any one of many exclusive marinas around the world, only this one was outfitted to receive cargo from vessels carrying his acquired weapons of mass destruction.

"My associates will be expecting payment upon delivery, of course."

"Of course. The money is secured in an overseas account and ready to be transferred in two weeks, as soon as the shipment arrives and is thoroughly checked by our scientists."

Isonov raised his glass at Orion. "To Cuba."

Orion smiled, and replied, "To keeping Cuba free of American imperialism."

16

Ron Wittica reached his company's building after a hasty drive from Lake Travis, where he had been enjoying a morning cruise in the company of Gail.

He keyed in the building's access code and rushed inside, waving at the security guard behind the counter as he ran across the lobby and into a waiting elevator, which took him to the third floor.

His mouth dry, his hands trembling, he knocked twice on the door to the Monitoring Systems Control Center. A guard opened it.

"Mr. Wittica?"

SoftCorp's CTO moved past the startled guard. "The Ryans . . . have they been home this morning?"

Two guards sitting in front of the monitors turned around, curious.

"Which one is the Ryans'?" Wittica asked, pointing at the monitors.

One of the two guards extended an index finger at a display before switching the audio for that monitor to the overhead speakers.

Victoria Ryan's voice filled the room. She was having breakfast with Michael Ryan in the kitchen. They were talking about the house they'd just bought and whether or not they'd be able to afford it.

Wittica exhaled, relieved. Hausser *had* to be wrong about his sighting at Town Lake. Wittica was about to leave when Ryan made a comment about his project, something about how he wasn't sure if he'd meet the deadline next Friday.

Next Friday?

Wittica frowned. Today was Saturday. The comment implied that Ryan had until the following Friday to complete the project. After the incident with Agi Maghami's security system that past Thursday, Wittica had given Ryan until Monday to finish it, changing the original deadline from last Friday—yesterday—to this coming Monday. Why would he think that he had until Friday?

He got closer, listening more carefully now.

"What is it, sir?" asked the young guard standing next to him.

Wittica shook his head. "I'm not sure." Ryan made another comment about how long he would have to work in the coming days just to stay on schedule, complaining once again about the deadline on Friday and how three weeks wasn't enough to complete this stage of the project.

"Could you give me a view from the other cameras installed at the Ryan's?"

One of the guards clicked a keyboard for a few moments. A view of the bedroom filled the screen. Then they switched to the foyer. Nothing abnormal.

Wittica still didn't like it. Something didn't feel right, but he couldn't quite put his finger on it. Maybe he was just being paranoid after the recent incidents both inside of SoftCorp with the security breaches, and outside of SoftCorp with the FBI probe. Now it seemed as if someone had spotted the Ryans at a meeting set up by the FBI—according to Washington sources.

The Ryans continued their conversation, chatting about their house, their plans for purchasing new hiking gear—

Wittica blinked. Did Mike Ryan just made a comment about *planning* to buy hiking gear? Wittica could have sworn that the other night, when he had been watching the monitors with the guards, Victoria Ryan had made a comment about *having purchased* new gear that day. It had been right after their lovemaking session in the foyer. Victoria had also made the comment about Rossini making a pass at her.

"Something isn't right," he finally said, tapping the monitor. "Can you replay the video from . . ." He closed his eyes, trying to remember. Then he did. It had happened the night before the security breach last Friday. "Play the one from last Thursday night, starting at around eight in the evening, and select the foyer camera."

The guard started clicking away again, but a moment later he turned around. "I can't replay that video, sir."

"Why not?"

"It's been erased."

"What?"

"Gone, sir. Look here."

Wittica placed a hand on the back of the guard's chair while leaning down and forward to look at the screen. The archive directory for the Ryan's video was empty.

"How . . . how can that be? Have we experienced a malfunction?"

"None that we have noticed, sir."

"Check everyone else's video records!"

All three guards now worked the keyboards, finding ten other employees with missing records.

Wittica began to rub his temples, his heartbeat rocketing. *What is going on? Why are so many video records missing? Is this related to the security breach the other day? Could they have gotten lost during the abrupt system shutdown triggered by the breach?*

Taking a deep breath, he said, "Check the video link to Mike Ryan's home." Then he grabbed the phone to call Shapiro, who had returned from Washington last night. Shapiro had given Wittica an intense fifteen-minute lecture on no more screwups. SoftCorp's CEO had implied that their lives depended on doing *everything* right from here on out.

No more screwups.

As Wittica dialed his boss's number he couldn't help but roll his eyes at the irony. The day had been *filled* with screwups.

193

Ryan almost spilled his coffee the moment his pager went off inside a coffee shop at the shopping center on the corner of Loop 360 and Beecaves Road.

"Who's paging you?" asked Victoria, setting down her mug, concern flashing in her hazel eyes.

Ryan grabbed the black pager and pressed a button while looking at the screen.

"Crap," he said.

"What?"

"Do you remember what I told you about the way I reprogrammed SoftCorp's video system to keep them from peering into our lives at home?"

She nodded while crossing her arms, obviously expecting something bad.

"I also added a special feature. If someone went browsing through this recorded file, which I had labeled as a live recording, the system would send me an alert of the attempted intrusion. It just did."

She stood. "What does that mean?"

He also stood, grabbing her hand while walking toward the exit. "It means that someone has found enough compelling evidence to warrant checking up on the status of our video file. It also means they've probably discovered that all video files were erased."

"Can they point this back to you?"

He shook his head. "First of all, mine aren't the only video files missing. I took the precaution of also deleting the records of ten other employees. I also left behind a software guardian who, in addition to alerting me, is also preventing anyone from reading the file. The guardian will also erase the recorded file and any evidence of my tampering, plus switch the camera's source back to actual live video—after making all screens go blank for ten seconds to make the switch less noticeable."

"Meaning we better be home when the switch takes place?"

He nodded. "Right, and we only have thirty minutes from the time the page was sent. I also get the strange feeling that someone from SoftCorp might be dropping by the house very soon to check up on us."

They got in their car and drove off toward Lakeway.

"Should we be going home, Mike? What if they somehow figured out it was you tampering with the video? What if they browsed through the directory because of what happened this morning?"

"You mean someone could have spotted us?"

Her eyes filled with fear as she gave him a slight nod.

"If someone did, then the video is our best alibi, which might explain why they were checking it in the first place. Otherwise they should have left it alone. But say for the moment that someone might have thought he saw us there at the meeting this morning, then the best thing we can do is go home and pretend nothing's wrong. Remember, we have no reason to be suspected of any wrongdoing."

"But . . . if they're really monitoring us, then all they have to do is call us on our home phone. If the phone rings but doesn't do so on the video, they will certainly know it's not live without having to get home."

Ryan smiled. "I took the phone off the hook this morning, Vic. Just in case. If they call, all they'll get is a busy signal."

She didn't reply as Ryan continued toward Lake Travis on Highway 71, taking a right on FM620.

"Do you remember what were you wearing last Saturday morning?" he asked just as he pulled into the neighborhood. Exactly fifteen minutes had passed since receiving the page. Ryan doubted anyone from SoftCorp, which was located farther east than the coffee shop, would be there for at least another fifteen minutes, if not longer. They had a little time, and they had to use it wisely to improve their odds of pulling this off.

"What?"

"What were you wearing? The guards watching the video have seen us moving around the house wearing something. They would expect us to be in the same clothes when they knock on our door."

"Let me think," she said, gazing at the scenery outside. The blue-green waters of Lake Travis appeared after a bend in the hillside road. "I was wearing my green silk pajamas. I think you were wearing one of your black Stanford football jerseys and a pair of gym shorts."

Ryan nodded. "That's what I remember too. And we changed into work clothes at around eleven and headed into work. That means we should be having our morning coffee in the kitchen now."

She also nodded.

"All right," he said, turning onto their street, seeing nothing abnormal, parking the rented car three houses away. "I think we'll be all right."

Victoria Ryan continued to hug herself while gazing out the window. "I hope you're right, Mike. I sure hope you're right."

Ryan *prayed* that he was.

Ron Wittica found himself behind the wheel of his black BMW racing back toward Lakeway, only he wasn't headed for his house. He was going to pay the Ryans a surprise visit.

He checked his rearview mirror and eyed the two sedans following him, one of them driven by an angered Todd Hausser. In all, six agents followed Wittica this morning per Aaron Shapiro's direct orders. That had left only one guard manning the Monitoring Systems Control Center.

But that should be enough, he thought, deciding that all the guard had to do was watch the video of the Ryans and call with any changes.

Wittica briefly closed his eyes at the thought of Todd Hausser. Bleeding from his side, the former lieutenant from the U.S. Special Forces had refused any assistance upon arriving at SoftCorp, field dressing the superficial wound himself with the first-aid kit in the lobby before demanding to know if the Ryans were home.

Wittica had noticed the pistols and silencers each guard had retrieved from the security vault—again under Shapiro's direct orders—and he had cringed then, as he did now, about the Ryans' likely fate.

This operation was coming apart at the seams, and Ron Wittica wasn't even sure if he would be able to keep his composure should Hausser and his men shoot the Ryans if anything—absolutely anything—indicated that they had not been home that morning, as was suggested by the home video, which continued to point to a live video source, though his men had been unable to access it. Wittica had tried calling the Ryans at home to see if the guards could pick up the phone ringing through the audio monitoring system, but the phone had been busy. Since the video showed the Ryans chatting in the kitchen the busy phone line could only mean that they had the phone off the hook. Unless, of course, the video source was not live.

He frowned. The only way to make absolutely certain that the video was live was by knocking on the door and verifying that the guard back at the Monitoring Systems Control Center could see him entering the house.

Otherwise . . .

Play it out, he told himself, wondering how long he would be able to keep up the race before he either ran out of steam or the FBI probe reached him—in either case making him a liability, just like Janet Patterson and her parents, just like Rubaker.

Just like the Ryans.

Michael Ryan unlocked his front door and stepped into the foyer, followed by Victoria. They rushed straight to the master bedroom and into their respective walk-in closets. Ryan found a black Stanford jersey and a pair of gym shorts. Victoria emerged from her closet wearing her silk pajamas. The actual color didn't matter much because the video cameras were black-and-white. As long as they were the right shade of gray on camera they should be fine.

He checked his watch. They had just under ten minutes before the software switched the video source. The question now was, where should they be? In the kitchen? In the living-foyer area? In the bedroom?

Ryan used his home PC to dial into work, accessing the network, quickly switching subdirectories, using his recently acquired passwords to link his PC's real-time video player to the file labeled Live Recording. Although he could link to the protected file containing one week's worth of video, Ryan couldn't view it without alerting the SoftCorp guards monitoring the directory. He needed a distraction, something to make those watching the protected file look elsewhere while he viewed the video that would tell him where to position himself and Victoria the moment the cameras switched their source.

A moment later the answer came to him.

20

The guard watching the monitor of the Ryans' home video grew tired. He had been there all night and Hausser had taken with him the morning shift that had been scheduled to replace him.

Great, he thought, drinking black coffee, struggling to remain awake, watching the boring video of Michael and Victoria Ryan also having coffee in their living room.

He returned his attention to the computer in front of him, which continued to deny him access to the live recording source of the video from the Ryans' house.

He was about to try again when all of the monitors flicked off for a moment before coming back on displaying the image of a gorgeous woman masturbating in bed. It looked like a porn flick and he was momentarily caught by it before he realized that something had gone terribly wrong. He immediately tapped the keys, switching to the main video directory to find the source of the problem.

21

Having achieved his distraction, Michael Ryan clicked the play button on his screen and fast-forwarded the video to the current time, 9:57 A.M.

"Here we go," Victoria said over his right shoulder as he sat in front of his small desk in his study and waited for the digital video stream to make it through his modem.

A moment later it appeared, showing a clear picture of himself and Victoria having coffee in the kitchen.

"We've got three minutes," he told her. "Make us some coffee. Quick."

Victoria rushed off while Ryan watched the video a little more carefully, checking their clothes, deciding that what they wore was close enough to pass inspection from the guards back at SoftCorp. He also took a peek at the living room and bedroom scenes, running back and forth to both rooms to make a few adjustments to match the video, including picking up the hiking gear Victoria had purchased late last week from the living room floor and shoving it all in the foyer closet, out of sight from any camera. He also rearranged the throw pillows in the living room and drew the curtains in the bedroom.

One minute to go.

He waited, watching his own pose on the screen, as well as Victoria's. They sat casually, mugs in hand, chatting about the recent home purchase.

Forty seconds.

Ryan deactivated the video short circuit, releasing the screens from the video of Agi Maghami's wife to their standard video stream, and logged off, running to the kitchen.

Victoria was already sitting in her seat holding a mug. Ryan took his place, also snatching his mug, his eyes on his wristwatch. Coffee had begun to drip in the coffeepot.

"Here we go," he said, "Fifteen seconds to go. Let's talk about the house and plans for improving it."

She nodded, whispering, "Show time."

He glanced at his watch and counted down from five to one with the fingers of his right hand, and off they went, forcing themselves to discuss plans to fix their yard. Ryan used the opportunity to comment on how much he loved working at SoftCorp and how excited he was about the opportunity to improve their security system. Victoria caught on right away, and also talked about her terrific job and how great a company Capitol Bank was, despite the pass made by its president, who had behaved himself ever since that one incident.

Then the doorbell rang about fifteen minutes into their conversation.

Ryan went to answer it while Victoria poured them coffee.

He acted surprised at seeing Ron Wittica in the doorway.

"Ron?" Ryan checked his watch. "Something wrong? I'd figure you'd be cruising the lake by now."

Wittica seemed quite apprehensive but forced the falsest smile Ryan had ever seen. "I'm actually on my way. Just thought I'd stop by and see how the house is coming along. I tried calling ahead to make sure you were home but the line was busy."

Ryan smiled, hoping that his smile didn't look as fake as his boss's. "I guess we're busted, boss. I took the phone off the hook so I could have some quality time with Vic."

Wittica patted him on the shoulder. "That's all right, Mike."

"But please come in and have some coffee with us."

He nodded. "Okay."

"Hey, Vic!" Ryan shouted toward the kitchen. "It's Ron. He's stopped by to say hi and have some coffee with us."

"Great! Just ignore the mess!" came back the reply.

Ryan tilted his head in the direction of the kitchen, closing the door after Wittica stepped into the foyer.

"Nice place," he commented. "Very nice."

"All thanks to you guys," Ryan replied, leading him toward the kitchen, where Victoria greeted them.

"My, my, you look lovely even in the morning," said Wittica as Victoria gave him a welcome hug.

"Liar, but thanks anyway," she said, handing him a mug of steaming coffee. "Cream and sugar?"

Wittica shook his head. "No, thanks. Black will do."

They sat in the living room, sipped coffee, and talked amiably about their jobs, about their new life, about their plans this coming summer.

"Mike," Wittica said, "Did you guys ever pick up your hiking gear? I remember you telling me how much you miss the woods since moving down here."

Ryan frowned internally at the question and sensed he was being tested.

Victoria answered before Ryan got a chance to speak. "I bought part of the equipment during my lunch hour this past Thursday. But I still need a number of items—only I couldn't buy them alone. I was hoping to convince Mike to come with me today—that's if you won't make him work this weekend. Maybe we could even get a chance to break it in."

Wittica grinned. This time it looked genuine. "It's really up to him. How are you coming along on your project?"

"Pretty good," he said.

"So, are you on schedule?"

"I'll be ready Monday morning. I'm even expecting the first set of hardware to make the initial installation at the IRS later in the week."

Wittica gave him a curious look, but then said, "Right. I also have a little surprise for you. Gam Olson will be joining us. He'll bring along a few IRS passwords to really kick the tires of your VR system."

Ryan rolled his eyes. "I wasn't expecting him until Tuesday, *after* you and I got a chance to test-drive the system. Monday's our dry run. Tuesday's the real thing with Olson."

Wittica reached over and patted his shoulder. "Relax. It'll be fine. He knows that the system's still in development."

"In that case," he said, "I'll probably be heading into the office sometime this weekend to tune a few things."

Wittica shook is head. "I'd rather you didn't."

Ryan dropped his eyelids. "But, Ron, I need to make sure that—"

Wittica held up a hand. "I'm confident that your program's in good enough shape, Mike. I really want you to take the weekend off. You have a very pretty lady here who needs your attention. Sounds like she wants to go hiking."

Victoria smiled.

Wittica glanced at his Rolex, and stood. "Time for me to go."

They said their good-byes and he was gone.

Ryan and Victoria spoke out loud about taking a shower and headed into their bathroom. Although Ryan had been forced to activate the live video monitoring again, at least he knew the safe areas in their house to hold private conversations.

"How do you think it went?" she asked after turning on the shower.

"Time will tell," he said, taking her in his arms. "Right now we have to be very careful and play along."

She hugged him. "I'm concerned, Mike."

"So am I," he said. "So am I. But I'll be damned if I'm going to let those bastards screw us over. For now, just remember where not to walk around naked or say anything that you don't want to be heard by Big Brother."

She nodded. "What about the woman at the park?"

He shrugged. "If she wants to contact us again, I'm sure she'll find a way."

22

"I still don't like it," said Hausser, sitting in the passenger seat of Wittica's BMW after they had driven to his house, several blocks away from the Ryans'. "I'm sure I saw them at the park."

"Impossible. Your own man back at the office confirmed it. The Ryans had indeed been at home all morning. The guard saw me visiting them just now."

"Then something went wrong. What about the strange problems we've been experiencing with the video system? The guard also reported that all of the screens started showing Agi's wife fingering herself. And it just happens to coincide with the monitors going blank just before you showed up."

Wittica shrugged. "Agi's security system is flawed. We've been having network problems for the past few days. In fact, we need Mike Ryan to help us plug the security hole in our system."

"What about the missing video files?" asked Hausser.

"There are files missing from eleven engineers, Todd. Is that reason enough to go kill them all?"

Hausser leaned back on the seat, a handheld radio in his left hand. His men were still deployed near the Ryans' house, waiting for the order to go in and eliminate them. "I say we get rid of them anyway. We should also get rid of Agi and his wife."

"Damn, Todd! Listen to yourself. You just can't go in and start shooting all of my fucking engineers and their spouses! Whatever went down at the park this morning has *nothing* to do with Ryan, Agi, or anyone else on my staff. They were home, dammit! Your own video monitors show that, even with a few technical glitches that need to be ironed out. You have no reason to kill my people!"

"Something tells me that they're responsible."

"Well, you show me something more than just a hunch, and we'll go through with it. Otherwise, stay out of their lives."

"Then we'll have to call Aaron Shapiro."

Wittica pressed a button on the BMW's steering wheel and said out loud. "Shapiro, home."

The BMW's car phone recognized his voice and preprogrammed words, and dialed Shapiro's private number.

Shapiro picked it up after two rings, his voice clear through the German car's speakers. "Yeah?"

Wittica spent a couple of minutes explaining the situation and the difference of opinion between Hausser and him. "You can't kill them, Aaron. Mike and Agi are very good engineers, and there's zero evidence of any wrongdoing on their parts. Besides, killing them may give the FBI agent more reason to stick around. It might give them clues. And what if someone manages to escape and reach sanctuary at the FBI?"

"We can eliminate the Ryans in less than a minute, sir," said Hausser. "We're in position now with silenced weapons. There will be no mess like with the Pattersons. The Ryans will simply disappear. The Maghamis will also vanish within the hour."

Wittica exploded. "Jesus Christ, Todd! Listen to yourself! You're out of your mind! You have no evidence—no proof—that they have done anything wrong!"

"What do you know about evidence? Your just a—"

"That's enough," said Shapiro. "I want no action taken against the Ryans or Maghamis. Is that understood?"

Hausser remained looking straight ahead.

"Todd?"

Wittica pointed at the overhead microphone. Hausser ignored him and continued to stare out the window.

"I know you're probably blaming yourself for what happened this morning, Todd," said Shapiro. "But killing the Ryans and the Maghamis will not stop the FBI agent from investigating. And if anything should go wrong, it might pique her curiosity even more. There's no evidence to force us to take that chance at the moment. Are you with me?"

Hausser exhaled, and said, "Yes, sir."

"Now," Shapiro continued, "I want them followed everywhere they go. And I mean every-*fucking*-where. Are we also clear on that?"

"Yes," replied both in unison.

"Although I've been ordered to take zero chances, we can't just start killing our employees for fear that the FBI might contact them. That could make matters worse. Keep your heads and focus on your respective jobs."

"There's also the issue of Esteban," said Hausser.

"Yes," Shapiro said after a short pause. "It is most disappointing that he missed his chance this morning. And so did you, for that matter."

Hausser dropped his gaze for a moment. Then he said, "It won't happen again, sir."

"I want everyone in my house in two hours, including Rossini, Myrtle, and Esteban. Can you arrange that?"

"Yes, sir,"

Then the line went dead. Hausser called back his men, except for one, whom he left guarding the Ryans' household.

23

Karen Frost had observed the activity at the Ryans' house from inside an outhouse in front of a residential construction site across the street and down the block, where a taxi had dropped her off ten minutes before the Ryans arrived.

Her abdomen and middle back hurt her every time she breathed the putrid air oozing from the latrine. She really should have gone to a hospital and got X-rays to make sure that the multiple wounds she had received in the past few days had not cracked a rib or caused other internal damage.

But doing so required time—time the federal agent couldn't spare, time the Ryans didn't have.

Karen had tried to call Palenski's cellular phone after hiding here, but she had gotten his voice mail. Either the director had turned it off, which was unusual, or he was out of range. She had then tried his office with similar luck. And when she'd finally called his house, Palenski's wife had told her that the director was golfing this morning. He obviously didn't want to be interrupted.

Swell. He's golfing while I'm stuck in this shit hole.

She would try him again later.

Based on what she had observed through the ventilation slits on the sides of this plastic enclosure, Karen decided that the young couple had come very close to disaster, to following the Pattersons' footsteps. And Karen could have done little to prevent it. Her Desert Eagle .44 Magnum, albeit among the most powerful handguns in the world, was no match for the men who had left the two sedans and staked out the place. The strangers, who Karen suspected were well armed, had monitored their target in a way that wasn't obvious to the untrained observer. Three of them had pretended to be inspecting the property for sale across the street. The other

conspiracy.com

three had gathered around the opened hood of one of the sedans, pretending to be working on it.

Professionals.

Just like the sniper. Just like the two guns trying to flush her out into the open at Town Lake.

What Karen had seen convinced her that the Ryans had not approached SoftCorp with her message. That definitely left only one possible source of the leak of her meeting this morning: the Bureau.

But who?

It couldn't possibly have been Palenski. The director was a cowboy, like her, incapable of being corrupted. Maybe his line was tapped—though she couldn't think how. Palenski's phone-line scrambler was state-of-the-art.

Then how?

Karen shook her head.

Regardless of how, the fact was that the information she had given her superior was potentially compromised, meaning anything she had acquired through FBI credit cards was also compromised, like her rental car. Her apartment might still be okay since she had paid cash for it. Still, Karen made a mental note to move right away. In her business it paid to be paranoid.

The stench made her cough suddenly, and her bruised ribs felt like a hot claw raking her insides. She winced in pain.

Damn.

Ignoring her protesting body, Karen continued to watch the street, the Ryans' house, and the lone guard left behind in a third sedan parked a half block away. The rest of the team had been recalled, departing in the first two cars moments after the third sedan arrived to monitor the Ryan's activities.

She wished she could warn the Ryans about the surveillance. Although getting a rental had been a smart move on their part, minimizing the risk of surveillance, if they used the car at this moment, while the guard was outside, it could spell disaster for them.

She actually wanted to do more than just warn them. She wanted to talk to them, to carry out the conversation she had planned for this morning.

She also wanted to get the hell out of this stink hole. There had been a time in her life when she would have spent a day or more in here with no problem, especially since it provided her with the perfect place to relieve herself while on a stakeout.

But not anymore, she thought, her eyes scanning the street, her mind trying to figure a way to reach the Ryans without alerting the surveillance.

Then she spotted a sign on the front lawn across the street, and she smiled for the first time today, reaching for her cellular phone.

24

The somber looks painted on the faces of the men present conveyed the concern hovering in the room. The FBI probe had managed to escape a second attempt, and for a moment Aaron Shapiro wondered if the repeated misses were telling him that perhaps he should pack it up and get the hell out of town while he still could.

Of course, he knew he couldn't—not without jeopardizing the lives of his family, especially his kids, who his superiors in Washington were having tailed to discourage exactly this type of action.

Bastards sure know how to motivate people, he thought, sitting at the head of the table, struggling to pick up the pieces. His eyes landed on Esteban, the Hispanic man sitting next to Hausser. Esteban had not revealed his last name and Shapiro had not requested it. In fact, for all Shapiro knew, Esteban might not even be his real first name. All that mattered was that he had been sent by Washington to help solve the problem, but the problem was still unsolved, and in a way Shapiro blamed Esteban for missing the FBI agent this morning.

Medium height, athletically built, clean-shaven, Esteban leaned back in his chair, eyes noncommittal, inspecting the group before settling his gaze on the bottle of mineral water in his hands.

"So, Mr. Esteban," Shapiro said, legs crossed, hands on his lap. "What do you suggest we do next?"

"Wait," he answered, his eyes still on the bottle.

"*Wait?* Wait for *what*? For the FBI to storm our offices and shut us down?"

"She will surface, especially after the event in Washington. She no longer has the support of his people. She is alone."

Shapiro inhaled deeply. Roman Palenski, the director of the FBI, had been killed in an auto accident this morning at the same time that the local

FBI agent was supposed to have been assassinated. He knew his superiors in Washington were powerful, but he never imagined they were *this* powerful. The realization of their apparently unchecked power both comforted and frightened him. On one side, such a powerful network, capable of killing the director of the largest law-enforcement agency in the world, couldn't possibly be threatened in any serious way by a single agent. On the other hand, this network would easily dispose of someone like himself if he didn't prove valuable in their eyes.

Of myself and my entire family.

Shapiro took another deep breath, struggling to relax, frustrated at his inability to do so. "How long do you suggest we wait, Mr. Esteban?"

"As long as it takes."

"And I take it that *next* time—whenever *next* time might be—you will *not* fail?"

All eyes turned to Shapiro—from Hausser and his men to the fidgeting Wittica, the perspiring Myrtle, and Rossini, dressed in a designer jogging suit. Shapiro didn't care. He was fed up. The big man in Washington demanded perfection from him, so why shouldn't he ask the same of those around him, including this supposedly top-notch assassin?

"Mr. Shapiro, you seem quite obsessed with causing trouble, especially for someone with so much to lose. Perhaps I should call Washington and explain my displeasure with the way you're handling this crisis."

Shapiro clenched his jaw, his blue eyes locked with the stare of the Hispanic assassin. "Leave me alone with Mr. Esteban."

In unison everyone stood and followed single file out of the conference room. Wittica went last, giving his boss a concerned stare before closing the door behind him.

Shapiro slapped the table. "Just who in the *fuck* do you think you are to come down here and speak to me this way, and in front of my men! Do you know who I am?"

Esteban remained calm. In fact, he almost looked amused at Shapiro's outburst, which only kindled Shapiro's contempt for the hired assassin.

"My record speaks for itself," Shapiro added proudly. "And Washington knows it. Over ten years of loyal service, creating hundreds of millions in revenue, and never *once*—not once—causing trouble."

Esteban grinned. "You don't even know who you work for, do you?"

"I never had a need to know, and I don't want to know. I have a business arrangement that—"

"That ends this minute if you force me to contact our boss."

"I refuse to believe you."

"*Believe*, Mr. Shapiro. I'm the only reason you're still alive today. Wasn't the little trip you took this week enough warning that something is seriously wrong? That bad things could happen to you *and* your family unless this situation is rectified? Our boss is giving you one more chance in return for all of the years of good service. And that chance is me."

Shapiro didn't answer.

"A single phone call, Mr. Shapiro. That's all I have to make, and within the hour your beautiful daughters and your lovely wife will be on a plane heading south. My associates down in Mexico are tired of the local whores. They'd love to get their hands on a few pretty blondes with blue eyes. Just picture that for a moment, would you? A bunch of horny Latinos screwing your girls twenty times a day, forcing them to do things that even I find distasteful. And your wife . . . they'll probably make her fuck a *burro*."

Shapiro suddenly found it difficult to breathe. He gasped, then coughed, his hands clasping the end of the table, struggling for control.

Esteban reached for his cellular phone and began to dial a number.

The sight of the phone brought it all into perspective, draining his anger, replacing it with raw horror. "No," he mumbled. "Please. Don't."

The assassin finished dialing and pressed the unit to his ear.

"For the love of God! *Please* hang up that phone!" He stood but was shaking so badly that he tripped, landing on his side on the floor.

Esteban ignored him. "Yes . . . it's me," he said into the small unit. "The operation is moving forward . . . yes . . . within the next two days. . . . Yes, he has been most cooperative. . . . No . . . no need for that yet. . . . Yes . . . Good-bye."

Shapiro staggered to his feet, grabbing another chair, sitting down, burying his face in his hands.

"I've just bought your family two more days, Mr. Shapiro. Do I have your full cooperation?"

"Ye—yes. I . . . my entire team is at your disposal."

"That's better, Aaron—may I call you Aaron?"

Shapiro nodded.

"Good," Esteban said, smiling, patting the executive on the back. "Why don't you take a minute to pull yourself together and then call your people back in. We have a lot of work to do."

25

Karen Frost smiled as the police cruiser steered in front of the parked sedan. She checked her watch. It had been exactly nine minutes since she had called the number on the Neighborhood Watch lawn sign. This was indeed a good area to live in.

The sentry remained seated behind the wheel as two officers got out and walked up to the sedan, exchanged a few words with the driver, and pointed toward the entrance of the subdivision. Reluctantly, the sentry drove off. The police hung around for a minute or so, and then they too went their own way.

That was Karen's cue.

She stepped out of the outhouse, welcoming the fresh breeze as she walked toward the Ryan's house. She had to hurry. The surveillance would be back very soon.

26

Michael and Victoria Ryan sat in their new patio set on the far corner of the rear deck, facing the crystalline waters of Lake Travis. They had stepped outside shortly after taking their shower and putting on fresh clothes, deciding to continue their conversation outside away from any surveillance cameras.

"What are we going to do next?" she asked, dressed in jeans, a turtleneck sweater, and sneakers.

Ryan vaguely inspected the wrought-iron pattern of the table. A week ago he had enjoyed sitting out here, admiring his domain. But now all he could think of was finding a way to get far away from all of this, to break free, to head back to California, to start over.

"We stick to our plan," he said, wondering just how close they had come from disaster. But Wittica had seemed fine, even chatting casually over coffee, though he did ask a couple of suspicious questions. Then Ryan added, "We try to figure out as much as we can about those accounts, but in a very unobtrusive way. The knowledge might serve us well later on."

"How?"

Ryan shook his head. "I'm not sure. It certainly can't hurt us to learn as much as possible about this operation. That way we're playing with our eyes open."

She slowly nodded. "It actually levels the playing field. They know pretty much everything about us. We know very little about them."

Ryan grinned. "They *think* they know everything about us. Don't forget that we have already made them react to our moves. That's the first step toward gaining control of our situation."

They gazed into the distance for a moment. Then Victoria took his hands in hers. "Do we really know what we're doing?"

He raised his eyebrows and exhaled. Ever since Wittica had left, Ryan had been wondering the same.

"Mike!" Victoria screamed, pointing toward the side of the property. "It's her again!" Victoria stood and took a step back. Ryan did the same.

"FBI!" the red-haired stranger shouted, walking toward them, holding a badge high in the air. "Please! Stay where you are. I mean you no harm. Please!" Her voice was deep for a woman, and on the rough side, as if she had swallowed sandpaper.

Victoria turned toward the house, getting ready to make a run for it. Ryan was about to do the same when something held him back. He wasn't sure what it was. Perhaps it was the eye contact he had just made with the alleged FBI agent. Or maybe it was the strange feeling that something had gone terribly wrong at Town Lake and that she indeed had not intended to point her gun at them. Instead of moving away, Ryan reached for Victoria's hand and clasped it, keeping her next to him.

"What are you doing? We need to—"

"It's okay, Vic. She won't hurt us."

The FBI agent reached the steps to the deck, climbed them, and approached the young couple.

She offered the badge to Ryan, who took it in his hands. "I'm really sorry about the incident at the jogging trail," she said in a low voice.

Ryan compared the photo on the badge with the woman in front of him. Karen Frost. FBI special agent. Washington, D.C. In the picture she had brown hair and eyes, but it was definitely her. She stood a few inches shorter than Ryan's six foot, her green eyes staring directly at him. But it wasn't her face, framed by shoulder-length red hair, that jogged Ryan's memory. It was her stance, which conveyed the same strength he had seen in her on the TV monitor at SoftCorp weeks ago—the strength that matched her somewhat raspy voice. Ryan recalled that she had been talking to an elderly couple right before the guards showed up. He opted to hold back that information for now.

He showed the badge to Victoria, who stared at Frost quizzically. "You're the woman who bumped into me at REI."

The agent nodded. "Very observant, considering that the contact lasted but a few seconds."

"But your hair," said Victoria. "It was blond."

Karen tilted her head. "You'll make a fine eyewitness. The changes are part of the job."

"What do you want with us?" Victoria asked.

"We must talk, but not here."

"Why?" asked Ryan.

"Because of the surveillance," Karen said, quickly explaining what she had seen outside their home.

"So we are in danger," said Victoria, crossing her arms, looking at her husband.

Karen nodded while pocketing the badge. "And we don't have much time before they come back."

"I know a place where we can go," said Ryan.

"Where?" asked Karen.

"Do you like the outdoors, Agent Frost?"

27

The place was Bastrop State Park, roughly thirty minutes southeast of Austin. Ryan and Victoria had been very careful about telling the surveillance cameras inside their home about their hiking plans for the weekend, confirming what they had told Ron Wittica. Then they loaded up Victoria's Honda and headed for the park, where they would meet up with Karen Frost, who had to borrow their rented car since her vehicle had been compromised.

They met, as arranged, by the ranger's station. Ryan paid for a primitive camping site at the park's headquarters and followed the directions on the map to their spot, buried deep in the woods, beyond the more "civilized" sites, which had running water and electricity. But the Ryans preferred to rough it, feeling closer to nature that way. The federal agent, however, was obviously a city rat, sitting uncomfortably on the ground littered with pine needles. She regarded the Ryans, dressed in T-shirts, shorts, and hiking boots. They had already set up their tent and other gear. Ryan offered Karen a small bottle of water, which she readily accepted.

"That was a very close call back at Town Lake," Karen began, taking a sip of water, regarding the tall pine trees around them native to the Bastrop area. The afternoon sun streamed through openings in the canopy. Insects buzzed nearby. "Didn't mean to scare you off."

"What happened?" asked Ryan.

"A sniper," she said. "Someone tried to kill me at the meeting."

The Ryans exchanged a glance. "Who?" they asked in unison.

"The people who also killed one of my agents. The people you work for."

The Ryans stared at each other once more before Victoria asked, "What are you after?"

"Proof," Karen said. "I need evidence of wrongdoing."

R. J. Pineiro

"First my wife and I need to know what we're up against. Who is behind the triangle of the IRS, SoftCorp, and Capitol Bank?"

"That's *precisely* what *I* need to find out." The slender agent extended a thumb toward her own sternum.

Ryan shook his head in disbelief. "And you want *us* to risk our lives to get information for you? Since when does the FBI use innocent civilians to do its dirty work?"

"We use informants all the time," Karen said. "I can guarantee your protection."

Ryan laughed. "How can you protect me from those guards if I'm caught snooping around in my own building?"

"Both of you will obviously have to use caution."

Ryan glanced at Victoria, who asked, "What's in it for us?"

"Freedom," Karen replied.

Ryan looked away. They were in debt up to their eyeballs and couldn't simply quit their jobs and walk away without declaring personal bankruptcy, staining their financial reputation for years to come. SoftCorp and Capitol Bank would certainly ruin their careers as well, assuming they let them walk away in the first place. Ryan was worried that this shadowy network would eliminate them and make it look like an accident if they tried to get away. They were simply stuck. They both knew it, and Karen Frost knew it too.

"I know the situation that you're in," the federal agent said. "I know about the house, the cars, the new furniture—all bought with credit, which just happened to be financed by Capitol Bank. They've got you, don't they?"

Ryan closed his eyes. "Shit," he finally said. "Yes, they do. We knew something was wrong . . . but, damn, we didn't expect it to be *this* bad."

"Did they really kill one of your agents?" asked Victoria, her arms crossed, fear tightening her features.

Karen breathed in deeply before saying solemnly, "His name was Dave Nolan. He was a good husband and a father of three. He had a stellar FBI career, until . . . anyway, the answer is yes. They killed him, and they shot me twice this morning."

"How did you survive?" asked Ryan.

Karen Frost raised her T-shirt enough to expose the black vest she wore underneath. "Bulletproof. But the energy from the impacts knocked me around—which is what you saw. When I reached for my weapon, I was simply trying to defend myself against the sniper, or anyone else who might be trying to kill me. I used the weapon to create a panic. The innocent people among the crowd—including you two—fled, leaving behind those who wanted to terminate me."

"And the shots that we heard?" asked Ryan.

"I fired at two men sent there to force me back into the open."

"Back to the sniper," said Ryan.

Karen nodded, breathing with obvious pain.

"Are you hurt?" asked Victoria.

She shook her head. "Just sore. The rounds bruised my ribs and my middle back." She then proceeded to tell them what she had just seen outside their house, and how she had temporarily gotten the surveillance off the area.

Victoria stood, continuing to brace herself, staring into the distance while Ryan simply glared at the ground in disbelief, finally realizing just how close they had come to being killed.

"These people are ruthless," said Karen, explaining how they had murdered not just Dave Nolan but also his informant and her parents as well. She also told them about the Rubaker incident. Ryan realized that the federal agent was trying to open the communications channels by being upfront first, by showing them her cards, hoping to instill confidence, trust. Still, he didn't see how they had a chance of making it against this apparently powerful operation. If this network was killing FBI agents and their informants, how could the FBI possibly protect them?

Apparently out of choices, Ryan decided to level with Frost, revealing the existence of the video monitors in the control center. He told her how he had temporarily disabled the electronic surveillance in his home—an action that he now realized had provided them with a life-saving alibi. Ryan also described his trips through the SoftCorp network, the last of which had yielded key bank account information.

"Work with us," Karen said. "Help us destroy this operation."

"We are willing to cooperate," said Victoria, leaning against her husband. "But how can you guarantee our protection?"

"And don't insult us with your witness protection program, because that is not a life, that is imprisonment," added Ryan.

"There is a way," Karen said, "to guarantee your freedom and also accomplish my end goal."

"How?" Victoria asked.

She regarded the young professionals for a moment, then explained her plan.

28

Thirty minutes later, Karen Frost left the Ryans at the state park and headed back to Austin on Highway 71, silently praying that her plan would work.

Over four hours had passed since her last attempt to contact Palenski. Hoping that that was long enough for the director to finish his golf game, she reached for the cellular phone and dialed his private number at the Bureau. She frowned when the call rolled over to another extension and Russell Meek answered.

"Russ, Karen. Where is Roman?"

"Karen? I guess you haven't heard."

This wasn't good. "Heard what?"

A moment later she pulled over to the side of the road while keeping the cellular phone glued to her right ear, her vision tunneling. Cars rushed by on the highway.

"When did it happen, Russ?"

"This morning . . . at ten, on his way to a golf game. His bodyguards were also killed," said Meek, his voice strained with anxiety.

She closed her eyes, feeling a headache creeping into her temples.

Roman Palenski dead?

Reaching for self-control, she asked, "Did you catch the driver of the truck?"

"Slipped away in the confusion, and the truck had been reported stolen a few hours before by a local construction company."

"Dear God," she said, the realization that 10:00 A.M. in Washington was 9:00 A.M. in Austin slapping her across the face. "Russ?"

"Yeah?"

"The timing, Russ."

"What timing?"

"Roman was killed at the same time that I was shot this morning."

Silence, followed by, "*You* were shot?"

"During a meeting that I had set up with a potential informant."

"Are you okay? Are you hurt? Do you need assistance?"

"I'm fine. Just a little sore. I wore a Kevlar vest."

"You're taking way too many chances, especially with no backup."

"We've covered that before, Russ. I have to do it this way for now. I'm a target and that makes everyone around me a target, including other FBI agents."

"But that deviates from standard—"

"We've also gone over that, Russ. I know the manual calls for backup, but if you send it, I'll guarantee you that within a couple of days you'll just have more dead FBI agents on your hands—and on my conscience. I've got to do it solo. That way I'm harder to find and I can move faster, react faster. It's my best asset and it's paying off."

"Sure. You almost got yourself killed this morning."

"I took the appropriate precautions. Besides, I *am* getting closer."

"I won't fight you on this, Karen. For now, that is. But not because I think you're right. I don't want to make any changes so close to Palenski's death. Besides, any changes I make might get reversed by whoever the president appoints next."

Karen didn't touch that. She didn't feel that Meek was qualified to run the Bureau, and she suspected that Meek knew how she felt.

"About what you said," continued Meek. "Are you *implying* that you and Palenski were scheduled to be terminated simultaneously?"

She regarded the highway traffic. "I'm trained not to believe in coincidences."

"So you *do* think that there is a connection."

After another long pause, Karen said, "Yes. I believe someone wanted to eliminate the two people within the Bureau who were pushing hard on this investigation. I also believe there is a leak inside the Bureau. Aside from my informant, who I know is clean, only Palenski knew about the meeting this morning. Somehow someone heard our conversation, our plans, and decided to kill us both."

"Jesus, Karen! Do you realize what you're saying?"

She nodded, though no one could see her. "It means that these people are very powerful."

"I need proof," said Meek.

"I'm working on it."

"All right. Keep doing what you're doing. Palenski kept a small dossier on your activities. I know how to contact you if I need to get in touch with you, and you obviously know how to get a hold of me. Right now I need to contact the rest of the agents involved in covert operations. I need to make sure that all efforts continue to move forward during this transition period."

"Smart move," she said.

"And by the book. Good luck, Karen."

"Russ?"

"Yeah?"

"Watch your back. Careful who you talk to about my activities. Remember what I told you about a possible leak."

"I can take care of myself. It's *you* that I'm worried about. I'm very close to pulling the plug on the operation. Innocent people could have been killed this morning by the sniper."

"I'm handling it, Russ. I just need time to get you the proof we need to expose them."

The line went dead, and Karen Frost got back on the highway, reaching Austin twenty minutes later, and driving straight to her apartment by I-35, where she retrieved her stuff, including her FBI-issued hardware. She shoved it all in the back of the rented Mustang, and spent two hours driving through downtown Austin, making sure no one had followed her, before searching for a new home. She found a run-down apartment complex with a vacancy sign on Woodward Street, across from St. Edward's University, in south Austin.

Karen paid cash for one month's rent and got a one-bedroom unit on the second floor, where she dropped off her gear before heading back out again. She planned to run some surveillance over the weekend on Wittica and Shapiro with the hope of learning something.

29

"You want me to *halt* the operation in Austin, Senator?" asked Russell Meek, sitting across from Jack Horton in the rear of the senator's stretch limousine, which had picked up Meek outside his office ten minutes ago.

They had spent the time driving around town while discussing Palenski's death, its implications.

"I'd met with Palenski the day before his death, Russ. We had an agreement. He would play it straight with me from here on out and I would do my best to get him the funding he sought for his federal agency. He was going to dismantle that operation—and several others—and restart them again, but this time going by the book."

Meek leaned forward, his eyes blinking suspiciously. He remembered Karen's warning clearly, and for a moment wondered if Horton could be involved.

"He did?" Meek finally asked, to see where this was headed.

"You sound skeptical."

"You're not the one who worked for the man. I tell you, he deviated from the book as often as he changed underwear. That was his standard operating practice, and I was against the way he was handling the operations—the one in Austin in particular."

Horton nodded thoughtfully. "Palenski mentioned that. He also said that you ran most aspects of the agency for him, including the generation of the congressional reports."

Meek nodded, leaning back, gazing through the tinted windows at the Washington Monument in the distance as they drove up Constitution Avenue. "Look, I can pull back the agent running that investigation—in fact I've just spoken with her. I can also call back the agents in other covert operations Palenski was running off the book, and restart them with the appropriate staff and procedures. But that means *nothing* if the next presidential appointee is going to reverse that decision. I'd rather stay the course and create zero waves until the president finds a replacement. With luck, the next director will have a little more respect for the rules."

Horton grinned. "That's what I wanted to talk to you about."

Meek tilted his head. "You've lost me."

"I'll be meeting with the president for breakfast tomorrow. I was considering recommending that you be appointed as director of the FBI."

Meek leaned forward. "*What?*"

"I think your time has come, Russ. I've watched your work be presented by Palenski and have always been impressed by its level of detail, by its thoroughness, by your attempt to present the truth."

"Just trying to do my job, sir." Was this guy serious about making him director of the FBI?

"And the way that you've modernized the agency's computer systems, setting it up to fight the increasing wave of cyber crime . . . that alone is enough reason to get you promoted."

Meek expanded his chest. "I'd be honored, sir. But will the president go with your recommendation? You and he have been known to butt heads on occasion."

Horton smiled. "The president and I both enjoy a good fight, but we have the utmost respect for each other. He'll go with it. Not just because it's a smart choice but also because he doesn't want to be embarrassed if Congress doesn't ratify his nomination for director of the FBI."

Meek nodded. "I see."

"I control Congress," said Horton matter-of-factly. "My vote has a way of swaying my colleagues. So start packing, my friend. You're going upstairs."

"How can I ever thank you?"

"By being honest with me about all covert operations. I'm putting my neck on the line by selling your name not just to the White House but also to Congress. I'm taking a huge risk with you, Russ, and in return you will provide me with insight on all key covert operations—enough to make me feel comfortable that nothing is about to blow up in your face. See, after I do this, and make it public that I support you and your policies, your success will be my success, and your failure . . . well, you get the point. It is my job—and yours for that matter—to make sure that all FBI activities are done by the book, without violating our taxpayers' constitutional rights. I've been doing this from the outside by controlling the FBI budget. Now I get to do it from the inside as well, by promoting your career."

Meek decided that Horton was probably okay after all. The leak had to be elsewhere. "That's it?" he asked.

"That's it. I'm a straight shooter," said Horton. "My whole career's been based on straight deals. I need your complete assurance that the FBI will fall in line with my management style. I also need your personal guar-antee that this arrangement will remain between us. No one else must know. *No one*. If the press gets word of this—regardless of our good faith and best intentions to do the right thing for the nation—it *will be* misinterpreted. With the way the press loves to twist these things around, I do not wish for something like this to stain my career, especially in the coming year. In return, you will get my full support—and my gratitude."

Horton extended an open hand at Meek, who shook it.

"Now," Horton said. "About the operations . . ."

"Where do you want to start?" Meek asked.

"Let's start alphabetically," Horton said, smiling. "How about Austin?"

30

Karen Frost was tired, drained, as she made her way up the mountain in southern Colombia. She moved swiftly, following the rugged terrain, past clusters of trees, through a sea of lush ferns.

She paused, controlling her breathing in this thinner air, remembering the directions a villager down in the valley had given her two days ago, before she'd begun this arduous climb. It indeed amazed her what a few American dollars could buy in this country.

The money had also bought her a small sack of coca leaves, which the villager had shown her how to chew, slowly, one leaf every couple of hours, mixing it with her saliva for strength, making it last.

Although the powerful narcotic bolstered her stamina, it would also develop an addiction, which she'd have to break. But by then it would not matter. By then the former New York mafia thugs occupying the estate atop the mountain would have paid for their crime, for killing her husband. Escaping south of the border mattered little to Karen, who had dedicated her life to catching these people who felt they were above the law.

No one was above her cold and hard law, especially Mark's murderers.

She reached the perimeter of the estate, running across the manicured lawn like a shadow, scanning her surroundings with her silenced Beretta, finding no guards in sight— and why should there be any? The new tenants had an agreement with the Colombian government. Protection and anonymity in exchange for monthly deposits in certain bank accounts—in American dollars.

Then she had spotted them, the head of the operation and his top lieutenants, drinking coffee in the front room, beneath slow-turning ceiling fans. And she had fired at them, the multiple spitting sounds of the bulky silencer tapping the darkness, drowned by the sudden reports from a dying guard, his index finger pressing the trigger while aiming his machine gun at the ceiling, its muzzle alive with rhythmic flashes, the staccato gunfire echoing loudly in the night, hammering her eardrums.

Karen Frost sat up in bed, soaked in perspiration, reaching for her Magnum, flipping the safety, aiming it at the darkness in front of her.

Something had awakened her, and it wasn't the dream. It was—

There it was again. The sound of metal scraping against wood. Someone at the front door.

But who?

No one knew she resided here, not even Meek.

Did someone follow me?

Karen had gone beyond her usual precautions after leaving the Ryans' yesterday afternoon. She had spent most of Saturday checking up on Ron Wittica and Aaron Shapiro, inspecting their estates from a safe distance. Her professional habits told her that the best way to prevent another attack was by monitoring the activities of her enemy. She had spent Saturday night, as well as most of Sunday, doing surveillance on the enemy, and had finally left for her new apartment just a few hours ago, exhausted. And again she had abided by her training, taking almost two hours to get there, making absolutely certain that she had not been followed.

Then how did they find me?

Analyze later. Move.

And she did, rolling out of bed, glad that she had taken the precaution of sleeping with her clothes on, even her sneakers.

Clambering across the carpeted floor, she reached her bedroom door, which she had locked, following another professional habit.

Wood splintered in the living room, followed by hastening footsteps.

They're in.

Hiding behind an old dresser, she thumbed back the Desert Eagle's hammer just as the door to her bedroom flew open from a kick, swinging on its hinges. Karen leveled her weapon at the three shadows detaching themselves from the entryway, positioning their bulky figures in classic special forces fashion, keeping the muzzles pointed up to avoid sweeping each other's heads as they stormed in, then lowering them once in position, and firing in silenced unison at the bed.

A cloud of white exploded as the bullets ripped through the mattress, tearing at the floor beneath like an army of angered hammers.

Karen fired once, the sound deafening as the powerful Magnum round nearly decapitated the closest intruder before striking the man next to him in the back. Both men collapsed as she fired a second time at the third intruder, but he had jumped back into the hallway.

Karen scrambled to her feet, pointing the weapon at the wall, firing

R. J.   P i n e i r o

once, shifting the angle a few inches and firing again. Both rounds went straight through the wall, one finding its intended target.

The agonizing moan reached her through the loud ringing in her ears.

Karen moved cautiously, the Magnum over her left shoulder, the muzzle pointed at the ceiling.

Silence, sporadically broken by the soft gurgling moan of a man drowning in his own blood, spurting from a gash across his neck. His body sprawled in the hallway connecting her bedroom to the living room, the operative gave Karen a narrow stare. Anger mixed with surprise. He was young, perhaps in his early thirties. And rapidly dying.

She kicked the weapon away from him, though he made no attempt to reach for it. His lips quivering, he mumbled, "My legs . . . my arms . . . I can't feel them."

A moment later Karen understood why. In the twilight of the narrow corridor, she saw where the round had pierced through his upper back, exiting just above his left collarbone, nicking his chin.

"Easy," she said, glaring at the open doorway, weighing the odds of helping this dying stranger instead of preparing herself for a backup team. Doing so would require her to leave this man alone for long enough to die before she could retrieve any information.

Screams echoed hollowly from other units. The police would be here soon.

Tearing off the lower portion of his trousers, and shoving the cloth against the neck wound, temporarily stanching the blood flow, Karen leaned forward, cupping his chin, forcing him to look at her.

"It's over," she said. "Only I can help you now, but only if you help me."

"My legs . . . I can't—"

"Listen! I can get you help—get you the best surgeon to patch you back up. He'll have you walking in a month! But you need to help me. Who do you work for?"

The young assassin locked eyes with her. Fear had replaced the anger and surprise—the fear of dying, or worse, of spending the rest of his life as a quadriplegic.

"Time's running out," she said. "Spinal cord damage has its best chance of being reversed during the initial hours after the trauma. Help me and I will help you! How did you find me?"

"Received message from . . . Washington."

Washington?

"So you didn't follow me here? Someone told you how to find me?"

"We followed . . . you."

Karen was confused now. "Followed me? But you said you got a message from Washington."

"Yes . . . but, you see—"

The man's words were cut short by a bullet to the head.

A fourth assassin!

Karen rolled away, her peripheral vision spotting a figure in the doorway. A silent bullet punched a dime-sized hole in the plasterboard where she had leaned just a moment ago. Another pounded the carpet. A third round nipped the collar of her shirt, the near miss buzzing by like an enraged wasp.

Diving into the bedroom, she crawled behind the large dresser once more. This time, however, no one entered the room. Instead, she watched in disbelief as a pear-shaped object skittered over the rug, rolling under the bed.

Grenade!

Karen leaped forward toward the large windows facing St. Edward's University, her mind blank as she planted her legs against the carpeted floor, launching her body against the glass with all her might.

The impact stunned her. Glass shattered, fell on her as she punched through like a missile, only then remembering that she was on the second floor.

She fell as the grenade went off above her, the deafening blast blowing out the window frame, followed by flames and inky smoke. Then the trees and the bushes below swallowed her.

31

Dressed in the uniform of an Austin Police Department officer, Esteban Yanez rushed inside the room seconds after the grenade went off, the spotlight attached to his silenced MP5 submachine gun sweeping the charred bedroom, searching for the FBI agent.

His anger spiraled when he failed to find her. She had escaped.

Again!

"*Mierda!*" he cursed.

Rushing to what was left of the window, Esteban aimed the MP5 at the shrubbery below, but could see nothing but darkness through the limbs of a huge oak. No sign of Karen Frost.

He ran out of the room, leaping over the fallen men, and reached the hallway. Several people were peeking out of their units.

"Police! Stay inside your homes!" he shouted, waving a fake badge.

Everyone vanished, and Esteban ran toward the stairs at the far end, climbing down to the first floor a moment later, where Todd Hausser and another one of his men covered the lobby.

"Did you get her?" asked Hausser.

"No!" Esteban shouted, his anger growing by the moment. He had spotted Karen Frost Saturday night, when the federal agent had staked out a surveillance on Ron Wittica. This time around Esteban had been careful, giving her the credit she deserved, biding his time, following her as he would have a professional operative, waiting for the right moment to strike. And she had still managed to escape.

Damn!

"Where is she?" asked Hausser, confused.

"She jumped out of the window! Go! Go and find her!"

Hausser and four of his men, also dressed in APD uniforms, turned to go outside.

"Wait!" Esteban shouted. "Todd, you and I will search for her. The four of you," he said, pointing at the muscular guards accompanying them. "You go back upstairs, plant the stuff, look for anything that might help us, and also get the bodies out of there! Now go! You have less than ten minutes before the police arrive!"

Before waiting for a reply, Esteban ran outside, breathing in the cool night air, cursing the obstinate federal agent.

32

Karen Frost ran like never before. She had lost her Desert Eagle during the fall and now clutched the compact Colt .45 pistol. Her instincts commanded her to retreat, to reach a safe hideout, to rest. Her right ankle burned from the fall. She had not broken it, but she had certainly twisted it enough for it to bring tears to her eyes every time she put weight on it.

But her survival instinct forced her to ignore the pain. In her years with the Bureau she had been punched, kicked, shot, and stabbed. Now she could add falling from a second-story window and almost getting blown up by a grenade to her repertoire.

The cool air tickled her nostrils as she filled her lungs, getting oxygen into her system, for a moment wishing for some of those coca leaves she had chewed in Colombia. She cut into the woods separating the St. Edward's University campus from I-35, slowing down after putting what she judged to be a hundred feet of vegetation between her and any potential pursuers.

Now it was time to wait, to listen—and to catch her breath and check herself for any other damage.

Her fingers ran up and down her body, feeling for anything that might resemble a stab, or a gash, or anything else that could cause bleeding. Her training told her that the adrenaline rushing through her veins would attenuate pain, which could be deadly if a wound bled profusely and she couldn't feel it.

She found a cut on her left leg, just above the ankle, now realizing that she had not twisted it after all. A stick—something—had stabbed her during the fall.

Karen felt the blood-soaked sock and frowned, quickly removing her sneaker and sock, and tying the wet sock around the wound, applying pressure against the inch-long gash.

Despite the wound, Karen considered herself lucky, having survived against four armed assassins without incurring a critical injury. The branch and the bushes had cushioned her fall, though she would certainly feel the bruises in the morning, compounding the ones she had received in Town Lake.

Slow down.

Karen nodded to herself while putting the sneaker back on and listening for possible threat. She had to slow down, take a day to rest, to regain her strength. Rest was a weapon, as powerful as the Desert Eagle she had lost in the shrubbery.

But then another thought entered her mind. Her apartment was probably being searched at this very—

The laptop!

She felt as if a two-ton truck had just landed on her shoulders at the thought of those men finding her laptop. Although the mobile computer system was protected by a series of passwords, someone with the right tools would be able to break in, access her Internet logs, electronically retracing her footsteps as she had searched for the right informant from SoftCorp and Capitol Bank.

The Ryans.

Karen had to warn them—had to pull them in. If the criminal ring managed to break her laptop's encryption, it would be just a matter of time before they learned about Karen's selection process, about her connection with the Ryans.

She also had to call Meek. Although the information from the dying assassin had been somewhat confusing, he *had* mentioned Washington. Someone in Washington had indeed betrayed them. And that someone was probably also responsible for Palenski's death.

Priorities.

First warn the Ryans.

The maimed body of Dave Nolan flashed in front of her, amidst the cedar trees and tall grass. She had to warn the Ryans. She had to . . .

Karen Frost began to feel light-headed, dizzy. Her thoughts grew cloudier. The woods began to whirl around her, like a bad dream—only it wasn't. Her body was giving in, falling victim to the abuse, the neglect, the physical stress. Maybe it was a delayed reaction from the gunshots. Or maybe it was because of how little food she had consumed in the past day. Or maybe it had been the fall, or the blood loss, or . . .

Her vision tunneling, Karen struggled deeper into the woods, realizing she was about to black out, crawling beneath a baby oak, beyond knee-high underbrush, ignoring the cuts, the scrapes, her tired mind following a single directive.

Hide.

And she did, just as the world around her spun uncontrollably, before all went dark.

33

Orion Yanez seldom lost his patience. There was something about spending the last fifteen years of his life away from his beloved homeland while building an empire in America that taught a man how to wait for the right opportunity to strike. And he had applied every rule he knew toward the protection of this well-oiled machine he had created over the past decade and a half—protection that required the immediate elimination of FBI Agent Karen Frost. Yet neither Shapiro's people nor the resourceful Esteban had been able to do the job. And Horton's attempt to get additional information from the FBI had proved fruitless. Apparently Karen Frost had grown quite paranoid, withholding information from her superiors on her whereabouts.

And why wouldn't she, he mused. *The last time she confided in someone at the FBI she was ambushed.*

Orion closed his eyes and took another sip of coffee, the strong, steaming brew relaxing him. He had to keep his head, just as he had done for so many years.

Up to now he had been using his own people to try to eliminate the maverick agent. Now he would enroll the help of the local law enforcement system to eliminate her—just as Castro had done when labeling his political enemies counterrevolutionary, convicting them, and then executing them.

It was time to apply *real* pressure.

book four

Crisis

When written in Chinese, the word crisis
is composed of two characters. One
represents danger and the other represents
opportunity.

—John F. Kennedy

Ryan had modeled his first official revision of the IRS's database access program on the solar system, only *his* solar system consisted of hundreds of planets, not just nine—and each with multiple moons—circling a single star, which represented the innermost database of the Internal Revenue Service. The planets, like the Earth-like representation of the SoftCorp network Ryan had hacked through last week, symbolized the many networks that would be of interest to the IRS's Internal Audit Division.

IAD Agent Gam Olson had pulled up to SoftCorp headquarters on time at 8:30 A.M. on Monday morning. Ron Wittica, however, was nowhere in sight, and neither was Agi Maghami. Ryan had decided to run the demo alone with Olson and bring Wittica and Maghami up to speed later.

Ryan had spent the past hour talking Agent Olson through the basic steps of their VR run, explaining what he would see, how to navigate, how to issue passwords, how to control his cyber agents, and insisting that during this initial run they remain together in case something went wrong and Ryan had to fine-tune the code.

"And if for some reason you begin to feel nauseated, just close your eyes and the feeling will pass," Ryan added. "Ready?"

Gam Olson nodded.

They jacked in.

"Wow," Olson said, revealing his first emotion since Ryan had met him. "This is . . . incredible!" The IAD agent floated next to Ryan over the galactic scene, complete with a backdrop of dozens of galaxies and millions of churning suns. "Amazing!"

Ryan grinned, staring into his cyber universe, into the stars burning with incredible realism, like a sea of candles, thanks to the digital footage he had downloaded from the Hubble telescope directory of NASA's Web page. Jacking into a run-of-the-mill VR environment for the first time was quite an experience for the average person. But doing so in Ryan's system, which was about the best among the VR environments to date, made it an unforgettable event.

"Pretty cool, huh?" Ryan said. "And quite practical as well."

"It really looks like I'm in outer space."

"That's the intent. The more realistic the experience the better the degree of immersion. On a scale from one to ten, I'd say we've achieved a degree of immersion of around seven or eight—as close as it can get to being there. Now, do you recall what I told you earlier?" Ryan turned to see his companion. The system displayed Olson as a metallic red figure. Eventually, each IRS agent would have his or her own custom suit. Behind them were two MPS agents, who would accompany them through this run. In the not-too-distant background, Ryan kept MPS-Ali ready to spring into action on demand.

"You said to look and blink, right?"

"Correct. The rest is pretty much automatic. The system will govern speed and the best approach route to your destination. We're using technology similar to the one used in fly-by-wire systems and smart helmets in fighter jets.

"So, the closer we get to the sun, the higher the security clearance required, right?"

"That's right. The outer planets are full of information, but are also public, requiring no access password. The middle planets require basic access passwords, like to enter a state database to get driver's license information or traffic violation history. The inner planets require more elaborate passwords to enter databases containing credit information, medical history, and even criminal records. In the middle is the hardest network to penetrate without a password, the Internal Revenue Service. Speaking of passwords, Wittica said that you would provide them today."

"That's right. I've got them all memorized."

"Good. Let's stretch the system's legs by using it to assist you on the first case you brought today."

Ryan watched Olson giving direction to an agent, an expert system designed to track the child support payments of one George Jerome Lewis from El Paso, Texas Mr. Lewis claimed child support payments on his income tax returns for all of last year, but his ex-wife, living in Houston with George's three children, claimed that he had not paid her a penny during the second half of last year and therefore had not reported that income on her own tax return. Someone was lying and it was the job of the IRS's Internal Audit Division to figure out who.

The expert system guided them at the speed of virtual light through the outer planets, past the middle planets, across the asteroid ring designed to mark the beginning of the inner planets, and finally to a planet that resembled Saturn, except this one only had two rings, flaming with colors, which expanded over the planet to form a hazy double atmosphere. The planet represented the computer network for the State of Texas Child Support Division. The atmospheric rings resembled two separate layers of security that anyone wanting access to the system had to go through. Unlike the relatively small and far less crowded SoftCorp network, the surface of this planet reminded Ryan of the Death Star in the *Star Wars* trilogy, crammed with structures, all visible from virtual outer space. The planet, of course, symbolized the thousands of offices and processing centers linked together in a huge network across the entire state of Texas.

Ryan was impressed with the clarity of the image, again thanks to his decision to merge actual footage with Java code and his C++ code.

Olson issued a silent password to the agent so that it could enter the first atmospheric ring. He followed with a second password, and the haziness dissolved, exposing an incredible level of activity below, like a global metropolis during rush hour. Unbeknownst to Olson, the expert system kept a temporary copy of each password, which Ryan's own MPS-Ali accessed a millisecond after the IRS agent had issued them.

Olson began to gather information from the database, using the expert system to accomplish in less than one minute what usually took him a half a day. The record from Mr. George Jerome Lewis indicated that he had mailed his payments just as he had claimed in his tax forms. Now it was time to check the receiving end to determine where the funds had gone. A search through the credit records of the former Mrs. Lewis yielded a single checking account with Bank of America. At Olson's request, the expert system took them to the network of Bank of America, a Jupiter-sized planet bordering the asteroid ring. Another password got them access to the bank's records, but in read-only mode. They could browse, but they could not alter any records. The expert system retrieved the bank records of the former Mrs. Lewis, who, as stated in her tax returns, showed child support deposits for only the first half of the year. Olson spent another minute reviewing the credit report and other financial information on her.

"Looks like both might be telling the truth," commented Ryan, secretly gathering passwords by the minute.

"One isn't," Mr. Ryan. "And I intend to find out who."

They headed to Mr. Lewis's bank in El Paso, Texas—a tiny moon in one of the middle planets—accessing it with the same password Olson had used to get into Bank of America. Apparently the financial industry had issued master passwords to the IRS for their convenience.

Using another one of SoftCorp's expert systems, Olson extracted vital information from the cashed checks. All checks had been mailed on time into the Lewis's law firm, Pryor, Jensen, and Associates out of Dallas, Texas. But the former Mrs. Lewis claimed never to have received the checks for the second half of the year.

"We're getting closer, Mr. Ryan," said Olson. "And that's only after ten minutes using your system. Very impressive."

Under different circumstances, Ryan would have felt proud of this early accomplishment, feeling that he was earning his high salary and other compensations. But not today, not when his wife's and his own life were at stake. "Thanks," was all he managed to say.

"Now it's time to go to the IRS. Let's review the records of Pryor, Jensen, and Associates."

Ryan's heartbeat rocketed. Olson was taking him inside the sun, into the core of America's tax system.

It required four different passwords, the last one thirty characters long. A moment later they made it beneath the sizzling surface, which would have roasted any unapproved visitor with a serious retaliation zap to the hacker's system—or to the head if the hacker happened to be wearing a head-mounted display.

And MPS-Ali had intercepted every password.

Ryan suddenly found it difficult to focus. He wanted to terminate this session and launch a new one solo, along with his pugilist ally. The passwords would give him enough privilege to scrutinize the activities between the IRS and SoftCorp. It would also allow him to visit the account numbers he had acquired last week.

Olson, an old hand at the IRS, searched through the records of the Dallas law firm, finding the Lewis file.

"Where are the checks for the last six months of the year?" asked Ryan.

"Mr. Lewis's bank shows them cashed by this firm, yet the firm denies it ever got them—at least that's what they reported to the IRS."

"So what are we doing next?" Ryan asked.

"You'll see."

Olson, who was rapidly growing comfortable with the system, found the bank used by the suspect law firm and then dispatched an expert system to track down bank transactions. Ryan's system performed beautifully, interfacing flawlessly with the expert system even though it had left the IRS environment to hunt down the bank. A moment later, the expert system returned with the information. The law firm, it appeared, had indeed cashed all of the checks for the previous year, but the funds for the second half of the year had gone to a different account than the checks for the first half of the year. Also, no checks had been written to the former Mrs. Lewis for the second half of the year.

"So they're at fault?" asked Ryan, fascinated by the process, and by the ease in which the IRS could probe into anyone's lives, now assisted by this handy VR tool.

"The plot thickens, Mr. Ryan. Why would the checks for the questionable second half of the year go to a separate account?"

Ryan regarded the relative brightness of the surrounding sun, dimmed by the layers of protection provided by Olson's multiple passwords, like stacked layers of tinted glass. No one but those with this quad-ply shield could endure the harsh environment Ryan had created for the innermost core of the Internal Revenue Service. "I can't think of a good answer."

"The reason, Mr. Ryan, is probably the same reason why the former Mrs. Lewis was able to afford, in the second half of the year, a new Lexus SUV—even though she had not received this vital income."

"What do you mean?"

Olson issued a command and the expert system replied by opening a holographiclike file in front of them. It contained the divorcee's financial and credit record. Her regular bank account couldn't explain how she afforded a forty-thousand-dollar vehicle, certainly not without the extra income provided by those missing checks.

"Unless she's now with someone else."

"If she is, she hasn't reported the income, nor has she moved to a new address. And the vehicle loan is under her name, but with a bank other than the one she uses regularly."

"But that's not unusual," said Ryan. "Sometimes people use different financial institutions for their car or home loans than their regular bank." Of course, in the case of the Ryans, everything was with Capitol Bank.

"True, but what's most unusual—in case you haven't noticed yet—is that the car loan is with the same Dallas bank used by the law firm."

"So," Ryan said. "You believe that Mr. Lewis sent his payments on time to the law firm. But for the second half of the year, the former Mrs. Lewis has gotten a secret deal going with the law firm, getting them to use their connections with their bank to finance her car while also claiming that she had not received a penny from her ex-husband."

"I think it's safe to say that the former Mrs. Lewis has been playing both sides of the fence, Mr. Ryan."

"But . . . but isn't that too obvious? Don't they run a high risk of getting caught, just like you did now?"

"No," replied Olson. "This is one of many cases we *never* get to because of the sheer volume, and her law firm knows it. Tracking this one down would have taken me and another agent probably a couple of days. But with your system I was able to do it in less than . . ."

"Fifteen minutes," said Ryan, checking the system clock.

They jacked out, both blinking rapidly when sunlight stung their eyes.

Ryan set his HMD on the desk, next to the workstation, Olson did the same. For the first time since he'd met him, Ryan saw a smile on the IRS agent's face.

"Very impressive, Mr. Ryan. Very impressive indeed."

"Thanks, but my job was merely interfacing the many expert systems into my virtual-reality environment."

"I saw what Wittica's expert systems could do before you got here, Mr. Ryan. While I'm sure that their systems were quite advanced, I could never figure out how to use them. They weren't user friendly, unless you happened to have a Ph.D. in computer engineering. What you've done— and done *very well*—is insulate me, the user, from all of the technogarbage that I could care less about so I can focus on doing my stuff. Good job, sir."

"Thanks," Ryan said.

"Are we getting the first system this week?"

"Yep. Did you get my E-mail on the networking requirements?"

"It's all ready, Mr. Ryan. A conference room has been converted into a VR room per your specifications."

"Good. Your initial system arrived over the weekend. I'm loading it in the trunk of my car in the next hour. I was planning to make a run to your building either this afternoon or tomorrow morning to install it. It's pretty small. Just a PC, the interfacing cables, and these HMD helmets."

"Great," said Olson, extending an open palm at Ryan. "Give me a call before you head over there so I can be expecting you. I'll have to escort you into the building."

"No problem."

"And again, good work. I'll call Mr. Wittica personally to express my satisfaction with your VR environment and with your professionalism."

Then he was gone, leaving Ryan gazing at the countryside extending beyond the smoked-glass windows.

Ryan smiled at the knowledge that he now possessed the electronic keys to access the core of the Internal Revenue Service's network.

That's where the trail begins, he thought, recalling all of the information he had gathered to date. The trail continued through SoftCorp, where, as Ryan had discovered on his last hacking excursion, his corporation was receiving far more money than they were reporting to the government. And that money went into certain accounts at Capitol Bank. Now he needed to see the next section of the trail: what happened to the money after it reached Capitol Bank? Where did the money go? Overseas?

Ryan wondered how Victoria was doing gathering passwords for his next hacking expedition.

2

Victoria got to Rossini's staff meeting early, a very risky plan forming in her head to copy the information on her boss's Palm Pilot V handheld computer, where she'd recalled seeing a directory containing passwords and other relevant information that might be useful to Ryan.

The conference room was located next to Rossini's office. It could be accessed either from the executive area's lobby or from Rossini's office. The door connecting to the latter was half-open.

As Victoria sat down near one end of the long mahogany table, Rossini stuck his head through the opening.

"Are we starting already?" he asked. The meeting didn't start until 10:30 A.M.

"I'm a little early," she said, winking at him. "Just making sure I got a seat next to you."

He smiled. "I'll be right there."

Since there wasn't prearranged seating—except for Rossini, who always sat at the head of the table—Victoria had selected the seat just to the right of her boss, who joined her a moment later, sitting next to her, patting her forearm, and setting down his Palm V and a binder in front of him.

"How was your weekend?" he asked.

"Noneventful. Yours?" she replied, her eyes briefly looking at Rossini's Palm V.

"I thought about you," he said, putting a hand over hers.

Victoria didn't push him away, but didn't withdraw her hand either. Her plan hinged on distracting him for long enough to swap Palm Vs with him, and she could only think of one thing that would distract this womanizer.

"Have you gotten a chance to think about our chat last week?"

Before she got a chance to reply, his assistant walked in. "Mr. Rossini, you have a call on line three."

He quickly moved his hand away and nodded. The assistant walked away, and Rossini winked at Victoria. "Don't go anywhere."

The moment he left, Victoria swapped Palm Vs with him, and began to peck away, browsing through his system—all the while half listening to Rossini mumbling away on the phone.

Her hands got clammy as she reached the same directories she had spotted last Thursday, right before he had made a pass at her. She beamed over to her Palm V the file with passwords, one with personal data, another with account numbers, and a fourth with miscellaneous information. She got so caught up in what she was doing that she didn't hear Rossini hanging up and returning to the conference room, catching her with his Palm V in her hands. Of course, unless Rossini paid close attention at the information on the tiny screen, he wouldn't notice the swap because on the surface both units were identical.

Victoria set the Palm V on the table, about a foot away from her own. She then stood, walking up to the front of the table to meet him, her heart pounding.

"About your proposal . . ." she said, glancing at the closed door at the other end of the conference room, making sure that no one was going to walk in on them. She positioned herself such that her body blocked his view of both Palm Vs.

A big smile spread across his tanned face. "Did you get a chance to think it over?"

She nodded, not sure if she was doing the right thing, but seeing no other option to temporarily distract him. Besides, this job was now very short-term given recent events. She decided to play it out, figuring that Rossini would not be able to accomplish much more than a kiss while in this conference room. She leaned back against the edge of the table, placing her palms on the smooth mahogany surface, directly in front of the Palm Vs.

"And?"

"And I think I'm ready to take the next step."

He reached under the table and pressed a button. Victoria heard the door locks snapping and her heart reached her throat. *What is he going to—*

Before she could react, Rossini moved onto her, wrapping his arms around her, kissing her. Victoria was momentarily startled, but controlled herself, forcing her lips apart, letting his tongue explore her mouth. She cringed when feeling his hands groping down her sides, sliding under her skirt. Instead of using her hands to push him away, she used her left hand to return the embrace while the right one reached behind her and fumbled to swap the Palms.

The moment she accomplished that, she tried to push him away, but gently, not wanting to arouse any suspicions—though she could already feel she had aroused something else.

Rossini kept his hands tight on her, a finger fiddling with the elastic of her panties while pressing his groin against her.

"Stop . . . Angelo . . . please . . ."

He moved from her lips to her left ear, nibbling her lobe, a finger brushing against her pubic hair. "I thought you wanted this . . . to promote your career."

Her skin goosebumped at his fondling. Then she said, "I do . . . but not *here.*"

"Door's locked, baby," he said.

"I'm afraid of . . . oh, God . . . stop." He moved his fingertips in slow circles, making her shudder. She was rapidly losing control, feeling warmth spreading between her legs.

"Besides," he whispered into her ear, "we have a few more minutes before—"

"Tonight," she said, forcing control, swallowing hard, pushing him away with resolve.

He smiled, removing his hands. Giving her a final kiss. "You're beautiful."

She didn't reply, embarrassment setting in.

"I'll be working late," he added, before licking his fingers while winking.

Feeling a heat flash, Victoria closed her eyes, dizziness clouding her mind, wondering what in the hell she had done. This man had had his hands on her!

Damn, Vic. Are you out of your mind? Was that really necessary? What are you going to tell Michael? Should you tell him anything at all?

"You look a little pale, Vic," Rossini added. "Why don't you go and freshen up before the meeting?" He patted her rear.

Victoria braced herself and took a deep breath. "I'll be right back."

"After a while it'll become second nature," Rossini said. "You'll learn to enjoy moments like this and then go home and also enjoy your husband. You'll see how terrific it is to have it both ways."

She nodded. *Right.*

"You have a lot of growing to do at this firm, Vic, and I'm very excited about helping you get there."

Her defenses momentarily down, Victoria just managed another nod—though she did have the presence of mind to snag her Palm V before heading out the door.

Rossini smiled and unlocked the door. "You bring that everywhere?"

Somehow she managed to flash him a smile while saying, *"Everywhere."*

"Can't wait to see what you do with it tonight," he replied.

She forced a laugh and stepped out. A few of her coworkers headed toward the conference room. Victoria smiled, though deep inside she felt they could see right through her. She received cordial smiles in return.

Going to her office instead of the restrooms, closing the door behind her, Victoria quickly E-mailed the files to Ryan before heading back to the conference room, swinging by the ladies' room on the way.

As the staff meeting droned on, Victoria Ryan had to put up with the occasional rubbing of Rossini's feet up and down her legs under the table, making her wish she had used another tactic—*anything* but this—to swap back the Palm Vs.

She had certainly unleashed a demon this morning, and she wasn't certain how she was going to control it.

3

Karen Frost woke up with the worst headache of her life. Not certain where she was, the federal agent sat up on the leaf-littered ground, staring at her surroundings, memories slowly creeping back.

The termination team . . . the fall . . . running in the woods . . . the laptop . . . the Ryans . . . I have to warn them!

She staggered to her feet, feeling dizzy, light-headed, grabbing on to a nearby branch for support, to steady herself, to regain focus. The throbbing from the cut above her left ankle made her wince, but at least she could put weight on the leg. She checked herself, grimacing at her soiled jeans, at the dried blood on the bottom of the left leg of her jeans, at the torn cotton jacket.

What do you expect after falling from a second-story window into trees and bushes?

She looked at her watch. Monday, 10:50 A.M.

Damn, I feel like shit.

She took a step, carefully, her senses slowly coming around, her eyes finding the Colt .45 pistol by her feet. She remembered losing the Desert Eagle .44 Magnum during the fall, running a hand over the empty chest holster anyway, perhaps hoping for a miracle.

Karen frowned. Not only had she lost her Magnum but also her cellular phone, preventing her from calling the Ryans right away.

Shoving the Colt in her ankle holster, she moved away, reaching the edge of the woods, peering through the shrubbery at her apartment complex, wrapped in yellow police tape. She contemplated her next move. Part of her training told her to head back to her apartment—the last place that her enemy would expect her to go.

Do the unexpected, turn the tables, perhaps capture and break a sentry who may have been left behind guarding the place.

She shook her head. Not only was she too damned tired to do that but doing so would consume time—time the Ryan's didn't have.

But she also needed to do something about her appearance. She could not be seen in public this way. Although her cotton jacket was a mess, the black T-shirt she wore underneath was in good shape. She used her pocketknife to turn her jeans into shorts, and again as a mirror to clean her face with her own spit, rubbing off grime with the cotton jacket. She sat down, inspecting the cut over her ankle, using her saliva and the jacket to clean it enough to avoid attention. She would have to disinfect it later. Last, she cut a long strip of white cloth from the back of the jacket and wrapped it around her head, like a jogger's sweatband.

She followed the tree line until it reached St. Edward's University and headed down Woodward, pretending to be a jogger, keeping a slow pace, turning left on Congress Avenue, ignoring the throbbing in her temples, in her head, reaching a small strip mall at the intersection of Congress and Oltorf. She went into a discount department store and emerged a moment later wearing a new pair of jeans, a clean T-shirt, and even a new cotton jacket, all courtesy of the four hundred dollars in cash tightly packed inside her money belt. Walking across the street, she found a public phone and called a taxi. While she waited, Karen called Ryan, but the computer engineer wasn't at his desk. Afraid to leave him a message in case it got intercepted, Karen decided to call Victoria instead, but she was in a staff meeting until noon. She hung up, cursing her bad luck.

The taxi arrived five minutes later, and Karen gave him directions to SoftCorp, offering the driver an extra ten bucks if he got her there fast. Karen Frost had to hurry. It was just a matter of time before they broke into her laptop and extracted the information that would seal the Ryans' fate.

4

Ron Wittica munched on a taco while glancing over Agi Maghami's shoulder as his subordinate ran a series of password-snatching programs through the laptop they had received early this morning from Aaron Shapiro. It had been found in the apartment occupied by the FBI agent who had been probing their affairs. Shapiro knew that inside the hard drive could be additional clues to the FBI's ongoing investigation.

It was just past eleven in the morning, but Wittica had already devoured two catered sandwiches. Tension always made him hungry.

"There," Maghami said, tapping the keys and pausing, then pointing at the laptop's screen. "I'm in. Where do you want to go first?"

Wittica put the sandwich away, thinking of the recent cyber break-ins. "Let's check the Internet log." If the FBI had been responsible for some of those breaches in the process of trying to acquire information, then the Internet activity would be logged in the system's Web browser directory.

They spent the following thirty minutes retracing Agent Karen Frost's Internet excursions. The agent had explored Capitol Bank's Web page, accessing the employees' roster, but without opening any of the files profiling each employee.

"She must have been just browsing through the names," Wittica said, grabbing a soda and taking a couple of sips.

Maghami nodded. "Then she accessed our company's public Web page and performed a similar browse through the names of our employees . . . and she did open one. . . ."

"Michael Ryan," said Wittica, his eyes glued to the laptop's plasma screen.

"Yes . . . and then she returned to Capitol Bank and opened the file for his wife, Victoria Ryan."

"Damn, Agi," said Wittica crossing his arms. "You don't think that the FBI contacted—"

"Michael and Victoria both went to Stanford, right?"

"Yes," replied Wittica. "Why?"

Maghami clicked to another Web site visited by Karen Frost. It was Stanford University, where she had apparently gotten special privileges to access the school records and anything else they had on file on the Ryans. Then Agent Frost had accessed their credit records.

"Sounds like the FBI is building up a dossier on them," offered Magh-ami. "I saw that in a movie. First they research their background and then they approach them."

Wittica wasn't liking this one bit. Perhaps Hausser's hunch on the Ryans had been correct after all. Perhaps they had been at Town Lake that Saturday morning. Perhaps Ryan had somehow managed to modify the video files, which would explain why there were so many problems with the video system that same day.

"What were the dates of the Internet incursions?" Wittica finally asked, feeling sick.

"The Internet accesses span almost three weeks. The last access was done this past Wednesday."

"Which," said Wittica almost to himself, "was the day before Mike's illegal breach—the one where your sentinel caught him and zapped him."

Before Maghami could say another word, Wittica patted him on the back. "Not a word about this to anyone, Agi. You've done us a great ser-vice, and Aaron and I will be rewarding you very soon."

Wittica grabbed the phone and called Hausser, urging him to meet him in front of Ryan's office. Then he left the room, racing down the hallway, reaching the elevators, opting to take the stairs up to the third floor. By the time he arrived in front of Ryan's office, breathing heavily, Hausser and two of his men were already waiting for him.

Hausser used his master key to unlock the door and everyone rushed inside. But Ryan wasn't there.

Wittica checked his watch. It was 11:30 A.M. "Where is he?"

"The rest rooms," said Hausser to his men. "Check them."

As the guards ran off, Wittica dialed the security desk in the lobby, ordering them to detain Ryan. The guard informed him that Mr. Ryan had checked out some equipment just a minute ago.

Wittica hung up, staring out the windows, scanning the parking lot below. "There!" he shouted. "He's by his car!"

While Hausser scrambled off in full gallop, Wittica dialed the lobby again. "He's outside, in the parking lot! Do not let him drive away!"

He hung up and was about to follow Hausser when he stopped and doubled back to the phone. He had to reach Angelo Rossini immediately.

5

Call it a sixth sense. Call it something else. Whatever it was, it made Ryan turn toward the front of the building after loading the VR hardware and software in the trunk of his Boxster. That's when he spotted two security guards running in his direction.

He froze, not certain of what that meant. He had signed all of the property transfer forms for the equipment. Had the guards forgotten something? Or was there another reason for their apparent alarm? Had they intercepted the E-mail he had received from Victoria an hour ago with the passwords from Capitol Bank? And why weren't they calling out for him, asking him to stop?

Ryan's eyes dropped to their hands, to the black objects they clutched. *Guns!*

He fought a rising wave of panic, forcing himself to run to the side of his car. Everything seemed to slow to a crawl, his fingers reaching for the door handle, pulling it. He got in, fumbling with the key, sliding it into the ignition, turning it.

The Boxster started right away, its low growling now mixing with the shouts from the security guards, both of whom stopped in front of the Porsche, pistols leveled at Ryan.

"Get out of the car, sir! Now!"

Leaving the engine running, Ryan opened the door, got out.

"Put your hands behind your neck!"

His heart racing, Ryan complied, looking toward the building, spotting the large blond guard running out of the building.

The report of a pistol cracked across the parking lot. Ryan watched the guard closest to him drop his weapon, clutch his bleeding chest, drop to his knees. In the same instant, the second guard turned his weapon to a spot to the right of Ryan, who froze, confused, terrified, not certain what was going on. In the distance, the blond guard produced a pistol and rushed toward them.

Another shot, like the crack of a whip, and the second guard also collapsed.

"Get in the car!" came a shout from behind.

Ryan remained still, his surroundings becoming surreal, dreamlike, the two guards sprawled on the concrete, the blond guard halfway down the parking lot, weapon in hand.

"The car, dammit! Get in it!" came the same warning again.

This time Ryan turned around, just as another shot thundered in the late morning air. The blond guard sought cover.

Ryan felt a hand clasping his wrists, which he still held behind his neck, just as he had been ordered.

"C'mon, kid! Snap out of it!"

Ryan turned around, stared at the face of Karen Frost. She was pushing him inside the Boxster.

"Drive!" she shouted while whipping around the passenger side, tugging on the handle, opening the door, her pistol pointed at the threat behind parked vehicles.

Something snapped inside of Ryan, and he found himself sitting behind the wheel again, putting the Boxster in gear, driving off.

Several shots followed. Ryan heard a hammerlike sound on the side of the car, as if he had hit a rock.

"Floor it!" ordered Karen, turning around, weapon pointed at the parking lot they were leaving behind.

He complied, the engine revving up, tires spinning furiously, propelling the sports car down the street, around the corner.

It wasn't until he had driven a few blocks that the thought struck him with the power of a gunshot.

Victoria!

Every time Victoria Ryan began to focus on the discussion at Rossini's staff meeting, her boss would distract her by rubbing her leg with his left foot. She certainly hoped that the passwords she had E-mailed Ryan were worth the aggravation she was going through. Had she known that Rossini would turn out to be such a horny bastard, she might have taken a different tack to swap the Palm Vs.

Rossini's assistant stuck her head inside the room at 11:32 A.M.

"What is it?"

"You have an emergency call on line one," she said.

"Tell whoever it is that I'm still in my staff meeting. I'll call them back."

"I've tried that, sir, but it's R. W. He says it's important."

Rossini nodded and stood. "I'll be right back."

Victoria breathed a sigh of relief. She began to formulate in her mind a way to reverse the damage she had done. She decided to simply resist, to blame it on a moment of confusion, of weakness—of anything that would keep his hands off her.

Rossini returned a minute later, a stolid look on his tanned face. "Something's come up," he said to the group. "That will be all for today."

Everyone got up to leave, including Victoria. Rossini leaned over to her. "Hold on, Vic. There's something I need to discuss with you."

Victoria pocketed her Palm V and crossed her arms, ready to let him have her rehearsed speech.

The moment everyone left, he reached under the table and locked the conference room doors.

"Look, Angelo," she began. "This is not going to work out."

"Really?" he said in a strange, somewhat sarcastic tone, walking right up to her.

"Yes," she replied, focusing on her speech. "I've worked very hard in college to get a good job, where I would be promoted based on my financial contributions to the firm, not based on—"

"Fucking me?"

She was momentarily stunned, recovering rapidly while blurting, "I really don't appreciate that language."

"And I really don't *appreciate* you trying to screw me!" He held her by the shoulders.

"I—I don't know what you're talking about."

"You don't, do you? Well, let me *show* you." In a single motion, Rossini slapped her with the back of his hand, sending her crashing next to the conference table.

Stunned, Victoria tried to sit up, bringing a hand to her burning cheek. "You . . . bastard!" How dare you—"

Rossini grabbed a clump of hair and pulled her back up.

She tried to scream but he slapped her again, throwing her on the table.

"You still don't know what I'm talking about, do you?" he asked calmly.

Dazed, her face burning as much as her torso from bumping against the side of the table, Victoria tried to say something, make him stop.

Before she could answer, Rossini reached under her skirt and tore off her panties.

"What . . . get off of me you . . . animal! You—"

He slapped her a third time. Hard. "Do you *now* know what I'm talking about?" he asked her.

"No . . . stop," she pleaded, punch-drunk.

"On your back, bitch! I'm going to teach you a lesson!"

"Oh, God. Please . . . no."

"I'm going to *show you* what it feels like to get *fucked*, just like you tried to fuck us by going to the FBI!" For a moment Rossini let go of her, his hands fumbling with his pants.

Victoria sat up, quickly coming around, finally understanding. Somehow they had found out, and now they were coming after her and Ryan. She had to get out of there, had to get this brute away from her, keep him from raping her!

Mustering resolve, she lifted her left knee, fast, driving it up in between his legs, kneeing him hard.

"*Agh* . . . damn!" he screamed, falling on his side, hands on his groin.

Breathing heavily, her face burning from the multiple blows, her ribs throbbing, her upper thighs sore after he had ripped off her underwear, Victoria pressed the button under the table and raced for the door.

A moment later she was dashing toward the stairways, hoping to reach one of the floors below, which belonged to other businesses. Ignoring the puzzled stares from fellow coworkers, she continue to run, her eyes on the large white door at the end of the corridor, next to the elevators.

She reached it, pushing the waist-high handle, pressing her left shoulder against the metallic surface, reaching the concrete landing.

Victoria bumped into three security guards, all tall, with broad shoulders.

"Going somewhere?" asked one of them.

"Please . . . help me," she said. "Someone just tried to rape me."

The guard looked at his companions. "Rape? Nah," he said, smiling. "I think Mr. Rossini was just having fun with you."

Victoria's mouth went dry, a sinking feeling descending on her. She tried to back away but bumped into Rossini instead. She was trapped.

"Oh, God. Please don't hurt me," she said, surrounded now.

"What took you so long?" Rossini asked, out of breath, a hand on his groin.

"We came as soon as we could," replied the guard.

"Now," Rossini said, turning his attention to Victoria Ryan, his features tight with pain from her kick. "Looks like we're going for a little ride."

"Van's waiting downstairs, sir," said the same guard.

"Take her away," he said. "I'll meet up with you later."

A hand reached from behind her holding a white cloth, burying her face. Victoria tried to fight it off, taking a deep breath, her nostrils burning, her mind quickly getting cloudier. Trembling with fear, slowly passing out, the coppery taste of her own blood from a busted lip mixing with the smell of a pungent chemical, Victoria struggled to free herself once more, before everything rapidly faded away. Her final thoughts drifted to Ryan, silently praying that he, somehow, had managed to get away.

7

Ryan cursed as he hung up the phone, setting it down on the Porsche's console while steering through downtown Austin. "Bastards! Damned bastards!"

"What did they tell you?" asked Karen, sitting sideways to him in the passenger seat.

"That she was tied up at the moment and couldn't come to the phone! That's a bunch of horse—"

"They've got her, Mike," said Karen, rubbing her temples, feeling terrible for the young professional, and also quite guilty, though she would never admit it. She had been the one who had gotten the Ryans involved in this mess, and she had accidentally tipped the enemy of their involvement by leaving an electronic trail in her laptop. For a moment she wondered if she just wasn't cut out for this line of work, having grown too old, too careless. She still didn't know how they had tracked her down last night.

"What—what's going to happen to her?"

"Right now she is being taken somewhere secret."

"I'm going after her," he said, turning the corner, heading for Capitol Bank's building several blocks away.

"It's too late for that," she replied. "You can't help her by going to the building. I've already told you she isn't there anymore."

"How can you be so sure?"

"I know how they operate. By now your wife is *nowhere* near Capitol Bank."

He pounded the steering wheel. "But—but I have to try something! Dammit, Karen, they've kidnapped her! I can't just sit here and let them—"

"If you go into that building you'll be kidnapped as well, and then both of you will be executed. As long as you remain free, however, Victoria will have a chance of staying alive."

"Why?"

"Because they will use her to *lure* you into a trap."

"A trap?"

"Even my own agents have fallen victims to their traps, often using an informant—or even a fellow agent—as bait." Karen closed her eyes for a moment, the maimed body of Dave Nolan flashing in her mind. She forced it away.

"What will happen to her in the meantime?"

"She's very likely to be interrogated."

Ryan pulled over, obviously unable to continue what had to be a very stressing conversation while driving. "Interrogated?" he asked, tight fists in front of his face, his eyes filling. "*Why?* She doesn't *know* anything. *I'm* the one who pierced their network! *I'm* the one who screwed with their video cameras! *I'm* the one who . . . who convinced her to come down here in the first place. All Vic did was get me more information on account numbers this morning."

"Account numbers?"

"Yeah," he said, his eyes wet with anger. "Last week I managed to get information on SoftCorp accounts at Capitol Bank, where the proceeds from IRS payments were deposited. Then Victoria got additional information this morning linking those accounts to other accounts overseas, where she believes the money might be getting transferred into. Now there's only one thing I can do."

"What's that?" Karen asked.

"When someone takes something you love dearly, the only way to get it back is by you taking something they hold dearly, and then set up a swap."

She had to give him credit. Despite his current emotional predicament, this kid was thinking objectively, like a pro. "You're on the right track, Mike. But what can you take away from them?" Ryan told her, adding, "And all I need is access to a high-speed telephone line, and these." He pulled out a tiny computer from his coat pocket.

"What's in it?"

"The bank account information," said Ryan, accelerating once again. "I'm going to hit them where it hurts."

Karen reached for Ryan's mobile phone.

"Who are you calling?"

"Backup. After you get your bargaining chip and a meeting has been set up to make the trade, we're going to need *plenty* of backup."

Russell Meek's private line rang three times before he picked it up.

"Yeah?"

"Russ, Karen. We've got problems in Austin."

"Karen? Jesus! Where are you calling from?"

"Never mind that," she replied. "I have a situation."

"No shit! I warned you and also Roman that this would happen one day. I should have stopped this operation while I had the time!"

Karen narrowed her gaze. "What are you talking about?"

"The cops, Karen. Jesus Christ, you killed police officers! I've got everyone from Congress to the White House breathing down my neck. CNN and the networks have been contacting my office for comment all day long!"

"Slow down, Russ. What are you talking about? Who claims that I've killed cops?"

Ryan shot her a look and Karen motioned him to keep driving.

"Where have you been? It's all over the news. You killed three Austin Police Department officers last night, and according to the report they weren't *just* killed. They were *executed*, shot in the back of the head. And then there's all of the drugs they found at your apartment. And the incendiary grenade that you set off to cover your tracks . . . What in God's name were you trying to do? This time you have gone too far."

258 Things were happening too fast for the federal agent. She tried to remain focused. "Listen carefully, Russ. An attempt was made last night against my life, and I did shoot three assassins, but in *self-defense*, and none of them identified themselves as APD officers. These were professional killers, Russ, and there were others right behind them. After I disabled their lead wave, more came and tried to flush me out with a grenade. I jumped out of the window and found shelter in nearby woods, then I passed out from exhaustion and from the wounds I sustained during the fall, until this morning. *That's* what happened, regardless of what you hear in the media."

"It's not the media, Karen. It's the evidence from the Austin Police Department. How do you explain the ballistics report we got a couple of hours ago from them? The bullets used to kill the officers match your FBI-issued Desert Eagle Magnum. And your fingerprints—only *your* fingerprints—are on the gun."

"I lost the Magnum during the fall. Russ, it's pretty obvious that I've been framed. This whole thing is a setup to try to keep me from digging any further."

"I'm afraid this one's out of my hands, Karen. All I can suggest to you is that you turn yourself in. We'll sort it out afterwards."

"Turn myself in? Are you out of your mind?"

"Look, if you don't stop—"

"If I turn myself in, I will be executed while in my cell, probably staged to look like a suicide."

"You're being paranoid. The Bureau will protect you."

"The Bureau couldn't protect Palenski and Nolan, Russ! How can they protect me?"

There was a long sigh. "You're still thinking that Palenski was assassinated?"

"What do *you* think?"

"I think that you've come up with plenty of theories but not a shred of proof."

"I'm working on the proof, dammit! I just need more time, and I also need your help."

"You're out of time. And I can't help you anymore."

"If you want proof, I will need your help."

"Sorry. This problem is past that stage. The media's comparing it to Ruby Ridge. I've gotten many calls from Congress and the White House threatening to restructure the FBI, kill our budget, and a host of other consequences unless I find a way to bring you in."

Karen couldn't believe this. "Would you consider what I've said if I bring you proof that exposes a conspiracy of unprecedented proportions?"

After a long pause, Meek said, "Yes. But how—"

"Let me worry about that. You just hang tight, and speak to no one of this. The only way that last night's termination team could have figured out my location was through an insider. I took the necessary precautions to avoid being followed."

"What are you saying?"

"That someone from Washington gave up my location."

"How can you be so certain?"

"Because one of the assassins last night told me so before he died," Karen said.

"I can't go on without evidence."

"I told you I'll get you the proof."

"Karen . . . please consider what I've offered. I can have a team of agents ready to pull you in. Are you sure you don't want me to help you? If you get caught by APD officers first I can't guarantee your protection. Cops are not nice to cop killers."

Karen closed her eyes, wondering how in the hell things ever got so out of hand. "I do need a team of agents, but to help me in my investigation."

"Proof, Karen. I need something to go on beyond just your word, particularly against such overwhelming evidence."

Karen frowned. The conversation had gone as far as it could for now. "I'll be in touch," she said, before hanging up, pinching the bridge of her nose with her index and thumb.

"What was that all about?"

"Let's just say that we need to get you on-line as soon as possible."

Ryan nodded.

"Do you have a place in mind where you can hook up your gear?"

"Leave that to me," he said.

"How long will it take?"

"That's one nice thing about my business," said Ryan.

"What's that?"

"We measure time in nanoseconds. It won't take very long at all."

8

Orion Yanez nearly spilled his coffee while sitting in his rocking chair.

"What did you just say?" he barked.

"Bra—Brazilian funds, sir," replied his accountant, a short and stubby man in his midfifties who'd handled Orion's overseas accounts for almost a decade. His face was ashen, his hands trembling. The ever-prudent Orion Yanez did not use Capitol Bank for such activities, limiting the Austin financial institution to getting the money out of the country and into specific accounts. From there on his personal accountant picked up the ball, controlling how those funds were managed in the foreign accounts. "Someone has just transferred the funds out of six accounts."

"What?"

"The funds—"

"Who?"

"I . . . I don't know!"

"How much?"

"One hundred and twenty million doll—"

Orion abruptly stood, grabbing his subordinate by the lapels, pinning him against the back of the house. "What in the fuck is going on? Where is the money?"

Orion's guards raced outside when hearing the shouting, only to step back away from their boss. No one wanted to be near the elderly Cuban when he was angry.

"I was doing a routine check . . . then the transactions came over the wire. . . . The passwords matched the—"

"Show me!" Orion demanded, releasing him before storming toward the door.

9

Ryan jacked out following a quick run through the financial world of this shadowy organization. He had managed to penetrate accounts in a few countries in the past half hour, since arriving at his neighborhood's clubhouse. Ryan had suggested the place, far enough from his own home, which he suspected would be under surveillance. At this time of the morning on a weekday, the building was empty.

Karen and Ryan had hauled two boxes' worth of VR hardware into the office in the rear, where he had hooked it up to the ISDN line in minutes before jacking in. The account information that Victoria had E-mailed to him had been Ryan's polestar, his magnetic north, guiding him from the Capitol Bank accounts into an overseas nirvana, where MPS-Ali had done the rest, not only acquiring access passwords in the same way in which he had broken inside SoftCorp's confidential directories but also finding the name of the owner. Once he reached the account's portal, MPS-Ali had handled the rest, setting off an alarm to lure the network's sentinels, intercepting their passwords before infecting them with a sleep virus. But just as with the previous break-ins, Ryan had only been able to do this for so long before the rightful owner caught up with him, not only changing the passwords but denying access through the Internet to force bank officials to contact the owner to verify the intended transactions. The resourceful Ryan, however, had used that intervention to capture the owner's E-mail address, a pivotal portion of his next phase to get his wife back. Once he intercepted the E-mail address, he dispatched MPS-Ali to the E-mail account's Internet service provider, obtaining the name of its owner, Orion Benjamin Yanez.

"That's it?" asked Karen Frost after Ryan spent a minute explaining what he had done.

Ryan nodded, extracting a floppy disk from the system and pocketing it. "Pretty amazing what you can do with the right information, and with the proper cyber help. And it all fits in here."

"So, what's next?"

"Time to send Mr. Yanez a message."

By the time Orion Yanez reached the accountant's suite and stared at the information on the screen, fourteen more bank accounts had been drained. Another one from Brazil, some from Mexico, a few from the Cayman Islands, and even a Capitol Bank account in Austin, where Rossini kept funds in transit.

Orion felt as if the room were spinning. Somehow someone had found a way to get to his money.

"Can't you . . . *stop it* ?"

"I did!" his accountant said, pointing a trembling finger at the new E-mail messages flashing on the screen. "The other banks have already denied access to anyone not in possession of new passwords. I've also requested that for the time being all transactions need to be confirmed by a phone call and a fax from this location. It's all in this E-mail I sent before I went to get you."

Orion read the E-mail, patting his subordinate on the back. "Sorry for what I did out there, my friend. You reacted well. Can we get those lost accounts back?"

The accountant shook his head. "We can try to trace them, but the money is likely to be funneled out through many channels. At least we managed to save the others."

Orion breathed deeply. His accountant had reacted as fast as humanly possible. This was not his fault but the fault of someone else. But who? Only Orion and his accountant controlled the passwords. No one else.

"How much have we lost?"

"Between the twenty accounts . . . roughly seven and a half billion dollars. That's roughly—"

"I know," he said. Orion's total worth overseas was estimated at around thirteen billion dollars. He had half as much inside the United States, but tied up in dozens of corporations like SoftCorp and Capitol Bank. The overseas funds were critical for his deal with the Russians. He *had* to get that money back.

Orion stared at the E-mails. Banks from the Cayman Islands, the Bahamas, Mexico, Colombia, and even Switzerland, had already sent confirmations of existing funds, plus password changes on their numbered accounts.

"What's that one?" Orion said, pointing at the last E-mail on the list.

The accountant shook his head. "It's not from any of the banks."

"Open it," Orion said.

The accountant did, and a moment later Orion Yanez screamed as loudly as his lungs allowed, "Esteban! I need to speak to Esteban!"

As his subordinate reached for the phone, Orion read the E-mail once again.

> To: Orion B. Yanez
> From: Michael Ryan
> Subj: Victoria Ryan
> I now have your attention and your money. If you want it back, return my wife to me. If you harm her, you lose the funds that I've taken from you. Details of the meeting will follow shortly.

"I've got Esteban on the line."

As Orion grabbed the phone he asked his accountant, "Can you trace the origin of that E-mail?"

He nodded. "I'm already working on it."

"Is this enough proof for you?" asked Ryan, holding the helmet-mounted display unit in his right hand, the fingers of his left hand rubbing his eyes.

Karen reviewed the information in her hands, the E-mails that Ryan had just printed using the clubhouse's office.

"What we have here," she said after a few moments, "is nothing more than information on overseas accounts, plus a name, Orion Yanez. This is what we call a *lead*, Mike, not evidence. We need to follow this up to *get* evidence."

Ryan clenched his teeth. "Then how are we going to get backup for the swap?"

Karen shifted her gaze out the window, which faced the clubhouse's large pool and tennis courts. "Calling my people won't do us any good at the moment. I need to show them proof."

Ryan began to don the HMD once again.

"What are you doing?"

"Going to get you the damned proof."

"Don't take too long." She pointed at the system, her index finger following the phone cable from the back of the computer to the wall. "They already know someone's screwing with them, Mike. If they're smart they will trace this connection and send a team over here."

"Then you keep an eye out for trouble. I need a few more minutes to check something out."

"Where are you going this time?"

"To a very *special* place. Here, take this pad and pencil and write down everything I tell you."

"Why?"

"Because where I'm headed is way beyond limits and I'm not capable of transferring any data out except for what I can see and dictate to you."

The office vanished and Ryan found himself orbiting the outer planets of his VR system, with MPS-Ali floating to his immediate right.

Ryan headed straight toward the sun, in the center of his cyber solar system, rushing at warp speed past the outer planets, beyond the asteroid ring, and right through the inner worlds.

As he cruised by a volcanic moon belonging to a magenta inner planet, Ryan received a warning from MPS-Ali. Someone had detected his run through his virtual-reality matrix. A further check revealed the user as Agi Maghami. His former supervisor, probably under orders by Wittica and Shapiro, must have been monitoring the cyber airwaves in case Ryan decided to use the VR hardware he had loaded up in his car this morning.

Ryan spotted him now, a bright violet-and-gold figure emerging through the light haze enveloping the volcanic moon. MPS-Ali immediately released a software shield around Ryan and itself, preventing any virus from penetrating them. In the same instant, MPS-Ali fired a freezing virus at Maghami, but the Indian programmer had taken similar measures.

Ryan frowned. Although Maghami couldn't attack, he could certainly follow him, and alert anyone of the network that Ryan was trying to penetrate. He didn't like the idea of Wittica and Shapiro learning that he knew how to access the inner directories of the IRS.

Ryan needed a diversion, a way to slow Maghami down, to lose him in this VR solar system, at least for long enough to access the IRS's network.

Instead of continuing in his current trajectory, Ryan went around the moon once, and headed for its planet, its shades of magenta filling his field of view. Surface detail followed, and a huge metropolis grew in size as he descended over it. According to MPS-Ali this planet represented the Department of Corrections for the state of Texas. The hazy moon circling it symbolized the prison system itself.

Ryan began to fly in between buildings, drawing Maghami into a highly detailed 3-D world, submerging him in a deep virtual-reality scenario, which pushed the envelope in terms of its required frames per second to keep the experience fluid for the user. Minimal latency, the delay between the user's head motion and the system's response to that motion, was a basic requirement at the speed in which they cruised through the city.

Maghami was protected against any virus that Ryan might fire directly at him, but the supervisor was not protected for a localized change in the parameters of Ryan's VR world.

At his command, MPS-Ali released a balloonlike cloud, its diameter roughly twenty times his size, locking its center to Maghami's user ID. The cloud engulfing Ryan's former technical advisor represented an alteration in the programmed frames per second and latency parameters of Ryan's VR system. It reduced the frames per second from the standard of twenty to just eight, changing the response of the environment around Maghami.

At the same time, Ryan increased Maghami's latency from the standard 0.05 second to one second. Every time Maghami turned his head to look around him, not only did the scenery appear like a movie in slow motion, lacking fluidity, but the information expected by his brain, based on his head motion according to the semicircular canals of his inner ears, no longer matched the image captured by his eyes. This conflict resulted in severe motion sickness and nausea.

Almost instantly, the cloud engulfing Maghami began to recede in the background, where it remain for another thirty seconds, getting even farther behind, until all Ryan could see was a dot in the cyber building. Then MPS-Ali informed him that Maghami had jacked out of the system.

Ron Wittica and Aaron Shapiro stepped back the moment Maghami began to vomit, ripping the HMD off his head.

"What in the hell is wrong with you?" shouted Shapiro.

"The . . . bastard," said Maghami, between convulsions. "Sorry . . . he . . . tricked me."

Wittica regarded his subordinate with contempt. "How in the hell did he do that?"

"Changed the parameters . . ." Maghami straightened up on his chair, wiping yellowish vomit from the corner of his mouth with the sleeve of his shirt. "Bastard changed the latency . . . the frames per second."

Wittica remembered the explanation Ryan had given him, and he now realized how Ryan had used that to his advantage. The kid was good, but not good enough. Esteban, Hausser, and two other guards were on their way to the clubhouse in Lakeway, where they had tracked Ryan performing this most recent cyber attack against them. A guard left behind by the Ryan's house in case he showed up was now guarding the clubhouse, waiting for the rest of the team to arrive. This time Esteban was determined to do it right.

"Where did you lose him?" asked Wittica.

"In the inner planets," he replied, putting on his HMD again, but removing it seconds later while rubbing his eyes and fighting another spasm. "I can't see where he went."

"Here," Wittica said, "let me try."

A multicolored city replaced his environment. Wittica gazed about him, watching the spastic response from the system as he tried to scan the area for any signs of Michael Ryan, instead feeling a knot forming in his stomach as his eyes grew heavier from the long delay between his head movements and the scenery around him. He lasted a minute before he removed the HMD and grabbed for a nearby table, dizzy, the room spinning around him.

"Son of a bitch," Wittica finally said, hoping that Esteban and Hausser had better luck.

13

Once Agi Maghami fell from view, Ryan resumed his trajectory toward the sun. MPS-Ali issued password after password, shielding them against the smoldering virtual heat, against the hostile environment they had just entered. MPS-Ali went off in a search of everything related to Orion Benjamin Yanez. His cyber agent returned moments later with an address in Virginia. Orion Yanez was a very wealthy man, owner of many corporations, including SoftCorp and Capitol Bank. The IRS, however, showed no flags against Mr. Yanez. He had built an empire from nothing in fifteen years and had religiously paid his taxes every year. A search on SoftCorp and Capitol Bank also revealed nothing out of the ordinary. From a previous run through SoftCorp's secret directories, however, Ryan knew that the high-tech firm had made much more money than what they were reporting.

Ryan was not that surprised when MPS-Ali detected hidden IRS directories on both corporations, each requiring additional access passwords, which Olson had not possessed. Once again, MPS-Ali was on the case, triggering alarms, drawing sentinels shaped like luminous figures, intercepting their passwords before freezing them in place like glowing wax statues incapable of executing their programs.

It was here that Ryan found the evidence that Karen Frost needed, the large disparity between SoftCorp's reported income and reality. The IRS had indeed paid SoftCorp huge amounts of money for its technical services, but only a fraction had been reported through standard channels—the areas checked by IRS workers and auditing agents like Gam Olson. It was within this hidden directory that Ryan found the truth, and the only individual with legal access to it was a man named Jason Myrtle, the director of the IRS offices in Austin. Ryan spoke out, relating to Karen Frost everything he saw, from passwords to invoices, payments, names, and dates.

He was almost finished when he felt a tug on his shirt. Ryan removed his HMD.

"We've got company," Karen said, folding the piece of paper with Ryan's dictated notes and pocketing it.

"Who?"

She pointed out the window. A dark sedan was pulling into the parking lot in front of the clubhouse, followed by a second car. One man got out of the first car, four climbed out of the other one, including the large guard with the ash blond hair.

"Is there another way out of this place?"

Ryan nodded, remembering the tour of the place that Gail, their real estate agent, had given them during their house-hunting trip. "But first there's something I need to do," he said, tapping the keyboard of the computer connected to the VR hardware.

"What are you doing?"

"Erasing my Internet log and also buying us time."

Esteban Yanez stepped out of the car followed by Todd Hausser and two of his men. The early afternoon sun reflected off the clubhouse's windows, making it impossible to see inside. According to the information they had received fifteen minutes ago, Michael Ryan had used a high-speed phone line to drain some of his uncle's bank accounts.

He further confirmed the claim when spotting the engineer's red Porsche, parked in front of the building by the glass double doors.

He reached for the cell phone and dialed Shapiro.

"Have you found him?" asked the elderly CEO, his voice strained.

"We're in position. Is he still logged in?" asked Esteban.

"Yes," replied Shapiro. "He's still on-line, though we can't tell where. You must stop him from digging any further."

"Will do." Esteban hung up the phone and pointed at Hausser and one of the guards. "He's still inside. Come with me." Then he aimed the cellular phone at the other two guards. "You two go around the back and make sure he doesn't try to leave through the rear door. Remember, we need him alive."

As the two men disappeared around the back, Esteban surveyed the area. No one was in sight. He slowly approached the house followed by Hausser and a guard, stepping up to the small front porch, trying one of the doors. It wasn't locked.

Unholstering his side arm, he went inside, rushing into the foyer, crashing into the closest door.

An empty conference room. He moved on to the adjacent room, with Hausser and his guard in tow. Kicking the door in, he rushed into an office, spotting a computer and other gear on the desk.

"That's Mike Ryan's equipment!" Hausser said. "I remember it from his lab back at SoftCorp."

"*Mierda!*" cursed Esteban, glancing at the flickering screen. "Spread out! Look in every room!"

Karen and Ryan had barely made it to the trees behind the clubhouse when they spotted two men coming around from the front of the building. She pulled Ryan down beside her, hiding in the bushes outlining the side of the swimming pool facing the forest.

"Quiet," she whispered, reaching for her holstered Colt .45, her thumb slowly flipping the safety.

Dressed in business suits, the strangers pushed open the waist-high gate of the club's chain-link fence and stepped onto the pool deck, their hands free, their shoes clicking lightly on the redwood decking around the pool. One of them paused by a wrought-iron table, looking around him before reaching for a radio inside his pocket and murmuring something.

A breeze rustled the canopy overhead, its sounds mixing with the droning from the pool's pump. Fallen leaves danced by their feet.

"It's working. They think I'm still inside," Ryan said. He had left something he called a script running on the computer. This script, as he had hastily explained while running out of the back of the clubhouse just a minute earlier, consisted of a set of keyboard commands in a loop, giving the appearance that someone was working on the system.

"You're right," said Karen after another moment. The two men flanked the door connecting the pool to the clubhouse. "Now, let's get out of here . . . nice and easy."

Ryan nodded, taking a step back, and another, slowly. Karen kept her weapon trained on the figures roaming around the back of the clubhouse until they disappeared from view as she and Ryan receded in the woods.

"What about my car?" asked Ryan, moving a bit faster now, trekking side by side with Karen as they headed down hill.

"Forget it," she said. "It was never really yours."

A few minutes later they were already a quarter of the way down the hill when Karen heard the men shouting overhead.

"I think they've just figured out your trick," she said, the hasty descent reminding her of the one she had made to escape from the late Rubaker's house last week.

"Will they come after us?" Ryan asked, moving between a wall of moss-draped limestone and the trunk of a tall cottonwood. Sunlight forked between its branches, casting a dim glow on the forest.

The turquoise surface of Lake Travis was visible between two ridges. Karen said, "Maybe. But we have enough of a lead." A butterfly fluttered around her face. She waved it off, momentarily watching its erratic flight before continuing their descent.

After another minute they cut left, going around the hill, until she had estimated they had put almost a half mile between themselves and the club-house.

"What are we doing next?" he asked.

She tapped the pocket of her new jacket, already frayed during their rushed getaway. "We're using this evidence to get you some backup."

"Have you thought of how we're going to get my wife back?"

"Priorities, Mike. First I need to get *you* out of harm's way. Then I'll contact my people, and *then* you'll contact SoftCorp and set up a meeting."

16

"What do you mean there was nobody there?" shouted Aaron Shapiro into the speaker box connected to the phone in his office, where Wittica and he had gone to await news from Esteban.

"His car was parked out front," came the reply from Esteban, his baritone voice flowing through the speaker box in the middle of Shapiro's desk. Wittica sat across from him. "But there was no one inside."

"But . . . the system," said Shapiro. "He was logged in and—"

"A script, Aaron," said Wittica, closing his eyes. "The bastard left a script running, making us think he was still logged in."

"Damn!" Shapiro protested, slapping his desk.

"Esteban?" said Wittica.

"Yes?"

"Is the monitor flashing different information?"

"Yes. It's changing constantly, as if someone's at the keyboard."

Wittica nodded, his eyes still closed. "Pull your people back. There's nothing else they can do out there except clean up. The little bastard tricked us again."

Shapiro gave Esteban additional instructions and then hung up. "Now what are we supposed to do?"

"Wait," said Ron Wittica. "Wait and follow Washington's instructions."

"The police are also coming up with nothing," commented Shapiro.

Wittica didn't say anything. He was aware that someone in Washington had pulled some strings to get the Austin Police Department in on this, but he was not sure how, and he'd rather keep it that way. The less he knew the better off he would be if things continued in this downward spiral.

"Is his wife all right?" asked Shapiro.

Wittica nodded, aware of that part of the operation. "She's asleep for now, from the chloroform."

"And do we know how Ryan got a hold of the account numbers?"

Wittica gave him another nod. "That's the first thing we checked. Although I haven't personally seen the video from Angelo's conference room, my men tell me that he tried to screw Victoria Ryan right there on his conference table."

Shapiro leaned forward. "You're *kidding* me."

Wittica shook his head, and added, "It appears that she got him distracted enough to swap Palm Vs with him. I guess he kept some accounting in it and she must have downloaded it, because she then E-mailed the info to her husband. We found the E-mail log thirty minutes ago. It contained several overseas accounts. He drained many of them before our people in Washington could intervene."

"How did he get the passwords?"

Wittica shrugged. "He must have hacked his way into the accounts, just as he hacked into our own security system. I guess all he needed was the account numbers, which he got through his wife from Angelo."

Shapiro frowned. "Stupid Angelo. I told that dumb bastard that thinking with his dick was going to get him in trouble one of these days. You simply don't shit where you eat, especially in our situation."

"I warned him too, Aaron, and he told me to mind my own business."

"Dumb," Shapiro said.

"What's going to happen to him?"

Shapiro put a hand to his forehead, dropping his gaze to his desk. "Ron, you don't want to know."

This was Russell Meek's first visit to the Oval Office, and the timing couldn't have been any worse. The most recent news indicated that his runaway agent had not only executed three police officers but had also stolen over two million dollars from Capitol Bank, a respected banking institution in Austin, Texas. The police found Karen's fingerprints at the home of the bank's president, Angelo Rossini, now missing. APD, working in conjunction with the local FBI office, suspected that Karen Frost might have abducted Rossini at his home and forced him to use his computer passwords and executive privilege to transfer the funds to an overseas account. They also suspected that Agent Frost may have disposed of Rossini following the transfer, and was now trying to leave the country.

Meek sat nervously on one of the sofas flanking a fireplace at the end of the room opposite the presidential desk. Senator Jack Horton sat next to him, trying to calm him down.

"Relax, Russ," Horton said. "He understands that you were handed a bag of shit and are now trying to deal with it. Just be yourself, be honest, and stick to the facts. He is very fact driven. No emotions or hunches. He hates that."

Meek nodded, feeling like vomiting. He had been quite confident in his position just an hour ago, to the extreme of even considering making certain recommendations based on his last conversation with Karen Frost, when the federal agent had informed him of the possibility of a conspiracy. But all of that had been thrown out the window the moment he had walked down the corridors of this intimidating place, full of so much history, Secret Service agents, and United States Marines. The placed simply *reeked* of power.

The president walked in through a different door from the one they had used. Dressed in a dark blue suit, he appeared thinner than on television. His white hair combed straight back, his face lined with the stress of two rough terms in the White House, the president shook hands with both Meek and Horton and took his seat on the sofa across from them.

"So, Russell," the president began right away, "Jack here tells me that you inherited quite a problem from your old boss."

Meek nodded solemnly. "It seems that way, sir."

"What are you doing about this alleged cop killer?"

Meek paused, considering his answer as the president inspected him with piercing eyes. Siding with Karen Frost at the moment would very likely end his chances of becoming director of the FBI. The evidence against his subordinate was overwhelming and he had nothing to counter it besides her word. He opted to play it safe. "We're trying to bring her in, sir."

"Have you been in contact with her?"

Meek nodded. "She called in once but refused to turn herself in."

The president leaned back and crossed his legs, looking at Horton. "I see. And now it looks as if she's added kidnapping and grand larceny to her portfolio."

"And the FBI is doing all the right things to fix this, Mr. President," interceded Horton. "Russ and I meet on a regular basis. I'm confident that he won't let us down."

The president nodded while frowning. "I trust your judgment, Jack. I always have."

After a moment of silence, the president turned to Meek. "I understand where you came from, Russ, and how the FBI got in this embarrassing situation. Roman Palenski was someone I inherited seven years ago from a previous administration, and we've managed to . . . coexist, but like yourself, I never approved of his maverick tactics. Jack here informed me that you also didn't approve of your former superior, and that's part of the reason why I nominated you over more qualified candidates. Jack sees potential, and after all he has done to help bring this office and Congress to the highest level of cooperation in the past fifty years, I couldn't deny him the opportunity of putting someone capable at the head of the FBI, a team player. So, I need you to go by the book here. No hunches, no emotions, none of the crap that got the Bureau in trouble in Waco, Ruby Ridge, and now Austin. You listen to Horton. He's a good man, and God willing he will be in this office soon. The two of you have a great opportunity to drive the federal law enforcement in this nation to a new level of excellence. Is that clear?"

"Yes, Mr. President," replied Meek.

18

Victoria woke up in a dark place. She tried to swallow to alleviate a burning sensation in her throat.

Where am I? she wondered, swallowing again, unable to quench her scorching throat. She desperately needed a drink. Her face also burned . . . no, it throbbed, and so did her ribs as she stirred.

Pain triggered recollection, the encounter with Rossini, the beating, her escape attempt, the chemical in the rag, her burning lungs. Then nothing.

And here I am.

But where is—

Victoria sensed movement, but not of someone or something around her. The entire room was moving, slightly swaying up and down.

For a moment she thought the chemical hadn't worn off, perhaps she was still dizzy. She closed her eyes, breathing deeply, rubbing her temples, trying to shake off the sensation, but the gentle rocking remained.

Slowly, she sat up, inspecting her surroundings, deciding that she was in a small compartment on a boat—a cabin. Reaching for the handle of a brown screen, she slid it aside, exposing a round porthole—and blinding sunlight. She pulled the screen close.

Darkness resumed.

She waited a moment before inching the screen just enough to let some light in, giving her a chance to verify her original suspicion.

Water extended beyond the opening, meeting with familiar hills in the distance, behind which a burnt orange sun slowly sank.

A boat on Lake Travis. Dusk.

What am I doing here? How long have I been out? What day is this?

She checked her watch. It was still Monday. Just after six-thirty in the evening.

Victoria stood. The cabin's ceiling was low, but she could still stand upright. She reached for the door handle but could not turn it. It had been locked from the outside.

Frowning, bracing herself from the pain of her ribs, Victoria sat back down on the bed, noticing a glass of water next to the bed.

She picked it up, sniffing it, wondering if it was safe to drink. It smelled like water. She took a sip, the cool water feeling like heaven on her throat. She drank some more, closing her eyes, breathing deeply, taking another sip.

Fifteen minutes passed. Victoria finished her water, glanced out of the small porthole again, and looked up at the early evening stars.

Just then the door opened.

A stranger stuck his head in, also flipping the light switch.

"Come," he said, disappearing from view, leaving the door open.

Blinking to adjust her eyes, Victoria set the glass on the nightstand and reluctantly followed.

She slowly walked into a spacious salon. Recessed lighting illuminated a galley opposite a dinette and a sofa next to a rectangular television screen hanging on the wall. Beyond it extended a large stateroom.

"Up here," said the stranger, going up the steps in the rear of the cabin. "Esteban wants you to watch the show."

Esteban? A show?

Victoria dropped her eyelids at the comment, climbing up the steps connecting the cockpit to the cabin. She froze at the sight of Angelo Rossini, his body wrapped in chains, a gag on his mouth.

"Hello, Mrs. Ryan. My name is Esteban."

Gripped by sudden terror, Victoria managed a brief nod, her gaze shifting between Rossini and this Hispanic man, roughly six feet tall with an athletic build. The lake breeze swirled his dark hair, sprinkled with white.

"Remember your friend, Mrs. Ryan?" asked Esteban.

She locked eyes with him for a moment before she looked away. Distant lights dotted the shoreline, merging with surrounding hills and the dark sky over central Texas.

"We wanted you to watch this," he said over the whistling breeze and the shallow waves lapping the sides of the yacht. "We thought you might like it."

"Oh, God. No," she said, feeling her throat constricting. "Ple-please."

"So you do have feelings for him, even after what he did to you?"

"It's not like that," she said, the lump in her throat swelling, her hands trembling. "Please, don't kill him."

"Then tell us where your husband is."

"I—I don't know where he is."

"C'mon, Mrs. Ryan. We know better than that."

"I swear it," she said.

"That's too bad. Because you see, Angelo got careless and let you copy those account numbers, which you then E-mailed to your husband, who in turn *drained* some of our overseas accounts. So, this is how it works: You tell us where your husband and the money are, and we forgive Angelo. Otherwise . . ." He shoved Rossini to the rear of the cabin cruiser, by the swimming platform.

"But I told you, I don't know," she insisted, a strange sense of control descending over her as she realized that not only was Ryan alive but he had managed to fight back, which meant that she still had a chance of making it out of this mess. But she dreaded what the immediate future held for Angelo Rossini.

"Last chance, Mrs. Ryan. You don't want Angelo's death on your hands, now do you?"

Victoria closed her eyes. "I don't know where my husband is, nor where he moved any money of yours."

Esteban removed the gag from Rossini's mouth. "You have one shot at this, *pendejo*. Go ahead."

Swallowing, licking his lips, Rossini looked at Victoria. "Please, Vic. I beg you . . . I don't want to die. Not like this. It can't end like this. Please tell them what they need to know. *Please.*"

Even if she knew, Victoria realized that she could not disclose Ryan's location because they would both be following Rossini into the lake. With Ryan at large she had a fighting chance, which probably explained why no one had mistreated her yet.

"I'm sorry, Angelo. There's nothing I can do." As she said this, Victoria realized that she would remember those words and this moment—the look of fear in Rossini's eyes—for the rest of her life.

The Hispanic man kicked Rossini overboard. The banker screamed before hitting the water. He sank immediately from the heavy weight strapped around him.

"Oh, God!" she screamed, hands over her mouth while watching him disappear below the surface, followed by a burst of bubbles. She fell to her knees.

Esteban said, "I knew it would be useless to show her this. She doesn't know anything. Take her back inside."

Two men flanked her, lifting her to her feet. Victoria jerked away. "Don't touch me! You—you animals!"

Esteban burst into laughter. "*Animals*, Mrs. Ryan? Angelo Rossini got off easy. He was a business partner who got careless. He was *not* an enemy.

You have no idea what's in store for our enemies." Then he glanced at his men, and said, "Get her out of my sight."

As they locked her back in the small cabin, Victoria wondered how in the hell Ryan planned to get her back without getting caught in the process by these characters.

19

The motel by I-35 and Oltorf Street looked like any one of a dozen possible overnight stays along this stretch of highway. Old, sporting a neon Color TV sign beneath a Vacancy notice, it blended well with its surroundings, providing adequate temporary shelter to Mike Ryan and Karen Frost following their hasty escape from the clubhouse at Lakeway.

Considering his options, Ryan stood by the windows watching the interstate traffic from his second-floor room. The kidnapping of his wife had finally sunk in, and Ryan found it increasingly difficult to concentrate, to remain objective. Suddenly nothing mattered anymore. Not the house, or the cars, or the furniture. All Ryan could think of was Victoria and how he could get her back, but every time he began to formulate a plan, her face would fill his mind, followed by waves of guilt. After all, he had been the one who had put them in this predicament. For a moment he wished he had never interviewed with SoftCorp, had never agreed to the Austin visit, had never—

"Idiots," mumbled Karen, sitting on one of two double beds. "If only Palenski was alive."

Ryan turned to face her. The brief call, which Karen had made using Ryan's cellular phone a half hour ago, had not gone well. The federal agent had started the conversation speaking normally and had ended it shouting. Frustrated, she had gone to the bathroom and showered, emerging five minutes later wrapped in a towel, apparently not caring about being seen this way. She had a second towel wrapped around her head. She just sat on the bed, crossed her legs, and became absorbed in her own thoughts.

"I guess the FBI won't be coming to our rescue," Ryan said, glancing at her firm legs spotted with bruises before looking back toward the windows, his eyes on the array of headlights cruising north and south on the interstate. Karen had not volunteered any information from the call and

Ryan had not pressed her, figuring that the federal agent would tell him anything relevant at the appropriate time.

"They want me to turn myself in," she said in her slightly raspy voice, turning her green eyes to him.

Ryan didn't say anything. Although his wife was the one missing, he felt sorry for the federal agent, who had no doubt been a very beautiful woman in her youth. But the years of fieldwork had taken their toll, drawing the fine lines of age that tightened as she grimaced. She was still a very attractive middle-aged woman. She added, "Meek claims that there is much more new evidence against me now." She lowered her gaze, rubbing the tip of her index finger across her right eye, and doing the same to her left.

For a brief moment Ryan thought she was breaking down. But then she lifted her gaze back up as she removed the towel wrapped around her head. She had just changed in front of his eyes from a redhead with green eyes to a brunette with brown eyes. This woman was a damned chameleon. "You're amazing," he said.

She grunted and shook her head. "If I was amazing, Mike, I wouldn't have been labeled 'beyond salvage' by my people."

"I heard you screaming 'beyond salvage' right before you slammed down the phone and rushed into the bathroom," said Ryan. "What's that?"

"A term used in my line of work when referring to someone who is so deep in trouble that their own network won't even try to help. It seems that I've reached that low point in my career."

"What about *our* evidence, the names, the accounts?"

"He didn't want to hear it. He said the FBI would review it, but only *after* I turned myself in. No deals before that."

"What about Vic? How in the hell am I supposed to get her back?"

Karen remained silent.

"So the FBI won't help us," said Ryan. "And neither will the police. That surely narrows down our choices."

Karen shook her head. "What do you mean?"

Ryan remembered Agent Gam Olson. He had seemed like a straight arrow, concerned with nothing but catching tax violators. If the SoftCorp-Capitol Bank operation was indeed as vast as it seemed, then the IRS agent should be very interested in helping them out.

"How about getting help from the IRS?"

"The IRS? But they are in this thing too."

Ryan frowned. "I can't believe that *everyone* at the IRS is in on it. I have a feeling that this is contained to some small group, an inner circle. I'm sure that we can get Olson to at least listen to us, which is more than you can get at the FBI."

"How are you going to do that?" she asked.

Ryan told her.

"And how do you know he isn't one of them?" Karen asked.

Ryan shrugged. "He seemed genuinely concerned with catching tax violators."

"So?"

"I have *quite* the prize to offer for his help," he said. "If Olson's honest, and he certainly seemed so during the two meetings that I had with him, then he should be very interested in the hundreds of millions in unreported income at SoftCorp, especially when they came from IRS funds."

"You've got a point."

"It should actually piss him off. SoftCorp isn't paying taxes on money they have stolen from the IRS. That's the ultimate insult to the most powerful agency in the United States. They won't go easy on the perpetrators."

"Of course, if he's crooked, then we're screwed," Karen said. "But there is one way we might be able to check that."

"How?"

She smiled.

20

The taxicab dropped them off at the intersection of Westgate Boulevard and William Cannon Drive, in front of a bowling alley. It was just past ten in the evening and Ryan found it increasingly difficult to keep his eyes open. He was simply exhausted. What had started as a typical Monday had turned into a nightmare of a roller-coaster ride from which Ryan wished to awaken. As they walked down Westgate toward the residence of Gam Olson, Ryan found himself missing Victoria terribly. He felt utterly alone, longing for her touch, her smile, for the simpler days at Stanford. Ryan chastised himself over and over for ever accepting SoftCorp's job offer, and vowed to do whatever was necessary to get her back.

"This is it," said Karen, pointing at the green-and-white street sign marking the intersection of Jorwoods Drive and Westgate.

Under the glow of streetlights, they strolled down Jorwoods, trying to remain in the shadow of the oaks and cottonwoods flanking the tree-lined street, which had been recently repaved. The smell of fresh asphalt prickled his nostrils.

"That's the one," said Karen, pointing at the number on the mailbox of a white-brick house across the street. It looked like an average middle-class house in a middle-class neighborhood, certainly within the salary range of an IRS employee. An old Chevrolet Caprice was the only vehicle parked in the driveway of the two-car garage. Light filtered through a crack in the drawn curtains on the windows to the right of the front door. The rest of the house was dark.

"If your theory's correct," said Ryan. "Mr. Olson should not be on the take."

"Cheap car and a cheap house," commented Karen. "I'd say that Mr. Olson's probably okay."

"Why do you say probably?"

"Because there's *always* the chance that he's stashing it all away somewhere else for the day that he makes a clean break and retires to live like a king."

Ryan frowned. "He certainly didn't fit the type when I met him. He comes across as a straight shooter, trying to do the right thing for the IRS."

"Let's go find out."

They crossed the street and arrived at Olson's front door. As previously agreed, Karen stepped aside, leaving Ryan alone in front of the door as he rang the bell. She would remain out of sight for a while, giving Ryan time to present his evidence without alarming Olson. After all, Karen Frost's face had been broadcast on every network since the morning. In addition, if Olson turned out to be crooked, then by remaining outside, Karen was in a position to assist Ryan.

The light in the foyer flickered and came on.

"Who is it?"

Ryan recognized Olson's stiff voice.

"It's Mike Ryan, from SoftCorp. I need to talk to you."

A lock snapped and the door opened. Olson, wearing glasses and a robe, regarded him with a puzzled stare. "Something wrong, Mr. Ryan? Do you realize what time it is?"

"I'm really sorry to bother you at this hour, sir, but something has come up that requires your immediate attention."

Olson tilted his head. "Something that couldn't wait until tomorrow morning?"

Ryan nodded. "How about if I told you that for the past several years SoftCorp has not reported over half of its true income to the IRS?"

Olson removed his glasses. "That's . . . *impossible*. We're their only client. They report exactly what we pay them. I've checked it myself many times. Are they moonlighting?"

"No."

"Then where's the extra money coming from?"

Ryan sighed. "May I come in? There's something I must show you."

21

Karen Frost grew impatient waiting outside while Ryan made a believer out of Gam Olson. The federal agent sat on the cool grass in the darkness, out of sight from the street, her back against the waist-high bushes hugging the house.

She thought of the conversation she'd had with Meek. Although he'd never admit it, Karen knew someone had gotten to him, and he had yielded, playing along, unquestionably accepting whatever proof was presented to him and choosing to ignore Karen's claim.

The question is who?

Who could exert such power over the head of the FBI as to sway him from the truth? The line of command was very clear. Meek now reported to the president of the United States, just as Palenski had.

She grimaced. Meek had either been persuaded through evidence or he had been threatened. The threat, of course, could have been quite subtle, perhaps along the lines of being allowed to keep his job in exchange for running this operation based on the fabricated information being fed to the media.

In the end it all pointed to Karen Frost. She had been chosen to take the fall here. Eliminating her meant eliminating the problem, the embarrassment, while keeping secret whatever agreements existed between this organization and the government.

Damn.

She had certainly walked right into the middle of a huge conspiracy, and for a moment she wondered if she would be able to walk away with her life.

The door opened.

"Karen?" Ryan asked.

"What took you so long?" she replied, getting up. Ryan had been in there for almost an hour.

"It took him a little while to cross-check my info. Now he wants to talk to you. But first you need to give me your gun."

"What?"

"It's the only way he'll talk to you."

"That's ridiculous! Doesn't he—"

"Look," Ryan said, "I've just spent the last hour convincing him of this conspiracy. He almost lost it in there when he realized that I had stolen his passwords from this morning's VR run, but I reeled him back when he saw the dollar amount in question—especially when the money came from IRS funds. Only after I'd gotten him comfortable did I mentioned you, and once again he went nuclear, coming this close to calling the police and having you arrested."

"But—"

"Wait," Ryan said, thrusting an open palm at her. "I've convinced him enough that he is willing to listen, but you also have to understand that he is a government man. He believes in the system and the rules. He is having a difficult time swallowing all of this and just wants a little insurance that you won't start shooting in there, just like the TV claims you did with the three cops."

"I didn't kill those—"

"That's besides the point! He's been trained to believe in the system, but he is also willing to keep an open mind, give you the benefit of the doubt—to some degree—only because of the information I've shown him so far."

Karen placed her hands on her hips. She was out of options. The police wanted her head, and the FBI would gladly take the rest. This was her only hope of being heard. As much as she hated doing so, she found herself reaching down to her right ankle and surrendering her weapon.

"I hope I don't live to regret this."

"Just a moment," he said, going back inside and emerging a minute later while adding, "Okay. Come in."

She followed him into the foyer, beyond which extended a nice-sized living room, sparsely furnished, with an old sofa, a television, and a pair of chairs. Gam Olson sat on one of the chairs, beneath an old chandelier, his hands holding a black gun, which Karen recognized as a 9-mm Beretta. Karen's Colt lay by his side.

Not particularly enjoying having a loaded gun pointed in her direction, Karen asked, "Is this necessary? You've already disarmed me."

Olson pointed the gun at the sofa. "It all depends on what you have to say. Now sit."

She did. Briefly inspecting her sparse surroundings, recognizing a glaring monitor atop a computer on the breakfast table to the left of the living room.

"Cross your legs and keep both hands beneath your thighs at all times."

Karen nodded. Olson was a pro.

"All right, Agent Frost. Give me one good reason why I shouldn't call the police. And be careful what you tell me. I can spot a liar from miles away."

"I am innocent," she claimed, adding in her raspy voice, "I've been framed."

Olson motioned Ryan to sit next to her. Ryan remained quiet, his gaze on the carpeted floor.

"You're going to have to do better than that," Olson said. "I also didn't believe Mr. Ryan at first, but he convinced me with hard evidence, which is the only reason I didn't arrest him for stealing my computer passwords—which is *also* the reason why I haven't called the police, yet."

"All right," Karen said, closing her eyes. She began to relate everything that had taken place from the moment she had arrived in Austin. She told him what she remembered about Dave Nolan's investigation and assassination, about the Pattersons', about Rubaker, about his Internet activity to zero in on the Ryans, about Roman Palenski's death, about the multiple attempts on her own life. She finished with the activity that had taken place in the past twenty-four hours, until the moment she had walked in the door.

"Now you know everything that I know," she said. "Between my story and Mike's—plus all of the evidence, which we gathered together—there should be more than enough ammunition to go after them. The problem is that my agency won't listen to me. They won't even give me the chance to explain unless I turn myself in first."

"Which you obviously can't do," Olson said, respect replacing the contempt in his eyes. "Or you will be executed before you can talk."

"Precisely."

"See," Ryan said. "She's one of the good guys. This whole thing in the news is just one big setup."

Olson breathed deeply, exhaling while lowering his gun. He stood, walked up to the computer on the breakfast table, picked up a sheet of paper, and returned to the lawn chair.

"Recognize this?" Olson asked Karen.

She nodded. It was the sheet of paper on which she had scribbled Ryan's information earlier in the day.

"I've always suspected something was wrong," he said, shaking his head. "I just never knew it would be *this* bad."

"Neither did I when I first took on this assignment," Karen confessed.

"You see, Agent Frost," continued Olson, flipping the safety of the Beretta back on before setting it next to her Colt, "on a few occasions during my thousands of audit investigations, I would stumble upon a confidential IRS directory, similar to the one Mr. Ryan found, for which I had no access password. Approval for the request-for-password forms resided with Mr. Jason Myrtle. On every instance, my request to access these mysterious directories was denied by Myrtle under the pretext of taxpayer privacy rights. Now I understand why."

"Tell her about the meetings," said Ryan.

Olson glanced at him for a moment before turning his tired gaze to Karen. "Mr. Shapiro, Mr. Rossini, and Mr. Myrtle met on a regular basis in Myrtle's office. No one really knows what was discussed there, but on a couple of occasions someone would accidentally overhear something or other about an account here, a special payment there. Once in a while an individual who may have mentioned something about those meetings would be let go, or transferred to another location. Mr. Myrtle seldom kept a secretary for longer than six months. He claimed that secretaries got sloppy over time. He got better service by replacing them often. I now think he didn't want anyone around for too long for fear of something getting out about his shadowy deals."

"What I don't understand," Karen said, "is how come Myrtle got away with it for so long, even if he swapped secretaries, even if he met with Shapiro and Rossini behind closed doors. Doesn't Myrtle have to account for his spending? Doesn't he need to *show* his superiors exactly how he spent his budget? How can someone not notice that the equipment and services that he was getting weren't worth the money he was spending? Isn't there a purchasing department that would bid out jobs and then select the best compromise between services and cost?"

Olson smiled. "That's the way it's supposed to work, Agent Frost."

"Karen, please."

"I prefer last names."

Karen looked at Ryan, who shrugged.

"All right. Please continue," she said.

"Like I was saying, that's the way it's supposed to work. Unfortunately, that's not the way it always works inside the IRS, particularly when acquiring technical services. For example, several years ago the IRS spent over eight hundred million dollars improving its computer systems. Yet, when asked by Congress to show how the money was spent, the IRS could only account for five hundred thirty million. What happened to the balance remains a mystery to this day."

"That's . . . amazing," said Karen.

"What's more amazing is that there's very little that Congress can do."

"Why?" asked Ryan.

"Because of something called Section 6103 of the federal tax code. It grants the IRS the right to deny disclosure of any information that may jeopardize taxpayers' privacy. The Service on occasion has abused that right by calling upon that section in times when it didn't want certain information made public. Now, this doesn't happen very often. In general, the Service is a very well run institution, efficiently handling mind-boggling amounts of information. But in such complexity there's room for wrongdoing, and that's what I'm afraid is taking place here. Myrtle has found a way to abuse the system. Somehow his budget for the Austin Processing Center gets approved by Congress every year. His numbers are never questioned, never challenged. As long as that happens, there's no reason to get grilled by his superiors in Washington. From their perspective, Myrtle is doing a fine job because he collects the taxes in his region, invests in equipment and services, and manages to show enough proof of his progress to Congress to keep on getting funded."

"That's unbelievable," said Karen.

"*Believe*, Agent Frost," he said. "The money is getting funneled right under everyone's noses. While the IRS applauds Myrtle's efforts, the fat bastard is robbing this country blind, sending the money to SoftCorp, where it gets funneled to overseas accounts through Capitol Bank."

There was a moment of silence, then Olson added, "My entire career I've been going after the corporate world, after their abusive tax-shelter schemes. Sometimes we won and sometimes we lost, but it was always us, the IRS, against them, corporate America. This case brings the problem too close to home. In hindsight, I guess I should have seen it coming. After all, the corporate world is used to buying its way into anything and everything, and sooner or later it was bound to corrupt some individuals within my agency, like Jason Myrtle."

Karen leaned forward. "What about corrupting someone in Congress as well?"

Olson tilted his head. "That's a strong possibility. Myrtle may have gotten away with his technical overspending *one year*, and avoided having to explain it to Congress by invoking Section 6103, but the following year Congress should have rejected his budget, should have made him account for every penny spent. Yet, year in and year out Myrtle gets his budget approved."

"Damn," Karen said. "So not only is the IRS involved but it now appears that so is Congress—or at least someone in a position to influence the congressional approval of . . ." Karen let her words trail off, suddenly remembering one of her last conversations with Palenski. Her former boss had complained to her about Congress ripping him a new one during the budget-approval process.

"Jack Horton," she said, more to herself than to Ryan and Olson.

"What?" asked Ryan.

"Senator Jack Horton," she repeated. "He's the man behind budget approvals."

"He's also very likely to be our next president," added Gam Olson with concern.

"That's right," said Karen. "Perhaps it wouldn't hurt to run an investigation on him. See what shakes out."

"Do you realize what you're saying?" Olson said, getting up, pacing in front of Karen and Ryan. "If what you say is true, then this conspiracy goes—"

"Very high," Karen said, also explaining how someone had been applying so much pressure on the FBI, threatening to slash its budget, to influence its mission. And that someone could certainly be Jack Horton.

"So," said Ryan, "if you assume for the moment that Horton is behind this, what would be his motive? He's already headed for the White House."

"Perhaps that's how he got on the road to the White House in the first place," Karen replied.

"Then that would mean that the proceeds from the illegal transactions between the IRS and SoftCorp and Capitol bank are somehow funneled to the senator," said Olson.

"At least some of the funds," said Karen.

"That's right," said Ryan. "And the rest could belong to the man whose name was flagged during my banking run earlier today."

"Orion Yanez?" asked Olson.

Ryan nodded. He had already briefed the IRS agent on this and much more during the hour they had spent together before bringing Karen in.

"He must be the one controlling the operation for Horton," said Ryan.

"Or maybe he *controls* Horton," offered Karen.

The three of them thought about it for a while before Olson said, "I need to do a little more research on Mr. Yanez, maybe that'll give us some clues about his role. I also need to investigate a possible connection with Horton."

"Fine," Ryan said. "But we also need to set the wheels in motion to get my wife back. You said you would be able to help me."

Olson nodded. "And you have my word on that. I need to call a few of my close associates and bring them up to speed on this. Then we'll set up a time for the exchange."

"How do you know they can be trusted?" asked Ryan.

"Because, Mr. Ryan, I will be contacting my friends in the IRS's Criminal Investigation Division. Those guys are the meanest group of men that you'll ever meet. They're almost a closed society within the IRS, and *no one* gets in their way. They live and die according to a single objective: nail any bastard who tries to avoid paying taxes."

"I thought that was your job," said Ryan.

"My job's to *find* violators and try to convince them to cooperate. If they do, and agree to pay their taxes, then it's settled. But if they try to fight it and even get cute by trying to run away and change names, or any one of thousands of schemes to avoid paying what they owe, then I turn them over to the CID."

"All right, then," said Ryan. "Let's get the ball rolling."

"Sounds like the ball's already rolling, Mike," said Karen as Olson dialed the phone in the kitchen. "The question is, will the IRS be strong enough to stop this conspiracy? The FBI sure wasn't."

Before Ryan could answer, Olson said, "There's something you don't understand, Agent Frost."

"What's that?"

"That there are two certainties in life. One is that you will die. The other is that you will pay your taxes. Everything else is uncertain. That makes the IRS the most formidable force in this world, up there with death itself. People can screw with the FBI and get away with it. People can cheat the police, Congress, and even the president, and get away with it. But no one—and I mean *no one*—fucks with the IRS."

295

22

They arrived one by one, introducing themselves by their last name. Ryan's initial suspicions about IRS agents had been correct. As in the military, these people were all last-name kind of guys. Some were older agents, like Olson and Karen. Others looked much younger, perhaps in their late twenties or early thirties. But all had two things in common: intensity in their eyes and side arms beneath their jackets.

Twelve of the finest agents from the IRS's Criminal Investigation Division now joined Karen, Ryan, and Olson in the living room, mostly sitting on the floor, listening intently at the tale of deception, assassination, grand larceny, money laundering, and tax evasion. Ryan explained everything he had seen and done since arriving at SoftCorp. Then Karen followed, and Olson wrapped up the discussion with a plan, a way to get Ryan's wife back and also bring this criminal network—and everyone associated with it—down hard.

By two o'clock in the morning the group broke up after having defined a strategy, which they would start executing immediately, deploying specific agents to carry out specific tasks, judiciously spreading the word and the evidence to additional selected members of the Criminal Investigation Division in Washington, D.C., Virginia, and New York. They wanted to attack in synchronized fashion, hit the enemy with a unified punch. When it came to losing tax revenue dollars—particularly of this magnitude—CID agents would do anything and everything possible, and do it right, even if that also meant bringing down some of their own people, like Jason Myrtle, who was apparently at the core of this conspiracy.

In the end, Ryan found himself once again sitting with Karen Frost and Gam Olson in the living room, going over their portion of the plan once more before they went to sleep. The following day would be very exciting and they all agreed that they needed to rest.

Ryan, however, couldn't fall asleep. Listening to Karen Frost snoring on the couch, he stared out the window, looking at the stars. Somewhere out there they were holding Victoria captive. The same feeling of immense guilt that had descended on him shortly after her kidnapping now smothered him with crushing force. In the final analysis it was he who had convinced her to come down to Austin. Greed had veiled his senses, his values, his decisions. Now it was all so clear to him, so obvious, that he wondered how in the world he hadn't seen it sooner.

When something's too good to be true it probably isn't. There has to be a catch somewhere. Ryan remembered Victoria's words after his original interview, when he had arrived at their apartment outside of Stanford.

Why didn't I listen?

Clenching his jaw, Ryan fought back tears of anger swelling in his eyes. This was no time to get emotional, to lose his head. Victoria had always complained that he was too logical, too calm, always looking at problems objectively, keeping his head, methodically solving them.

Now of all times she needs you to keep your head.

Ryan needed to remain focused, thinking ahead, reviewing the plan in his mind, slowly, carefully, for he would only get one chance at getting her back.

And he didn't intend to fail. He would get Victoria back.

Or die trying.

23

Perspiration dripped down Karen Frost's neck as she crawled into the backseat of an old, rusted Ford Pinto, both its doors missing. Exposed springs scratched her abdomen through the ripped upholstery as she inched forward, pressed both elbows against the seat, and lifted her binoculars to scan the meeting grounds from the other side of the vehicle.

She wiped the rolling beads of sweat from her forehead and pressed the rubber ends of the binoculars against her eyes. Old automobiles came into focus as she turned the small adjusting wheel in between the lenses and panned over to the dusty clearing in the middle of the junkyard in south Austin, where the exchange would take place.

She checked her watch and frowned. Shapiro was not there . . . at least, he wasn't showing himself, she noted, pointing the binoculars to the far left section of the large yard and spotting Olson and two CID agents setting up an observation post and also a sniper rifle from inside a wrecked car at the precise location Karen had told them to be: out of the way and with the early morning sun behind them. A second sniper team had positioned itself on the north side of the yard. The rest of the CID agents covered the perimeter of the place, but were careful to remain out of sight to keep Shapiro and his team from realizing that Karen and Ryan had backup. They had debated last night on the proper number of agents to deploy today. Too few would run the risk of getting overrun. Too many might telegraph their presence and scare off the enemy.

She crawled out of the Pinto and walked down the small hill in a crouch. She zigzagged her way around heaps of wrecked relics.

Karen stopped once more, brought the binoculars to her eyes, and trained them on a clearing two hundred feet away, spotting Shapiro, flanked by four large men carrying automatic weapons. The group stopped in the middle and looked around.

She approached them under an already bright sun, remaining out of sight. The oil-stained ground leveled off as she moved swiftly, keeping her head below the roof level of the hundreds of automobiles arranged in long radial lines that projected out from the clearing at the center of the yard.

She spotted one limousine a few hundred feet behind Shapiro's group, and decided to move sideways, circling the clearing three hundred feet away until she positioned herself next to the glossy-clean vehicle.

There was no one guarding it.

She retrieved the tool that Olson had given her earlier in the day and removed the valve stems of all four tires, which deflated right away.

Pausing, she checked her watch. It had taken her just under five minutes to eliminate Shapiro's getaway. Now it was time to face him and his guns.

"Shapiro!" she shouted as she stepped into the clearing. Their backs were to her.

Almost in unison, all four bodyguards brought their weapons around and trained them on the federal agent.

"Would you tell your gorillas to relax? I'm unarmed!"

"Stop where you are!" shouted a Hispanic guard next to Shapiro.

"What is it with all the precautions? I thought we had a deal?" she shouted.

"That all depends on whether you have the package with you or not," replied Shapiro.

"The package is nearby, with Mike Ryan. Where is Victoria?"

"Nearby too."

"Be reasonable, Shapiro. I'm alone with Ryan, and unarmed, just like I said I would be. I'm also a fugitive, so I have little to lose. You, on the other hand, not only have a lot at stake but also have enough hardware around you to stop a tank. You don't really expect me to just hand over the package, shake hands, and walk away with the Ryans, do you? I need insurance that you won't terminate us after we give you what you want."

"How do I know you're not holding back part of the package and plan to double-cross me?"

"You get all of your money back, except for five million dollars so we can leave the country, vanish from your life forever. Consider it your payment to buy our silence."

"All right," said the Hispanic guard to Shapiro. "We'll play it her way."

Shapiro reached for a handheld radio and brought it to his lips. Karen tried to hear what he said over the radio, but the CEO of SoftCorp was too far away.

A few minutes went by. Karen just stood there, roughly fifty feet away from them.

Suddenly, the low flopping sound of a helicopter rotor became audible in the distance, growing to a deafening sound as the craft hovered a hundred feet over the clearing.

Karen realized at that moment that her plan was in jeopardy. She had not considered the possibility of a helicopter.

24

Ryan remained hidden from view, per his agreement with Karen. But now he wondered if that was the best course of action given the unexpected arrival of the helicopter, its rotor stirring up dirt and debris, creating a column of dust that temporarily clouded the clearing.

He got on the radio and called Olson.

"What should we do?"

"Stay in position, Mr. Ryan," replied the IRS agent. "We're trying to assess the situation. Remember that our men have the place surrounded."

"But that doesn't do us any good if they leave in the helicopter!"

"Stay put. I'll get back to you."

"Olson!" insisted Ryan. "How in the hell can the sniper team see the clearing with all that dust?"

"We can handle it. Now, stay put and leave this channel open," said Olson.

Ryan frowned. This was bad. Real bad. He wondered if there was something he could do besides just stand there.

Putting away the radio, Ryan decided to walk around to the other side of the yard, squeezing himself in between stacks of wrecked cars, moving parallel to the clearing.

Sweat filmed his face as he crawled past an old truck, through the rear seat of a rusted sedan, slowly repositioning himself, reaching a vantage point at the edge of the clearing between Shapiro's party and the landing helicopter.

The white craft touched down gently, its rotor continuing to swirl up dust, ruining the line of sight of the sniper teams.

A side door swung open. Through the thick haze Ryan watched the slim silhouette of Victoria stepping out of the craft, hugging herself. She was no more than fifty feet from him and getting closer as she walked toward Shapiro and his team. One of Shapiro's guards, barely visible in the swirling dust, moved in Victoria's direction.

Ryan narrowed his gaze, realizing that the same dust that ruined the snipers' line of sight would also limit the visibility of Shapiro and his men.

Shifting his gaze between the blurry shape of the guard, roughly a hundred feet away, and Victoria, now less than thirty feet from him, Ryan readied himself to alter the plan. If he could barely see the guard, then the guard would also have a difficult time seeing him.

He waited, biding his time, letting Victoria get a little farther away from the helicopter, yet still a safe distance from the incoming guard, who was almost perpendicular to Ryan while walking toward his wife.

He held himself back until the guard had passed his position before lunging, racing as fast as his legs would go, the helicopter noise masking his sounds. His eyes, mere slits of glinting anger, focused on the dark figure moving toward Victoria, weapon in hand.

Ryan brought both hands to the middle of his chest, elbows extended, his upper body leaning heavily in the direction in which he sprinted, just as he'd been taught at Stanford.

He struck the guard's torso with his left elbow, much harder than he would had done as a defensive back, hearing bones crack, his forward momentum powerful enough to lift the guard off the ground. As he did so, Ryan also jerked upward while keeping his elbow dug deep into his victim's side, flipping him upside down before letting go. His old coach would have been proud.

The guard groaned, releasing the gun, landing headfirst, going limp.

"Vic!" he shouted over the deafening noise, rushing toward her, his left arm throbbing, the adrenaline rush heightening his perception, magnifying every detail.

The helicopter's rotor rumbled in Ryan's chest, its blades slicing through the dust, which swirled about him like a cyclone. Victoria stood frozen like a wax statue, her short hair fluttering as if someone held a giant leaf blower behind her.

Ryan kept his momentum after the tackle, leaning into his wife, extending his arms, snatching her light frame, throwing her over his shoulder as he sprinted toward the cover of the—

A gun cracked, its sound muffled by the craft's turbine.

Victoria screamed.

Ryan rushed faster, his lungs burning, his bad knee protesting every step, Victoria's body drilling a hole in his right shoulder. But he couldn't slow down now, not with those animals so close nearby.

A second shot, a near miss, buzzed past him, impacting the metal rubble just ahead.

"Mike!"

"I know!" Ryan shouted, risking a backward glance, spotting a few figures jumping off the helicopter, rushing after them.

Cutting left after running beyond a large heap of wrecked vehicles, and swinging right after clearing what had once been a black limousine, he kept up the zigzagging rhythm for two more minutes, listening to the multiple shots in the distance mixing with the helicopter noise.

His bad knee trembling, Ryan realized that he had pushed it as much as it would go.

Leaning down, he set Victoria gently on the ground, breathing heavily, gasping for air. He was definitely out of shape. "Are you . . . okay?" he asked, embracing her.

She hugged him back. "Yes, my darling. Yes, I'm fine!"

Then he took a close look at her for the first time. Anger replaced exhaustion and fear. He tightened his fists at the sight of her facial bruises, at her busted lip. "Bastards!" he hissed. "I'll get even for this!"

"Come," she said, tugging at him. "Let's get away from here."

Ryan put a hand to her face. "That's right, Vic. We're getting the *hell* out of here."

Just then a gun went off behind them.

Karen didn't realize something was wrong until the first shot was fired from inside the cloud of dust. Two of Shapiro's men reached for their weapons.

Damn!

She raced for cover as multiple reports cracked through the clearing, as the ground exploded to her right, then her left. She reached a wall of cars, diving the last five feet, landing next to a pile of rusted axles, skinning her left shoulder.

She scrambled to one side of the nearest wreck, the remnants of a green truck.

Ignoring the hammerlike sound of bullets ricocheting off its front fender, she rolled to the rear of the vehicle, her left shoulder burning. Karen peeked around the rear bumper and produced her Colt.

Screams and shouts filled the area, mixed with sporadic gunfire. Two dark silhouettes ran toward the other side of the wrecked car, their faces hidden in the expanding cloud of dust.

She fired once, twice. One of the figures fell. The second dove for the cover of a nearby pile of metal scrap and returned the fire.

She ran away, cringing in pain as gravel and glass from broken windshields tore at her. She reached a new vantage point, a large heap of crushed cars almost as tall as a house. Racing around it, she reached the spot where Ryan was supposed to be waiting for her.

Where is he?

After making sure that she had lost the second guard in the maze, Karen grabbed her radio. "Mike! Where in the hell are you?"

Static, followed by, "I've got Vic! Hurry! They're after us!"

"You've got her? Where are you?"

"Running toward the north fence!"

Karen took off in that direction, listening to the steady *chop-chop* of the helicopter.

Moving to her left, she ran parallel to the clearing, her Colt leading the way, but keeping her finger resting against the trigger casing to prevent an accidental discharge.

"Olson! Talk to me!" Karen shouted.

"Can't see a damned thing from up here!"

"Damn it! Then get *down* here!"

26

Ryan gripped Victoria's hand tight as they raced down a corridor formed by walls of scrap metal, keeping the helicopter noise behind them, turning left and right at random, continuing their jagged approach toward the perimeter of the junkyard.

He had to lose the figure he had just seen going after them, the one who had fired moments after Ryan had set Victoria on the ground.

The afternoon sun blinded him as they lurched forward as fast as they could go until it seemed as if the wrecked vehicles on either side of him fused into solid walls.

A gunshot struck a car just ahead of them, the screeching sound of metal against metal.

"This way!" he shouted.

They cut left into a narrow alley, turned right into another one, and made their way up the shallow incline toward the fence, away from this graveyard of rusted machines.

Victoria reached it first. Beyond the ten-foot-tall chain-link fence extended a grassy field sloping down to I-35. He frowned when he failed to see any IRS agents.

Where are they?

They hopped on the roof of an old Mustang. From there, Ryan helped her up on the fence and then began to follow.

"Stay where you are!" a voice tinged with a Hispanic accent shouted behind them.

Victoria was at the top, one leg on the other side. She froze. Ryan let go of the fence and turned around, standing on the roof of the car, looking down at a dark-complexioned Latino in his forties, as tall as Ryan and similarly built.

"Leaving so soon?" he asked.

"Didn't like the party," replied Ryan, trying to control his anger.

The Hispanic man became serious, leveling his gun at Ryan. "My name is Esteban, Mr. Ryan. You're wife knows that I mean what I say. Now, hand over the accounts or I'll shoot you both."

Ryan produced a small gadget, roughly the size of a portable CD player. He held it up in the air with both hands. "Amazing where you can fit billions of bucks these days."

Esteban held out his hand. "Just pass it over."

"Do you even know what this is?" Ryan asked.

He didn't reply.

"It's a diskette formatter. Inside I have a floppy disk with the information you seek. However, all I have to do is press this button and the data are erased."

"Don't do anything stupid, Mr. Ryan."

"And I suppose giving you the only thing that's keeping us alive isn't stupid?"

"Nice and easy now," Esteban insisted, taking a step toward Ryan. Gunfire erupted once more behind them. The IRS agents had engaged the criminals.

"One more step and you can kiss your money good-bye."

"All right," he said, lowering the weapon. "What do you wish to do?"

"Vic?"

"Yes?"

"Get to the other side and run out of sight."

More gunfire filled the air, multiple reports echoing off the walls of crushed metal.

"Not without you."

"Damn it! Just do it!" Ryan shouted, wondering where in the hell were Olson and his IRS agents. He wanted to reach for his radio, but not only were both his hands occupied with the disk formatter, using the radio would imply that Karen and he had found help. He wanted to keep Esteban under the impression that they were alone with the fugitive Karen Frost until after Victoria was safe.

Keeping his attention on Esteban, Ryan listened as his wife climbed down the other side.

"Mike?"

"Run!"

She did.

After a moment, Esteban said, "All right, Mr. Ryan. She's out of sight. Get down from there. You're coming with us."

"What?"

"You didn't really think that we were going to just take a diskette from you. For all I know it could be filled with garbage."

"This was a trade. Nothing more."

Esteban smiled. "You don't understand. We *are* trading. You for your wife."

"You're the one who doesn't understand. This place is surrounded by federal agents."

Esteban smiled. "Nice try, Mr. Ryan, but the FBI, unknowingly, happens to be on our side, as well as the local police."

"Who said anything about the FBI?"

Esteban gave him a puzzled look.

"I was referring to agents from the Internal Revenue Service. Some of the meanest guys you'll ever meet."

Esteban seemed momentarily confused now.

Ryan pointed toward the junkyard. "Do you *really* think that all of that commotion is being caused by *just* Agent Karen Frost?"

Esteban didn't reply.

"It's over," Ryan said. "The IRS knows everything. They know about Orion Yanez and Senator Jack Horton."

Esteban took a step back, then another, slowly shaking his head. "That's—"

"Impossible?" said Ryan, feeling a surge of confidence now that he detected fear in the stranger's stare. "At this moment Orion Yanez is being taken into custody, as well as Senator Horton, and dozens of business associates, like Ron Wittica and Jason Myrtle."

"You—you lie!"

It was Ryan's turn to smile. "*Do I?* Then turn around and convince yourself. At this moment you have three guns pointed at the back of your head."

Esteban slowly looked behind him.

Ryan threw the formatter at him, striking a direct hit in the left shoulder.

Esteban fired his gun once as Ryan jumped off the roof of the Mustang, landing on him.

Ryan cringed in pain, his right shoulder burning as he tackled Esteban. Warmth spread over his chest.

Pinning him down, Ryan drove his left elbow into Esteban's chin before the assassin pushed him away.

Staggering to his feet, Ryan began to turn around to face Esteban once again.

Another shot whipped through the dusty field. Ryan watched Esteban on the ground, his weapon pointed at Ryan for a brief moment before dropping it.

A second later he understood. Karen Frost stepped away from the protection of an old truck, her gun still leveled at Esteban, who had gone limp.

Ryan began to feel dizzy and light-headed, dropping to his knees. "Karen," he said, before collapsing on his side.

His vision beginning to blur, Ryan saw Karen Frost shouting on the radio but could no longer hear her. Then a cloud of dust engulfed them.

27

"Go! Go! Go!" shouted Karen as the helicopter airlifted them to a nearby hospital.

Gam Olson sat in front, a gun leveled at the head of the pilot. Victoria knelt in front of the last row of seats, where Ryan rested face up while she pressed a towel against his gunshot wound. Karen had seen worse. She felt certain that Ryan would make it, as long as he didn't lose too much blood. Olson had already alerted the emergency staff at Brackenridge Hospital in downtown Austin, which had a large helipad just across from the emergency entrance. With a little luck they should get there in time to save this brave kid's life.

Two other IRS agents sat in the second row, in front of Karen, who occupied the third row. The rest were busy sorting things out down in the yard, in the company of several cruisers from the Austin Police Department, which had arrived just moments after Ryan was shot.

Karen leaned over and felt Ryan's pulse. "It's still strong," she told Victoria, who nodded, keeping the pressure against his shoulder while whispering something in his ear.

She turned around, dialing Russell Meek's private line with Olson's cellular phone. According to Olson, three high-ranking officers from the Internal Revenue Service had paid Meek a surprise visit two hours ago. This time around, she found Meek quite agreeable.

"Jesus, Karen! Is this all true?"

Gazing into the blue skies over Austin, Karen said, "I tried to warn you, Russ."

"I know, I know. I'm still learning. But Horton? Who could have ever thought?"

"He was just a puppet, Russ. Orion Yanez was pulling the strings."

"I saw the reports," he said, referring to the information an army of

IRS agents had managed to gather in a few hours on Orion Yanez's operation in the United States. While it appeared quite legal on the surface, it had quickly become evident that Yanez had funneled huge amounts of money overseas from dozens of American corporations, SoftCorp and Capitol Bank being just two of them. And with the help of Jason Myrtle and the directors of two other IRS processing centers, Orion Yanez had been able to keep his operation a secret. Once Karen Frost had established a possible connection between Jack Horton and Orion Yanez, it didn't take the IRS long to probe into Horton's campaign contributions and discover that Yanez, through his many corporations, had essentially financed Horton's political career—as well as the careers of three other senators, two governors, five congressmen, and a large number of judges. In return, the politicians had used their influence to bolster Orion's empire. The IRS, now assisted by the FBI and the CIA, were probing deeper.

"When are you going to bring the crooked politicians in, as well as Orion and his mob?"

"My people are working with the IRS on that right now. I'm also about to head for the White House to see the president. Are the informants okay?"

"One is. The other's been shot, but he should be fine."

"Looks like I owe you a huge apology," said Meek. "You and Palenski were right all along."

Karen smiled as the helicopter began its descent. "We'll sort it out when I get back to Washington, Russ. Just make sure you grab Yanez and Horton and also clear things up with the press and the police."

"It's being taken care of as we speak."

Karen hung up the phone as the helicopter touched down and paramedics wheeled Ryan away, followed by Victoria and two IRS agents.

"Is everything all right in Washington?" asked Olson.

Karen Frost regarded him and smiled while giving him a single nod. "Everything is *just* as it should be."

epilogue

Two months later.

Michael Patrick Ryan stepped out of the doctor's office and into a clear and cool northern California day. He was thrilled at finally shedding the cast that doctors in Austin had applied to his arm following a three-hour-long surgical procedure to repair the damage done by a 9-mm bullet. Victoria had wanted to come along, but a last-minute meeting had been called at her job. Since this was only her second week with the Bank of San Francisco, the Ryans had decided that it would be best if she didn't miss work so soon. After all, they both wanted to create a good impression at their new jobs.

His arm ached as he moved it. According to his doctor it would take roughly three months of physical therapy to get it back to normal, but the good news was that there would be no long-term damage.

Ryan inspected his arm, not only pale for having missed sunlight for the past sixty days but also thinner than his left arm from lack of exercise. Still, it was good enough to move and hold objects, as long as they weren't too heavy. Best of all, he would not have to use his left hand to write again, though he had become fairly proficient at doing so in the past weeks, including one-handed typing.

Ryan exhaled while flagging a taxi and giving the driver directions to take him back to his home in Mountain View, just a half mile away from Stanford.

Settling in the rear seat, he momentarily closed his eyes. The past weeks had indeed been interesting for the young professional. The domino effect that he had triggered still continued to ripple across the country. First to go down had been Jack Horton, caught at Dulles International Airport while trying to board a plane headed for the Cayman Islands. Orion Yanez had put up quite a fight when the FBI had shown up on his doorstep in Virginia. In the end, he had been taken into custody, along with a dozen of his bodyguards. In Austin, his old bosses Ron Wittica and Aaron Shapiro had been arrested on charges ranging from grand larceny to murder one. Jason Myrtle had also been arrested but committed suicide in prison—at least according to the media. Then more politicians were arrested, along with dozens of business executives from several corporations, some, like Horton, while also trying to flee the country. Everyone was awaiting trial. The finest defense attorneys in the country were all headed for the courtrooms of America to defend high-profile cases. And CNN was there to cover the action in vivid color.

The media's going to have a field day with this, Ryan mused as the taxi entered Highway 101 and headed north. He watched the streets of Silicon Valley rush by. Fortunately for Victoria and him, Ryan had worked out a deal with the FBI and the IRS to keep their names secret. The young couple wanted to start over again and didn't need the hassle of dealing with *anything* that had to do with their previous lives.

Almost anything, Ryan admitted to himself. The Ryans had convinced the IRS to let them retain the interest accrued on those accounts over the six-week period that it took the IRS to gain control of the funds. Even at the going rate, several billion dollars could generate quite a bit of interest in that time. Ryan had told Olson to consider it payment for services rendered. A grateful IRS had not only allowed the Ryans to transfer that money to a California account—tax free—but also to keep their cars and sell their Austin home for a small profit.

That's the least they could do, Ryan decided, thinking of the billions of dollars that the United States government had seized from Orion Yanez's empire following his arrest, and especially the arrest of his personal accountant, who made a deal with the feds to save his own hide, in the process disclosing the locations of dozens of other accounts, which total had yielded over ten billion dollars at the last count.

"Take a left at the next intersection," Ryan told the driver as he exited 101. "Then go up one block, take another left, and drop me off at the next corner."

A moment later, Ryan stepped away from the taxi in front of a ten-year-old, four-bedroom house—quite new and very large for this area, and on a corner lot. Best of all, the house was two-thirds of the way up the mountain, not only providing him with a great view of the valley, but also a great resale value if the Ryans ever decided to move. In the valley, home prices went up exponentially with altitude. The same house at the top of the mountain would sell at four times the price of one at the foot. Living two-thirds of the way up wasn't doing badly at all, especially for a young couple.

Ryan smiled, staring not at the house but at the detached three-car garage. He looked forward to driving his red Boxster for the first time since the shooting. But first he needed to log in to work and check E-mails. His boss at Cisco Systems had been kind enough to let him take the day off for medical reasons. Ryan was still on the hook for keeping his new virtual-reality project on schedule.

Ryan shoved his right hand into his pocket, smiling at the feeling of metal against his fingers. It felt good to grab his house keys again with his right hand.

As he did so, he noticed someone standing in the shadow of his front porch.

"Hello, Mike."

Michael Ryan stopped in midstride, for a few seconds staring at a slim woman with short ash blond hair and eyes as hazel as Victoria's, wearing large silver earrings. After a moment of surprise he said, "Karen? You're . . . you're about the *last* person I expected to see at my doorstep. How have you been?"

"I've been fine. Thanks for asking."

Ryan smiled. "I see we're still changing?" He pointed to her hair and eyes. It also looked as if she had lost a few pounds—not that she needed to lose any before. But her face was thinner, which made her look five years younger.

"The job," she said, shrugging. "I was in the area and thought I'd stop by and drop this off." She approached him holding an envelope. The federal agent climbed down the steps separating the porch from the walkway leading to the sidewalk. She wore tight black jeans and a maroon jacket over a black T-shirt. She also wore boots and most likely a couple of guns. Her blond hair contrasted sharply with her golden tan, which radiated health, a look that was miles away from the last time he had seen her at the hospital in Austin. "I wasn't expecting you to be home in the middle of the day."

"I took the day off to get my cast removed," Ryan said, flexing his right arm. "Good as new . . . or will be shortly." Ryan then narrowed his gaze at her. "What are you *really* doing in this part of the world, Karen?"

She looked away and then back at him. "Well, it seems like the Bureau liked the results of my last high-tech case so much that they've assigned me a new one. I'm investigating a local company for possible industrial espionage."

Ryan shook his head. "*Please,* don't tell me it's Cisco Systems!"

Karen smiled. "Relax. Cisco's clean."

He exhaled in relief. "For a moment there . . ."

"I'm glad to see that you and Victoria are doing fine."

Ryan tilted his head. "It all seems like a bad dream now."

"If it's any consolation, it's been a *nightmare* for the bad guys. I'm predicting that Wittica and Shapiro will get at least twenty years each. Fifteen other employees at SoftCorp and twice as many at Capitol Bank have also been arrested. Plus many more across other corporations, the Internal Revenue Service, and even Congress."

"I also heard about the governor of Louisiana and Illinois."

She nodded. "This is definitely what I call a serious house cleaning. And the more we look, the higher the number of rats that surface begging to make a deal, pointing the finger at more rats. This is just the kind of vicious cycle that criminal networks dread. Once a few people start talking and pointing fingers, it's all over for them. The problem is always getting the momentum started. You helped us do that, putting a lot of people behind bars."

Ryan frowned, remembering that cruise on Lake Travis during his recruiting trip. He was at least glad that he hadn't been at SoftCorp long enough to become friends with anyone. That would have made this ordeal all the more stressful. Still, there were now a lot of wives and kids who would have to suffer while their husbands and fathers did jail time. "Did you ever get to the bottom of Orion Yanez's scheme?"

Karen handed him the envelope. "We figured that you should know what it was that you helped prevent."

Ryan tore it open. It contained a hand-written note from Russell Meek, director of the FBI, attached to a newspaper article. The note thanked Ryan for his help in stopping the shipment of nuclear weapons to Cuba. The article, printed in yesterday's edition of *The New York Times,* described how a U.S. Navy destroyer intercepted a Russian merchant ship five hundred miles from the coast of Cuba. Buried deep in the cargo compartment American sailors found enough spare parts to manufacture a half dozen short-range tactical nuclear missiles, each capable of delivering a fifty-kiloton warhead to within five hundred miles. There was, of course, no mention of this incident having anything to do with the largely publicized Orion Yanez case—though it was just a matter of time before someone made the connection.

"Jesus," said Ryan. "Was this what Yanez planned to do with the cash?"

"Part of it, anyway. He was also investing heavily in Cuban resorts to bolster that country's economy, according to his accountant. Although Orion has not admitted it, the CIA thinks that he might have been next in line to take control after Castro. Orion was slated to continue the reign of terror, the human rights abuses, torturing and imprisoning those who dared speak against him."

Ryan shook his head in disbelief. "And he was doing it using our taxpayers' money."

"Incredible, isn't it?"

Ryan looked away.

Karen patted him on the back. "You've done your country a great service, Mike."

He sighed. "I don't want to sound antipatriotic, but hopefully this is the first *and* last time that I help Uncle Sam . . . aside from paying my taxes."

She smiled, waving at someone down the street. A sedan parked a few houses away rumbled to life and began to move in their direction. "Good luck to you and Victoria."

They shook hands before she climbed into the passenger seat.

Michael Patrick Ryan watched her drive away before turning around and going inside his house. Victoria would be home in a few hours, giving Ryan enough time to catch up on his work in the meantime.

He logged into his system and checked his daily E-mails, browsing through them to decide which he would open first. Most were from his new job, which didn't offer the huge payoffs and benefits of SoftCorp, but it was honest work and he didn't have to worry about surveillance cameras in his bedroom. Besides, with his house and cars paid for thanks to Uncle Sam, the Ryans could afford to live in the valley and still build up their savings.

One E-mail caught his eye. To the untrained observer it appeared to be a string of letters and numbers. However, Ryan launched a software descrambler, provided to him by the Bank of London just four weeks ago as an exclusive service to holders of numbered accounts. He read the very brief electronic statement, like the first one he had received last month, showing the balance and accrued interest. No deposits and no withdrawals.

Ryan stared into the distance for a moment, still uncertain if Victoria and he had done the right thing by secretly funneling the funds from one of Orion Yanez's smaller accounts in Colombia to London. The few million dollars had been lost in the shuffle of several *billions*.

Ryan and Victoria were financially well off as it was, and they were both young, bright, and holding well-paying jobs with good prospects. But the future was always uncertain, unpredictable, and it never hurt to have a golden parachute beyond everyone's reach but their own.

Perhaps in five years, or ten, or longer. After they were tired of working, of developing their careers, of running in this rat race called the high-tech industry, maybe, just maybe, they could consider retiring to a remote place in Europe, perhaps in southern Italy, while they were still young, and . . .

Ryan smiled. *Perhaps one day.*

He closed the E-mail and began his work.